YOU'RE SO DEAD TO ME

GRIMDALE GRAVEYARD MYSTERIES, BOOK 1

STEFFANIE HOLMES

Cover Design: Covers by Aura

ISBN: 978-1-991099-28-0

❀ Created with Vellum

YOU'RE SO DEAD TO ME

What do you do when three hot, possessive ghosts want to jump your bones?

I'm Bree, and I see dead people.

Not all dead people. Only those with unfinished business. They're everywhere – I'll be eating my breakfast and a poisoned heiress glares over my Cheerios, and I can't even enjoy the wilderness without being accosted by chattering ex-hikers who don't understand which mushrooms are edible.

I've returned to my hometown of Grimdale to cat-sit for my parents while I plan my next move. I'm looking forward to raiding their fridge, hanging out with their two mischievous kittens, and staying far, far away from anything supernatural.

But I forgot that I'm never alone in Grimdale.

The three ghosts I used to play with as a kid are back in my life again. Only now I'm their age and they're *infuriatingly* attractive.

There's the *slightly* psychotic Roman soldier who loves the Great British Bake Off, the bossy, aristocratic royal prince who demands the finer things in life (er, death), and the blind Victorian gentleman adventurer who doesn't have a mean bone in his body (or any bones, for that matter).

But my three ghoulish houseguests are the least of my problems. I've landed a job giving tours of the historic Grimdale Cemetery, and on my very first day, I stumble into a fresh corpse.

The dead guy's ghost needs me to solve his murder so he can cross over, but sticking my nose into spirit business might see me to an early grave.

As for my three hauntingly hot friends? It turns out their unfinished business...is me.

You'll Be The Death of Me is the first in a darkly humorous paranormal romance series by bestselling author Steffanie Holmes. If you love a sarcastic heroine, hot, possessive and slightly unhinged ghostly men, a mystery to solve, and a little kooky, spooky lovin' to set your coffin a rockin', then quit ghouling around and start reading!

JOIN THE NEWSLETTER FOR UPDATES

Want a free bonus scene from Bree's school dance and Bree's playlist? Grab a free copy of *Cabinet of Curiosities* – a Steffanie Holmes compendium of short stories and bonus scenes – when you sign up for updates with the Steffanie Holmes newsletter.

http://www.steffanieholmes.com/newsletter

Every week in my newsletter I talk about the true-life hauntings, strange happenings, crumbling ruins, and creepy facts that inspire my stories. You'll also get newsletter-exclusive bonus scenes and updates. I love to talk to my readers, so come join us for some spooky fun :)

For my dad
Who is my first hero

But our love it was stronger by far than the love
Of those who were older than we—
Of many far wiser than we—
And neither the angels in Heaven above
Nor the demons down under the sea
Can ever dissever my soul from the soul
Of the beautiful Annabel Lee;

— EDGAR ALLAN POE

I

BREE

"Go on, dearie. Let me have a little sniff of that salty goodness."

"No," I snap under my breath as I snatch the pretzels from the tray table and stuff them in my pocket.

For your information, I'm not hanging out in the world's grossest sex club. (That was two years ago in Amsterdam. My shoes stuck to the floor.) I'm sitting in my seat on a flight somewhere over the United Arab Emirates, minding my own business and trying to ignore the ghost of a blue-haired old biddy who is annoyingly fascinated by my airline snacks.

"Pleeeeease? Just hold the bag out so I can have a whiff."

I glare at her before turning my body toward the window. Outside, the world is dark – the kind of deep, unsettling darkness that makes you remember you're hurtling through space at a gazillion miles an hour with only a computer, a hopefully not-drunk pilot, and the laws of physics standing between you and a fiery, dramatic death. We're somewhere over the Middle East, but the cloud cover is so thick that it looks like we're flying into a black hole.

Most people in the cabin are settling down to sleep, but I

won't get any peace as long as Chatty Cathy insists on a running commentary of my snacks.

"I know you can see me, dearie," she sighs. I watch out of the corner of my eye as she hovers over the empty seat beside me. "My good friend the headless pilot told me all about you. Well, he didn't tell me so much as gesticulated. He said your thighs were much bigger. You should eat more, put some meat on those bones – starting with those pretzels in your pocket."

I groan. Stupid ghosts. They have no right to be gesticulating about the size of my thighs, which are perfectly fine as they are, thank you very much.

It figures that airplane ghosts talk to each other. There aren't that many of them compared to, say, hospitals, old asylums, and Starbucks stores. They generally stick to the plane where they died but they can hop off at airports and float around in the terminals like some kind of spectral hen party, swapping gossip about their flights. The Headless Pilot and I had a run-in on my flight from Bali last year, and it was not a pleasant experience. I was on the loo, reading a smutty romance novel on my phone and enjoying hour three of *absolutely no dead people* when he stuck his torso through the bathroom door and shook his neck stub at me. I screamed bloody murder because that's what you do when you have a see-through neck stub in your face, and the stewardess had to break down the door because she thought I was having some kind of fit. They didn't believe my story about seeing a spider, and I've been banned from that airline for life.

Ghosts are nothing but trouble.

Usually, airplanes are one of the few places in the world where I'm blissfully free of ghosts for a while. Statistically, not that many people die on planes. It's one of the reasons I decided to leave my small British village of Grimdale the moment I got my GCSE and embark on a backpacking trip around the world.

It wasn't the most pressing motivation, but it definitely factored high on my 'reasons to get as far from Grimdale as possible' list.

And now, after all this time, I'm heading *back* to Grimdale, a place I very much do not want to be, because of the terrible thing...

No. I squeeze my eyes shut. *I don't want to think about that. If I burst into tears on this plane, Chatty Cathy will never let me hear the end of it.*

"Excuse me, ma'am?"

I open my eyes and see the reflection of a man in a business suit in the window. Ghosts don't have reflections, so it's a real live person talking to me. That doesn't happen often – my resting bitchface is so legendary that sonnets have been composed in its honor.

I spin around. Businessman McArmaniPants flashes me an apologetic smile. He leans forward and puts his arm on the back of the seat, right through the old lady's spectral head.

"Argh, watch where you're putting those skinbags, you rotten oaf!" She jerks away, holding her head as she hops angrily down the aisle. She looks like a chicken with her bony elbows jerking wildly. I cough into my hand to cover my smirk.

Businessman McArmaniPants flashes me a megawatt smile. "I didn't mean to startle you. I noticed that this seat is empty. I wondered if I could sit next to you – I'm near the back and a kid spilled his orange juice and now everything is sticky—"

"Sure." I pat the seat, grateful for his presence. He'll act as a buffer between me and the old lady ghost. "Please, make yourself at home. Stay as long as you like."

"Do not make yourself at home!" Chatty Cathy huffs, glaring at the man as he lowers himself into her seat. "This is my chair. I claimed it first. Get your own snacks to sniff."

"Do you want some pretzels?" I crack open the bag and offer

it to my new seatmate, knowing that the ghost won't want to risk getting close enough to sniff them now.

"Sure." He takes a handful. "Hey, why are you poking out your tongue?"

"Oh." A blush creeps across my cheeks as the old biddy huffs away. "No reason."

ARE you ready for a little ghost lore? I'm on the second leg of my thirty-two hours of flying from New Zealand to London, so I have time to kill.

Time to kill. Ha ha. I'm a comedian.

Here's the skinny on the spirits of the dead, aka, Bree's Ghost Rules:

1. Not everyone who dies becomes a ghost. You have to have unfinished business. Often, you don't remember what that business is, which I'm sure must be annoying.

2. Ghosts hang around the location where they died. There's an invisible force I call ghost mojo (it's a highly technical term I came up with when I was eight, shut up) that acts like a rubber band that pulls them back to the location of their death. They can wander away from their death location, but the ghost mojo gets worse the further they go until it becomes painful for them to remain away and they get sucked back to their death place again.

3. Some ghosts, like my childhood friend Ambrose, aren't tied to a death location but instead, a place

that's important to them. I don't know how it works, so I blame it on ghost mojo.

4. Ghost mojo is also why ghosts can fly through airplane bathroom doors but don't fall through the floor and out into space. Ghost mojo keeps spirits standing on the ground the way they did when they were alive.

5. Only very powerful or very angry ghosts can interact with the human world by moving things or flickering lights or writing on mirrors. Mostly they just waft around being annoying.

6. Despite not having noses, they can still sense strong smells, so they're forever lingering around when people are eating and begging to sniff my salty nuts.

7. Ghosts hate it when humans walk through them. *Hate. It.* Sometimes I do it just because I know it pisses them off so much.

How do I know so much about ghosts?

Because I'm the only person who can see them.

I had an accident when I was five years old – I fell off my bike and cracked my head on a rock – and ever since I've been able to see the dead. See them and talk to them and be infinitely harassed by them—

"Go on, dearie," the old lady pokes her head out of the luggage rack. "Just a little sniff."

I'm Bree Mortimer. And it's going to be a long flight.

2

BREE

T step off the plane at Heathrow, bleary-eyed and with skin like an elephant's arsehole. I broke down in hour three and left the open pretzel bag on my tray table for the old bird to sniff. But the businessman reached across me to adjust his airflow and accidentally bumped it off, so I spent the rest of the flight picking pretzel bits out of my compression socks.

Just another day in the life of a ghost whisperer.

I collect my backpack from the luggage carousel and step onto the tube, which is relatively empty of real people at this time of night. One ghost sits in a seat in the far corner, his head bowed as he stares at a pair of sneakers on his feet that are so '80s retro they'd be worth a fortune if they were corporeal.

I slump down in the opposite corner and turn on my phone to check my messages.

Sure enough, there's a long text from Mum.

Mum: Hi honey! Hopefully you'll see this after you land. I'm so sorry we couldn't be there to greet you, but you know what they say – the last one to Paris is a rotten egg! I've kept your old room exactly how you left it, the key is in the squirrel, and we'll call you in a couple of days. Albert and Maggie are happy to help with anything you need. Try not to burn the place down, and we'll see you soon!

She's attached a picture of her and Dad standing beneath the Eiffel Tower. Dad's wearing his signature Led Zeppelin t-shirt and beaming like an idiot. A hard lump forms in my throat, and I navigate away from the photo and start a game of Woodoku.

I have to change trains thrice, and my second train is late. Ah, England, how I have *not* missed your blasé approach to train schedules. It makes me long for the four months I spent living in Hamburg. Germans know how to run trains.

By the time I arrive at the Crookshollow interchange, I almost bowl over a nun as I sprint to platform 4 to catch the last train to Grimdale.

Great. As if I need any more reasons for God to smite me.

I step off my final train just as the Grimdale village church bells chime 10PM. The little shops lining High Street are all shut up for the night. The only lights on come from the village pub – the Cackling Goat, which is in a wobbly old Tudor building on the corner that's hopping with people. *Ah, the famous Monday Night Aunt Sally Tournament. Some things never change.*

As I pass the door, I catch a whiff of roast beef with all the trimmings.

My stomach – which had gone on strike after nearly two days of airplane food – flares to life again and demands I go inside. But I'm not sure I'm ready to face the entire village two pints in, during a heated argument over whether Davey Jenkins stepped over the line when he threw his batons. I cut across the parking lot, hoping no one saw me, and am just about to turn onto Railway Row when I'm distracted by the sight of three ghosts with their noses pressed up against the windows.

"Ooh, they've got haddock on the menu tonight." Lottie Bishop jumps up and down, her bonnet strings flapping wildly about her face. "They haven't served haddock in at least two moons."

"Come on, come on, sit by the window," urges Mary Kemp, rubbing her stomach gleefully. "Let us smell the delicious deep-fried potato fingers and the mushy peas..."

"Pah, who wants to smell a pile of green snot?" scoffs Agnes Waterhouse, her long, hooked nose passing through the glass as she sniffs around for something more to her taste. "It looks like Walpurgis threw up a hairball on the side of their plate."

Walpurgis is Agnes' cat. He's black as midnight and is also a ghost, because Agnes is every witch stereotype come to death. Agnes, Lottie, and Mary were hanged as witches on the village green in the sixteenth century. They're old enough that they have some decent ghost mojo and can travel to the very edges of Grimdale without a problem. They cause a lot of mischief around the village. Of all the ghosts I encounter, they're some of the few I actually sort of consider...friends.

Of course, right now they're too distracted by haddock to notice me. Story of my life – Bree Mortimer, invisible even to ghosts.

At the sound of his name, Walpurgis slinks out from beneath the hem of her skirts and mews with delight when he sees me.

"Hey, Walpurgis." I glance over my shoulder to make sure no one is watching, then slide my heavy rucksack from my shoulders, squat down, and run my hand over his spine.

Remember what I said about ghosts hating you walking

through them? This is true – it's very intense and painful for them, and it always happens when they're unprepared. But sometimes lightly touching their ghosty skin will feel quite nice. When you touch them, you might get a little tingle, or a little warm or cold depending on what they think of you, and they can feel it, too.

Don't ask me how I know this – it's a long story involving a naive teenage Bree and her imaginary childhood friends, and my cheeks grow hot just *thinking* about it. So I won't think about it. Especially not since I...

No. Not thinking about it.

Walpurgis purrs and flops down on his belly, letting me scratch him under the chin. I check over my shoulder again, but I'm still alone. No one living can see me tickling the concrete.

"Walpurgis, stop that," Agnes snaps. "You're supposed to be a servant of Satan, not a gibbering pup."

Agnes, bless her immortal soul, is still a little pissed about the whole being hanged as a witch thing. She told me once that if she'd known she'd be accused of consorting with the devil, she'd have been much more wicked during her lifetime. Now she's determined to make up for it in death.

"Meow." Walpurgis take no offense to being called a pup. He's used to Agnes. He rubs his ghost cheek against my fingers, and a soft warmth floods over my skin.

"Who's got Walpurgis all gooey?" Lottie turns from the window. Her soft amber eyes widen when she sees me.

I stand up and give a little wave. "Hello, Agnes, Lottie, Mary. It's nice to see—"

"Bree Mortimer!" Mary exclaims as she tears her round face from inside the window. "We thought you'd run off to join a troupe of traveling minstrels."

"*I* said that our Bree wouldn't be caught dead singing Hey Nonny Nonny. You obviously became a harlot," Lottie pipes up, looking over my outfit with a nod of approval. "You do have the kind of ankles that would make men weep."

"Don't be ridiculous," Agnes snaps. "She could never be a loose-legged woman in those hideous clothes she wears. How will a man find her cunny in those skintight pantaloons?"

I laugh as I plant my hands on my hips, showing off my comfiest pair of leggings with a pattern of black cats. Agnes has made it clear on several occasions that she does not understand the modern woman's love of leggings.

"I did run off, but not to become a traveling minstrel *or* a harlot." I keep my voice low in the hope that no one will walk past and see me holding a one-sided conversation with the Cackling Goat's wall. "I've been exploring the world, seeing the sites, hiking the trails, climbing the mountains, eating exotic things—"

"I hope you steered well clear of *France*," Agnes says with a sniff. "French people live there."

I decide not to tell her about the six blissful weeks I spent working in a vineyard eating my body weight in cheese and fucking the village baker under the vines every night.

"I've been all sorts of places – to Germany, the Czech Republic, the Netherlands, Vietnam, Cambodia, Peru, Bolivia, Chile—"

"Those aren't the names of countries," Agnes scoffs. "On the day of my trial, there was a map of the world above the magistrate's desk, and there aren't even that many countries on Earth. You're making this up."

I ignore her, which is the best way to deal with Agnes. "— Bali, New Zealand, Australia—"

"Oooh, I've heard of Australia!" Lottie rubs her hands together in excitement. "Mrs. Doolhan says her son went there for something called surfing. Did you do a surfing? Did you hug a koala bear?"

"Did you have to disguise yourself as a boy to escape from pirates?" Mary sounds concerned. "Is *that* why you're wearing those clothes?"

"No, Mary. Those are her normal clothes," Agnes sounds exasperated. "We've explained a million times that in the *modern world*, women may dress as men now, and no one bats an eyelid or hangs you as a witch. Please at least pretend to pay attention, dear."

"Oooh, we're just so happy you're back," Lottie squeals. "We want to hear all about your travels. The furthest I've ever gone from Grimdale is apple-picking in farmer Tilby's orchard..."

They all crowd around me, pressing their ghostly bodies into me until I'm tingling with warmth. Another important ghost rule is that a spirit's feelings alter their temperature. That's why you get cold spots in haunted houses – those are pissed-off ghosts. Happy ghosts make warm clouds, but no one ever puts those down to hauntings, because if you live in England you take any opportunity for warmth you can get.

"Did you go to Amsterdam?" Mary asks. "We watched a documentary about Amsterdam through Lizzie Duncan's window. You won't *believe* the things they get up to over there—"

"I did visit Amsterdam, but I obviously wasn't hanging out with the cool ghosts, because I didn't get up to anything crazy," I say quickly, not wanting to get into a long discussion about cannabis cafes and that horrible, sticky-floored sex show. "Listen, I'd love to stay and catch up, but I've just got in after a thirty-six-hour flight from New Zealand and I need sleep—"

"In my day they hanged women for flying," Agnes barks, folding her arms. "Very well. You get to bed now, but you'd better return to us with stories of all the foreign men you seduced with your *leggings*. And I trust you brought us presents."

"I..." *Fuck.* "I sure did. I'd never forget my favorite terrible trio. I'll bring your presents tomorrow."

Now I have to get them presents? What souvenir do you even give to a ghost?

"You'd better," Agnes growls. Walpurgis shoots me a filthy look before darting back beneath Agnes' skirt.

"I promise I will. We can go to the park, and I'll tell you all about the Australian wildlife photographer with the snake as long as—"

I'm interrupted by a tittering sound behind me. Cold dread runs down my spine as I whirl around to see three women standing in the doorway to the pub, staring at me as I talk to thin air and badly muffling their laughter.

And not just any women – Kelly Kingston, Leanne Povey, and Alice Agincourt – the three villainous queen bees who made my high school years miserable. Of *course* they'd be at the pub tonight. It's God's way of getting me back for the nun thing.

"Oh, look, it's Cheddar Cheese!" Kelly collapses into giggles, and just like that, I'm back at Grimdale Comprehensive again, being tormented by the three of them.

Their favorite joke was to only refer to me by the names of different cheeses. Get it, because I'm called Bree? Hilarious. John Cleese is taking notes.

That is, when they weren't stealing my things or drawing ghosts on my locker or whispering rumors about me, or taking secret videos of me talking to my 'invisible friends' and sharing them on the internet...

It shouldn't get to me, but I'm fighting jet lag and an overdose of the undead, and I am *done* with this shit. Of all the people, why did Kelly Kingston have to be the one to see me talking to a lamppost?

And in what universe is it fair that she looks like a movie star with her perfectly-straight hair and designer sweater dress, while I'm a gremlin wearing saggy-arsed leggings and compression socks filled with salted pretzels who looks like she's been hit by a bus?

I plaster a fake smile on my face and throw my hair over my shoulder, knowing that this situation is past saving. "Ladies, I didn't see you there. I was too busy catching up on the village gossip with this lamppost here."

"Excuse me, I'm no lamppost!" Mary splutters, sashaying her hips. "I have beautiful curves. My husband's best friend always said so."

"Still talking to spirits, Camembert?" Kelly says with a smirk. "Or is that your new boyfriend? It's no surprise that the only guy you can get to go out with you is inanimate. I bet he *lights you up.*"

"Awwww, look, he's got *wood* for Gouda," Leanne pipes up. The two of them clutch at each other, cackling like the drunken bitches they are. Mary circles around them, leaning in close to sniff them.

"Fools," she snaps angrily, stepping back. "You ordered the Caesar salad. No one orders the Caesar salad."

"Come on, you two." Alice is searching for something in her bag. She pulls out a set of jangling keys "I want to get you home before you throw up in my car."

Alice doesn't even acknowledge I'm here, which is her particular brand of psychological warfare. While her two friends were of the 'bludgeoning with snottiness' school of bullying, Alice ignored me. No, she didn't ignore me – she looked through me in a way that made me feel like *I* was the ghost.

Sometimes, when we were thrown together on a history project or performed opposite each other in the school's Shakespeare festival, I saw another side of Alice. She was whip-smart and sarcastic as fuck, and we even had a couple of normal conversations about bands and TV shows we liked, but then she'd go back to Kelly and Leanne and those little moments of connection were forgotten.

"I don't wanna go home, Alice. You're such a spoil-spooooort," Leanne moans. She does sound drunk. "I wanna stay here and get Bree's hairstyling tips. I've always wanted to look like a ferret stuck in a light socket."

They burst into more cruel laughter. I straighten my back and run my fingers through my hair. It feels like it did after a week of not showering when I hiked through the Andes. *Perfect.*

Agnes tsks. "You're going to let someone wearing whore's trinkets talk to you like that?"

"Merrrrw," Walpurgis agrees.

I mean, Leanne's earrings *are* quite large and gaudy.

"I just got off a plane," I snap back. "A plane is a big flying contraption that takes people far away from the shitty one-horse village where they grew up to places where they can have adventures, eat glorious food, and sleep with hot AF foreign men. But I forgot, you don't know what a plane is, because none of you have even set foot outside of Grimdale."

"Oooooooh," Lottie rubs her hands together gleefully. "I love it when Bree gets spirited!"

"Invoke Satan!" Agnes pipes up. "That always sends them running."

"I went to Paris for my honeymoon," Leanne says defensively. "It was dirty and the creme brûlée tasted like vomit."

"Whoop-de-do." I kick my battered rucksack for emphasis. "Forgive me for not jumping up and down with excitement. Let me guess, the most exciting thing in your life is meeting up at the Goat after work and bitching about all the people you know who are more interesting than you. What have you three done with your lives? Oh, let me guess. Leanne married that loser Simon she was dating in high school, and she's positive he's cheating on her with the secretary at his father's London office but she's too afraid to investigate in case it's true. Kelly is probably still trying to get Riley Jenson to notice her, and she works at the plus-size clothing store on High Street, which is the closest to New York Fashion week she's ever going to get—"

"I'm an assistant manager now," Kelly says with a smirk. "And I'm *dating* Riley, who is captain of the Grimdale football club and is even hotter than he was in college. Alice works at the Grimdale museum, and *she* studied at *Cambridge*. What have you done, freak? Spend the last five years sleeping with stoner hippies, meditating on mountaintops, and getting bedbugs from grubby youth hostels?"

She's annoyingly close to the truth. I ball my hands into fists. I hate that Kelly can get under my skin and make me feel like all my dreams are weird and stupid.

"She can't talk to you like that," Agnes snaps. "Hex her!"

"She can't do that, Agnes!" Lottie gasps. "We don't want our Bree to be hanged—"

"Fine, then you should pinch her nose," yells Agnes.

"I'm not pinching her nose," I snap. "Just shut *up*."

Wrong thing to say. Kelly's eyes narrow on me.

"Still talking to ghosts, I see."

"No, I—"

"You should give up the act, Gruyere," Leanne juts out her hip. "You're not special. You're just weird."

"Push her down the steps!" Agnes screams.

"Go away, Blue Vein," Kelly smirks. "You're stinking up the village with your rotten cheese scent and your creepy invisible friends—"

"Bree Mortimer, is that you?"

Great. Because what I want right now is for more people to join this little party. "Hello, Albert, Maggie."

I turn to the couple who have come out of the pub behind Kelly, Alice, and Leanne. Albert and Maggie Fernsby are my parents' next-door neighbours. They're a lovely couple – Albert's retired from the Grimdale bank and Maggie makes herbal bath products and runs every committee and charity baking event in the village (and there are many). They hold hands as they push through Kelly and her friends, and Maggie rests her head on Albert's shoulder. Even though they've been married for eleventy million years, they are still so adorably in love. I've always secretly hoped that one day I'd meet a guy who made me feel giddy about him in the same way.

"It's wonderful to see you again, dear." Maggie leans down to kiss both my cheeks. She smells of smudged sage, rose petals, and honey – one of her own concoctions, no doubt. Out of the corner of my eye, I notice Mary leaning in close to get a good whiff. "Your mother said you'd be home this week to look after the cats. We promised we'd keep an eye on you while you're here, didn't we, Albert?"

"You look upset, dear." Albert grabs my shoulders and leans in to inspect my face. "Have you been getting enough sleep? Perhaps you need some of Maggie's prune tarts. They're absolutely delicious and they keep you regular—"

My cheeks flush hotter as the girls laugh behind them. "I'm fine, thanks. No prune tarts required. I'm jet-lagged after the flight. I think I'm going to head to the manor now—"

Albert tugs on his jacket. "We'll walk you home."

"Oh, no, that's okay. I enjoy being by myself—"

"We insist. It's the middle of the night. You don't know what kind of creepy strangers might be hiding in the darkness."

Agnes hops angrily, pointing a gnarled finger at the couple.

"Are they talking about me? They'd better not be talking about me!"

Albert grunts as he lifts my rucksack onto his back, and Maggie grabs my arm and practically drags me down the street. Kelly's laughter rings in my ears. I pray for the god Jupiter to send a nice lightning strike in her direction, but he's busy watching telly or something because he doesn't answer my prayers.

"You must tell us all about your travels," Maggie gushes as we round the corner and start along the winding village streets up the hill toward Grimwood Crescent. "Albert and I went on a round-the-world cruise on our silver wedding anniversary, but poor Albie was so seasick we didn't stray far from our cabin! We went to Glasgow on the bus once, didn't we, Albert?"

"That we did, lovey." Albert huffs as he struggles behind us with my bag. I try to take it off him but he won't hear of it.

"That we did. I didn't much care for Glasgow." Maggie shakes her head. "It was dirty and I couldn't understand a word anyone said. Albert and I always say, why travel when you already live in paradise?"

"I couldn't agree more, lovey."

We pass the blocked-up old railway tunnel in the hill and another familiar ghost – the squashed navvy. He looks away from us as we walk past, which is nice of him because the whole right side of his face is caved in, and it used to terrify me as a kid. Mum never understood why I ran screaming every time we passed this corner, and I'd learned by then that I had to keep my ghostly sightings secret, because my stories made adults uncomfortable and got me taken to 'special' doctors.

Thankfully, the three witches decided to hang around the pub and sniff some more haddock. I'm so done with ghosts tonight.

"...of course, we were upset when we heard about your dad,"

Maggie is saying, drawing me back to the conversation with a start. "But it's good that he and Sylvie are having their little adventure now. They deserve it. They've worked so hard keeping the B&B going all these years. And it'll be nice of you to see the old family home again, I'm sure."

"You've picked the perfect time of year to return to Grimdale. I know you didn't have the best time of it growing up here, but I think you'll enjoy village life."

"I'm not staying long," I mutter. "Just until Mum and Dad get back."

But even as I say it, a pang shoots through my stomach. I don't know how long I'll stay. The reason I came home isn't even here now, and I don't know how long I can live in that house with...

Luckily, Maggie and Albert are oblivious. They keep on chattering away. "—we've got the Grimdale Bake Off next week to raise money to repair the church roof. Maggie will be cooking her award-winning scones—"

"Oh, Albert, I haven't won yet."

"—but you will, my little flower petal. You always do. Twenty-two years, my Maggie and her scones are undefeated. And did you hear that Maggie's Bath and Body are taking off? Her healing oils and body butters are now being stocked at 'Basic Witch' in the village, and they're constantly selling out. They're amazing – her products smell so yummy and have ancient healing properties from the herbs she uses. She makes this special one for my arthritis, and I slather it all over myself every night."

I shudder at the mental image of Albert slathered in body butter.

"Oh, Albie." Maggie plants a kiss on his cheek. "You don't have to be my salesman. Bree, I'll drop off some products for you tomorrow. You look like you could use a little pampering.

I've got a balm that will do wonders for your jet lag. Will you be joining our team for the Wednesday pub quiz? We always need young people to answer celebrity questions. Albert has no idea what a Kardashian is—"

Albert and Maggie keep up a steady stream of chatter as we walk through the narrow, cobbled streets of the village, bringing me up-to-date on all the Grimdale gossip. I barely hear a word of it. I'm too busy trying to keep my eyes open and stop my pounding heart from leaping out of my chest in terror.

Because every step brings me closer to my childhood home.

Closer to...*them*.

And after seven years, I'm not sure that I'm ready to face what I left behind.

3

BREE

I drag my feet as we turn into Grimwood Crescent. Here, the houses are further apart and set back from the road, partially or fully obscured by the thick woodland surrounding this part of the village. Grimwood was once considered a bit of a holidaying spot for London's elite – the woods were a favorite hunting spot for earls and dukes, and many landed families had homes around Grimwood Crescent. They're mostly sold now, the grand houses divided into flats or rented out on Airbnb.

My boots crunch on fallen leaves. My heart thunders against my ribs. *I can't do this. I can't go back there. What if I see them? What if I don't see them? This is a big mistake—*

But the Fernsbys don't stop dragging me along, marching me toward my doom.

We round the final corner, and there she is in all her disheveled glory: Grimwood Manor.

Home.

Yes. I grew up in a manor house. The Addams Family would be right at home at Grimwood with its stone turrets, gothic mullioned windows, trailing ivy, carved wooden staircase, heavy oak beams, and secret passages.

Grimwood has been in my mother's family for generations – apparently, her great, great, great grandfather was the local game warden, and he won it off the previous owner – Lord Bentley – in a hunting bet. We're not a noble family by any stretch of the imagination. No one sleeps with anyone's cousin or drinks their tea with their pinkie pointing out.

The problem with manor houses is that unless you have piles of cash and endless time on your hands, they're pretty difficult to keep running. Something's always breaking, caving in, or being eaten by rodents. Back when I was still in diapers, my parents were dead broke and the bank was knocking on the door, so they decided to take drastic action to keep the place and turned it into a B&B.

Posh travellers to Grimdale stay in the fancy Queen Elizabeth Hotel on the high street or the Instagrammable Honeysuckle House at the other end of the Crescent, but all the bohemian, odd, crunchy folk stay at Grimwood – often for weeks or months at a time. I've grown up with travellers coming and going from the west wing bedrooms and my mother cooking stacks of sausages and black pudding every morning so the guests have their proper English breakfast before they go off rambling. We live in the east wing, but I spent most of my time hunched beside the fire in the guests' sitting room, listening to the travellers' tales and wishing for the day I'd be old enough to kiss Grimdale goodbye and go off on my own adventures...

And how did that turn out for you?

"What do you think? How does the old girl look?" Albert slides my rucksack off his shoulder and leans on the gate, peering up at the house with an expression of awe. "I bet she hasn't changed one bit."

Apart from a fresh paint job on the Victorian conservatory added by Mum's great-grandfather and a few more gaudy gnomes painted by my dad in the front garden, Grimwood looked the same as the day I left. The same sheer walls of stone and brick jut out from the top of the hill – a fortress protecting those inside. But it couldn't protect me.

It didn't protect Dad, either.

"If those walls could talk, I bet that house would tell us all kinds of stories," Maggie adds.

That's the problem. This damn house doesn't shut up.

I swallow hard, fighting to keep down the panic welling up inside me.

It's now or never.

"Thank you very much for walking me home." I grip the handle of my carry-on so hard that my knuckles turn white. "I'll leave you to enjoy the rest of your evening. Those poor kitties must be desperate for their dinner."

"Yes, yes, you get inside out of this cold." Maggie leans in to give me a warm hug and a peck on both cheeks. "I'll pop around tomorrow with a shepherd's pie and some of my bath products. You get some sleep now."

Unlikely.

I wave goodbye and wait until they've gone inside their house – a cute little stone cottage that was once the manor's gatehouse but was sold off by my grandparents to pay down the manor's mortgage – before climbing the steps to Grimwood's front door. I'm so exhausted that ascending those twenty-two steps feels like climbing Mt. Everest (which I was going to try, but it was expensive and scary, and I chickened out and went to Bali instead).

Or that might be the cold dread settling into my bones.

I lift up the chipped squirrel statue from a menagerie of concrete animals and pick up the key. My boot creaks as I cross the porch and insert the ancient key in the lock and turn the handle.

My whole body tenses.

What am I going to find in there?

Part of me longs for the peace and tranquility of their silence, and another part of me desperately wants to see them again...

Stop it, Bree. You're being ridiculous. You'll find what you find. Just open the door.

I suck in a deep breath and shove the door open. The hinges creak loudly.

I stare into a black void of emptiness.

I step over the threshold.

My rucksack makes a heavy thud as I drop it on the tiles. I squint into the gloom, trying to make out the familiar shape of the sweeping carved staircase and the cobweb-coated chandelier we never get around to dusting and the antique chair my mum uses to store her junk-sale purses.

Home sweet home. Grimwood Manor. It's strange to hear the house so silent – no guests yelling at each other as they fight over the bathroom, no parents shuffling about with spare towels and hot toddies. No whispered voices that only I can hear.

I'm used to the living *and* the dead making a lot of noise here. *I wonder if—*

"MERRRRROW!"

I scream as a tiny ginger monster leaps from the gloom, sharpened claws stretched toward my face. I manage to duck in time, and the furry demon slams into the wall behind me before dropping to the marble and landing on all fours in a daze.

"You must be Entwhistle. You're a little shit, aren't you?" I admire the claw marks he'd gouged in the wood. "Mum is going to kill you when she sees what you've done."

"Meow." Entwhistle trots over and rubs his cheek against my leg, like he hadn't just tried to gouge my eyes out.

"I'm glad to meet you, too. Where's your sister at?" I pick up the little mischief ball and cradle him in my arms as I move deeper into the house, flicking on lights as I go. I can hear a cat meowing plaintively from somewhere deeper in the house. According to Dad, this is Moon's favorite game – she takes great delight in wiggling into an impossible nook and then making the hapless humans rescue her.

I only have one job, and it's to keep these two cats alive until Mum and Dad get home. Please don't tell me I've failed before I even begun.

I move through the downstairs rooms of both wings, turning on the lights and peering behind the curtains and under every chair. I tell myself I'm hunting for Moon, but it's a lie. My whole body tingles with anticipation. Every time I turn on a light I expect to see them...but nothing.

They're not here.

They're standing by our agreement.

Grimwood Manor is empty of ghosts.

I finally locate Moon in the kitchen, hiding inside the coal scuttle. I clean her off as best I can and set her and her brother down with some wet food while I drag my rucksack up the winding carved staircase and down the eastern hallway to my old room in the turret. Above my head, something creaks and bangs. *It's just some critter that got into the attic, nothing to worry about.*

In this house, no sound is innocent, especially when I'm alone, and it's dark, and...

Scrabble scrabble *BANG*.

"Shit!" I jump ten feet in the air and fling open the door.

The room is a shrine to seventeen-year-old me. Posters of my favorite bands adorn the walls, the corners curling over where the sticky tape has pulled away. They're interspersed with a bunch of terrible photocopier prints of Voltaire's poetry and National Geographic spreads of UNESCO sites I dreamed of visiting. The bed is covered in a giant pentagram duvet, and a bunch of felt bats dangle from a mobile near the wraparound gothic windows.

Yep, I was a teenage goth. You try growing up in a creepy manor next to a graveyard with the ability to see dead people and *not* get attracted to heavy metal and emo boys with eyeliner. It's impossible.

I flop down on the bed and stare at the ceiling. I had more posters glued there – things I wanted to dream about before I went to sleep. In between a photograph of the Giza pyramids and Machu Picchu is a series of initials carved into the plaster.

B + P + E + A = 4EVA.

No.

I leap off the bed like it's made of lava. Tears spring in my eyes.

I can't do this. I can't sleep here. Why did I come back?

I know why I came back. But the reason for my return is currently in France, probably trying to order escargot using Google Translate and making Mum snort wine up her nose. And I'm all alone in this house with reminders of *them* everywhere—

This is a mistake.

I can't do this. I'm getting out of here first thing in the morning.

I'll tell Albert and Maggie that I'm meeting my parents in France. They'll understand, and I'm sure they'll be happy to feed the cats for me. I'll spend some time with my dad, eat some cheese, and be back on the road and forget all about this place...

I glance at my phone. It's nearly eleven. The trains have stopped, the reception at the Queen Elizabeth will be shut up for the night, and the next closest hotel is several miles away in the village of Argleton. Even if I manage to get an early flight or train tomorrow, I'm stuck at Grimwood Manor for the night.

I slam my bedroom door and drag my rucksack back down the stairs and into the west wing. I push open the door to the nearest guest room. It used to be the old drawing room where the ladies of Grimdale Manor would play cards and do their needlepoint and receive visitors. My mother has replaced the heavy furniture with a huge bed from one of the other rooms and decorated it in the bland earth tones and organic textures Airbnbers go nuts for. I dump my rucksack beside the blanket box and flop down on the bed. The ceiling here is freshly painted and free of graffiti.

They're not here.

They're not here.

I'm all alone, and I don't know how I feel about that.

4

EDWARD

"What do you see, Edward?" Ambrose jostles me as he tries to settle in beside me behind the balustrade.

"Stop drooling in my ear, fiend." I shove him away. "You dare touch a royal without permission? I'm well within my rights to cut off your hand."

"You can't cut off my hand." Ambrose waves the offending appendage in my face. "It's not corporeal."

"Fine. Then I'll get Pax to enact some ghoulish Roman punishment on you. Just because you're a ghost doesn't mean you can't feel pain, and you know he'll enjoy inflicting it. Perhaps that one where he peels your skin off—"

"You don't have to be so mean." Ambrose pouts, adjusting the collar of his morning jacket. I hate him for dying in his finest attire, for if I must be truthful, he looks quite dapper in that jacket, and as a blind ghost, he can't even appreciate himself, whereas I, a prince of England...

No. I'm not thinking about my lack of fine accouterments now, not when our Brianna is wandering about downstairs...

"I heard my name." Pax stomps out from the upstairs sitting

room, his Roman sandals flapping on his enormous feet. A ghost shouldn't be able to make such a racket, but Pax manages it. "By Saturn's hairy scrotum, if you are accusing me of scaring the cats again, I did not. It's not my fault they can't appreciate the scent of real Roman flatulence—"

"Sssssh." I hold my hand up to silence the oaf. "Do you want her to hear you?"

"I want everyone to hear me. That is the problem with being a ghost. Only Bree could hear me and she's gone—"

"She's *here*," I hiss, jabbing my finger at the figure dragging an enormous item of luggage toward the drawing room. "Brianna has returned."

"By Venus' golden cunny, is it truly her?" Pax immediately plops down beside me, folding his legs so that his short tunic flaps open and gives me a rather unpleasant view of his monstrous Roman tackle. "I cannot see her face beneath that wild hair. That's a huge rucksack she has – I didn't even carry half that amount of luggage on campaign! I bet it's full of shoes. She did always love her shoes. She looks weary, as though she has marched many miles. But look, she has grown buxom! And her hair...it's so long I could wrap it in my fist and—"

He yelps as I slam his head into the balustrade. He goes right through it, but the uncomfortable sensation of his cranium passing through a solid object momentarily shuts him up.

Pffft. Romans. So uncouth.

"If you stay silent for *one moment*, we will find out why she has returned," I snap. "And *close your legs*. You're worse than Lady Pendelyn with the Loamshire cricket team."

We all watch (well, Pax and I watch. Ambrose wafts anxiously across the landing, waiting for us to tell him what we see) as Brianna disappears into the drawing room, but she doesn't shut the door behind her. If I stretch out my neck, I can see her in the room, lying on the very bed where I once fornicated with Lady Pendelyn *and* the cricket team, her luscious hair fanning out across the pillow like a halo. My fingers itch to paint her, to pose her on silk cushions and render her curves in oils the way I did with the Countess de Boufflers...

And then I remember what the countess and I did during that particular portrait sitting, all that paint in strange and wondrous places, and her creative use for my opium pipe...and I'm overcome with a sensation that's become increasingly elusive to me during my spectral years.

I'm *horny.*

Concupiscent.

Downright lustful and randy.

No, those words are too crass, too primal for the sensations that assail my ghostly being. There's a bald friar in my britches, certainly, eager to make his prayers at the altar between her thighs. But my dry throat and trembling hands suggest something more...especially since I don't actually possess a throat.

I'm humming with magic, brimming with vigor, positively *overflowing* with urges that involve this new, buxom Brianna and an opium pipe...

I'm *entranced* by her. Oh, Brianna.

Our Bree has returned to us.

I stand up. "I'm going to sneak closer. Do not break anything while I'm gone."

"Why do you get to go?" Ambrose demands.

"Because I am a prince of the realm and I owned this house," I shoot back. It's my trump card, and I use it whenever I fancy. What is the point of being trapped as a spectre if you can't make your fellow ghosts dance to your whims?

Before either of them can stop me, I float down the staircase, careful to remain in the shadows. I've become used to not hiding from the Livings, but Brianna's no ordinary Living. If she comes out of the room now, she'll see me, and I'm...I'm not ready for her reaction.

As much as my maypole is desperate to dance with her, I'm *not* ready for her to hate me again.

As I approach the door, I sink into the wall, passing through the decorative plaster and knots of electrical wire and internet cables. A tingle runs through my body as I wrap my hand around the wire, and when my head pops out the other side of the wall, the lights flicker.

It's one of my favorite ways to pass the time since the house got electricity in 1936 – I hang out in the walls, letting the electricity hum through my body, and taking cruel pleasure in watching the humans searching in vain for the loose wire that causes the lights to flicker wildly. If I stay hooked up long enough I can sometimes feel my scepter lengthening and hardening...but I can never achieve anything like the princely shaft of delight that's standing to attention now.

Don't judge me. Being dead for four hundred years with only an oafish Roman centurion and a blind Victorian adventurer for company gets rather dull. I must make my revels where I may.

I hover in the wall above Brianna's head, only my face and the head of my scepter sticking out of the wall, but she's turned over to face the opposite wall now, her body curled in on itself. She breathes steadily, her long lashes fluttering. It looks as if she's fighting the urge to sleep.

Why are you here? Why have you come back?

The urge to reach out to her, to brush my fingers over her warm cheek, is overwhelming. My hand reaches out, and I'm flush with joy as I remember the warmth of her, the pleasure of holding her hand while we walked around the garden and she listened to my poems...

My hand hovers in midair. I'm frozen, torn between what

my heart so desperately wants and the one oath I swore I'd never break.

I may be a rake of the first order, but I made a promise to a frightened girl, and I won't go back on it just because she's returned and she's...

...she's...

...the most beautiful woman I've ever laid eyes on.

After her accident, we talked to Brianna all the time. We used to touch her and tease her and invent games for her. When she came home from school upset because Kelly Kingston teased her, we cheered her up. Pax and I enacted elaborate sword fights and Ambrose told her stories about when he rode an elephant or was chased through Russia by the Tsar's men.

After so many years with only those two nitwits for company, it was nice to have a Living who could interact with us, even if she was a little girl. Bree could touch the world in a way we could not. She could turn on the TV for us and request our favorite foods and teach us about things like mobile phones and microwave popcorn.

And now...now she is very much not a little girl anymore. Now my memories of her are sullied by the way her tight t-shirt clings to her breasts, and the rod in my britches is harder than if I spent a whole morning sitting in the electrical box—

Stop this, Edward. That's Bree. You cannot feel that way about your Bree. It's not chivalrous. Not that you've ever been chivalrous in your life. That's how you ended up where you are. So you'd better start now, because if you cross over, you don't want to end up in the fiery place with a pitchfork up your arsehole. She's Bree and it's not right—

Brianna sighs and rolls over. I jerk back through the wall before she can see me, and race back upstairs to join the others, my non-existent heart clenching in my chest.

"Well, what did you discover?" Pax demands, waving his

sword around. "Why is she back? Why is she sad? Who do I need to stab to make her smile again?"

"How do you know she's sad?"

"I see her face from here."

I peer over the railing and through the door at Brianna's face. Pax is right. She *does* look sad, and I was too distracted by her bosoms to notice.

That's not the Brianna we used to know. Our Bree was full of life, bursting with the need to adventure, to experience everything she could before she met her own end. Our Bree didn't lie around in bed feeling sorry for herself.

What's happened to her? How has the world hardened her? If someone has hurt her I will haunt their arse so hard they won't be able to sit down for a *month*.

"I'll go talk to her." Pax's face brightens. "I'll cheer her up with one of my stories, like the time Marcus Septus got so drunk that he passed out, and so I tucked him into bed with a sow and when he woke up—"

"No stories." I glare at him. "We made a promise, remember? A prince never goes back on a promise."

"What about when you promised all those peasants that they'd have fresh drinking water?" Ambrose asks. "And then you drained their well to create a swimming pool at the palace—"

"Or the time you collected all the money from your friends with the promise you'd spend it on Christmas gifts for the children's orphanage," adds Pax. "And then you purchased that peacock-feather hat—"

"That was different." I fold my arms. "I'm a prince of the realm. I'm in charge here, and I declare that we stay away from Brianna."

Pax nods, but he looks unhappy. "I miss her."

"We all do." Ambrose's eyes swim with pain – of all of us, I think he misses Brianna the most. He'd have given anything to go with her on her adventures instead of being tethered to this house. "But Edward is right. We made a promise and we must keep it."

Good. I'm pleased we're in accord. I'm about to suggest we return to the sitting room and sniff the liquor cabinet in celebration before it occurs to me just how impossible this task we've set ourselves is.

It's been seven years since we made our promise to Brianna, and five years since she walked out the doors of Grimwood and never returned. We've got used to having the run of the house without any of the Livings seeing us. Pax sits with Mike and Sylvie every evening to watch the *Great British Bake Off*, and no one bats an eyelid when he starts yelling about Deborah using Howard's custard instead of her own. Ambrose listens along to Sylvie's smutty audiobooks while she does the cleaning, and I spend my days watching the guests shower and fuck, and sniffing the liquor bottles until I feel the shadow of a buzz.

But now, everything's changed. We can't do any of that stuff *and* keep our promise to Bree.

We'll have to go back to living in the attic, and I swore I'd never set foot in there again after the last time. Have you ever lived in a small enclosed space with a Roman centurion who thinks fart jokes are the height of culture?

And that's not to mention the horror that awaits us up there – the yellow-eyed fiend who kept us in a constant state of terror for two long years. I swore I would never cross his path again, but now...

How are we going to keep our promise to Brianna?

5

BREE

My eyes fly open. Light streams through the curtains across the bed. I'm in a large, unfamiliar room, which is not uncommon for me in my travels. It takes a couple of moments for me to remember where I am.

I'm at Grimwood.

I'm home.

I sit up and roll my neck, which cracks in protest. I slept at a funny angle, curled up in a ball, still in the clothes I wore on the plane. I smell *delightful*. I grab my phone from the bedside table and check the time.

1:47PM.

It's past *lunchtime.*

I slept for over twelve hours.

My stomach growls, reminding me that the last thing I fed it was airplane food. I haul my sorry excuse for a body out of bed and drag myself into the bathroom. Shower first, then food.

I turn the shower on, toss my clothes in the laundry basket, and step under the stream. I yelp with shock – it's ice cold. I forgot about the temperamental water in the house. The down-stairs guest shower has two settings, ice cold and boil-your-flesh-from-your-bones. I grit my teeth against the chill as I nudge the mixer a millimeter at a time until the water turns scalding, then I soap myself down and get out of there as quickly as I can.

I wrap the towel around myself and pad back to my room. I look all around – behind the curtains, under the bed, in the wall sconces, but I can't see them anywhere.

It's been seven years since you last saw them. Maybe they've crossed over.

Or maybe they're abiding by their promise to you.

It's on the tip of my tongue to call out to them. I know if I speak their names, they'll come running. Ever since the day I woke up after the accident and saw them looming over me, I knew I could count on them to be here for me, no matter what.

At least if I call out, I'll know that they're still here. I'd be able to put to rest this gnawing, twisting loneliness that squirms in my gut.

But then, I wouldn't have the silence. Grimwood wouldn't be a refuge from the noise of the restless dead. It wouldn't be the place I need to relax and take stock and endure the pain of what's to come and figure out what the fuck I'm doing with my life.

I snap my mouth shut. *Not today.*

When I walk downstairs to the light-filled kitchen at the back of the house, I'm struck again by how strange and silent it is. All my memories of this kitchen are of Mum and Dad frantically running around filling guests' orders, or of Pax storming through everything, swinging his sword about and demanding I make him his favorite meal of spaghetti and meatballs so he can sniff it.

It's *too* silent. I can't stand it.

I boil the kettle and pour my coffee into a thermos. I tuck my book under one arm and head out the back door and down the crumbling path. The path winds through a small patch of Grimdale wood and comes out in the eastern corner of the Grimdale cemetery. It's one of my favorite places in the world.

Goth kid, remember?

Grimdale isn't your ordinary graveyard. It's one of the grandest Victorian cemeteries in the country. In the middle of the nineteenth century, the inner-city London cemeteries were overflowing with bodies to the point that they were a health hazard, especially during the winter when rivers of...human *stuff*...would leak from the ground of cemeteries and flow through the streets. It became the fashion for the wealthy and well-connected to have their earthly remains shipped out of the festering metropolis to a pleasant final resting place in the country. And Grimdale – with its picturesque woodland and connections to the royal family – was *the* happening place to be dead.

Because of its illustrious clientele, the Grimdale cemetery is filled with all manner of grand gravestones, sacred statuary, and marvelous mausoleums. Archaeologists and historians come from all over the world to study funerary architecture, and it's the village's most important tourist attraction.

It's also my favorite place in the whole world, and I've been away for far too long.

I cut through the hole in the back fence that Mr. Pitts hasn't fixed and wander between the towering mausoleums and along the neat rows of Victorian graves. I breathe in the fresh, damp air and the scent of moss and rotting leaves.

I remember.

A pair of angel statues at the end of this row – a female with a flowing dress, and a male with wings unfurled – bend their heads toward each other as if they're deep in conversation. As a kid, I used to make up stories about the angels gossiping about the other statues when they thought no one was listening, and mocking the tourists who take tasteless photos posing on the graves.

Sometimes, Ambrose would walk with me around the graveyard. Ghosts don't like being in cemeteries – it reminds them of their own painful deaths. Edward and Pax had their own reasons for avoiding the cemetery. Edward didn't like being confronted by his own grandiose and garish grave erected by his friends, since his family disowned him (although he did occasionally deign to stand on the edge of the cemetery to give a suitable backdrop for his morose and terrible poetry).

And when Pax was alive, the cemetery land was the site of a bloody battle between the Roman forces and the Celtic tribes where he was slain, and he can still hear the Celtic war cries as they mowed down his friends...

Ambrose is also buried in the Grimdale graveyard, but if he felt uncomfortable so near his own grave, he never complained to me. He liked being out in the open air where there were fewer things for him to accidentally walk through, and he ran in the same circles as some of the famous Victorians buried here. He had stories about the Van Wimple family that were definitely *not* appropriate for an eight-year-old to hear.

I wish he was here now... I wish they all were...

No. I shake my head. *No, I don't wish.*

I've spent my whole life running away from ghosts, trying to be normal. I finally have some semblance of peace and quiet, and I have this huge, horrible sadness gnawing away inside me, and I'm not going to make my life even harder just because—

"Bree Mortimer, is that really you?"

I whirl around, startled out of my daydreams. "Oh, hello, Mr. Pitts." I wave to the cemetery warden as he hobbles down the path toward me. Mr. Pitts is one of those old people of indeterminate age who seems as if he's carved from the same stone as the graves. "It is me. I'm staying with my parents for a little while."

He tilts his head to the side. "I thought they were in Europe, on their big adventure?"

"They are, I mean, I'm staying in their house, looking after Dad's new kittens. Eventually, they'll come back."

I hope.

"That's good. It's good they're making the most of things. Such sad news. I couldn't believe it when I heard. You bearing up okay?"

I swallow hard. "I'm fine."

"That's good. You always were a tough girl. What are you doing with yourself these days, Bree Mortimer?"

"Oh...nothing." My cheeks burn. "I mean, I might help my parents run the B&B over the summer. I'm sort of between jobs at the moment. I don't know how long I'll be in Grimdale for..."

"Oh, dearie me," he tsks. "I'm not trying to embarrass you. I'm asking because I'm in a bit of a pickle, and I wondered if you can help. You see, I hired a young lass from the village as a tour guide for the season, but she's run off to London with that Fitzwilliam boy, and so I don't have anyone to run the tours. An' I thought since you know these old stories so well, maybe you'd like to—"

"I'd love to." I perk up immediately. This is better than I could have hoped for. I needed a job, and working in Grimdale Graveyard meant that I wouldn't have to be harangued by the dead every minute of my workday.

Plus, I really do love it here.

"Thank you, Bree. You'd be doing me a huge favor. I'm afraid I can't pay much—"

"That's okay, I've got free rent for the summer, so I don't need much." *Just enough to get me far away from Grimdale, as soon as possible.* "It's my pleasure. When should I start?"

49

"Is tomorrow too soon? I've got a busload of American tourists booked in, and I was hoping not to have to cancel on them." He leans against his rake. "Come back to the office with me. I have some maps and brochures for you. We got a new one printed up just the other month – you'll love it."

I don't need a brochure, as the stories are ingrained in my subconscious, but I follow my new boss through the Avenue of Tears, past the witches' monument and the Van Winkle mausoleum, to the tiny stone cottage where the Victorian warden used to live, but now serves as a combination ticket office and garden shed.

"If these stones could talk, eh?" Mr. Pitts taps his rake on the corner of the witch's monument. "These old ghosts are as happy as I am to have you back."

I'm not so sure they are.

6

AMBROSE

"What's she doing now?" I ask desperately.

"She's walking around the cemetery with Mr. Pitts," Edward says in that insouciant voice of his, the one that pretends to be thoroughly bored with the present situation. "Perhaps he wishes to bed her now that he's encountered her ample bosoms—"

I stick my tongue out at him. It's not very gentlemanly, but I don't feel kindly disposed to Edward today.

We're hiding in the woods behind the manor, on the steps that lead down to the public walking trail at the bottom of the gully, watching Bree on her first day back in Grimdale. And despite his feigned indifference, I know Edward is just as curious about her return as I am.

Okay, if I'm being honest – and a writer should always be honest, at least with himself – I'm more than curious. I'm filled with a raging *desperation* that I haven't known since the day my friend stuck me on the back of an elephant, handed me the reins, and told me to "hold on tight, old chap."

Bree is *home*, and she smells of sadness and adventures. All I want to do is talk to her in that easy way we've always talked, but I *can't*. So I'm resorting to spying on her like a degenerate.

"What's about now?" I ask through gritted teeth. Edward knows I need him to describe what's going on — we've lived together in Grimwood Manor since my death one hundred and forty-eight years ago. But he enjoys leaving me in the dark. I guess he's used to the people around him existing only for his amusement, for he certainly takes pleasure in my misery.

At least *I* died with dignity, unlike our resident prince, who shuffled off mid-opium binge after he tripped over his own pantaloons and fell out of the turret window. When you become a ghost, you walk around for eternity wearing the clothes you died in. Edward's doomed to spend eternity with his white shirt hanging open, his codpiece crooked from the fall, and a large piece of glass sticking out of his posterior.

I much prefer Pax's company on an outing. Pax loves explaining every detail and learning about what's changed in the world since he bought his one-way ticket on the Charon express. But unfortunately, Pax can't join us on our covert mission, because we must stay hidden, and our Roman friend's booming voice and sizable shoulders are anything but subtle.

"...they're just talking...and that chap with the strange saucer on a stick device is walking along the path now, waving it back and forth across the ground..."

"I don't care about him. Tell me about Bree." On a normal day, I'm very much interested in the man with the saucer on the stick. He walks through the forest most weeks, often straying from the path to push his saucer under bushes and pick at the dirt with a knife. I once heard Silvie swear at him once to get his 'metal detector' off her land. But today, I can think only of Bree.

"...Oh, now Pitts has handed Bree a stack of pamphlets," Edward says with a sigh. "Perhaps she's his new assistant.

That's how Livings in this age like to have their affairs – I saw it in the moving picture box. Of course, in my day, we didn't have to hide our illicit liaisons. The more women I took to my bedchamber, the more my esteem rose in the minds of my people oh—" he jerks away and grabs the back of my neck, shoving me forward. "Duck. She's coming this way."

I flatten myself on the ground and hold my breath, even though I don't technically have breath to hold. I can hear Bree puffing as she walks back up the path. At the top, she meets her neighbours – the Fernsbys – as they set off on their daily walk through the woods to collect herbs and wildflowers for Maggie's apothecary. Maggie tells Bree that she's left her a shepherd's pie and some scented candles on the kitchen counter. Bree thanks her and moves on toward the house, and the Fernsbys continue on down the other fork in the path, deeper into the woodland.

I wait until I can no longer hear Maggie's pealing laughter or Bree's puffing. I sit up, rubbing the back of my neck where Edward had held me down. Ghosts might not be able to interact with the Living world in any meaningful way, but we can certainly feel each other.

"That was close. It reminds me of that time I joined the circus in France and accidentally walked into the tiger's cage on my way to the water closet—"

"Yes, yes, I've heard all about it a thousand times," Edward huffs. "But you're right, that *was* close. I've seen a flaw in our plan – it's going to be very difficult to avoid Brianna while she's living here."

"I've been thinking the same thing, old bean," I say, with less than my usual enthusiasm. "We might have to consider the possibility of—"

"No," Edward says firmly.

"But I think it's the only way we can avoid—"

"We are *not* moving back into the attic, and that's final. Consider it a royal decree."

"Okay, okay." I adjust my cravat. I don't particularly want to move to the attic. We lived there for two years after we made our promise to Bree, and at first it was cramped and miserable. But now that He lives there...it's downright *terrifying*.

"Although..." Edward says thoughtfully, and even though I can't see him, I'm positive he's rubbing his chin. "The attic does give me an idea. We can avoid Brianna if we adjust to a nocturnal schedule. We'll sleep during the day, and while she's sleeping we can get up and do our ghost things."

But then we won't see her, I want to say. But, of course, that's the point. I nod. "A most ingenious plan. In fact, I think I'll go get started on my evening nap right now."

"Ambrose, wait up! Hey, Ambrose, you have to be careful that you don't walk in on her—"

As if I don't know that. I'm more attuned to her than you will ever be.

I beat Edward up the path and float through the conservatory wall, listening carefully for Bree's presence. She's in the kitchen, humming to herself as she clatters dishes, puts the shepherd's pie in the oven, and chops vegetables for a salad. As quietly as I can, I slip away down the hall into the west wing, heading for my bedroom.

It wasn't easy being a blind man during the nineteenth century – most people thought I should have been locked away in an institution, instead of traveling around the world and writing books about it. I carried a walking stick with a brass tip that I tapped on the ground. The sound produced by the echoes helped me to discern obstacles and find my way on my own, and I could also sweep my cane in front of me to feel undulations and textures in the ground's surface, and thus navigate around obstacles.

But being a living blind man is a fiddle compared to being a dead one. As far as I know, I'm the only blind ghost in existence, but I base this conclusion only on the paltry research I've been able to conduct – chatting to the other ghosts floating around Grimdale and overhearing the podcasts about true hauntings Bree used to listen to.

For some reason that we don't understand but attribute to 'ghost mojo,' my cane accompanied me into the afterlife. Pax, also, still carries his sword. Although my hands will not connect with objects, the tip of my cane will, and so I navigate the house the same way I did in life – by sweeping and tapping. This produces sounds that are audible to Livings, but they put it down to knocking in the pipes or the house 'settling.'

I also have a more attuned sense of touch than the other ghosts – while Edward and Pax fall through any object without feeling it, I can sense the edges of things with my fingers, some-times even enough to move very, very light things. I don't believe I'm more powerful than the other ghosts, especially since I'm the youngest. I certainly can't do Edward's rather salacious *thing* with the electricity. But I needed to sense the walls and objects, so I developed the ability to do that.

I listen in the kitchen for a while, cursing myself for my lurking creepiness. Her footsteps fade from the kitchen, down the hall, and into her bedroom. I follow. I'm drawn to her as a moth to a flame.

I pause at the door to the guest room Bree is sleeping in, allowing myself a few moments to drink in her scent. Even though she's all grown up now, Bree still smells exactly the way I remember her – like a warm, crackling fire on a stormy night, like a pear and almond tart and mulled wine straight from the pot, like comfort and home and the juiciest parts of a good book.

I want so badly to curl up on the bed and talk to her. I want to hear all about her adventures. I wonder if she's been to Australia. We always talked about going to Australia—

But I *promised*.

I have to get away from her, away from temptation. I'm making myself crazy standing here smelling her. And she could turn and see me at any moment.

I tear myself away from the door and head down the hall to my bedroom.

Last century, all three of us chose rooms for ourselves in distant corners of the house – sanctuaries where we could go to be away from each other. We're not allowed to enter each other's rooms upon pain of pain.

(There's not much you can threaten a ghost with, and certainly not death, but we all have ways of making each other's bodies feel pain, so that's our currency.)

Edward claimed the master suite in the guest wing for himself, because of course. It's the most expensive guest suite in the house, which means that it's usually empty save for when it's occupied by newlyweds. Edward says he's learned many new tricks that make even his libertine sensibilities quake.

I'm too much of a gentleman to ask him for details.

Pax's room is upstairs in the turret. It's directly above Bree's old bedroom and has floor-to-ceiling windows that look out over the cemetery and the woods. He says that he likes having a defensive position over the landscape, but I'm certain he chose that room because it's close to Bree.

And possibly also because it was the very room from which Edward fell to his death. Pax was very annoyed at Edward the day we chose our rooms.

My space is accessed through the back of the closet in one of the guest rooms – it's a secret room Bree found one day while she was exploring the house. She thinks it might be something called a priest hole – Grimwood Manor was the residence of a prominent Catholic family during Elizabeth I's reign, where Catholics were forbidden to practice their faith and any priest found performing the rites would be sent to the tower. Rumor has it that many priests hid from Elizabeth's soldiers in the walls of Grimwood, before the family was eventually imprisoned and the house gifted to Edward, who wasted no time turning it into a den of sin and debauchery.

Before we stopped talking, Bree placed a few things inside the priest hole that she thought I'd like. Some scented candles and soaps, their smells long faded. A strange device called an MP3 player that's supposedly loaded with audiobooks, although I've never been able to press the buttons hard enough to get it to work. And a tactile globe – the continents are raised from the surface, and if I concentrate very hard I can feel the edges with my fingers. Bree traced the path of my travels using pins and string, and I can feel that, too. I can speak aloud the names of the places I visited and remember all my adventures, although it carves my chest hollow.

How splendid it would be to be a ghost if only I could travel further than the edge of Grimdale village! Alas, it is my own personal torture to have infinite time to explore the world's joys and yet, not be able to go anywhere at all.

And Bree understood. She understood me in the way no other person ever has, living or dead. But then she told me never to speak to her again, and then she left and never came back...

Until now.

I tuck myself into my little hidey-hole, set down my cane,

and hover over the pile of dusty duvet covers Bree kept in there so she could curl up and read to me.

Bree. That blazing almond and pear scent of her still dances on my senses. Her smell pulls me deeper as I drift into a dream-filled sleep...

7

BREE

Mum: Bree, darling. I hope you're settling in okay! Just a couple of quirks about the house you might not remember.

1. If you hear a clanging, tapping noise, don't worry about it – it's just the pipes.

2. The power seems to be on the fritz. I've had Sam look at it and he says nothing's wrong. So don't freak out if you see the lights flickering.

3. If you hear any strange noises coming from the attic, it's just Ozzy. He's a bat who moved in up there and your father decided to give him the run of the place. We're off to Versailles today – hopefully your father won't get his head chopped off for one of his tasteless frog jokes.

Talk soon!

I sink down further in the bathtub, breathing in deep, letting the scent of lavender and bergamot from Maggie's 'Calming and Relaxing' candles soak away the tension in my body.

Ah, this is the life.

I can't remember the last time I had a bath. I've been sharing bathrooms with other backpackers for the last five years, and let me tell you, it gets old. One of the draws to coming back here was the guest bathroom with its enormous clawfoot bathtub, fluffy towels, and Maggie's homemade candles, all of which I'm taking full advantage of right now.

I cross my feet on the end of the tub, sink deeper into the bubbles, and crack open one of Mum's smutty romance novels. I have a glass of wine and St. Vincent playing on my portable speaker, and the best thing of all is that there isn't a single ghost in sight...

I could get used to this.

I turn the page and reach for my wine and—

"Argh!"

I come face to face with the brilliant blue eyes and noble features of a slightly see-through Victorian gentleman who's fallen through the wall and landed half in my bathwater.

"Argh!" cries the ghost.

The water temperature rises ten degrees as he struggles to pull himself out. I'm aware of his arms thrashing in the water, dangerously close to my lady bits, and just how much that makes my heart leap.

It's the hot water, that's all, the water is too hot...

"I'm sorry! I'm sorry!" Ambrose cries as he flings himself away from me. Unfortunately, because he's blind, he doesn't see the candles and ends up falling through them, causing the flames to flicker out, plunging the room into near darkness.

"I'm naked!" I splash him with water, which falls straight through him. "And I have open flames in here! What are you doing?"

"I didn't mean to intrude. I smelled something delicious in my sleep, and I must've floated through this wall by mistake. I'll leave you be. I promise you won't see me anywhere again."

Ambrose's shoulders sag as he dusts himself off and turns back to the wall. My heart aches. Here's Ambrose, my childhood friend, and it's the first time I've seen him since I told him to leave me alone forever and he's...

...he's fucking *hot*.

"Wait."

Ambrose freezes, his frock coat flapping around his thighs.

"Just...hang on a second, will you?"

I rise out of the tub, my heart pounding. I'm aware of every hair on my body standing on end as I move, naked and exposed, across the slippery floor to the stack of towels I placed on the vanity.

Why are you afraid? It's Ambrose, and he won't hurt you.

I'm not afraid of him – my childhood friend, my closest confidante, my fellow restless soul.

I'm afraid of what seeing him and talking to him is doing to me.

I'm afraid of the way my body is reacting to seeing him again. I'm terrified of the quickening in my heart and the deep ache that swells inside me. I'm frightened of the way my skin burns where his ghostly fingers brushed me.

You haven't slept with anyone since New Zealand, that's all this is. You're sleep-deprived and horny, and any man or ghost will do. You'll get over it in a day or so.

I hope.

I wrap a huge, fluffy towel tight around my body, making sure that everything is covered and tucked in. I right the candles, noting with dismay the splotches of wax on the tiles I'll have to clean up before we open for guests again.

"I can go," Ambrose murmurs, his voice strained. He still hasn't turned away from the wall. "I didn't mean to—"

"You're here now. Let's..." I search for the right words. "Let's catch up. It's been a hot minute—"

"—seven years, two months, and twenty-four days—"

My heart skips. "You've been counting."

He nods. His shoulders hitch. "I started when we lived in the attic. There wasn't much else to do up there."

"Wait, when did you live in the attic?"

Ambrose opens his mouth, but I interrupt him. "You know what, we're not talking about this here, in the bathroom, with water everywhere. Do you want a drink?"

"Yes." His face perks up. "A glass of ale. You can drink ale now, can't you?"

I grin. "I sure can, and an ale sounds like the perfect thing. Can you wait outside?"

Ambrose floats out through the wall, his cane making its familiar tapping noise on the ground – the noise that every guest in the house writes up in their reviews as ghostly happenings. We tell everyone it's the pipes, but for once, the overactive imaginations of tourists are right.

I move quickly, so I don't have time to question my sanity. I pull on clean clothes – a pair of tight black jeans and a long t-shirt with the band Blood Lust on the front, because even though it's supposedly moving into summer, it's also *England*. When I open the bathroom door, Ambrose is still waiting there. He turns to me, his eyes the azure blue of the ocean around the tiny Greek island where I spent a month skinny-dipping with a Spanish tour guide, dappled with sunlight – such warm, expressive eyes for a man who is blind.

I notice other things about him, things that had started to stir in teenage Bree but I'd convinced myself with time and distance didn't matter. I notice the sharp edges and perfect tailoring of his Victorian clothing, perfectly hugging his body to accentuate his trim figure, narrow waist, and broad shoulders. So different from the scruffy men in t-shirts and flip-flops I usually found.

I notice how long and sure his fingers are, and my skin buzzes with the memory of his touch. It's not even a real touch, not skin on skin, and it's affected me more than any of the living men I've been with over the last four years.

I *definitely* notice the wide, genuine smile that lights up his whole face, and the way it softens his jawline. A smile that's for me and only me.

My heart does that flippy thing it hasn't done in a very long time.

He touched your tits. A ghost touched your tits.

It was an accident.

It may have been an accident, but I can't deny the fact that my nipples are hard under my t-shirt thinking about it. How is that even possible? He's a *ghost*.

I'm messed up in the head.

"Hello," Ambrose says, his voice low, unusually harsh.

"H-h-hello." I swallow once, twice. My mouth feels like a foreign object. I've been staring at him for Hades knows how long without saying anything. "Shall we, um, get that drink?"

Ambrose steps aside and sweeps his hand in the direction of the kitchen. "After you, m'lady."

I head downstairs to the kitchen and pull out a craft beer from the fridge. Ambrose taps his way over to the counter and inserts his face in the glass as I pour the beer inside.

"Aaaaah," he sighs. "That hit the spot."

I pour another for myself and carry them through into the snug. It's this small area off the kitchen containing shelves filled with airport books, brochures for attractions around Grimdale, and the best reading nook in the house. One entire corner of the room is given over to a bay window that juts out into the woodland. The window seat is large enough for two people to lie next to each other, and it's covered with enough cushions to send Laurence Llewelyn-Brown into a tailspin.

I flop down into the pile of cushions. Ambrose sits gingerly on the edge beside my feet, floating in midair, about an inch above the surface of the cushions. It's a little disconcerting, but I'm used to this sort of thing.

I set his glass on the windowsill beside him so he can sniff it to his heart's content. Entwhistle leaps up and curls up in my lap, purring happily. I bring my own glass to my lips and take a long drag, but I don't think beer is going to quench the thirst I feel at seeing him again.

He's exactly the same ghost I saw as a kid – the same Victorian gentleman in a natty frock coat with his pocket-watch chain hanging down and his golden hair combed neatly back from his face. And yet, I don't remember ever looking at him and feeling the way I feel now, as if the floor has fallen out from beneath me.

When I made the decision to come back to Grimwood, I didn't know if I wanted to see the ghosts again. But now that I'm sitting beside Ambrose, I...I realize just how much I *wanted* this.

I missed him. I've thought of him every time I landed in a new country or saw a brilliant sight. I cried at the base of the Great Pyramid of Giza because I was with this super annoying Belgium guy and I really wanted to be there with Ambrose.

But I can't say that. Not yet.

"So..." I take another long sip of beer. "How are...things?"

"Oh, excellent, excellent." Ambrose gestures to the window. "It's all the same around here. Pax wages war against an imaginary Celtic army, Edward recites his appalling poetry and orders us around, and I eavesdrop on the guests' tales of adventure."

"You know..." I grin. "I've had some adventures myself. I finally did it, Ambrose. I did exactly what we said all of those years. I walked out of here with my clothes strapped to my back, went to the airport, and booked the first flight to anywhere that wasn't here. And it was everything I dreamed of."

Until it wasn't.

Ambrose holds my gaze with too much intensity for someone who can't see. My skin hums like my blood is made of bees. His lip curls into another panty-melting smile as he slides closer, his knee brushing mine. The bees dance beneath my skin.

This is crazy. I'm not supposed to feel like this about a *ghost*.

Especially not a ghost who's seen me cry over school bullies and puke up my eighth birthday cake after I got a stomach bug.

Ambrose's too-pretty lips open, and I know he's bursting to ask me about my travels, about all the things that made his blood run hot when he was alive. Instead, he jerks back and turns his head away. "That's nice," he mumbles into his cravat. "I'm happy for you."

That's nice?

"You...you *don't* want to know about my travels?" I hate how desperate I sound. All the stories I've told myself about what I wanted from Grimdale crumble as I stare at his tense shoulders.

Everywhere I travelled, I met new people. In the youth hostels and backpacker bars, I was surrounded by laughter, partying, excited conversation. But it's all shallow, surface connections. Nothing feels real. Nothing *lasts*.

Even when you think you connect with someone on a soul level, you move on or they move on, and as soon as you're away from the magic of a Greek sunset or a remote New Zealand bush cabin, your memory of them fades into sepia. They become another postcard on your journey, existing only in two dimensions, as if they never even had a soul at all but are merely an extension of your own searching.

But not Ambrose.

He's never been sepia to me.

His shoulders shudder.

"Ambrose, please, turn around."

He shakes his head. "I can't."

"Why not?"

"I shouldn't be here, with you, like this. I'm breaking my promise."

My heart twists. I did this. I made him feel like this. "You made that promise to me seven years ago, and then I left. You're released from your oath to me. Please, Ambrose, talk to me. I swear that's what I want."

The words rush out before I can stop them, but I don't take them back.

Ambrose inclines his head, focused on his long fingers clenched on his knees, as if he's desperately holding himself back from something. "Why are we doing this, Bree? Why are we having a drink together?"

"I missed you."

His lips puff out, and he makes a sound like he's in pain. "But you said—"

"I know what I said," I growl, slamming my glass down on the windowsill. Beer sloshes over the side. Ambrose winces at the sound, but Entwhistle knows he's on to a good thing so doesn't move a muscle. "And I stand by it. The three of you were making my life miserable. I just wanted to be a normal teenage girl. But you kept showing up everywhere, making me look like a freak. And then Trevor—"

The memory flashes back to me. It was the night of my first real date – I was a flat-chested fifteen-year-old in the middle of my goth phase when Trevor Sutcliffe invited me to the school dance. We stood in the corner most of the night while he laughed with his friends and put his arm over my shoulder, and Kelly Kingston glared daggers at me across the room. It was the greatest night ever, even if a hulking Roman Centurion did tail us the whole night with his sword tip waggling dangerously close to Trevor's crotch.

Then, Trevor walked me home along the woodland path. At the bottom of the garden, he turned and pulled me in close and kissed me. It wasn't an earth-shattering kiss – in fact, it was kind of gross, way too much spit – but it was my *first kiss*. And Trevor was popular, and he made me laugh, and he was a normal, *corporeal* guy.

But then the three ghostkateers showed up over my shoulder and started talking about how he wasn't good enough for me, and Pax tried to stab him, and I yelled at them to leave me alone and Trevor thought I was talking to him. He called me a freak and ran away, and I knew that the next day at school he'd tell everyone and I'd never get another date to a dance ever again.

So I told Ambrose, Pax, and Edward to leave me alone. I said they'd had the run of the house for too long. All my life I'd catered to their whims. I made their favorite snacks to sniff and played with them and listened to their stories. And now I wanted some time for myself. I wanted quiet.

I wanted them to go away.

And they obeyed.

For two years, they left me alone. I don't know where they went, but I never saw them in Grimwood Manor again. Edward wasn't practicing his poetry while I tried to memorize physics formulas. Ambrose didn't sit in the corner of the guest lounge listening to the travellers' talking. Pax wasn't at the foot of my bed when I went to sleep every night, guarding me against the monsters.

I missed them terribly, but I needed the break. I did better at school. I went to a few parties. I saved every penny I made cleaning rooms in the B&B, and the day after I graduated high school, I packed up my things and hopped on a plane to Germany.

And now I'm facing Ambrose, and all these complicated memories and new feelings, and I want to explain, but it's hard, so hard...

"I don't think you understand how bad things were for me." I stroke Entwhistle's tiny body with more force than is perhaps required. "I felt like my head was going to explode from all the noise. Sometimes I felt like I didn't know who was more real, the ghosts or the kids at school. I just needed to exist in the real world for a bit and—"

"Bree, it's okay. You don't have to explain yourself or pretend that you want to talk to me. I know how you feel. I made a silly mistake falling through the wall. I'll be more careful in future. We're trying to stay out of your way—"

"You are? All of you?" Is this why I haven't seen or heard a peep from them since I got back? "Pax and Edward are still here, too? I thought after all this time, one of you must have crossed over, or you didn't care about me, or—"

"We'll never stop caring about you," Ambrose says gruffly.

He turns to me, and my chest tightens. His eyes brim with blue fire as he fixes on me as if he can see me. Ambrose always has this way of looking through me, as if I'm the see-through one and not him, as if he of all people can see right into my bones.

"I wish you could have come with me." My eyes brim with tears.

Ambrose swallows, his ghostly Adam's apple bobbing. "Me too."

A silence descends between us. Ambrose and I are rarely silent. We always have so much to talk about – places we long to travel to, people we think are interesting, stories we've heard and wish to share. He reads so many books and knows so much about so many things, and he's always interested in what's changed since he died. But now...I'm so *aware* of him that all my words die on my tongue.

I take a deep breath and battle through my raging emotions for something neutral to cling to. "So do you want to hear about the time I was stranded in Istanbul with no passport and only one change of underwear?"

A thousand emotions play across his features. I hold my breath, afraid he'll turn away again or disappear through the wall. Instead, he leans forward, his knee setting the bees in my veins a-buzzing where it touches mine. "Please, Bree, tell me *everything*."

8

PAX

"She talked to me! She talked to me! She—argh!"

Ambrose skids into the room, so excited that he swings his cane around like a gladiator on *kill-one-get-one-free* day at the Colosseum. The cane's tip catches on the edge of the table and sends him flying into the chair where Edward is hovering.

"Meeeerrww!" Moon barrels out from under the chair, leaps on top of the liquor cabinet, and glares at us with glimmering sorceress eyes.

"Get off me, you fiend!" Edward shoves Ambrose off him.

I burst out laughing. It's always hilarious when prissy Edward gets knocked around.

"How dare you touch royalty, you oaf?" Edward makes an attempt to smooth down his rumpled white shirt. "Don't think I won't cut your hand off again—"

"Do that and I'll cut your mint stalk off with my sword *again*," I growl at him, cracking my knuckles. "And you know how much that tickles."

Edward pales and plops back down in his seat, his hands cupped protectively over his squashed codpiece.

"She *talked* to me," Ambrose paces back and forth excitedly, too engrossed in what he's saying to notice that he's walking through the fireplace. "I saw her in the bathroom and she invited me—"

"You were in the bathroom with her?" Edward and I exchange a glance. That's not *fair*. We all agreed that we wouldn't spy on Bree in the bathroom.

It's not fair that the only person to see Bree naked is the one who can't even appreciate her glorious bosoms.

"Get your minds out of the gutter. I accidentally fell through the wrong wall. It was completely innocent." Ambrose waves a hand, but a blush forms on his pale cheeks, and it takes a lot to make a ghost blush.

"What did you do to Bree?" I leap to my feet, my hand flying to the hilt of my sword. "By Jupiter's gnarly gonads, if you've spoiled her virtue with your ghost verpa I will mince it and feed it to Entwhistle and then you'll never get it back—"

"I swear, I didn't do anything!" Ambrose throws his hands up. "She was in the bath all covered in bubbles, and I fell in and my hand just *grazed* her and—"

"What did she feel like?" Edward asks softly.

"Like the smoothest Chinese silk." Ambrose sighs.

I fold my arms. I don't want to talk about what Bree feels like, because we'll never truly get to feel her. Not in any way that matters. And now my verpa is standing at attention, and ghosts can't jerk their own cucumbers, and it's very annoying. When I get annoyed, I like to stab things. "Does she want to see us?"

Ambrose looks sheepish. "I didn't ask."

"What do you mean, you didn't ask?"

"We were too busy talking about her travels. Oh, Edward, she's been *everywhere*. She even went to the Parthenon in Rome just because I said that she'd like it—"

"She went to Rome?" I perk up. "Did she speak with the consul about my pay, because I'm due seventy-five denarii and—"

"Dead soldiers don't get paid, Pax. We've been through this before. Why is Brianna back?" Edward says. He's always called her by her full name; he says that no one ever wrote a brooding love poem for someone named Bree. "If she's had this amazing life, then why did she come back to the place where we caused her so much pain?"

"I didn't get to that, either." Ambrose's face falls. "All I did was mention Mike, and she went all quiet and burst into tears and ran away to her room."

She's upset?

He upset her?

No, no, no, no. This won't do. Bree can't be upset. I don't know why her father's name would upset her, but that's not the important thing here. Our Bree shouldn't have to be sad, *ever*.

If she's upset, she'll leave us again. I don't want her to leave again. The last seven years without her have been the most awful in my entire afterlife, and that includes the fifty-eight years after my death when the Druids used the battlefield for their sacred rituals and I saw enough naked Druid butts to give me nightmares for eternity.

"I want to talk to her!" I sheath my sword and move for the door.

Ambrose sticks his cane out, and I trip over it and go flying through the ottoman. *Ooof, that hurt.*

"She's asleep." Ambrose folds his arms. "And I don't think either of you should talk to her. Not until she says it's okay."

And leave Bree's happiness in the hands of the blind ghost? No – if a Roman centurion has a problem, he takes a stab at it himself. Often literally.

"What say you, prince?" I turn to Edward. "We have ways of

making her talk. Remember when we used to tickle her until she'd tell us what we wanted to know?"

"As much as I detest saying this, Ambrose is right. We made a promise, and I will not break it unless Brianna wishes it." Edward strokes the edge of his open shirt. His usual haughty expression is pensive. "Now, if you'll excuse me, I'm in the mood to write some poetry—"

"Do it in your room," I growl. "Far away from us."

Edward's poetry is like naked Druid butts – if they must be endured, best in extremely small quantities and while very, very drunk.

"I must do it here," Edward declares, leaping to his feet. "The lighting is just perfect and the gloomy atmosphere stimulates my creative juices—"

"Fine, Fine." I do not want to be anywhere near Edward's stimulated juices. I perform my perimeter check of the house and head to my bedroom, which is located in the turret, directly over Bree's old room. She is not sleeping in her old room, and that makes me nervous, too. She has chosen the guest room closest to the front door, so that she can run away faster. It's an old army trick I taught her.

I don't want her to run away again.

I pause in the doorway of her old room, performing my nightly ritual of checking for monsters under her bed and bogeymen in her closet. She asked me to do that when she was six and afraid of the dark, and I've never stopped. I've stood watch beside her bed every night.

And the others don't know that after she told us she didn't want to see our see-through faces again, I'd sneak down from the attic and stand guard outside her window.

A soldier follows orders, especially when those orders make his Imperator's face light up.

I float over the bed to touch my hand to the inscription in

the plaster – Bree scratched it there one night when she couldn't sleep and the three of us were telling her stories to cheer her up.

$$B + P + E + A = 4EVA.$$

"By Jupitor's Thorny Nutsack," I swear my nightly ritual. "I will always protect you."

No monsters found. I ascend to my room – also known as the 'box room' or the 'room of dust and despair.' Edward calls it a gloomy, rat-infested shithole and refuses to set foot inside. To me, it feels homely. It reminds me of my tent while out on campaign. And unlike Edward's 'boudoir' (I don't know what that means, but it's what he insists we call his bedroom), it's not filled with copulating newlyweds.

It is, however, becoming increasingly full of random objects Mike and Sylvie have no use for anymore. They used to put those things in the attic, but since Ozzy moved in, they're too nervous to go up there.

I don't blame them.

I have faced the most terrifying enemies on the battlefield. I have been outnumbered ten to one and lived to tell the tale.

But Ozzy gives me the shits.

I step around a stack of stringed instruments called 'guitars.' Mike was using this room as a music studio. He plays the drums, which I approve of – nice rhythm to keep step while on the march! He hasn't touched his guitars in a couple of years, a fact for which I'm eternally grateful. Sleep comes much easier now that he's no longer trying to master a song called "Stairway to Heaven,' which reminds me too keenly of the ghastly, discordant music enjoyed by naked Druids.

I stand at the window and look down over the woods. Below the house, the cemetery stands silent and still. Sometimes, spotty-faced youths come to the graveyard to drink. I yell at them that if they have time to layabout, they should have joined the army, but of course they do not listen.

I blink. When I look again, I do not see the gravestones or the little souvenir stand by the gate. I do not see the mature trees crowding. I see the open battlefield, the Celtic warriors lining up on the other side, their skin painted blue with woad and their leaf-shaped swords sharpened and calling for blood. I hear my general issuing orders, feel the weight of my plumed helmet as I fit it on my head, and the heft of my sword in my hand...

I blink again and stare down at my hands. Without realizing it, I have taken out my sword. It no longer feels heavy.

It has no weight at all.

I tear my shield from my back and leap across the room, practicing my maneuvers. After so many centuries, the movements are still fresh in my mind, the slashes and stabs I used on the field that day alongside my brothers, my comrades...I stab at the air, remembering the sheer bloody joy of sliding my sword into the heart of my enemies, but all that makes me think of is sliding my *other* sword into Bree...

CRASH.

BANG.

SMASH.

"Knock it off, thou foul knave!" Edward yells from his bedroom. "You ruined a perfectly good couplet with your racket!"

I stare from the sword in my hands to the pile of splintered guitars. Sometimes, if I can work up the battle lust, my sword will connect with objects in the Living world. But it's never been powerful enough to slice and smash through a wooden instrument.

Until now.

80

It's because of her. Because she's here.

I want to talk to Bree. But they say no, not while she's sleeping. Fine, I shall talk to her tomorrow. I shall make her see that she belongs here, with us.

But tonight, I have a duty to perform. I affix my shield to my back with its leather straps, slide my sword into my belt, and float downstairs and through the front door. The thick wood smarts something fierce as I pass through, and the pain jolts me back to reality.

I must stay sharp.

I drop beneath her window and raise my head slightly. She's lying in bed, her gaze focused on the magical rectangle in her hands, the screen glowing with its powerful sorcery. While her attention is not on me, I slip through the wall, wincing with the pain of passing through the stones, and settle myself into position behind the heavy curtains.

A soldier always follows orders.

I have a duty to my Bree.

No monster will get through my guard. I will *always* watch over her.

THIS JOB IS HARDER than I remember.

And the job is not the only thing that's hard.

My be-testicled lance is ready to wage war. I'm harder than I've ever been as a ghost, *and* all I'm doing is standing behind this curtain, listening to Bree sleep and watching the graveyard battlefield for the enemy.

Fine, fine, if I'm being honest, I *might* have let my gaze

wander over to her. But only a couple of times! And only to check that no monsters have snuck up on her.

Not at all to focus on the way her ample bosoms rise and fall with her breath.

Not to marvel at the peaceful expression on her face, so different from the sadness clutching her when she walked into the house earlier.

Definitely, absolutely not to imagine myself lifting the blankets and drinking in the sight of her womanly body before crawling in beside her to stroke her until she screams my name...

She makes these little noises as she sleeps – squeaks and moans and murmurs that make me curse Venus for all the wrong and lustful things I imagine doing to her.

I grip the hilt of my sword. My *actual* sword. I ignore my verpa's demands.

I *will* perform my duty, no matter the temptation to do otherwise.

Something moves at the window. I snap to attention, but it's only Albert, the elderly neighbour. He dances wildly down his garden path toward the graveyard, no doubt under the influence of Bacchus' mushrooms. Some delightful varieties grow in the woodlands around the battlefield. My men and I had a jolly time eating them on the eve of battle and toasting the downfall of the Britons.

If I had known it was to be my final battle, I might have had double the amount!

Unfortunately, as a ghost, I can't join Albert on his midnight frolic. But he's given me an idea.

What I need is a drink, just to take the edge off.

To dull the blade of my *little sword*, so that I can focus.

A drink of fine Roman wine would help a soldier to withstand a long watch or lonely outpost. Unfortunately, as I no longer possess a stomach or throat, I cannot partake. But Edward learned that a ghost can still get a little...

I notice the strange contraption in the corner. Mike left his failed homebrew gin experiment within. He had a great idea to sell the guests little bottles with the Grimwood Manor logo on them as 'sooo-vin-ears,' but gave up after he pronounced the brew less like gin and more akin to 'rocket fuel.'

I don't know what rocket fuel is, but it sounds like exactly what I need to get me through this watch.

I check one more time that Bree's asleep, and then I float over to the still and shove my head inside.

I WAKE WITH A START. My hair is damp and plastered to my face. My head pounds like a Druid is dancing on my temples. What is wrong with me? Have we been attacked? Where is my sword—

"Oof." I trip over my sandal strap and topple backward on the floor. My vision spins, and for a moment I don't know where I am. I leap to my feet, sword drawn, and cast around me at the flapping velvet curtains, the mussed guest bed, the gin still, and women's clothing strewn across every surface. Last night's events hit me like the blow from a Gallic war-axe.

I stop undead when I realize that Bree's bed is empty. She's not in the room. I cross into the bathroom and stick my head through the door, feeling only the slightest twinge of guilt. Bree told us that under no uncertain terms were we to spy on her in the bathroom, but this is life or death—

Bree isn't in the bathroom, either.

Panic seizes me. Has she already left? But her rucksack is still here, her clothing strewn across the room. That would never be allowed in camp – a soldier must always be disciplined in his personal habits.

Bree came here. Bree talked to Ambrose, and then she got upset. I was supposed to watch her, but I filled my head with rocket gin fuel and now she's gone. She's left us again.

No, it's not too late! Not if I catch her first! I am excellent at catching things.

I whirl around to face the door and nearly keel over again. I must have fallen asleep in the gin still. That is disgraceful for a soldier on watch.

When he first appeared in the house after his death, Edward fell asleep in a bath full of champagne and realized that we could get a faint sense of drunken invincibility if we immerse our spectral bodies in alcohol. We still can't bring ourselves fully to climax because the afterlife is cruel and Pluto is a dick... but we can get a little joyous buzz.

Since then, Edward's moved on to attempting to box his one-eyed gladiator using the electrical circuits. But I...I am a man who appreciates the traditional Roman pastime of drinking oneself into oblivion.

I regret my decision now as I shake off the few droplets of gin that cling to my ghost skin. I march downstairs, full of purpose. Bree cannot have gotten far without her things. I am Pax Drusus Maximus, and I am heading to the battlefield to win back my woman—

"Pax?" Ambrose cries as I pass him in the entrance hall. "What are you doing?"

"Where is she?" I demand. "You have driven her away by allowing her to see you."

"She hasn't left us, Pax. Well, she has, but only for the morning," Ambrose says with a shrug. "She's gone to her job."

"Job? What is this job?"

The only jobs women in Rome had were as servants and prostitutes.

My hands ball into fists at the idea of disgusting men touching Bree's bosoms. "I will kill that man who hired her for this 'job'! I will kill all who touch her or even look at her or—"

"You're not that powerful, Pax." Ambrose grabs my wrists. I thrash about, ready to throw him through a wall so I can run off to rescue Bree's virtue, but he quickly adds, "And even if you were, her job isn't what you think. Remember that thing called feminism that Bree told us about once? Well, that means she doesn't have to service men to earn a wage. She's working in Grimdale Graveyard as a tourist guide."

"That sounds made up! Why would people pay to visit a field of dusty bones?"

I don't like it. That feels wrong. I know what tourists are because many of them stay at the manor. They are loud and have magical rectangles that cast bright beams of light, and they make silly poses and ask endless questions and leave rubbish everywhere. I don't want them walking over the bones of my brothers!

What if they're walking over my unburied bones, and I don't even know it?

A shudder runs through my body. Sometimes, during those dark days after Bree told us to leave her alone, I wished that my bones would be found – exposed by a rainstorm or dug up by someone's dog, so maybe some Living would take pity on a Roman soldier who died far from his home and give me a proper burial so I could finally cross over and join my brothers in Hades.

Now that Bree's back, I'm not ready to give up on ghosting. But the battlefield is sacred to Mars – it must be respected!

"It's not made up. People come to visit the cemetery because it's old and interesting," Ambrose says. "Bree will make sure they're respectful. And I bet you can see her from the window. So don't worry about her – she's fine, and she's coming back."

"No! You don't understand about that place. It changes you." Visions of my comrades flash before my eyes, their bodies trampled beneath the Celts' horses, their bones dragged off by the Druids for their bloody rituals. "People don't come back from there. I must save her!"

Edward and Ambrose don't understand that Bree needs me. *I'm* the one who taught her how to stab her enemies in the guts so they bleed out slowly. I'm the one who coaxed her as she climbed to the top of the tallest tree and then got too frightened to come down. I'm the one who held her hand while she explored the secret passage in the back of her mother's closet for the first time. Ambrose may be her adventuring friend, but I'm the one who protects her.

And I'm going to protect her now. She is sad, and I don't know why. She needs comfort! I give the best comfort! Everyone I threaten with my sword says so!

"Pax, come back!"

"I'm not afraid of no dead bones!" I shout back. "I'm going to bring our girl home!"

9

BREE

"...**A**nd here we turn into Poet's Way. The large angel statue guards the grave of the famous English poet, Robert LeBeau. Robert was a friend and contemporary of Byron and Shelley, and some say that his work was much more influential at the time, although he's now faded into obscurity. He briefly owned Grimdale Manor, which you can see on the hill—" I point to the roof of the house visible over the tops of the trees. The tourists 'oooh' and 'aaah'. "—and he often entertained the literati and libertines of London in lavish parties on the property. Many of the men and women buried along Poet's Way stayed in the house."

I stand back so the tour group can take their photographs. My very first tour as an official Grimdale Graveyard guide is a busload of American tourists and a couple of goth girls up from London. Immediately, an older American wearing a stars-and-stripes t-shirt and white socks with sandals starts peppering me with questions about military graves. "I don't like all this namby-pamby poet nonsense," he says. "I want to hear about guns and wars!"

"Oh, Gary, can't you leave the poor girl alone?" his wife

chastises him. I decide I like her, but then she drapes herself over LeBeau's grave and flips her hair while her friend takes a million pictures.

"Certainly, sir." I try to stifle a laugh at their antics. "We move to the military section near the end of the tour. I have one more grave to show you here, first."

My chest tightens as we pass by Edward's mausoleum – the grandest structure along Poet's Way, if not the entire cemetery. He was actually the first person buried here, back when the land where the graveyard and Grimdale Manor lie was part of his estate. Edward's libertine ways made him the black sheep of the royal family, so after his untimely death in the manor, they decided to bury him here without ceremony instead of in Westminster in London. His towering monument is draped all over with chubby cherubs and dancing skeletons – and I can see the goth girls staring at it forlornly.

But I only have the strength to talk about one of my childhood friends on this tour, and after last night's conversation, I know who it's going to be today.

I feel bad about how I ran out on Ambrose last night, but he mentioned my dad and it all suddenly caught up with me – that I'm talking to him again, that I'm home in Grimdale, and *why* I'm home in Grimdale. I went to my room and tried to call my parents, but if their present behavior is any indicator, they were probably out dancing in some Parisian nightclub and weren't picking up their phone.

If Dad can even dance anymore.

No. I don't have time to break down about this now. Not in the middle of my tour.

I lead the tour group down to an unassuming grave at the end of the row and point to the simple quote attributed to Saint Augustine carved beneath the name.

THE WORLD IS A BOOK, AND THOSE WHO DO NOT TRAVEL READ ONLY A PAGE.

I suck in a deep breath. It feels important, somehow, that I get this story right. That I make them *see* him.

"Here is the grave of the famous Victorian adventurer, Ambrose Hulme. Hulme was training for a career as a naval officer when he went blind at the age of eighteen from a degenerative disease. Blind people were not treated kindly in Victorian England, and he faced poverty and life in an institution, but Hulme chose instead to set out on a life of adventure and discovery. He brought passage on the first ship out of England and spent the next five years walking around Europe, the Middle East, and across Russia. He travelled on foot, by himself, with a brass-tipped cane that he tapped on the ground to help him discern objects and obstacles. In this way, he became one of the most extensive pedestrian travellers the world has ever known."

"Wow!" The Americans snap their pictures. I suck in a breath and continue.

"Braille hadn't been invented yet, so after he became blind Ambrose Hulme taught himself to write again by using a frame with pieces of string tied across it that he'd place over a blank page. The string would enable him to write in a straight line and know where he'd already written. Using this device he penned one of the world's first adventure travel guides to Europe, which is sadly no longer in print, as the only known copy was destroyed in a fire at his publisher's office in the fifties. He was working on another book about his Russian travels when death claimed him."

My throat closes up, and I have to cough a few times before I can carry on.

"Ambrose Hulme had all kinds of adventures – he walked

the steps of the ancients in Italy and Greece, fought the slave trade in Africa, and even hunted rogue elephants in Ceylon. He survived a harrowing journey across the frozen Russian landscape, only to be killed in Siberia when the Tsar became convinced that he couldn't possibly be a blind man travelling alone for travel's sake, and that he must be a spy."

The camera flashes go wild as the group crowd around for photos of Ambrose's grave. I can't help but feel a little bit of pride. Although Ambrose's travel book was popular in his day, it was mainly as a curiosity – people called him 'the blind adventurer,' but they didn't take Ambrose seriously as an explorer even though that's exactly what he was – and he died in obscurity.

Telling his story helps people remember him for the remarkable person he was. *Is.*

"That's so inspirational," the wife coos to her friend as I lead them to our next destination – a long, low stone building decorated in a Neo-Classical style. "I mean, if that fellow can walk around the world and he's blind, there's no excuse for me, is there?"

That's not the point of his story.

"I know exactly what you mean," her friend says back. "It's so brave of him to go and do all those things with his disability."

I want to yell at them all that I'm not telling them about Hulme so he can be their inspiration porn, and that Ambrose is brave not because of his lack of eyesight but because he literally rode elephants. He wanted to see the world and he did it, and he is kind and excitable and endlessly curious and hot AF and *so much more* than a blind man.

But that's not part of my job description.

So I grit my teeth as I fumble the keys in my pocket and finally manage to insert the right one in the rusty old lock, only to find that it's already open. Mr. Pitts isn't the best at remembering to lock up.

"Here's one of the most interesting areas of our cemetery," I say, eager to change the subject. I swing the wrought iron gate inward. "I need to warn you that if you're claustrophobic or afraid of the dark, you might like to wait outside."

No one ever waits outside.

"Oooh, is this where you keep the ghosties?" Gary rubs his hands together. The two goth girls push to the front of the group, their pale faces lit with excitement.

"These are the catacombs." I walk deeper into the cool, vaulted building, and my group tentatively follows me. "Because the cemetery became so popular and rich Londoners wanted to be buried here, the cemetery director wanted to look at ways of selling more plots without having to purchase more land. And so the catacombs were built as a way to offer people that coveted Grimdale plot at a cheaper price."

"Bree, is that you?" Someone steps out of the gloom toward me. It's Albert, and he looks a little confused.

"Albert, hi." I give him a little wave. "I didn't see you on the tour."

"Bree, you have to help me!" His voice rises in distress.

With a start, I realize what's happened. When Maggie dropped the shepherd's pie and bath products off yesterday, she told me that Albert is in the early stages of dementia. Since he's alone, and he's never without Maggie, I suspect he's wandered the wrong way from his house and become lost.

"I'm nearly done with the tour," I tell him. "You stick with me and I promise when I'm done I'll get you home to Maggie."

"Who's she talking to?" the wife turns to her husband. "Is Maggie some famous dead person?"

I turn back to the tour group and indicate the niches set along both walls of the catacombs beneath curved brick arches.

"Each niche houses nine coffins – the coffins are sealed behind these capstones, but some of the capstones have broken off, allowing us to glimpse the coffins beneath. Each coffin has three layers – a hardwood lining, a lead coffin, and an outer wooden layer that's often finely decorated—"

My words die on my lips as an enormous shape bursts through the wall and barrels straight at me.

"Bree Mortimer," the shape booms, and I recognize the leather armor, impossibly-broad shoulders, and plumed helmet of my childhood ghost friend, Pax. The Roman centurion storms through the tour group, uncaring that he's walking through their bodies. He's such an old ghost and in so agitated a state that he manages to knock the annoying American man over with the pommel of his sword. "I want to talk to you! Why won't you speak to me? Why are you only speaking to Ambrose?"

Please, not now.

I shake my head, hoping he'll get the message. Pax isn't exactly attuned to subtlety. *Just finish the tour and then you can deal with all this.* "These tombs were extremely popular with the mercantile classes, who wanted to demonstrate their newfound wealth by burying their dead in such a sought-after locale—"

"Why do you still ignore us? We are your friends. We only ever wanted to be your friends. We were always so good at cheering you up when you were sad. You're sad now and you don't want us to cheer you up?" He draws out his sword and stabs it around. "I will slay all your enemies if it will make you smile again!"

"—and you could pre-purchase a tomb to ensure your final resting place—"

"Is *he* your enemy?" Pax strides right up to Albert and waggles his sword in his face. "Because if he's hurt you, I'll crucify him. No, crucifixion's too good for him. I'll feed him to a starving lion, we'll just have to find a starving ghost lion somewhere—"

"Argh!" Albert covers his face with his hands and cowers beneath Pax's rage.

"Pax, stop," I hiss. "Could you please go home and wait for me there, and I'll talk to you."

"I will *not* go home. The tour isn't finished yet!" Gary booms, striding up to me and getting right up in my face. "You haven't taken us to the military graves. And you've been talking more than enough and not answering my questions. My throat is dry trying to get your attention. You'd better sell Coke at your souvenir shop or I'm going to leave a 1-star review!"

"I will not go home," Pax stamps his foot. "You ignore us at home, as you did before you left. All except Ambrose. How do we know you're not going to leave again? I am staying until you give me answers." He folds his arms and glares at me.

And so help me, but as I glare back, I can't help but notice the way his leather armor accentuates those enormous shoulders of his, and that proud, fierce expression as Pax does what he's always done – protect me.

Damn, why did I never notice how hot my old ghost friends were?

The thing with Pax is that he may be kind of psychotic, but he's a soldier. He responds to commands. I fix him with a death stare and point my finger in the direction of Grimwood Manor. "You will turn your Roman arse around and march back up that hill, and I will deal with you later. Disobey me and you will suffer. Just because you're undead doesn't mean I won't kill you."

"That's not any way to speak to us," Gary's wife huffs. "You'll be hearing from our lawyers! Take us to the war graves right now!"

"Bree, please, you have to help me," Albert pleads.

I whirl around and yell at Albert. "In a second!"

"No, *now!*" Gary's ready to explode. The rest of the tour group recoil in fear. I'm not afraid, I'm *pissed off.*

I can't even get through one tour without ghosts causing trouble and everyone thinking I'm a freak.

"But there's a man waving a sword around." Albert is trembling. "Isn't that dangerous?"

I freeze. "You...you can see Pax?"

"If he's the stabby fellow, then yes, I can see him," Albert nods vigorously. "Now will you help me?"

Hang on a second...

I've been so distracted, I didn't even notice...

Before, when Pax walked up to Albert, he cowered. *He cowered as if he could see Pax. But that's impossible, the only people who can see ghosts are me and other ghosts...*

I hold my breath as I look at Albert. Really look at him. And I realize that I can see right through him to the wall behind him, where one of the goth girls is poking some object that's been stuffed into an empty niche.

"This is a very realistic mannequin." The goth girl tucks her black braid behind her ear. "I approve."

No, not a mannequin.

A body.

A human body.

A human body wearing Albert's distinctive striped sweater.

Gary's wife starts to scream.

It looks like for the first time in over seventy-eight years, Grimdale Graveyard has a fresh corpse.

Albert looks between his body and my face. "See? I told you I needed your help."

10

BREE

Mum: Hi honey, I see we missed a call from you last night. Is everything okay? Did Ozzy chew through the wires again? We have to get that repaired before the first guests arrive in two weeks.

We made friends with a lovely German couple and they took us out on an evening dinner cruise, and it was so fun. We'll try and call you today, but we've got a jam-packed schedule of art galleries! I'm excited!

Your dad, the heathen, is excited about the wine on the menu in the art gallery cafe.

"Thank you, Bree, that's all we need from you for now." Inspector Hayes nods sagely as DS Wilson closes her notebook with a snap. "Please don't leave the shire for the next few days. We might need you to come down to the station to give a formal statement."

Albert's dead.

That's Albert's corpse being lifted carefully from the niche and placed into a white bag.

I've been surrounded by death my entire life. But this is the first time I've come face to face with an actual corpse. It's so... alien, an empty husk. The eyes open and empty – a void where a person should be.

Albert's dead.

And his ghost is currently trying to steal the inspector's hat.

I rise to leave. "Thank you. I hope you catch the culprit soon."

Because there *has* to be a culprit. Albert didn't just go for a walk, break into the catacombs, climb into one of the empty niches, and die in his sleep. The SOCO team has roped off the catacombs, and men and women in white sperm suits are walking everywhere, dusting and scraping and taking samples, *and* I distinctly heard them refer to this as a homicide.

Someone killed *Albert* – the kindliest old man in the village, giver of sage financial advice at the pub, chief of the tombola at every village fete, captain of the Grimdale over 60s cricket team, and the man unashamedly making other husbands look bad every February 14th with his huge public Valentine's day surprises for Maggie...

Oh, gods, someone will have to tell Maggie. She'll be devastated. I should find her and...

"Help!" Albert waves his arms in front of Sergeant Wilson. "Why can't you see me? Why are the police here? And why was there a fellow dressed like a Roman centurion? Is my wife okay? Have you seen my wife?"

"You're dead, Albert," I try to whisper out of the corner of my mouth. "That's why Wilson can't see you. You've kicked the bucket, finished the race, and checked into the Horizontal Hilton."

Great. I spoke too loudly and now Sergeant Wilson is glaring at me from across the catacombs, her mouth set in a firm frown.

She thinks I'm a suspect. It makes sense, I guess – only Mr. Pitts and I have access to the keys to the catacombs to open it. But then why would I bring the tour group down here if I knew this is where I'd hidden his corpse?

But I know how a village like Grimdale works. Logic doesn't matter – if Wilson decides to ask around about me, everyone in the village will tell her about weird Bree who talks to herself and claims to see ghosts. By the time Kelly Kingston and Alice Agincourt are done flinging shit at me, Wilson will have me for every unsolved crime on her books.

"But I can't be dead," Albert cries as he awkwardly shuffles over to me. "I haven't had a chat with St. Peter or seen a bright light. And you can see me!"

"That's because you're a ghost, and I can see ghosts. You haven't crossed over, because you have some kind of unfinished business in this world. I promise I'll explain everything if you come with me." I incline my head toward the SOCO team. "It probably has something to do with whoever murdered you."

Albert's hands fly to his mouth. "If someone murdered me, then they might be after Maggie."

"We don't know that. Come on, Albert, we need to leave—"

But Albert is in full panic mode. He's hopping around so fast that I have to jerk my head to keep an eye on him, which means Wilson can now see me doing some strange headbanging routine and probably thinks I'm on drugs.

"You have to help me." Albert tries to grab my shoulders, but his hands go right through me, sending a stab of ice through my skin. "You have to help me keep Maggie out of danger until the cops solve the murder. I'm sure that's why I'm still here. As soon as I know she's safe, I'll be able to cross over."

"Of course I'll help you," I grit out. "But I can't do that until we get away so the police don't see—"

"Bree!" Pax calls out. "I have brought reinforcements!"

101

I look over and see Pax fly through the wall of the tunnel, followed by Ambrose and Edward.

"Oh, great," I grumble under my breath. "All the merry men are here."

"See, there's that Roman costume fellow." Albert jabs his finger at Pax. "He's probably the murderer. Look at his sharp sword! Tell the police about him!"

"That's Pax, and he's not the murderer. He's a fellow ghost."

"Brianna, are you okay?" Edward asks, his insouciant voice trembling with concern. "Pax told us that Albert was murdered. Oh, hello, Albert."

Edward. Oh, Edward. I swallow. He's hot, too. Godsdamnit. He's rather hot with his long, wavy hair all rumpled and messy, his pouty lips and sharp cheekbones, his eyes of black, fathomless obsidian that at this moment are studying me like I'm a wild muse he's determined to tame.

"Bree, why is this fellow with the open shirt and socks down his pants talking to me?" Albert's voice cracks.

"It's a codpiece." Edward glares at Albert as he cups his hand over his crotch. "And I'll have you know it is the height of fashion."

"Albert? Albert's a ghost? Albert, old buddy, it's nice to finally meet you in the not-flesh." Ambrose thrusts a hand out, but he's pointing in the complete opposite direction. "I'm Ambrose Hulme, and I'm pleased to make your acquaintance, old bean."

"Ambrose Hulme, the adventurer?" Albert's got that rabbit-in-the-headlights look. "The one buried in Poet's Row?"

"So you've heard of me? That's amazing! Hardly anyone remembers me. We're going to be fast friends."

"Where is this murderer?" Pax booms, unsheathing his sword. "I would like to introduce his bowels to the pointy end of my sword."

Edward rushes toward me, studying my face in that intense way of his that always makes me feel like spilling my darkest, most depraved secrets. "If a murderer is loose, you must go home immediately. As your prince, I order you to go straight to your bedroom, lock the doors, put on a really skimpy night-dress, and await my next instructions."

Why, why, why, when Edward speaks in that haughty, commanding voice, does my body so desperately want to obey him?

No, no, no. Panic wells inside me. *This can't be happening. I cannot deal with them all now.* "Thanks for your concern, guys, but I've got this—"

"Bree?" A female voice calls my name. "It is you, right? I saw someone talking to a wall and figured it must be Bree Mortimer."

"Danny?"

My old high school friend runs over and envelops me in a giant bear hug. I haven't spoken to Danny since I left Grimdale – she's not on Facebook, and we lost touch. But I inhale her coffee and amber scent, and even though her voice sounds different, suddenly I'm transported back five years. Danny was the one good thing about high school.

"It's Dani with an 'i' now." Her voice is definitely different – the masculine edge has gone. She pulls back, and I gasp as I get a good look at her. "I'm officially using she/her pronouns. And look at these puppies."

Dani leans back and pokes out her chest to show off her breasts.

"Oooh, those are sexy AF." I look into my friend's warm brown eyes and see something that I often only glimpsed back in school. Dani is *happy*. She's finally living as who she truly is, and it looks damn good on her. "So what else has been going on apart from you embracing your fabulous self?"

"Oh, so much. I'd love to chat, but I'm actually here on business." She holds up a briefcase. "I'm the funeral director. I've just spoken with Maggie, and I'm here to talk to the police about releasing Albert's body so we can prepare him for burial. But can we meet up tonight at the Cackling Goat? We've got so much to catch up on."

"I'd love that so much." I whip out my phone, and Dani and I swap numbers. As she leans in to hug me again, she whispers, "I'm so sorry. I heard the news about your dad. It's horrible."

I stiffen. "Yeah. It is."

Dani lets me go and, with a little wave, she wanders over to Hayes and Wilson and bends her head to speak to them. They talk in low voices so I can't hear what they're saying.

I'm not surprised Dani became a funeral director. She loved Grimdale graveyard almost as much as I did, and she was kind of obsessed with forensic shows and true crime podcasts. Plus, she's just about the nicest person you could ever meet. I bet she's great at talking to grieving families...

I'm sorry about your dad.

Tears well in the corners of my eyes. I blink them back, but one escapes and topples down my cheek.

Edward's eyes harden. He reaches up to wipe the droplet away. His finger brushes my cheek, and I brace myself for the warm, tingling sensation I remember from them.

Instead, as he makes contact, as his ghostly fingers slide over my skin, never quite touching, an electric charge hums through my body – a jolt that pulses through my bloodstream. A trail of tiny explosions that lead from my cheek straight to *that spot* between my legs.

Um, what the fuck?

Edward jerks his hand away and floats back, his eyes wide. He felt it, too.

He's not supposed to feel like that.

That surprised him, and nothing surprises Edward.

I touch my hand to my cheek, my skin still buzzing from where he touched me.

Something's different. I sensed it yesterday when Ambrose fell into the bath and the temperature grew hotter than the Egyptian desert on the one day you realize the only clean pair of pants you own is lined with fleece. I felt it when I sat with Ambrose and his knee touched me. We touched. We *connected*.

That's not normal ghost mojo. Something has changed. Ghosts aren't supposed to feel like this. We're not supposed to be able to *touch*.

"Brianna?" Edward studies me with those poet's eyes of his.

I swallow again, rubbing my cheek. "I think...I think we have a problem."

I I

BREE

Mum: Gosh, why didn't you warn us that Renaissance art is wall-to-wall naked breasts! It's really quite salacious. Your poor father has a crick in his neck from staring at his shoes.

We need to get to the bottom of what's going on, and Albert desperately needs to get the skinny on the ghost rules. But the cemetery is still crawling with people, and I can't hold a ghost confab without attracting all kinds of unwanted attention. As nonchalantly as I can, I lead the ghosts away from the catacombs and whisper to Albert.

"As we move around, you might feel a kind of pulling sensation inside you, drawing you back to where you were murdered. That's your ghost mojo. It's like a supernatural boomerang, always bringing you back to the place you're haunting. But it's nothing to be afraid of, okay?"

Albert nods miserably. He follows us back up the hill. He's still trying to walk up the steps like a Living, and grunts in frustration as his feet refuse to stay where he puts them.

"It will take some time to get used to floating," Edward says with more kindness than I've ever heard from him.

"The new ghost is doing a funny dance," Pax says happily. "Like a Druid summoning, only with more flailing about and less blood-drinking."

Somehow, we make it up the hill without me throttling them all. We enter the kitchen. I indicate for Albert to have a seat at the island before remembering that he can no longer sit. It's been a hot minute since I've had this much interaction with ghosts.

Albert hovers in the middle of a stool and stares glumly out the window at his house.

"It's going to be okay, Albert," I say as I pick up the kettle. "Edward, say something reassuring."

Edward shuffles forward, the edges of his white poet's shirt flapping open to reveal a sculpted slit of pale chest. His pantaloons slide down his thighs as he straightens to show off the edge of a corded V of muscle. I swallow – I must be seriously sex-deprived if even foppish Edward with his rumpled black curls and pretty-boy sneer is enticing to me.

"Albert, you're dead now," Edward says in his haughtiest, princeliest tone. "So the good news is that you'll never get syphilis from a Covent Garden floozy."

Albert makes a choking noise. I sigh as I fill the kettle and set it on the element. "Thank you, Edward, that's very helpful. Albert, I'll make you a cup of tea and tell you all about being a ghost—"

"But I can't drink tea!" To demonstrate, Albert swipes his hand through an empty cup on the counter. He winces at the pain. The cup wobbles a little bit but doesn't tip over. "I'll never have a cup of tea again, or win the Cackling Goat pub quiz, or touch my wife in an intimate way. Oh, Maggie." He swipes at the cup over and over again as his voice grows more agitated. "I can't believe I've left you all alone—"

"Stop doing that," I scold him. I haven't met a newly minted ghost in a while, but I remember the first stage of ghouldom is being an annoying twit. "All you're going to do is hurt yourself. You can't drink the tea, but you *can* smell it. Smelling familiar things is soothing to ghosts, so let me—"

"We'll make the tea." Ambrose leaps up and gets an umbrella stand through the crotch. Pain flickers across his features for a moment, but then his easy smile is back.

We always assume that any of our bodily imperfections will be sorted in the afterlife. But that's just humans being ableist AF and assuming blindness is something that needs to be 'fixed.' To Ambrose, being blind is completely normal, so of course he'd be blind as a ghost, too, which means he constantly falls through objects, like umbrella stands and bathroom walls.

"You can't make me tea," I say.

"Why not?"

"Because you're *ghosts*."

"How little faith you have in us," Edward says with a mischievous wink. "We've been practicing."

"*You've* been practicing?" I narrow my eyes at him. "You, the royal prince who orders around servants like it's an Olympic sport, you learned how to roll up your sleeves and make tea for someone else? This I've got to see."

Edward cracks his knuckles like a prizefighter stepping into the ring. He moves into the kitchen and shoots me this look that turns my panties wet as he plunges his hands into the wall. A moment later, there's an electrical 'zzzzz' noise. The lights flicker and the electric kettle begins to boil.

"Um, excuse me, what is *that?*" I don't recall Edward ever performing that trick before.

"I can do remarkable things with these fingers," he says with a smirk.

I swallow.

I've read practically every book and article that's ever been written about Edward. It's hard to resist, especially since so many writers love to luxuriate on the salacious details of his libertine lifestyle. One thing writers are pretty unanimous on was that he had half the courtiers in London lining up for an invitation into his boudoir. One quote claimed he made a woman scream so wildly with pleasure that she traumatized the king's hounds and they refused to hunt for a month.

For thirteen-year-old Bree, the stories were gross. But now, when he's looking at me like he wants to eat me for breakfast, my stomach flips, and I think I might just let him.

"My turn." Pax bounds over, sword drawn. I'm confused by why one needs a sword to make coffee, but then Pax – who can sometimes get the tip of his sword to manipulate the Living world if he wants it bad enough – uses it to knock the top off the tea container, scoop out a bag, and dump it in the cup I'd placed on the bench. He does the same with the sugar, dipping his sword inside and removing it carefully with mounds of sugar balanced precariously atop the blade. As he moves it across to the cup, most of the sugar ends up on the counter, but he does get a few granules into the drink.

"Hey, that was easier than normal. Milk?" Pax shouts at Albert.

"Er, yes please—"

"*No.*" I'm not sure how Pax intends to get milk into the cup using only the tip of his sword, but I can guarantee it will be messy.

The kettles whistles.

"You're up, Mr. Adventurer," Edward says.

Ambrose tap-tap-taps with his cane, floating around me. He

wraps his hand around the handle of the kettle while Pax nudges the cup closer with the tip of his sword. Ambrose's brow furrows with concentration. He sucks in a deep breath and screws up his face, then lets out a mighty howl.

He manages to lift the kettle an inch above the stand. He tips it. Water sloshes from the spout and mostly goes into the cup.

Mostly.

"That's...it..." Ambrose puffs. He drops the kettle with a bang and sinks to the ground.

Pax blows on his sword like it's a smoking gun.

Poor Edward looks even paler than usual.

"I...I can't believe it." I stare at the coffee cup, the dusting of sugar and splatters of water across the counter. "You did it. You really did it."

"You'll have to carry it to the table for Albert yourself," Ambrose's shoulders sag from the effort. "We haven't quite mastered that part yet. Although Pax was right, it was easier this time. Maybe I'm getting stronger."

"But how did you learn to do that?" I can't believe it. "You've never been able to move objects like that before."

Ambrose taps his head and smiles shyly. "Your mother has been listening to lots of meditation podcasts, and I've been following along. It's all a matter of focusing your mind."

"Sometimes, I can hook the cups on the tip of my sword," Pax says, obviously not wanting Ambrose to get all of the credit.

"And let's hear it for my electrical skills," Edward adds, sticking his chest out proudly.

I roll my eyes at him. "Let me guess, you only discovered you had electrical abilities because it makes you hard, right?"

Edward folds his arms. "You try being a ghoul for three hundred years without a single Duchess to stroke your scepter and see how you like it."

"Bree, dear," Albert pipes up. "While this is fascinating, if we might get back to the issue of my untimely demise?"

"Right." I grab the mug off the counter and take a sip, trying not to think about all the places Pax's sword tip has been. And yes, I know, dirty. "Okay, so you're dead. You're a ghost and I can see you. I'm the only human I ever met who can see ghosts, so don't even bother trying to get anyone else's attention. You're stuck with me. Now, being a ghost comes with a few ghost rules, which you'll learn about as you navigate your after-life. Rule one, which we've already kind of discussed, is that you're a ghost because you have unfinished business, which we think is that you have to protect Maggie from your killer. Rule two is about how ghost mojo works—"

My phone rings. I pull it out of my pocket and am about to hang up the call when I see who it is.

My parents.

My heart leaps into my throat. "Shut up, all of you. I have to take this." I shunt the ghosts to the other side of the room and set the phone on the kitchen counter, propping it up with the skeleton salt-and-pepper shakers, and click ACCEPT on the video call.

Mum and Dad crowd into the tiny screen. My eyes zero in on Dad, who's lying on a sun lounger, wearing a terrible Eiffel Tower t-shirt. His beard's grown longer and it's not as neat as he normally trims it – it's crooked on one side. He flashes me a huge smile that makes my throat tighten.

"Bonjour, Bree-bug," Dad waves with one hand. He clenches the other against his chest. His voice sounds a little slurred, like he's had a few drinks.

"Bonjour!" Mum fans herself with a large souvenir paper fan covered with drawings of French bulldogs.

"Hey, you two." I wave back. "Look at you, using your French words. You sound like locals."

"We love it here." Mum waves her arm around. "We're at a resort in Marseilles with our new friends, Hans and Erina. We toured a castle and I've eaten my body weight in cheese and I've never felt better. And last night we all snuck onto a private beach and went skinny dipping—"

"Argh." I jam my hands over my ears. "I don't need to know that."

"Oh, darling, I didn't know you were such a prude." Mum blows me a kiss. "We're having the best time. I understand now why you were in such a hurry to go out and travel. This is great fun. I can't believe we lived beside France for so many years and didn't know about the cheese! Why didn't we do this sooner?"

"Because of the French people?" Dad grins at her.

"Exactly. Because of the French people."

My parents are delightfully, annoyingly British.

"So how are things at the manor?" Mum asks, holding the fan up high and waving it at the top of her head. She looks deranged, but Mum does not care.

"Things are fine with the house. Entwhistle's been following me around, making sure I do everything to your exacting standards."

As if responding to a cue, the ginger cat leaps up onto the table and headbutts the phone. I pull him into my lap and set the screen upright again.

"Moon spends most of her time hiding and leaping out at me when I least expect it. Oh, and I caught up with Dani today..."

I trail off as my eyes fall on Albert. He's standing by the window, looking across the garden and down the hill to the cute little gatehouse on the edge of the cemetery. More police cars are pulling up. Albert's face is a picture of misery.

I don't want to talk about it like this, with him in the room. But my parents would want to know.

"There's some sad news, too," I say quietly, hoping Albert isn't listening. "Albert Fernsby died."

"Oh, no, that's awful!" Mum clucks, switching her fan to the other hand and whacking Dad in the face with it. "Poor Maggie must be distraught."

"I imagine so. I can see the police cars arriving now. I'm going to go and talk to her in a sec. It only just happened. I um, actually, discovered the body..."

"Oh, Bree-bug." Dad's face tenses up a little. I know he's thinking about his strange daughter talking to dead people and hanging out in the cemetery too much. All my teachers and his friends would tell him I was morbid and lived in a fantasy world and needed to see a professional, but Dad always defended me. *Having an imagination isn't a crime,* he'd tell them proudly. *Bree has more fun with her pretend friends than most of us have with our real ones.* "That sounds awful. We can get on the next plane home to be with you. Maggie probably needs some help, too—"

"It's fine!" I cross my fingers behind my back. "Really. I'm doing fine. You don't have to cut your holiday short or anything because of me. Dead people don't bother me."

It's a lie – they bother me all the time. Right now, Pax is making silly faces at me and Edward is trying to pick up a jar of peanut butter, but is only succeeding in moving it closer to the edge of the counter.

"Don't be silly, Mike. We don't need to come home." Mum raps Dad lightly on the shoulder with her fan. "Albert's dead, so we're no use to him now. Maggie has the whole village to help her, and Bree has been living on her own for five years – she's perfectly capable of handling the realities of getting old. But speaking of our holiday, we were wondering if we could talk to you about an idea we had."

"Oh, yeah?" My stomach sinks. My mum's ideas usually involve chaos and mayhem for everyone involved.

"Hans and Erina want to show us around southern Germany. Apparently, it's filled with castles and chocolate-box villages, and there's less cheese but better beer, so your father will appreciate that. And we thought, what the hell? Why not? But it means we'll be gone a little longer than we expected. We were wondering if you could possibly keep things ticking over while we're away? You'd have to check in the first summer guests all on your own, but I told Mike that you're more than capable—"

I swallow. "Sure. I'd be happy to help out. Or, you know, we could put the B&B on hold this summer and I could come over and meet you. Maybe we could travel around Germany together. We haven't had a family holiday in years—"

"Oh, no, darling, we don't want to put you out. We know you don't want to spend your life hanging out with your fuddy-duddy old folks. Besides, this is like a second honeymoon for us." Mum leans forward and whispers conspiratorially, "You won't believe how randy your father gets after a couple of glasses of French wine—"

I don't mean to tempt fate, but kill me now.

"Sylvie!" Dad's cheeks flush with embarrassment.

"What? Bree's an adult now, she can handle a little salacious talk."

"I really, really can't." I jam my hands on my ears.

"You think that's salacious?" Edward leans in beside me and makes a face. I catch the faintest glimpse of his lingering scent – burnt sugar and opium and sweet summer blossoms. Refined and elegant with a twisted, corrupted core.

"Oh, for heaven's sake, you two are as bad as each other." Mum rolls her eyes, then flounces offscreen. "I'm going in the hot tub. Mike, come and join me when you're finished."

That's my mum – she has the attention span of an ADHD goldfish.

I'm left with Dad on-screen, and suddenly I don't know what to say to him. I've been thinking about him every moment of every day since they told me the news a month ago. I've read everything the internet can tell me on the topic, but faced with the reality in front of me, all that information flies out of my head. All I can think about is the time that he made me a set of stilts out of scrap wood from when he repaired the roof, and we spent the day lurching around the ballroom together, trying to learn how to walk in them. I don't know if I ever laughed so hard in my life.

I don't know if I'll ever laugh with him again.

This disease is robbing me of everything, even my relationship with my dad.

"Hey, Bree-bug," Dad waves.

"Hey, Dad." My throat's gone all dry again. I cough into my sleeve.

"Don't mind your mother. You know how she is. She's having the time of her life over here. I really should have taken her travelling sooner."

There's a wistfulness in his voice that turns my stomach, a sense that he's given up something. I *hate* it. I've always looked up to my dad because he enjoys his life so much. He blasts his classic rock albums while he's doing repairs around the manor and sings along, out-of-time and completely off-key. He always has some new hobby he's trying, and when Mum's being too crazy, he'll retreat into one of the manor's many rooms and immerse himself in wickerwork or home brewing or his model train set. And no matter what he was doing, he'd always drop everything to take me for a walk in the woods or teach me how to whittle or make a batch of scones together.

How long until he doesn't have any of those things anymore?

I swallow down the memories. They taste tart, bitter. "Tell me more about your travels."

I don't want him to stop talking. I want to soak in every moment of him being here and alive and my dad. And yet, hearing the slur in his voice getting worse and seeing the tremor in his hand tears me apart inside.

I should have been here for him.

We have so little time left.

Dad chatters on about a rock concert he and Hans are going to in Germany. He's a huge music fan. He took me to my first concert when I was eight years old – we saw Jethro Tull at the Barsetshire Odeon, and I listened to most of the show with my face buried in Dad's arms because while Ian Anderson hopped around on one leg with his flute, some old hippie ghost with one side of his face caved in was jiving on stage beside him.

More memories sting in the back of my throat. Dad might not have always got me, but he was always there when I needed him. But I couldn't return the favor. All these years when he's been dealing with this huge, awful thing, I've been off having my adventures, completely oblivious to the fact that every day he loses a bit more of who he is.

It's too painful to look at him, so I flick my gaze away. Big mistake. My eyes land on Albert in the window, ghostly tears streaming down his cheeks as he watches police officers move up the path to the gatehouse. My own tears bristle in my eyes.

Pax sees me wiping them away. "You are crying again."

"I am not," I say before I can stop myself.

"You're not into Blue Oyster Cult anymore, Bree-bug?" Dad asks quizzically. "That's a shame. I was going to bring you home a t-shirt."

"No, Dad, I still love them. I wasn't talking to you. I was..." I fish around for an excuse, and quickly swipe the cat from the counter and gather up him in my arms. "I was talking to Entwhistle."

"Oh, hey buddy!" Dad leans in close to wave at his cat.

Entwhistle recognises his voice and headbutts the phone again, sending it skidding across the table. I grab it before it smashes on the tiles.

"Dad, it's a little crazy here, and the police are down at Maggie's. I should go."

"Sure, Bree-bug. I love—"

CLICK. I toss the phone on the table and bury my face in my hands.

It's not fair.

It's not *fair*.

"Bree, what's wrong?"

Ambrose's soft voice brushes my earlobe. That does it. The tears spill over, crawling down my cheeks and splattering on my dad's batter-stained family cookbook.

"It's...nothing," I sob.

It's *everything*.

"If it was nothing, then you wouldn't be crying," Pax says triumphantly. "I have won this battle of wits, therefore you must tell us who has hurt you so I can feed them to the starving lion."

"No one's hurt me," I sniff. "It's just...if there are gods, they have a sadistic sense of humor."

"Which god has hurt you?" Pax unsheaths his sword and stabs it at the sky. "Was it Jupiter? He can be a real dick. Or Mercury, that trickster. I don't care if they're divine beings, I will crush their skulls in my hands and use their testicles for tiddlywinks."

I bring the cup of tea to my lips so Pax can't see the smile bursting from my lips. No matter how sad I was, he could always make me laugh. If only this could be solved by crushing skulls.

The tea tastes remarkably good. I take another sip. Ambrose and Edward watch me expectantly while Pax dances around behind them, pretending to slay the gods for my honour.

The drink warms my stomach and fortifies me. No wonder Britain has gone to war over tea – it's magic in a cup.

I set the cup down.

"My father has...has Parkinson's disease."

There. I said the words out loud.

They hang in the air, heavy and sad.

"We heard that," Edward says. "We heard him discussing it with Sylvie. We do not know what the word means."

Of course they don't. They all died young, in the days before modern medicine.

"It's a neurological condition," I say. "Basically, Dad's brain is losing nerve cells that control movement and coordination. His limbs are stiff and he's developing a tremor in his hands, so he can't do delicate tasks that require precision. His balance is affected, his voice is going quiet, and his speech slurring. Surely you've noticed him changing?"

"He gave up learning the guitar," Ambrose says. "But we were too busy being grateful to learn why."

"He was rather awful." Edward waves a hand. "Has he had a course of leeches and laudanum? That should sort him out."

"We don't use leeches anymore, Edward, and even if we did, it wouldn't help. There's no cure for Parkinson's disease. He's never going to get better. He's going to keep getting worse and worse and..." I swallow. "At some point, he won't be able to walk without a wheelchair, won't be able to speak, or make things, or play drums in the pub band...all the things in life that he enjoys...he won't have them anymore."

And I won't have my dad anymore.

The three of them exchange a look. I can read their thoughts on their features. Ambrose's stricken face tells me he's thinking of the horror of being trapped in a body that won't do what you want it to do. Edward is calculating how much sex he could have before his body literally expired from exhaustion. And Pax, Pax is casting his eyes around, desperate for something to stab that will solve the problem.

Not all problems can be solved with bloodshed.

"How long?" Ambrose asks quietly.

"He has two years left before things become really bad, maybe three. My parents have known for three years already, and he's been on medication that helps his brain to manage symptoms. But eventually, the medication won't work anymore and he'll...he'll..."

Another sob escapes me. Something warm lands on my shoulder. I glance up and see Ambrose's hand – and the counter and window through it – rubbing small circles on my back. My skin tingles where he touches.

Ever since my parents called me a month ago and gave me the news, I've been carrying around this weight. It feels like I swallowed a stone and it's expanding inside me, squeezing out every breath, squashing the food I eat and crowding out every happy thought I try to chase. Dragging me down, down, down into the center of the Earth.

But when Ambrose's fingers dance so lightly over my skin, a touch that is not really a touch at all, the stone becomes lighter, as if he is taking a little of the weight to carry himself.

I've been alone for so long, far away from anyone who knows me in a deep, intimate way. I've been holding Dad's diagnosis inside me ever since they told me, swallowing it down, keeping that stone inside myself as it grows mould that festers and infects me with this overwhelming helplessness.

Just talking to the three of them makes the pain recede. Maybe...maybe I don't have to carry this weight all on my own any longer.

"They didn't tell me," I whisper. "My parents knew for three years and they didn't tell me."

"I'm certain they didn't want you to worry while you were off on your adventure," Ambrose whispers.

That's so close to what Mum said when they gave me the news that I start crying harder.

"They shouldn't have made that choice for me. If I'd known, I would have come home. Instead of traipsing all over the world with my possessions on my back, working shitty hospitality jobs and scrimping every penny and shagging every boy with a pulse and a combi van—"

"—what boys?—" Edward growls, his eyes flashing.

"—I could have been *here*, making the most of the time he has left with his body. I would have gone for walks with him in the woods every single day, and taken him to all the rock concerts, and got him guitar lessons, and helped him build his model train, and..." I swallow down another heaving sob. "I missed so much time with him. I should have been here for him, and now I *am* here and they're gone, and I don't hate them for it, I *don't*. Dad always wanted to travel, and he thought he couldn't because he had to take care of our family and the house, and now he can. But I just wish..."

The hand on my back keeps making those circles, and the warmth of it spreads through my skin, wrapping around my heart, crowding out that stone with his unique spicy, summery scent – a scent that carries a little from every place he's travelled.

I suck in a deep breath and...I can't explain it, but as the stone inside me shrinks, it's as if the weight moves into his hand, and it feels so solid and safe, so much like a real hand, that I look up with a start.

Straight in Ambrose's kind azure eyes.

He's looking right at me, and even though he can't see me, his eyes swim with tears – a reflection of my pain.

"I wish I could do something," Ambrose whispers. "You're hurting, and this isn't like the times you fell over and scraped your knee and we could make you laugh until the pain went away. I wish I could take you in my arms and tell you that things will hurt for a while, but they'll get better. Your dad is still your dad. He has always found joy in life no matter what's going on. He will continue to find that joy. He hasn't yet given up his ghost – you still have so much time with him, so many beautiful memories to make and adventures to have. We'll help, too. Whatever you need, we're here. We're always here—"

"Bree? Come quick!" A distressed voice cries, breaking through the spell of Ambrose's kindness. "Something's wrong!"

Shit.

Albert. I completely forgot about him. Some ghost whisperer I am. I wipe my eyes and rush over to the window, where Albert is pacing through the kitchen sink and wringing his hands.

"Albert, what's wrong?"

"It's Maggie!" He jabs his finger at the window. "The police are dragging her out of the house."

I2

BREE

I wipe my eyes with the back of my hand and peer out the window. Sure enough, Hayes and Wilson are standing on the path leading to the gatehouse. Two squad cars are parked behind them on the road, lights flashing, and a bunch of officers surround the house while two of them roughly drag Maggie down the garden path and beneath the rose trellis toward the cars. Sunlight glints off a flash of metal on her wrists.

She's handcuffed.

"Don't worry," I tell Albert, even though I am very much worrying. "This is all a misunderstanding. I'll fix this."

I run out the front door and down the driveway to the gatehouse, four ghosts hot on my heels.

"My darling, what have they done to you?" Albert reaches for his wife's arm, but his hand goes right through her. His whole face crumples. I've never seen a man look so desolate.

"Can I have a jacket, officers?" Maggie asks, shifting her arm. "I just got a chill."

Albert howls so loudly I can barely hear myself think.

"Could you shut him up?" I snap at Edward under my breath as I barrel toward Hayes and Wilson.

"Me? What do you expect me to do?" Edward folds his arms. "I suppose I could drug him, but you never stocked the house with laudanum like I specifically requested."

"Recite some of your poetry?" Pax offers. "That should put him to sleep."

"Or it will give him another existential crisis to focus on," Ambrose adds.

And they wonder why I ran away?

"Excuse me, Sergeant Wilson," I puff as I catch up with them. "What's going on?"

"Please go back to your home, Ms. Mortimer," Wilson says curtly. "This isn't your concern."

"Bree, they're arresting me!" Maggie cries as the officer places his hand behind her neck to lower her into the car. "My darling Albert has been brutally murdered and they think I did it!"

13

BREE

The ghosts and I watch glumly as the police drive away with a distraught Maggie. Albert half-runs, half-floats after them, but only gets to the end of the street before his ghost mojo pulls him back. He collapses on the manor's overgrown front lawn, his head in his hands.

"This is a nightmare," he moans. "Any moment now I'm going to wake up in bed, and Maggie will bring me a nice mug of tea and a container of her lavender healing balm, and everything will be normal again."

"I'm afraid not. But don't worry. We all know Maggie would never hurt you. I'm sure after they question her, they'll figure it out, too." I try to sound soothing. The truth is, I'm worried, too.

Albert's chin wobbles. "How could they believe that my Maggie would lay a finger on me?"

"Everyone in the village will tell the police how devoted you two were to each other. I'll go down there and give them a statement myself." The Fernsbys have lived in the gatehouse my entire life. I saw them nearly every day, and they are the most kind, loving couple you could ever meet. They adore each other and dote on each other. I've never even heard them raise their voices in their anger.

There's no way Maggie would murder her husband. There's just *no way*.

Albert turns to me, his face stricken. "This is what you were talking about. This is my unfinished business."

"What is?"

"Clearing Maggie's name! Please, Bree. You have to help her. She didn't murder me. I know it."

"I know it, too, Albert. But I'm not a police officer. I know nothing about solving murders. We just have to wait until the police piece together the clues—"

"No! I won't wait! Not while Maggie is sitting in a prison cell for a crime she didn't commit." His lip wobbles. "What will they do to her in there? She's such a beautiful woman, what if some criminal brute decides to ravish her? Do you want that on your conscience?"

"Well, no, but I don't think that's likely—"

"Are you saying that my Maggie isn't pretty enough to be ravished?" Albert glares at me.

Behind Albert, Edward is cracking up.

"That's not what I'm saying at all." I glare at Edward, and he arranges his face into a picture of innocence. "I'm simply saying that we need to leave this to the experts—"

"You know," Ambrose rubs his chin, "we could help you solve this murder. We can fly through walls and listen in to the conversations Livings think they're having in private."

"I'm very good at convincing people to do things they wouldn't normally entertain, such as enticing innocent maidens into removing their garments and upstanding gentlemen to indulge in hedonistic opium binges." Edward rubs his hands together with glee. "If you think that will be useful."

"And I can stab people until they confess!" Pax cries. To demonstrate, he swings around and tries to slice the Fernsbys' letterbox. All he succeeds in doing is making a tiny dent in the metal.

"Oh." Pax stares at that dent in surprise. "I didn't expect that to happen."

Pax has obviously been honing his powers so he can affect the Living world. I touch my shoulder, remembering the weight of Ambrose's fingers there, how he felt so real, so human. Edward's eyes are a fathomless cave as he sweeps his gaze over my body, and the stone inside me shrinks a little more as my heart lifts.

My three childhood friends. I've missed them. And everything in my life may be completely messed up, but they're here with me. If we do this together, it'll be just like old times, and maybe that's exactly what I need.

Albert sniffles.

"Okay." I sigh. "I guess we're solving a murder. Where do we start?"

THE FIRST, most obvious step, is to find out exactly what the police know. The ghosts volunteer to go to the police station, float through the wall, and listen in to Maggie's interrogation. Unfortunately, the police station is in Argleton, the next village over, and their ghost mojo won't allow them to travel that far.

But I have another idea. I glance at the time. "Stay here and look after Albert," I tell the ghosts. "Talk him through all the ghost rules. I'm going out."

"You can't leave the house," Pax commands. "A murderer is roaming around the village."

I should give him a lecture about feminism and letting women make their own decisions, but he looks so goddamn adorable standing at attention, his muscles bulging from his leather armor, that I stick my tongue out at him. "I'm going to the pub to get answers, and you can't stop me."

"I'm going with you." Pax pats the sword at his side. "I'll slay anyone who looks at you funny."

"Then you're going to be busy," I sigh. "Everyone in this village looks at me funny."

"That's because they wish they were as beautiful and special as you," Edward says.

Um...

Well...

Fuck.

Edward used to say things like that all the time. He *is* the poet prince. But they never made me feel like this before, like my blood is filled with honey.

In New Zealand, I visited this beautiful city called Queenstown at the foot of the dramatic Southern Alps. A bunch of travellers at my youth hostel wanted to go bungee jumping, and I tagged along. I stood on the edge of the platform, overlooking this insanely beautiful canyon, as the wind whipped around me. My body screamed 'not fucking happening,' but something in the wind beckoned me, and I leaned forward and my heart stopped and I was falling...

...and falling...

...and falling...

I'm falling now, waiting for the bungee cord to spring back, to remember that I'm strapped in and soon this ride will be over and I'll be back safely on the ground.

But the cord doesn't spring.

The silence after Edward's statement becomes a barbed, toothed creature that takes up the whole room. My cheeks flush with heat. Ambrose elbows Edward in the arm.

"Take Pax with you," Edward says drolly, looking away. "He's right – there is a murderer out there. Ambrose and I will look after Albert."

My heart hammers. I don't know what to say, so I nod. I nod and I nod and I wonder if I truly have lost my mind.

I leave the ghosts in the guest lounge on the second floor, take a quick shower, pull on a black sleeveless shirt and patterned wrap skirt I ought in Bali, and head downtown to meet Dani with a see-through Roman soldier marching at my heels.

14

BREE

The Cackling Goat is *heaving*. The beer garden is standing-room only, and I have to battle the laws of physics to make my way to the bar. Word will have gotten around the village about Albert's death and Maggie's arrest, and everyone has shown up to get the gossip. My ears prickle at mentions of my name, but I don't stop to chat.

"Bree, over here!"

I turn, and feel a surge of love for Dani as she waves at me from a table she's snagged under the window. I fling myself toward her and manage to squeeze myself into the seat opposite. She's already nursing a pint of cider, her deep purple nails tapping against the glass. "I got here early. I knew the place would be a madhouse. Sorry, I didn't get you a pint, but all I remember you drinking was that godawful apple scrumpy shite, and I assume your palate has at least slightly refined."

"I'm not sure refined is any way to describe me," I laugh as I pick up her glass and take a swig of dark ale. "But yes, my scrumpy days are over. I'm so happy we could do this. I didn't expect you to stay in Grimdale."

"Neither did I. I did a couple of years at business school in

London, but the city life wasn't for me. Mum was always trying to convince me to move home, and after two years of battling the tube and never being able to afford more than a packet of crisps, she convinced me." Dani's mum had her when she was sixteen, and they're more like best friends than mother and daughter. "When the apprenticeship came up at Wighams, I leaped on it."

"How do you like the death business?"

"Is it wrong to say that I love it? Because I do. It's such a privilege to be there with a family as they farewell a loved one's soul into the next life. Ever since you and I..." Dani lowers her voice as she waves her hand at me, "you know...I guess I've been fascinated by death."

I nod. Apart from when I was really little and I assumed everyone could see the see-through people wandering around, Dani's the only living person in the whole world I ever told about seeing ghosts. She didn't believe me at first, and we had a big row and actually didn't speak for a year. But then her grandmother died, and I went to the funeral because that's what you do for your ex-best friend who you miss terribly. During the service, Dani's grandmother Pearl sat beside me and told me that she was a lesbian but she'd always been too afraid to come out because of the social stigma from her generation.

"Why are you telling me this?" I hissed at the old woman. The priest shot me a dirty look.

"Because you two shouldn't be fighting," she says. "My grandchild needs people like you in her life, people who understand her and accept her for who she is, and you need her, too. Let her accept you for who you are, Bree. So stop fighting over things that don't matter. That's all I have to say. And tell her to wear that purple nail polish she loves. It suits her."

After the service, I found her in the graveyard and whispered everything her grandmother told me. And we were friends again, and have been ever since.

"I'm so happy for you." I beam. "So how's your latest... client? Is that what you call them – clients? What did the police say about Albert when they handed him over? I heard them say it was a homicide, but he had dementia so couldn't he have just wandered over to the cemetery and—"

Dani tilts her head and flashes me a brilliant Dani smile. "Albert's a ghost, isn't he? That's why you're peppering me with questions. Is he here right now? Hi, Albert!"

She glances over her shoulder and waves at a potted plant. A couple of patrons stare at us, and I feel the familiar prickling in my skin of people talking about me.

Let them talk. I'm here with my friend, and that's what's important. Who cares if people think we're weird? We have more fun than anyone in this room.

Oh, and I guess Pax is here, too. He can't come into the bar – too many people will walk through him and cause too much pain, but he's watching through the window. I give him a little nod and he flashes his sword, just to show me he's hard at work guarding me against murderers.

"Okay, you got me." I smile as I slide the menu toward me and peruse the burger options. "And Albert's not here. He's back at Grimwood with Edward and Ambrose. Pax is outside the window, though. He wants me to solve his murder."

"Who, Pax?" Dani waves at him, even though she can't see him waving back.

"No, Albert. He's convinced that Maggie couldn't possibly have done it and that she's in danger from the killer."

I hear something scratching at the window. I look up to see Mary, Lottie, and Agnes elbowing Pax out of the way so they can squish their faces up against the glass. Mary jabs her finger frantically at the mushy peas in the 'sides' section.

I snap the menu shut.

"The police seemed awfully sure it's homicide," Dani says. "And you know what all the true crime podcasts say – poison is a woman's weapon."

"He was poisoned?"

Dani makes a face. "I'm not supposed to tell you this."

"Please, Dani. If you've seen the body and spoken to the police, you can help me. It will help Albert cross over. He thinks that his unfinished business is to catch the killer so Maggie is no longer in danger."

"That's sweet." Dani taps her nails on her glass. "They were such an adorable couple. I don't really believe Maggie could have done that. But I'm not talking murder on an empty stomach. What are you having?"

"Bangers and mash. And a pint of cider, please." I grin. "And make it extra scrumpy-licious."

"You are ridiculous." But Dani's laughing as she shoves her way through the crowd to the bar to put in our order. She returns a few minutes later with a table number and a pint of cider for me. She leans across the table and lowers her voice.

"You can't repeat any of this or tell anyone where you got the information, or I could lose my job. Albert was poisoned with atropine, which is found in the leaves and berries of the belladonna plant."

"Belladonna? That sounds like something from Agatha Christie."

"Agatha did use belladonna in her stories," Dani – ever the murder mystery fan – says. "Its common name is deadly night-shade, and it grows everywhere in Grimdale wood. The pathologist, Jo, says that they found no trace of the poison in Albert's stomach. It's hard to get people to swallow belladonna because it has a horrible bitter taste. She thinks the poison might have entered his system in another way, but she didn't say how."

"Why do they think Maggie poisoned him?"

Dani shrugs. "Probably because of her knowledge of herbs. Everyone knows she foraged from the woods to make her body lotions."

"That can't be all they're going on!"

"I'm sure it's not. The last time anyone saw Albert alive, he was out on his morning walk along the woodland path with Maggie. The Fernsbys were home alone all day. Maggie went out to the pub quiz at the Goat, and told everyone that Albert's arthritis was playing up so he decided to stay home. The police think she was establishing an alibi. No one else saw Albert until he turned up dead in the catacombs. Apart from that, I don't know what other evidence they have."

I screw up my nose. "There has to be some other explanation. Maybe someone snuck into the house while Maggie was away, or maybe Albert was drawn out to meet someone in the catacombs..."

"If you say so, Sherlock Bree. Admit it, you can't stand the thought of their love story ending so unhappily." Dani leans across the table and pats my hand. "That's the real reason you're so upset by this, isn't it?"

Dani peers at me with her warm brown eyes, and I know what she's really asking. Am I throwing myself into solving this murder for a ghost because I don't want to think about my dad's condition?

And the answer is: yes, of course. I'm all about healthy coping mechanisms like completely ignoring my feelings and running away from my problems. I should write a self-help book.

"Damn right I'm upset by this. Aren't you?" Our food arrives then. Mary sticks her head through the window and tries to plunge her face into my plate, but I stick a fork through her nose into my sausage. She jerks back and makes a sour face at me, then disappears. "I've got a heartbroken ghost who had to watch the love of his life carted off by the police for his murder. If I can set the record straight, Albert could cross over. And that would be one wandering spirit I could actually help. That is, if you'll agree to—"

"Of course I'll help." Dani takes a big bite of her burger and smiles at me across the table. "All in the name of love. What can I do?"

"We need to know everything about the poison – what is it, how was it administered, who could possibly know about the properties of belladonna. And we have to find out why the police are so sure Maggie is the killer. Can you get information like that through work?"

"It'll involve some illegal fidgey-widgey with Albert's records, but sure. What are you going to do?"

"I'm going to dig up all the dirt I can on Albert," I say. "He's got to have more enemies, someone who wants him dead who the police haven't considered. Luckily, I'm able to go direct to the source."

15

BREE

When Pax and I return from the pub, I find the ghosts in the upstairs sitting room. Ambrose paces in front of (and sometimes in) the fireplace, delivering an impassioned lecture about ghost rules, while Edward makes a great show of slouching across the chaise lounge, looking every bit the spoiled, indolent prince. Although I know him well enough to know that he's precisely arranged his body to appear as flattering as possible. His shirt hangs open, his codpiece freshly polished, and from this angle, I can't see the bloodstains or the piece of glass in his arsecheek.

My fingers itch to run along the pale skin on his chest. Although...it's not skin. I know that my fingers will just pass through him. So where is this urge coming from?

The cider's gone to my head. That's it. That's what's happening.

"I will show you an important thing about being a ghost that Ambrose hasn't told you." Pax puffs out his chest, strides across the room, and plunges his head into the liquor cabinet.

This is ghost behaviour I'm used to. Centuries ago, the ghosts discovered that holding their head inside a bottle of liquor will make them a little tipsy. They didn't do it around me much when I was a kid, but as a rebellious teen, I did sneak bottles from my parents' cabinet to share with them.

"Move your head. I need to get in there," I tell Pax. He snaps his head out of the cabinet. I rummage around until I find a bottle of old Scotch. I dust it off and pour myself a glass.

"I don't know how you drink that stuff," Edward wrinkles his nose. "What about fine French wine? I used to keep a cellar of exquisite vintage in this very house. Some of those bottles were worth two whole pounds! I wonder what happened to it."

"I read that your friends drank them all at your funeral," I tell him, and he sighs.

I flop down on the sofa and nudge Albert with my foot. My skin tingles where it passes through him, and he whirls around to face me. Touching him feels exactly the way ghosts normally feel. I don't understand why it's different with Edward and Pax and Ambrose.

"How was your first day as a ghost?" I ask Albert as I raise my glass to my lips.

"Miserable," he says as he floats over to where Pax has his head in the liquor cabinet. "Can you step aside, son? I'd like to have a go at that."

"It's got to be better than my first day," Edward says conversationally. "I was supposed to be bedding the Countess Marie de Rothschild. Instead, I woke up on the lawn with a shard of glass in my arse and no matter how many times I pull it out—" he reaches behind him and yanks out the triangle of glass. "—it comes back."

"Or my first day," Ambrose pipes up. "I was sitting beside the fire at an inn in Irkutsk, trying to get warm after a hard day's ride across the frozen landscape, and writing a chapter on my Russian adventures for my next book, when the Tsar's men broke in and forced me to drink something foul. Everything went dark and I woke up here, without my manuscript but with a newfound talent for falling through walls."

"Or mine!" Pax yells, unsheathing his sword and dancing across the room in a dramatic retelling of his final moments. "I was stabbing Britons left and right, smashing skulls and exchanging insults, and then I felt a sharp pain in my head, and everything became dark." He falls through the coffee table onto the floor, causing the decorative candlestick to wobble. "When I awoke, everyone had gone from the battlefield, and the Roman corpses were piled high as mountains. We lost the battle so magnificently that my men didn't have the time to give me a proper Roman burial. I will never rest until my bones are found and given the proper rites—"

"Er, yes. Thank you for the hospitality," Albert's chin wobbles as he stares at Pax in horror. "But I think I'll go home. In twenty-five years, I've never slept apart from Maggie. If tonight's the first night, then I will at least be in our bed."

"You do what you need to do, Albert," I say. "I know you have a lot on your mind right now, but tomorrow morning, I want you back here first thing. We need to sit down and have a talk about who might have wanted you dead."

He disappears through the wall. I hear him gasp as he falls through the air into the garden below. Ambrose shakes his head sagely. "That's what you get for not paying attention to my lecture on ghost gravity."

I turn to my three childhood friends, suddenly aware that for the first time since I returned to Grimdale, I'm alone with them. The weight of our seven years apart hangs in the air, and something else, too. Something that's been fizzing beneath my skin since Ambrose first fell through the bathroom wall.

Something I feel strange admitting.

They got *hot*.

Well, more accurately, I grew up, and now I'm noticing how

hot they are. Before, they were like my annoying older brothers who made me watch their favorite TV shows and made me laugh when I fell and scraped my knees so I'd forget about the pain. I remember Edward trying to teach me to dance under the moonlight before my school formal, and Pax dreaming up elaborate punishments he wished to inflict upon Kelly Kingston and her posse of mean girls.

But now...

Edward was twenty-seven when he fell out that window, and Ambrose was twenty-five when the Tsar ran him through. No one knows anything about Pax's age. I think you'd have to cut him open and count his rings, but he can't be older than thirty. And he's *ripped*. If there was a swimsuit calendar for the Roman Legion, he'd be January, February, *and* March.

They're hot and they're looking at me expectantly, and my mouth's gone dry, and what am I supposed to do?

"Um. Hi." I wave shyly.

"Bree! Bree is back!" Pax bounds toward me, arms wide. I brace myself for his ghost hug, and I'm surprised when he wraps his arms around me and the heat sears my skin. When ghosts are happy, they give off warmth, but Pax's warmth is tinged with something else...a hard, dangerous edge that makes my skin tingle.

His hands fall into me, the warmth passing through skin and bone and blood vessels. I don't usually let ghosts anywhere near me because I can't bear the thought of the invasion of their *bits* inside me. But I've been friends with these three for so long that I know they can't help it, and I'm used to the feel of them.

At least, I was. But as Pax's hands stroke down my back, and his fingers pass through my skin and actually touch my spine, the delicious warmth radiates through my whole body. I find myself relaxing against him, letting him in.

I lift my arms and wrap them around him, hoping I'm not

hurting him. I can feel the edges of his skin, but I can't hold him. It's like popping a bubble – as soon as you try to touch it, it's gone.

I close my eyes and steady my breath. In. Out. In. Out. Pax's scent invades me – a woodsy, earthy scent. Leather and musk. The sweetness of grapes from the wine he drank before battle. All of it tinged with something sharp and metallic. *Blood*.

My head spins, and a memory assails me. I'm sitting on a three-footed stool inside a leather tent. A man named Marcus Flavius stands before me. He's speaking a foreign language, but to my ears, it's perfectly understandable.

"—we must move swiftly to cut off the power of the Druids," he tells me, his features grave. He scratches the scar where his left eye once was. "They've already united the Silures, Brigantes, and Iceni tribes against us, and their forces swell every day. We cannot allow them to reach London before our reinforcements arrive from Rome."

"But the Caledonian Legion hasn't arrived." Commander Publius Scapula has sent a legion of men from the border to help us protect the province, but they are still two days' march from our current position.

"I do not think we can wait for them. We are a legion of battle-hardened veterans, and although we're outnumbered, we're facing uncouth barbarians armed with rocks and sticks. I see a swift and decisive victory for us, one that will go down in history. Perhaps you will even have your own triumph back in Rome." Flavius winks at me, although he might just have something in his eye. Can a one-eyed man even wink? "It is your decision, *Primus*. The men will follow you to the very gates of Hades."

I grip my sword, the weight of the hilt familiar and sure. "We fight!"

This isn't my memory.

My eyes fly open and I hurl myself away from Pax. My glass flies from my hand, and I topple over the back of the sofa and land hard on my knee.

"Bree, are you okay?" Ambrose cries. He runs through the sofa to get to me and doubles over in pain.

"What is wrong?" Pax's face crumbles.

"Nothing," I breathe as I rub my throbbing knee. "I'm...I'm just a little overwhelmed by today, is all."

I'm not quite ready to tell them what I saw.

I was inside Pax's memory.

I was in his body.

That's never happened before.

Flustered and confused, I crawl across the rug and pick up the shards of my glass. There's a brown stain on the rug from the whisky, but the rug has been in the house since Edward's day and is basically held together by stains now. One more wouldn't hurt.

I straighten up. Ambrose steps forward. "I won't hug you and risk more crystal flying, but you should know that we're so happy you're home, even if it is in unfortunate circumstances."

Home.

My cheeks flush as I remember my little breakdown in the kitchen earlier. "I don't know how long I'm going to be here." I stare at my shoes. "This has all been very sudden. Mum and Dad called a month ago and told me the news about Dad's diagnosis. He put on a brave face in the video, but all I could think about was how gutted he must be. I was working in a youth hostel in Queenstown, New Zealand. I was surrounded by all this beautiful scenery, and I felt like the world was swallowing me..." I search for the right words. "I felt *wrong* being on the other side of the world. I wanted to give Dad a hug. So I decided to come home. Only, when I give them the news, they inform me that they've bought a one-way train ticket to Paris and they're cashing out their retirement savings to go on a holiday, and would I cat-sit for them while they're gone? And I'm so happy for them. I am. They spent years trying to keep this place running, listening to travellers talk about their adventures without going on any themselves, and looking after me and all my weirdness. I want them to have the most amazing time, but I just..."

"You miss him," Ambrose whispers.

"I miss him." The tears prickle again. "I miss my daddy. Isn't that pathetic?"

"It's not pathetic at all," Ambrose says. "My father was a remote, unpleasant man who worked from sunup to sundown. He was a stranger to me, and after I became blind and refused to live in the rat-infested almshouse, he disowned me and refused to give me a cent. If I had Mike as a father, I would miss him, too."

"My father was a soldier." Pax pounds his chest, his voice swelling with pride. "He rose to become a *legate* and won many battles. It was an honor to be beaten by him."

"My father wasn't much for affection," Edward says. "Hugs and affection are not the proper way for a king to behave, especially not a king who's going mad from syphilis."

"Perhaps if your father had hugged you more as a child, you wouldn't write such insufferable poetry," Ambrose shoots out.

"Perhaps if you'd been hugged, your face wouldn't bear a resemblance to a mangled hamster," Edward snaps back.

"I love hugs!" Pax barrels into Edward, knocking him through the liquor cabinet with the force of his affection.

I can't help the smile spreading across my face. I have missed this — the four of us hanging out, ribbing each other.

I might not have my dad with me, but I'm not alone anymore.

"I should go to bed." I stand up, cupping the shards in my

hand. "It's been a long day, and I have a murder to solve in the morning."

"We're going to help." Ambrose's face breaks out into his signature determined smile. "Sylvie and I listened to a fascinating podcast about a man who didn't push his wife down a staircase. I feel as though I've been training my whole afterlife for this moment."

"Don't look so excited about it. Murder is a messy business. Someone was always getting murdered at court, and it took the servants weeks to remove the bloodstains. So undignified." Edward performs a deep bow. "Goodnight, m'lady."

I giggle as I hold my hand up, the way I used to do when we were kids. "High five?"

Edward presses his fingers against mine. Again, I'm expecting the feeling I remember – a slight brush of warm air.

What happens is that hot, needy tingle. It starts in the tips of my fingers and rockets down my arm. My body responds in ways I don't expect – the bees are humming beneath my skin, building their hive between my legs.

I leap back in surprise, and instantly regret it. That tingle felt so good...

From the expression on Edward's face as he stares down at his hand, I know he felt something, too.

"That's...different," I breathe.

"It is," he whispers. "It is very different."

Edward steps toward me again, and the look on his face morphs into something more like the Edward I remember. His hand reaches for my cheek.

My heart thuds, because as Edward leans closer, I feel sure that he's going to kiss me, and that I want him to kiss me...

THUD.

CRASH.

BANG.

"What the fuck?" I turn to the ceiling, where the noise had come from. Ambrose yelps and dives into the bookshelves. Edward scrambles away and cowers behind a trembling Pax.

The tough-as-hobnails centurion is *trembling*.

"What the fuck was that?" I glare at them. Pain splays across my palm, and I look down to see that I'm clenching the shards in my fist. "Is it the bat?"

"N-n-not a bat." It doesn't seem possible, but Edward is more pale than usual. He points a shaking finger toward the door. "A creature of supreme evil. You should go to bed. Quickly. And take the back staircase."

"But—"

"Go!" Edward barks. "Your prince commands you! We shall keep the fiend at bay!"

"Okay, okay, I'm going!" I run out of the room, still unsure exactly what I'm running from. Behind me, I can hear the ghosts screeching with terror as the banging and crashing noises continue.

Just another day in Grimwood Manor.

As I pound down the staircase, blood dripping from my palm where I'm squeezing the shards, I'm aware of the skin on my fingers tingling, and the ache between my legs that cannot be about me being attracted to Edward. Because, sure, he's hot. But he's also a ghost. He's expired. Deceased. Shuffled halfway off this mortal coil. He's rung down the curtain and joined the choir invisible. He's no longer counted on the census, and is severely living-challenged.

I cannot fall for a ghost.

I will *not*.

I'm back in this house, with my father's illness taking up rent in my brain, and now Albert's murder to solve – it's too much already without adding kissing a ghost to the list.

Not to mention that this is Edward. *My* Edward. Edward the

rake and wastrel of the finest order. A kiss would complicate everything, and...

...and what would kissing him even feel like? Would it be like the tingling in my hand? The warmth inside me when Pax hugged me? The humming bees when Ambrose's hand brushed my tit?

And what about Ambrose and Pax? What would they—

No. No no no no no.

NO.

I should go back and talk to them. Hash this out right now. But if I look into Edward's obsidian eyes or feel his ghostly touch on mine again, I will lose all my resolve.

I push my door open, throw off my clothes, and crawl into bed, my mind a tangle of emotions. I've been back in Grimdale for two days and already I'm embroiled in a murder and narrowly avoiding kissing a ghost.

And what is up with the way they touch me? Why do they feel so different? Why are they so much more powerful than they've ever been before?

What the fuck am I doing?

16

EDWARD

I don't sleep all night.

I'm not sure what we ghosts do is even considered sleep. If I retreat into the depths of my memories, I can place myself into a restful, trance-like state where I'm oblivious to the Living world for several hours. It's not quite as blissful as the opium pipe, but it's not far off.

But tonight, rest does not come. I lie in the middle of the enormous, four-poster honeymoon bed and think about Brianna down the hall, curled up in her own bed, her lustrous hair fanned like a halo around her face, and her breasts rising and falling with every breath.

My fingers still tingle from where I touched her.

I've wafted around the whole house, touching every object I can find, trying to recreate the sensation of my fingers dancing in hers. But all I get is the jarring cold that sucks all the pleasure from the air. This leads me to believe that whatever has changed between us to create this magic sensation, it is not because of something I've done.

It's *her*.

I've always known Brianna is different. Ever since her accident, she's been able to see us. In the four hundred years I've been dead, I've never known another human who could see ghosts.

Even before her accident, Bree had a presence in the house that called to me. Beneath her tiny baby's chest beat the heart of a poet.

I spent my whole living life chasing every pleasure that crossed my path, always searching, always yearning for that which was new and exciting and different. I wanted one thing only – to be in opposition to everything my father stood for. And all I achieved was a footnote in history and a shard in my posterior.

Brianna Mortimer is everything I have always dreamed of being. But whereas I embraced everything unusual and different and forbidden, she has always been desperate to be normal. And now...

...and now the connection between us is stronger than ever...

I almost kissed her.

I would have kissed Brianna if that blasted monster hadn't messed it up by coming down the chimney to torment us. And if I kissed her, I would have ruined everything. I would have frightened her so much that she'd run away and *never* come back.

I have to get myself under control.

Not that I've ever succeeded in controlling my carnal urges before, but there's a first time for everything, right? An old prince can learn new tricks.

I hold my hand up and turn it over, staring at my fingers, wishing for things to be different. But I know what I must do.

I must try *not* to seduce a woman.

A COUPLE of hours after sunrise, grumpy and dishevelled, I'm dragged from bed by the overpowering scent of butter and cream. I haul my princely visage down to the kitchen to find Brianna boiling the kettle and flipping drop scones in the frying pan.

"Good morning," she sings out. "I made your favorite. I thought you'd appreciate it."

She sets a small plate of drop scones opposite her at the counter, all made up with butter, jam, and clotted cream. I lean over and inhale the scent. *Ahh, that's delicious. It's almost as good as...*

...as the seductive, scandalous scent of Brianna that fills the room and makes my ghost heart do strange things.

Without my other senses, smell has become a way to navigate the world. In a way, all ghosts become like Ambrose. We learn to see in new ways. Brianna smells like tangled bedsheets and the flickering of candlelight. She smells of wild nights and fingernails dragging over my skin. Her scent glides against my ghost skin like the edge of a blade.

Brianna sits down opposite me and tucks into her own scones. We eat and sniff in silence. I long to bring up our almost-kiss, but she's got that look in her honey-colored eyes – the look she'd get sometimes when she arrived home from school that meant she'd endured a day of taunts from the other children. It was the look my horses gave when my father went out to ride them with the whip in his hand – the look of someone who wanted to bolt.

"Albert's already been over," she says. "He and I had a good chat. He has no idea who might've wanted to kill him, but he believes it might have to do with his work as a freelance financial consultant. Apparently, he's been supplementing his pension by giving villagers investing advice."

"Maybe it was a jealous lover," I say. "That's how my friend Percival met his untimely end – his wife found out about his mistress and so she snuck a knife into their marriage bed and cut off his gentleman's sausage and he bled out—"

"Albert doesn't have a jealous lover. He was loyal to Maggie." She squints at me. "You don't know anything about loyalty."

"Excuse me, m'lady, if you must know, in the past four hundred years since my argument with the second-story window, I have only had one woman in my life, unless you count Moon." I grin down at the cat as she wanders in from outside, the tail of a field mouse dangling from her mouth.

When I was a Living, I never had much time for cats. We kept some in the palace to ward off the rodents, but they were just annoying furry things that got underfoot and jumped on the bed while I was *in flagrante delicto*.

But Entwhistle and Moon kept us ghosts entertained, especially during the boring winter months when the B&B was closed to guests. They rule the house with regal dignity and have Mike and Sylvie completely under their paws – an achievement for which I can't help but feel a sense of pride.

Entwhistle is more like me – the entertainer, the buffoon, the one who always has to pull the craziest stunts. Entwhistle will be licking his arsehole one moment and then it will suddenly occur to him that he should climb the curtains or dive into a freshly baked pie. Moon is the Pax of the pair – the bloodthirsty one, the devourer of flesh. I tell her often how much I admire her ability to get her paws dirty to protect our little

Grimwood kingdom, although I'd never say such a thing to the Roman.

"Albert was a manager at Grimdale Bank," Brianna says as she shoos Moon and her present back outside. "He helped people with their investments and retirement accounts. But he has – *had* – dementia. He shouldn't have been giving financial advice to anyone. I bet there's someone who's lost money and blames him."

"You should talk to the three witches," I suggest. "They know all the gossip in the village. I bet they've seen something."

"Edward, you're a genius."

"Obviously." I puff out my chest. "As well as being the most handsome personage in this household, and the most, I always happen to be the cleverest. You should hear my latest poem. It's about Moon hunting in the mid-afternoon sun. There are many references to the celestial bodies and a rather fetching comparison to the untrimmed bush of Lady Penelope Londsdale—"

"Edward, you are...you are..." Brianna leans forward, and her lips brush my cheek. It's something she used to do as a kid – she'd try to kiss the surface of us and giggle at the heat or chill on her skin.

When her lips graze me, I get that same strange and lovely tingle, the same sense that I'm more solid and real than I've ever been. And as she leans over to reach me, her breasts also graze my arm.

Well, that puts a little life into my scepter!

A woman in my time would never be so brazen as to kiss a prince unless she was a prostitute. Even then, she risked having her hand cut off if she displeased me.

But Brianna lives by her own rules, always. And now, the rules have changed, and her touch...it does things to me. Things I haven't felt in a long time.

Things I'm desperate to feel more.

I turn my head, slowly, trying not to scare her away, aware of her lips hovering just over...

"Fuck." Brianna clamps her hand over her lips and pulls away. Her honey eyes dart toward the door. Panic churns inside me. I have to keep her here.

"Am I interrupting anything?" Ambrose hovers there, fresh from his morning float around the woodland. "I smelled drop scones and—"

"It's fine!" Brianna leaps up and pulls out her chair. "Sit here opposite Edward and have my scones. I'm...I'm not hungry anymore. I have to get ready to go to the village. It's the Great Grimdale Bake Off today, so it's a good chance to catch the latest gossip about Albert's case."

"We'll come, too. Won't we, Edward?" Ambrose beams in my direction. "Pax will love the competition, and it will be good for us to get out of the house, stretch our legs."

"We don't have legs." I slump my face into my plate of scones, bracing myself against the pain. It does nothing to lessen the fire of Brianna's touch against my cheek.

I need to find some way to control myself, and fast. Before my lascivious ways end up chasing Brianna away again...for good.

17

BREE

Mum: Bree, darling, I hope you're doing well and taking good care of Maggie. I don't know if you remember, but the Grand Grimdale Bake Off is happening this weekend. You should go along – it will be heaps of fun.

Maybe there will be a cute boy you can ask out – ideally one who can cook, because I'm sorry, darling, but your domestic skills are severely lacking.

After I clean up the kitchen and check that Moon has eaten her mouse, the four of us set out for the village. As we pass the gatehouse, I look up and see Albert in the top window, slumped half in the sill, staring over the graveyard and looking miserable. I want to invite him along, but honestly, he's in a bit of a state and I'll get more done without yet another ghost to wrangle.

The village is bustling with people setting up for the Bake Off. Bright-colored streamers crisscross High Street, and the village green is overrun with scaffolding and white awnings from the fairground rides and fete stalls being set up for the weekend. I've had my eardrums assaulted at the international ukulele festival and been pelted with tomatoes at La Tomatina in Spain, but I still feel a little burst of nostalgia that I'm home for this ridiculous Grimdale tradition.

The festivities begin tomorrow. Amateur bakers from around the village run stalls selling their wares, and they have until the main event on Saturday to put forward their entries to the judges – this is so they can choose their best day's baking from the week and the villagers can sample everything without having to go into a diabetic coma if the event was a single day. At Saturday's grand fete, the judges will announce the top pies, biscuits, cakes, and pastries, as well as the crown for Grimdale's best baker.

Although it won't be the same without Maggie. She's won every year with her incredible scones, and she's also the head of the organizing committee. Judging by all the people swarming around the green, at least she'd be proud to know that the festival is going on without her.

But it shouldn't have to. And that's why I'm here. Get to work, Bree.

I find the three witches hovering near the duck pond on the other edge of the village green. Lottie has her skirts pulled up and is dangling her legs in the water, swinging her legs and pretending to make splashes. The ducks take a wide berth around them. Ghost rule number seventeen: ducks have an uncanny sense for the presence of the undead. Everyone thinks it's dogs who can sense ghosts, but it's really ducks.

Trust me, I know these things.

Pax and Edward wander off to inspect the setup for the Bake Off in the marquee behind us (i.e., shove their ghosty heads into some cakes). Mary rushes after them, rubbing her belly with joy.

I sit down beside Agnes and Walpurgis, while Ambrose

wanders obliviously into the pond. Walpurgis looks up at me, his eyes full of cat disdain, as if to say, "aren't ghost men daft?"

Yes. Yes, they are.

"For heaven's sake, Lottie, stop that," Agnes pouts as Lottie swings her legs again. "If I wanted to get motion sickness I'd join Bree on one of those ghastly carnival rides."

Lottie sticks out her tongue. "You're just jealous because I have the most comely ankles."

"Hrmmmmph," Agnes snorts. "With those chicken's feet? I think not. *This* is what a real woman's ankle looks like."

She hikes up her skirt, revealing a pair of wizened legs and narrow, bony ankles shoved into worn leather boots. I stifle a laugh.

"Bree, you must settle this for us," Lottie declares. "Who has the most comely ankles?"

"Um..."

"Leave her out of this. She's wearing a sack." Agnes frowns at my hoodie. "She has no eye for these things."

"Agnes is right. Sorry, ladies." I smile, grateful for a way out. "Perhaps Edward can judge your ankles instead. I brought you that present from my travels."

The two witches lean over as I pull out an empty pickle jar I was using to store my Amsterdam stash. The weed is long gone, but the jar still reeks of it. I pull the lid off and the ghosts take a whiff.

"Oooh!" Agnes flaps her hand in front of her face. "That brings me back to my witching days, dancing naked in the woods. Why, did I ever tell you that I saw a unicorn once..."

"Only three thousand times," Lottie says, elbowing Agnes out of the way so she can get a whiff. "I don't feel anything except hungry. Maybe I'll go check out the cakes—"

I throw out an arm to stop her. "Before you do, I was

wondering if you might be able to help me with something. I require your expert skills."

Lottie immediately perks up. She kicks her legs and actually manages to make a couple of ripples in the water. "Is this something to do with the new ghost in the village?"

"How did you know about the new ghost?" As far as I'm aware, Albert hadn't left his house since last night, and he certainly wasn't strong enough to make it all the way into the village. Which is just as well, because I didn't want the three witches – or any of Grimdale's other kooky, post-death residents – to scare him.

"We were over at the Anderson house, spying on Mr. Anderson's new mistress, when we heard Mrs. Anderson and Mrs. Dewey talking about the murder at the graveyard."

"And that 'crazy Mortimer girl who found the body and was talking to herself at the crime scene.' We figured that means we have a new victim...er, *friend*." Agnes rubs her fingers together with glee. "Who is it? Please let it be that randy old vicar – I have a few lessons I'd like to teach him about being a whore of Satan..."

"No, it's Albert Fernsby," I say quickly, before she can go into detail.

"Oh, that's a shame. Poor sweet Albert," Lottie frowns. "He always ordered an extra side of mushy peas – now that's my kind of man. Poor Maggie must be distraught."

"She's more than distraught. She's in jail. They think she killed him with poison." I lower my voice because I'm not in the mood to deal with any more villagers seeing me talking to the ducks and spreading the word that crazy Bree Mortimer is back in town.

Agnes tsked. "When will women learn? Maggie was always swanning about with her herbal remedies and healing balms, making it known she understands plant magic. And then she's foolish enough to use poison? Amateur mistake. The first person they blame for poisoning is the local wise woman. I guess she'll have plenty of time to ruminate on that error while they're leading her to the witch-hanging tree. Now, if she'd had the audacity to bludgeon him with a rock, then she wouldn't be in this mess."

I blanch. Sometimes Agnes scares me. "We don't hang people as witches anymore, Agnes. And I don't think Maggie killed Albert. I just can't see her as a cold-blooded murderer. They were far too in love. But the police seem so sure they have the right person and, well, Albert's a ghost now, and he's insisting that I help him clear his wife's name. Dani's going to find out what poison killed him, but in the meantime, I was wondering if you might have heard anything around the village. Anyone with an axe to grind with Albert or Maggie?"

"Oh," Mary sits up. "We have, as a matter of fact—hey! Mmmmmpffff."

She struggles as Agnes clamps a hand over her mouth.

"We might be able to help you with your little mystery, dearie." Agnes peers up at me with a glint in her eyes. "But it'll cost you."

"Meow!" adds Walpurgis.

"Mmmmmph, mmmmmmmmmmmph," cries Lottie.

I sigh. "You'd be helping a ghost cross over. Isn't that payment enough?"

"You know that it's not. Nothing in the afterlife is free."

"Fine." I whip out my phone. "What'll it be?"

"We want a feast," Agnes says. "We want all our favorite foods laid out on a table so we can sniff them to our heart's content. Starting with a dozen cupcakes from the market."

"And a Victoria sponge!" Lottie cries.

"And some bangers and mash from the Goat," Mary appears on my other shoulder. She rubs her belly in anticipation. "And maybe a lamb shank, too. Oh, and what about a slice of strong cheddar?"

"I'd also like a glass of the finest cider," Agnes says. "And a bowl of pottage."

"—I don't know if I can get 'pottage'," I say glumly, my fingers whirring as I frantically type out their shopping list.

"You'll get pottage or we'll keep our secrets," Agnes growls. "And a pickled haddock."

"And a lemon muffin!"

"And cookies-and-cream ice cream!"

"With fish sauce on top!"

"And extra mushy peas!"

"Fine." I shove my phone into my pocket before they can add anything else. "Come to Grimdale Manor tomorrow evening, 6PM sharp, and I'll have a feast prepared. It's nice to know that charity begins with ghosts."

18

BREE

The next morning, my phone alarm wakes me three times before I throw it against the wall in disgust.

I am not a morning person. Or a mourning person. Get it? I'm hilarious.

As I trudge over to my pile of clothes and fumble around for something to wear, I catch movement out of the corner of my eye.

I whirl around.

The curtain flutters. Five huge toes in a Roman sandal disappear from beneath it.

"Pax?"

I stare at the curtain, my heart hammering in my chest.

It can't be.

He can't still...

When I was a little kid, I was terrified of the dark. When you realize you can see ghosts and no one else can, and every children's book you read depicts those ghosts as terrifying, chain-rattling monsters who frighten people to death, you develop an unhealthy fear that other fictional monsters will eat you in your sleep.

Not sleeping sucks. I was grumpy all the time. I'd smash things, break my toys, hurt myself. The slightest noise would set me off. Once I fell asleep in the sandpit, and a teacher had to dig me out before the other kids buried me.

My parents were distraught. They thought my not sleeping had something to do with the trauma of my accident. In a way, they were right. They took me to sleep doctors, psychologists, and even a psychic to try and get answers, but I refused to talk about what was really bothering me. No one believed me when I first started seeing the ghosts. The child psychologists my parents took me to prescribed drugs that made me feel woozy. So why would things be different now?

But I talked to Pax and Ambrose and Edward. They were the only ones who understood.

Every night after my parents kissed me goodnight, Pax would unsheathe his sword and check under the bed, in the closet, and in my toy chest for monsters. Then he would take up his position at the end of my bed, hand on the hilt of his sword, steel grey eyes scanning the shadows for danger.

I slept.

With him there, watching over me, I could finally sleep.

My parents called it a miracle. But it was my friend, Pax, taking care of me.

My throat closes up. How many times while I've been traveling have I woken in a cold sweat in the middle of the night, terrified of something I couldn't see? How many times had I missed feeling safe, knowing he was nearby?

He's still watching over me.

"Pax," I take a step toward the curtain. My fingers graze the heavy linen. I sleep naked. Did he—

Did he see anything?

My cheeks flush. The thought of him watching me sleep should gross me out, but instead, it turns my veins molten hot. I tug on the curtain. "Pax, it's okay. You can come out now. I'm not a little kid anymore. I don't need you to protect me from monsters under the bed—"

"Get up! Get up! Get up!"

"Argh! Albert?" I drop the curtain to clasp my pattering heart. "You gave me a heart attack."

"Hyperbole is unbecoming on such a lovely young lady. You're still alive, which is more than I can say for me." Albert hops around the room. "You're going to solve my case and get my wife out of jail. You promised."

"I'll solve it this afternoon," I growl as I throw a pillow at him.

Ghosts – can't live with them, can't throw them out a window.

I locate some jeans that don't smell like airplanes or New Zealand (I really need to do some laundry) and head down to the kitchen. Grimdale cemetery is closed to the public again today, so I have all day to create a ghost feast.

The three ghosts float into the kitchen as I hunt around in the cupboards for something to eat. Pax refuses to meet my eye, and I'm not going to bust his ass for being in my room in front of Edward. I don't want anyone to think I'm playing favorites, especially not after all the strange things that have been happening.

Albert hovers impatiently near the door. The ghosts make a cup of tea for me while I feed Moon and Entwhistle and write out a shopping list. Most of the food I can order from the Goat once the kitchen opens, and the baked goods I can get from the fete. But the pottage is going to be a little more difficult.

"I don't even know what pottage is," I moan, my head in my hands.

"It's the dross that peasants eat," Edward explains with his typical haughty tone. "It's oats and barley and vegetables all mushed together. We ghosts could probably whip up some for you while you procure the baked goods."

"You'd do that?"

"I think we can if you line up all the ingredients on the counter." Ambrose's brow creases in worry.

"I will stir." Pax whirls his sword around.

"And I shall supervise, as is my proper place as the prince. We're pleased to do it. Anything to help Albert cross over." Edward bows again. I narrow my eyes at him. I've never known him to think of anyone else. "Perhaps in exchange for our magnanimous cooking skills..."

"Ah, I knew you didn't have an altruistic bone in your body."

"I have no bones in my body." He lowers his voice. "Except for the other night, when you touched me—"

My cheeks burn with heat. "Spit it out, prince. What's this going to cost me?"

"All I'm suggesting is that you might include a few of our favorites in this little feast of yours? I can't tell you how much I've been craving braised quail—"

"No weird tiny birds," I snap. "You get a piece of Victoria sponge cake, and that's it."

Edward breaks out one of his signature devilish grins as he bows again. "Brianna Mortimer, I am forever in your debt."

"I'm not certain what any of this has to do with solving my murder," Albert points out frostily.

"That's because you lack my murder-solving skills, Albert," I say as I grab my purse. "You can follow me to the village if you like, but I don't think your ghost mojo will let you get any further than the end of the lane."

"Albert gets to go? No fair. I wanted to go to the fete," Pax grumbles. "The *Great British Bake Off* is my favorite moving picture show."

"It...is?"

I didn't know ghosts had favorite moving picture shows. When I used to live here we hardly ever watched TV, mainly because it's very hard to concentrate on a show with three ghosts whispering about historical inaccuracies (Ambrose), trying to stab the villains (Pax), and demanding every female actress remove her undergarments (Edward).

Pax beams. "*The Great British Bake Off* is the kind of battle that poets sing about, except instead of wooden horses and cutting off the heads of enemies, there's buttercream and finger sandwiches. Will there be finger sandwiches at the fete? By Jupiter's hairy butthole, I'd love to try a finger sandwich. Who knew fingers could look so appealing?"

"They're not made from real fingers, you indolent oaf," Edward sneers. "And you can't go because we need you to chop the vegetables for the pottage."

"Can we pleeeeeease go now?" Albert pleads. "I want to see if my, ahem, ghost mojo is any stronger today. Maybe I'll be able to train myself to get to Argleton so I can see her in jail?"

"I doubt it, old bean," Ambrose says as he flexes his fingers, ready to pour the oats. "I haven't been able to get outside the village, and I've been a ghost a lot longer than you."

I get out the ingredients Edward specifies – luckily, we have everything – and leave them to it with no shortage of trepidation.

They're not even corporeal. Surely they can't do too much damage.

Albert floats behind me as I march toward the village, talking a mile a minute about various insane theories on how someone might have poisoned him. Luckily, he only makes it to the squashed navvy's corner before he disappears, leaving me to the blissful peace of my own thoughts.

Without my ghostly retinue in tow, I'm able to quickly shop

at the market for aged cheddar and pop into the Cackling Goat with my order for delivery at 5:30PM before heading over to the fete.

The tent is filled to bursting with people oohing and aahing over the baking on display. The judges have already sampled the entries, so the bakers can offer their goods to the public. People glance at my face and quickly look away. I spy Kelly and her husband beside the sponge cakes. She meets my eyes and bursts into cruel laughter.

Great. No matter how long I'm away, I'll always be Bree the weird kid who talks to imaginary friends. And by now people must have heard that I'm the one who found Albert's body and that Maggie has been accused of his murder. Everyone probably thinks I did it...

At least I have Dani on my side. And the ghosts.

I stop in front of a display of mouthwatering cupcakes. *Those would be delicious for the feast...*

"Hello, Bree Mortimer," Linda Bateman smiles broadly from behind her cupcake booth. "It's so lovely to see you back in the village. Your parents must be thrilled to have you home again."

"They are," I smile back, relieved to be having a normal conversation for once. "Actually, they're in France at the moment, having a well-deserved holiday. I'm cat-sitting for them at Grimwood Manor for a couple of weeks."

"That's wonderful, dear." Linda comes around the side of the table and whispers conspiratorially. "I heard that you were the one who found poor Albert's body at the cemetery. Was it utterly dreadful?"

"It was pretty awful." A shudder runs through my body as I remember it. Even though I've been surrounded by death my whole life, it's hard to come face to face with the body of a friend, and then to have that friend haunt you.

"It's such a terrible shame about Albert," Linda shakes her

head sadly. "He was such a lovely man, and so devoted to Maggie. You know the police have arrested her? I just cannot believe she would do such a thing. She really was the heart of this village – always a kind word for everyone, the head of every committee, the flower show coordinator every year. And those herbal body butters of hers! Did you know that she was the main organizer of the fete? It's no wonder that her scones always win. But it just goes to show that you think you know someone and they can be hiding all kinds of surprises. Would you like a cupcake? I'm afraid that with Maggie gone, I'm going to win the competition this year, although it'll be a hollow victory. I'd much rather have our dear Albert back and Maggie out from that nasty police cell."

"Sure. I'd love a cupcake, thanks." I bite into the raspberry and dark chocolate concoction she hands me. Wow, that is some cupcake – buttery and crumbly and absolutely divine. "This is amazing. Can I take four of these to go?"

While Linda boxes up my cupcakes, I spy Dani down the other end of the row of stalls, helping her mother at her cider stall. She waves me over and hands me a cup of something that smells like apples and rocket fuel. "Pinch your nose and drink it really fast."

I oblige and immediately regret my decision. The cider burns all the way down, and not in a fun way. I cough and gratefully accept the cup of water Dani hands me. "What was that? It tastes like apple crumble and sadness."

Dani laughs. "Mum has many talents, but cider brewing isn't one of them. She does cater to a certain crowd, though."

I peer at the line of grizzled-looking old men who have lined up at the stall, behind the sign that reads 'Four drink maximum.' Dani hands the first four cups and he downs them all right there in front of her and moves to the back of the line for his next round. Dani rolls her eyes at me and it's all I can do not to burst into laughter. It is so wonderful to have her in my life again.

"There you are, dearie." Linda bustles over with the package of cupcakes all tied up with a pink bow. "They should stay safe on the ride home. I hope you'll stick around for the judging. I can't believe how sad I am that I might actually stand a chance of winning this year."

She skips off. Dani glances around the room. "It is strange to be here without Maggie. She really was the force behind all the kooky events in the village."

"Hopefully we can clear her name and have her back running things soon." I hold out the package. "Do you want a cupcake? I got them for the ghosts, but they can't eat them so they won't care if one is missing."

Dani bites into it eagerly, her eyes popping out of her head. "Omg, that is *amazing.*"

"Right?"

"So..." Dani waits until her mum is busy with another customer, then she grabs my hand and pulls me over to the jelly mould stall. "I found out some information last night about the case. I didn't even have to resort to covert ops. Jo, the pathologist, was at our lesbian film club in Argleton last night. I bought her a couple of pints, and she told me all the gossip. Unfortunately, it's not good. The police have pretty damning evidence that Maggie did it."

"What's the evidence? I thought the point of poisoning someone is that there's no way to tell who gave it to him."

"This is true, except that remember I told you how Albert didn't ingest the poison? So it wasn't put in his food. He absorbed it through his skin."

"Is that even possible?"

"It is if you slather yourself in body butter made with a high concentration of belladonna berries and then fall asleep."

Shit.

That's...that's *horrible*.

Surely, Maggie wouldn't have done that to Albert?

"So it's not a mistake?" I stare down at the cupcakes, suddenly not hungry. "Some belladonna got into the mixture by accident?"

"Jo says no, this is deliberate. The butter was one Maggie made Albert specifically for his arthritis. And Maggie knows about herbs and plants – there's no way she'd accidentally use something so poisonous."

"Then someone must have tampered with one of Maggie's bottles. That's the only explanation..."

"Jo says that's possible but unlikely. The person would have had to know how to extract the juice from the berries and what concentration to mix it. The police are warning every shop in the village to stop stocking Maggie's products in case she poisoned her whole batch."

"So Maggie gave Albert the poisoned balm, waited until he went to sleep, went off to the pub quiz, and then came home and stuffed him into the catacombs? She's not exactly a body-builder – how would she even have lifted Albert's body into the niche?"

"The current theory is that Maggie intended to come home and wash the belladonna off his body and then call the ambulance and say he died of a heart attack, which is technically true. His death would have looked like natural causes and no one would have thought to look for the poison. But Albert woke up and ran out into the cemetery. Belladonna can make you hallucinate. He probably let himself in through the unlocked gate and crawled into the niche himself."

"And what's Maggie's story?"

"It matches up pretty closely. She says that Albert was sore from his arthritis, so she ran him a bath, gave him the balm to slather all over himself, and left him sleeping with the door ajar while she headed off to the pub quiz. She came home and found him missing. She said that one of the downstairs windows was wide open, but the police dusted it for prints and only found Maggie and Albert's prints and some traces of flour. But there's flour all over the house because Maggie was baking for her fete entry."

Shit. That really, really does not look good.

Dani continues. "Maggie claims that she noticed a pot of her healing balm missing a week or so ago, but then it seemed to reappear, and she thought perhaps she'd just counted wrong. Old age, you know? But now she's telling the police that someone stole that pot and then returned it laced with belladonna. For her story to be true, the real murderer had to have visited her house twice in the past week."

"That's something. I can ask Albert. Hopefully, he remembers."

"You could also talk to the kooky woman who owns Basic Witch, that crystal and magic shop in the village," Dani suggests. "She sold Maggie's scented candles and balms, and she might know who else in the village would know how to poison with belladonna."

"That's a good idea! And the three witches think they have some leads on Albert's enemies, but if I want them to talk I have to cook them an epic feast." I perk up. "Hey, did you want to come over to my house this evening? I going to have enough food to feed a Roman legion, and it's all going to go to waste."

"Yeah, I'd love to." Dani pauses. "Could I...could I bring a date?"

"Hell yeah, you can!"

After visiting a few more stalls, I waddle home from the village, stuffed with finger sandwiches, laden down with my purchases, and in somewhat of a good mood. I may be so confused about my love life that I'm lusting after three ghosts, but at least Dani's putting herself out there. Maybe I could even make dinner more romantic, put on some soft music, light some candles...

No. I think of poor Albert, missing the love of his life. *No candles.*

Fine. A hedonistic, sugar-soaked bacchanal it is.

"Hey, ghosties, I have good news." I fling open the back door. "I got cupcakes! And we have a new lead on Albert's—"

I stop short.

"What the—"

The kitchen is a disaster. Every pot, pan, and pie dish has been torn from the cupboards and dumped on the floor. There is oatmeal mush stuck to the oven, the cupboard doors, the floor, and splattered across the ceiling. Pax stands over the counter, slamming his sword down on some poor defenseless carrots with such force that carrot shrapnel ricochets off the tiles. I watch in horror as he swings his arm back with such force that he embeds his sword into the wall behind him.

"Pax, stop!"

"I must chop vegetables finely," Pax says, frowning at the lumps of carrot as he raises his sword again. "Just like they do on *Bake Off.*"

I reach for the sword at the same time as Pax. My hand touches his, and a hot tingle courses down my arm. Pax leaps back, staring at his hand as if it's haunted.

"What was that?"

"I don't know. But it keeps happening." I take one look at the ruined kitchen, and it all rises up inside me again. Dad's disease. Albert's death. Being back in Grimdale. Kelly Kingston laughing at me at the fete. Seeing the ghosts again and all these strange new feelings that brings up.

And now this new ability – this sense that the distance

between me and the ghosts is closing, that they've pulled me deeper into their world, and they're more real to me than ever.

It's too much.

I run from the room before I let the ghosts see the tears falling from my eyes.

19

BREE

After a long bath (with none of Maggie's balms and no ghost interruptions) and an hour practicing the meditation techniques I picked up on a yoga retreat in Bali, I feel calm enough to tackle the mess in the kitchen. Edward and Pax make themselves scarce, but Ambrose sits at the table while I chip oatmeal off the stools, and regales me with one of my favorite stories from his travels – riding elephants in Ceylon.

A knock on the door at 5:30PM startles us both. For a moment, I'd forgotten that I was in the Grimwood kitchen. I was on the back of that elephant with him, being bucked about and dragged off into the wilderness without a hope of finding his way back. Ambrose has such a way with words. He makes the whole world come alive with his enthusiasm. I wish more than anything that we had a copy of his book so that other people could come on his adventures, but sadly there are no copies left.

I yank open the heavy front door. "Principal Gibbons?" I cry in surprise. "What are you—"

"It's Mr. Gibbons now. Here's your order," he says gruffly,

handing over my takeout bags. Gibbons was the principal of my old high school. He's one of the most prominent figures in the community; first tenor in the church choir, bowler for the cricket team, and never seen without his pristine three-piece suit he had tailored on Savile Row.

But today, there's no suit in sight. He wears a polo with a tomato sauce stain on the collar. He thrusts the brown paper bags at me like he's anxious to get out of there, which isn't an uncommon feeling when people knock on the door in Grimdale. But still...it's weird.

"Princ—er, *Mr.* Gibbons...why are you running deliveries for the Goat?"

"I had to get a job, didn't I?" he growls. "That blasted neighbour of yours lost all my money. I hope he rots in hell. No tip?"

I fish around in my pocket and pull out a couple of pound coins, which I drop into his fist. "Thank you. How are you enjoying your retirement—"

But he'd already disappeared down the path. He drags a bicycle from behind the hedge and swings his heavy frame into the seat.

He's riding a bicycle? He used to ride about in a vintage Bentley.

And he's angry at Albert for losing his money. Hmmmm. I think I might have lucked onto another suspect.

I don't have time to mull it over. My ghostly and Living visitors will arrive any moment now. I set the food on the counter and busy myself dishing it into bowls and platters. We're going to eat in the dining room.

Grimdale's formal dining room seats twenty and looks like the room where a vampire would host a dinner party. We basically only use it on Christmas or during that ill-fated year my mother decided Grimdale was going to do weddings.

I set the table with knives and forks and the nicest china.

The light from the chandelier is muted so I decide that actually, we are going to have candles. I find some fake tea-light candles in a drawer and rest those in the sconces. I notice Mum has stacks of Maggie's scented candles, but after everything Dani told me, I'm not ready to trust them.

I believe Maggie's innocent.

I do.

But I've seen enough true crime TV to know that it's always the person you least suspect.

"The table looks beautiful," Edward says as my ghosts float into the room, followed shortly afterward by Albert. They take seats down one side of the table. Pax eagerly eyes up the platter of cupcakes.

"No sniffing until our guests of honour arrive."

"They're nothing compared to Maggie's scones," Albert says with a sigh. "What I wouldn't give to taste her baking once again..."

I set down the final dish of mushy peas at 5:49. I pour myself a pint of cider. At 6PM on the dot, the three witches float through the wall, Walpurgis purring around their ankles. Agnes inspects the table and pronounces it 'adequate,' and we all sit down to eat.

Well, I sit down. Moon and Entwhistle head to their bowls. Walpurgis shoves his head through a bowl of cream I left for him, and six ghosts dive into the food.

It is very, *very* strange to sit at the head of a table for twenty and see only faint, see-through outlines of people floating around you, sniffing the food and shoving their faces *through* the dishes. As hungry as I am and as good as at least two-thirds of the food smells, I don't serve myself.

This is for them.

"Sooooo..." I ask once the room is filled with disgusting sniffing sounds. Edward shoves his entire face into the Victoria sponge and wobbles it around. "Any gossip about Albert and Maggie you'd like to fill me in on?"

"We heard that Albert was taking on some private clients, and he made bad investments," Agnes says as she wafts through the table, her eye on the sharp cheddar and water crackers I'd set out.

"They weren't bad investments!" Albert cries. "It's a growth market. I learned all about it from an expert on YouTube!"

"Something about bitten coins?" Mary's voice is muffled because she has her head inside the cheddar. "Who would want coins with teeth marks in them?"

"You mean, bitcoins?"

"Hmmmph. I wouldn't know. All I know is that it's been the talk down at the Goat. Most people only lost a little money, but a couple of people lost thousands. Albert got into the bitten coins because he and Maggie have been struggling to pay their mortgage."

"You still have a mortgage on the house?" I ask Albert in surprise.

"The cost of living is so high these days!" he frowns. "I guess I don't have to worry about that anymore."

"Apparently, you remortgaged ten years ago to pay for a round-the-world cruise for your silver wedding anniversary. Maggie wanted a new car, and to redecorate the bedroom. And Maggie likes a new outfit for every event she puts on in the village. Oh, and the labeling machine for her healing balm business cost a pretty penny." Lottie is trying in vain to lick the bowl of mushy peas. "You went into debt to finance it all, Albert. Whatever Maggie wanted, you'd pay for it, no questions asked."

"I love my wife!" Albert puffs out his chest. "She deserves the best of everything."

"Oh, don't think I'm judging. I'd love a man like that,

instead of my ungrateful husband who had me hanged as a witch because I burned his meat one too many times—"

"He accused you of witchcraft because you burned his dinner?"

"No, not his dinner." Lottie winks.

Gross.

"Just last week, Maggie met with a man in a black suit at the Goat, and they looked over something called en-shore-ants," Mary says as she drags her ghostly fingers through the mushy peas. "She was most interested in en-shore-ants on Albert's life. She increased whatever that is to three million pounds."

"This isn't helping." I lay my head in my hands. "All of this is incriminating Maggie, and the police will know about the insurance policy. I either need something that proves Maggie couldn't possibly be the murderer, or I need another suspect."

"What about Principal Gibbons? I bet the police don't know about his threatening Albert and Maggie," Agnes says proudly.

I perk up. "He did?"

"I don't remember this," Albert says despondently.

"Sometimes ghosts don't remember things that happened close to their death," Edward explains. "For example, I cannot for the life of me remember the poem I had composed about the Countess Marie de Rothschild's bosoms. It was to be my masterpiece, but poof, it's gone forever."

Yes, and Albert was in the early stages of dementia, so that probably makes it worse.

"It happened in the square, late at night, about a week ago, as Albert and Maggie were walking home from the pub. Gibbons jumped out from behind a post, got right up into Albert's face, and said that he would make him pay for ruining his life."

"Yes, he said that Albert lost all his money on bitten coins and that he was going to make sure Albert knew exactly what it felt like to lose everything."

"Thank you, that's exactly what I'm after." I think about Mr. Gibbons at the door in his stained polo shirt. So that's why he's working at the Goat – Albert lost his retirement fund. That's enough motive to kill.

But how could Mr. Gibbons have made the healing balm and got it into the house?

I turn to Albert. "Did Mr. Gibbons visit your house?"

He screws up his face. "I'm afraid I...I don't remember."

"Mr. Gibbons is that man who came to the door earlier, to deliver the food?" Pax asks.

"Yes."

Pax thumps his fist on the table. Well, he tries, but his fist sinks through the wood. "I saw him at the Fernsby house six days ago."

"You did?"

"It's my job to keep watch, notice everyone coming and going, and put my sword through anyone who threatens the peace of the citizens of the Roman Empire."

Now's not the time to remind Pax that the Roman Empire no longer exists, nor to point out that it wasn't particularly peaceful. "What was he doing?"

"Dropping off takeout food. He stood on the doorstep and yelled and shook his fist. I was going to go over there and give him the old Roman greeting—" Pax jabs his sword in the air. "—but Maggie invited him in and gave him a cup of tea."

So Mr. Gibbons was inside the house. He could have easily ducked off to the toilet and taken one of the pots of balm. "Did he visit a second time?"

Pax nods. "Maggie really likes the steak and kidney pie from the Goat."

"That's true, she does!" Albert beams. "It has the perfect crust and just the right amount of filling."

"Ooooh, that sounds delicious." Mary rubs her stomach. "Bree, how come you didn't get us a steak and kidney pie?"

I sigh. "And who else visited the Fernsbys in the last week?"

Pax counts them off on his fingers. "Man with smushed face delivering parcels from boutique in London. Women in flowery dresses having meetings about the Bake Off, man with cup on long stick to see about the blocked latrine. Woman with ice-blonde hair and pointy-toed shoes, asking about square footage—"

"Great, so half the village then."

"I remember the pointy-shoe woman," Albert pipes up. "She's Annabel Myers, a real estate agent. Her husband is in the metal detectorist society – he found a Saxon brooch out near the Babbage farm once. He was showing it off down at the pub, pleased as punch, he was, but then he had to give it over to Henry Babbage because he found it on Henry's field and he didn't have permission to be there."

"A fascinating story," Agnes says, in a tone that implies the opposite.

"What about Annabel?" I ask Albert. "Were you and Maggie going to sell the gatehouse?"

"Oh, no, no, no. Annabel came to the door months ago, telling us how much we could get for the house if we sold it. But we would never! Maggie loves it so much."

"Well, she doesn't love it as much as she loves French silk dresses," Agnes snaps. "Because she told her girlfriend Mabel in the pub that she invited the agent around to appraise the house while you were at bingo. I guess now that you're dead, she'll be able to do what she likes with the house."

"That's not Maggie!" Albert cries. "She doesn't do things behind my back. This makes no sense."

"Just because Maggie spoke to a real estate agent doesn't mean that she's a murderer," I say. "The agent was probably pressuring her into it." Real estate agents are known for being sharks. But still, it's odd. The gatehouse is quite lovely, but the Grimdale market has been in a downturn for years. Maggie wouldn't exactly get a huge return out of it. "We'll figure all this out. We can set up a murder board the way they do in crime shows, and Dani and I will—"

"You know who you should talk to," Agnes says. "Mina Wilde."

"Who?"

"Mina Wilde. Mina's a dear girl about your age who lives in the village across the valley. She runs a dusty old bookshop with a grumpy man who has forearms like tree trunks, a dark-haired artistic sort, and a suave, tall, tattooed fellow with a mind for criminal shenanigans and a body for sin."

"Mmmm, yes. Morrie. I'd like to climb Morrie like a tree," Lottie pipes up.

"You can have him. Give me the dark and surly one. I'd bake him into a pie." Mary licks her lips.

"Can we get back on topic? Why should I talk to Mina?"

"She's a strange girl." Agnes takes a long whiff of cheddar before continuing. "Aside from consorting with her three hand-some lovers and embroiling herself in every village scandal and murder, she's often seen talking to a raven. If she were born in my time they'd have hanged her as a witch long ago. You two will probably get on like a witch on fire—"

"Agnes!"

"Yes, yes, sorry. Anyway, I think Mina might be able to help you figure out the mystery of Albert's murder. We had a bit of trouble with a vampire a few months back, but Mina took care of him. And she's always solving this or that murder—"

"Wait a second, vampires are real?" I can barely keep up

192

with the three of them. I grab my glass of cider and clutch it for dear life.

"Not anymore," Agnes nods sagely. "I tell you, Mina and those men of hers know how to get the job done. If you need some advice on investigating this mystery, you'd do well to consult with her."

"I can't just walk up to some random girl and ask her to help me solve a ghost's murder," I say as I start filling my own plate with food. I take a wide berth around the heaped bowl of mushy peas.

But the things they told me swirl around in my head. There's a girl in the next village who runs a bookshop and solves mysteries and talks to a raven. A girl who has *three* boyfriends. I think of the way it felt when I touched Edward, and when Ambrose fell into the bath, and how Pax is still watching out for me, and how happy and anxious and confused I feel about them. And I think of Albert's forlorn expression as he watched his wife being dragged away by the police.

Maybe this Mina person can help me more than I realize.

"Okay." I pull off a leg of chicken and point it in Agnes' direction. "I'll talk to her. Now, if you have no further gossip for me, the feast for the ghosts is over. Dani will be here any minute with her date, and I don't want her to have to explain why her friend Bree is talking to the furniture—"

"Bree?"

I glance up, expecting to see Dani bounding into the house, her long blonde hair streaking behind her. Instead, Alice Agincourt stands in the doorway, hands on her hips, looking at me like I've grown two heads.

"What are you doing?" Alice sneers at the table laden with a strange assortment of food and my chicken leg. "What the fuck is this food? Who are you talking to?"

193

20

BREE

I leap to my feet. "What are you doing in my house?"

"Dani invited me. The front door was open. I should have known better than to accept an invitation to Grimwood. I mean, who serves mushy peas with ice cream? This is a culinary hellscape." Alice's eyes flick to me. "I've been here for five minutes trying to get your attention, but you've been too busy talking to your imaginary friends about Albert Fernsby's *murder,* like you're some kind of psychic detective."

Jupiter, just kill me now.

My mouth opens and shuts, but I can't think of what to say, what to do. Alice's cruel green eyes bore into mine, and I'm not in my own home anymore, I'm back on the playground at Grimdale Grammar with her and her friends standing over me. *Freak. Crazy. Wednesday Addams. She still has imaginary friends. How pathetic. She should be locked up.*

"Don't let her insult you," Ambrose says. "You're so amazing and you know it."

"Eviscerate her with your impressive wit!" Edward growls.

"I'll run her through!" Pax leaps toward her, sword drawn.

"No!" I throw myself in front of him. If he's angry enough,

that sword could do real damage, especially with the way the ghosts seem to have grown stronger. I don't need to explain why Alice Agincourt died in my dining room after being struck by a weapon that went out of use two thousand years ago.

"No what?" Alice backs away. Fear flickers in her eyes. "What's going on, Bree? Are you having some kind of episode? Do I call an ambulance or an exorcist?"

I ball my hands into fists. "Get out of my house."

"You read my mind." Alice grabs her purse and runs for the door.

Dani walks in a moment later. "Why is Alice's bike pulling away? Did you scare off my date?"

I gesture to the table. Dani's eyes widen as she takes in the spread of strange foods. "Ah, I should have known the ghosts wouldn't want anything normal."

"Yes. You should have known." I slump into my chair, my head in my hands. "She was standing in the doorway listening to me talk to the ghosts about Albert's murder. Why did you invite *Alice?*"

"Because you said I could bring a date."

"You're dating Alice?"

"Not yet. I want to date her. And I think she wants it, too. She's different when you get her away from Kelly and Leanne. We both go to this queer film club over in Argleton, and we usually sit together and mock the pretentious films, and last week there was this moment when..." Dani slumps into a chair and starts filling her plate with food. She won't look at me. "I know she was a cow in high school, but she's changed. I thought maybe tonight would break the ice between the two of you, and then the three of us could hang out or something and you'd see that she isn't so bad. You just don't know her like I do."

I groan. I have no desire to get to know Alice Agincourt.

Dani hunches over her plate, her dark curls covering her face.

"*She* eats like us," Mary says triumphantly.

"She's not sniffing her food," Agnes snaps. "She's upset with Bree."

"Thanks, Agnes." My cheeks burn. I hate that Dani's upset. "I'm sorry, friend. I didn't mean for your date to get an extra dose of crazy. You'd think after five years away from Grimwood, I'd be at least halfway normal, but from the moment I stepped back through those doors, I've been drawn back into the ghost world, and...sometimes I don't know how to shut it off. I don't know how to be normal."

"S'okay," Dani mumbles.

"It's not okay. Look, Alice was awful to me in high school, but I'd be a hypocrite if I judged her based on who she was five years ago. I promise that the next time we meet up, I'll give her a chance and try not to do anything crazy in front of her. Okay?"

Dani reaches across the table and throws her arms around me. "It's good to have you home, Bree. I missed your face."

"I missed your face, too. As much as I love this hug, you're pulling me dangerously close to the mushy peas."

Dani grins and helps herself to a giant pile of peas, as well as a cupcake, a pork pie, and a tiny dollop of pottage. I fill her in on everything the ghosts told me about Albert.

"This is good stuff," she says between mouthfuls. "It demonstrates that someone could have taken a container of Albert's balm and then replaced it. Which reminds me..."

She digs around in her purse and pulls out a small container sealed in a clear plastic bag.

"If you let it slip that you have this, I will lose my job, and then you will finally be able to dance with Edward because I *will* kill you, got it?"

"Got it." I mime zipping my lips. "What is it?"

"It's some of the healing balm left in the bottom of the container that killed Albert. I stole it from the lab when I went to pick up Albert's body. I thought it might be useful when you visit Basic Witch. But do not touch it, or let the old hag touch it – that thing contains so much atropine it could down an elephant."

"Got it." I take the plastic and stare at the fluffy cream inside. It looks so innocent. How could someone be so cruel? "Thanks for this, Dani."

"No problem. Maybe it will help. But we still don't know how Albert got to the catacombs that night—"

"I saw him," Pax says proudly.

"Pax says he saw Albert." I whirl around to face Pax. "Why didn't you say something?"

"You did not ask. It was the second night you came home, and I was in hour three of my watch. He emerged from his front door dressed in his night toga, skipped down the path, kissed a raccoon statue, sang a song about a horny bunny rabbit, and then danced away into the cemetery."

"A proper danse macabre," Edward muses. "How poetic."

"I skipped down the path?" Albert frowns.

"You did. Like this!" Pax begins dancing wildly around the room, flailing his sword around. He catches the curtains with the tip and tears a long gash. Dani gasps.

"Bree...that curtain just tore on its own."

Shit. I plaster a smile on my face. "That's Pax. He's demonstrating what Albert looked like that night—Pax, no!"

Too late. Pax climbs onto the table, dancing between the dishes. Edward throws his body over the cupcakes to protect them.

The tip of Pax's sword catches on the chandelier, and he flies backward. His body crashes on the table, half on, half inside it. Food splatters everywhere. Jelly smears across the portrait of my grandparents over the fireplace. Spaghetti dangles from the sconces. Victoria sponge decorates the antique sideboard.

Entwhistle pounces on the crumbs of cheddar on the rug, while Moon claws her way up my spine and burrows into my hair.

"Oops." Pax grins at me.

"Pax!"

"Fuck." Dani wipes mushy peas out of her eye. Her face is almost as pale as the ghosts. "They are real."

"Of course they are!" Her comment stings. "I haven't been talking to myself all these years."

"I know. I believe you, but it's just..." Dani picks up the shredded curtain. "Look at these. That's a real sword cut. It's different hearing you talk to them than it is seeing them do ghost stuff. What does this mean? How long have they been able to affect the Living world?"

I wince. "I've noticed it since I got back, and they seem to be getting stronger. Yesterday, Pax could only move things with the tip of his sword, but this time, his body made the food fly everywhere. I have no idea why they're suddenly more powerful, but it's scary. Maybe this Mina Wilde will be able to help figure it out. Apparently, she slayed a vampire."

Dani's eyes widen. "Vampires are real?"

"I guess I'm going to find out tomorrow. Mina's bookshop is in Argleton and—"

"Oh, are you talking about Nevermore Bookshop?" Dani runs her finger through the Victoria sponge and licks off the cream. "I've been there before. You'll love it. It's this huge old house filled with books, and the other owner is super grumpy but in the way you'd imagine Heathcliff from Wuthering Heights, all dark and brooding."

I smile. "I can't wait to meet him."

"I heard he has the Black Death," Edward says seriously. "I don't think you should go."

"I don't think so, either." Pax folds his arms.

"Jealous?" I grin at them.

"Let me guess, the ghosts don't want you to meet Mina's handsome boyfriends?" Dani winks.

"It's not that," Edward says quickly. "It's simply that—"

"—we're coming, too," Ambrose finishes.

"But you can't get to Argleton!"

"We don't know that. If you're right and we're more powerful now, then maybe our ghost mojo will let us leave the village." Ambrose's voice rises with hope. "It's worth a try."

"But not because we're jealous," Edward adds. "Just because we could do with the fresh air."

"If I can leave the village, I can protect you wherever you go!" Pax drags his sword blade across the edge of the table, leaving a deep gash. Dani scoots her chair away.

"What are the ghosts saying?"

I sigh. "They're saying that they're absolutely, definitely, not at all jealous of Mina's handsome boyfriends, and that we're all going on a field trip tomorrow."

21

BREE

I peer in the window of the Nevermore Bookshop, but all I can see are shelves of dusty books. There's not a soul in sight. "Is it even open?"

"This is boring," Edward moans. "I can't believe we're wasting our newfound hanging out at this dingy closed shop. Can we go to a whorehouse? Or a—hey!"

He yelps as Pax clonks him on the back of the head with the hilt of his sword. "Bree wants to go to the bookshop. We go to the bookshop. If you have a problem with that, I will—"

"—string me from the nearest tree by my testicles in the Roman tradition. I know, I know."

"I think this is a wonderful outing," Ambrose beams. He puffs out his chest and throws his arms wide. "I haven't been outside of Grimdale in a hundred and forty-eight years. I'm so happy to be on a new adventure. Everything smells different, don't you think? And what about these cobbles? They're a different shape from the cobbles in Grimdale. Can someone draw a map of the village green? There are so many people about – do you think that has anything to do with the Shakespeare festival in the village? I want to write a long journal entry about today's adventure, and I'll need a map. Can we stop for ice cream? Oh, do you think this bookshop will have a copy of my book?"

The hope catches in his voice.

"I don't know if we'll be able to find out." I frown at the door. "The sign says it's closed."

"It always says that," a woman walking past flips the sign over and winks at me. The other side of the sign also says 'CLOSED.' "Heathcliff doesn't like customers, but he does have a nice arse, so we tolerate him. Talk to Mina if you want someone to actually help you. She's the lovely lass behind the counter."

"I will, thank you." My stomach flip-flops. Why am I doing this? Why am I harassing some poor girl about Albert's murder just because a ghost thinks she slayed a vampire?

I push my way inside, stepping around a display of Shakespeare books that take up practically the entire hallway. Argleton village is hosting a Shakespeare festival at the moment, because our town isn't the only one with kooky traditions.

I turn right and end up lost in a warren of shelves, tables, baskets, and mismatched chairs. Books are stacked on every surface. A lady ghost wearing a beautifully embroidered Victorian corset, her hair pulled back severely with a velvet ribbon, reads over a man's shoulder and mumbles at him to hurry up and turn the page. A black cat luxuriates across a stack of National Geographic volumes. Her yellow eyes follow me as I make my way through the shop, hunting for the elusive Mina Wilde.

"This place smells amazing." Ambrose follows behind me, sniffing every shelf. "Like knowledge and academic rigor, and quiet nights beside the fire..."

"It smells like the inside of a codpiece," Edward makes a

face. "Where's the poetry section? I want to see if they have my poetry in stock."

"They won't—"

But he'd already gone.

Edward wrote a small pamphlet of erotic poetry that got published purely because some enterprising publisher knew he'd make a killing off the prince's erotic shenanigans. It's difficult to find in print these days because it is, quite frankly, terrible, and was probably used for kindling for the Great Fire of London. But that also means it's quite collectible, and Edward is always excited to see how much a copy sells for.

Unlike Ambrose, whose life's work didn't survive.

We don't often talk about why the ghosts haven't crossed over. It's a bit of a sore point with them. We know Pax has to be reunited with his bones for a proper Roman burial, but with the graveyard built over the original battlefield, that's unlikely to ever happen. Edward's unfinished business is a complete mystery since I'm pretty sure he partook in every licentious and depraved act imaginable during his short life, so he has nothing waiting for him to finish in death.

But Ambrose...

I've never told him, but I think Ambrose's unfinished business is about his manuscript. People never appreciated his contribution to exploration during his lifetime, and I wonder if he can't cross over until he gets the recognition that he deserves. I think that's why he haunts Grimwood Manor instead of the rooms in Siberia where he was killed – because he wrote the book in the house, while he was visiting with one of my very distant relatives who owned it at the time.

Even though I know it's hopeless, I always check secondhand and rare bookshops on my travels in case a copy of his book happened to survive. I sweep my eyes along the labels on the shelves, searching for the travel section and noting with interest that all the shelf labels are also written in Braille—

Nice hoodie.

I whirl around, looking for the person with the rich, throaty voice who complimented my hoodie, which has a picture of a cute ghost and says 'You're My Boo.' But there's no one there except for my ghosts.

"Edward, did you say that?"

"Say what?" Edward wrinkles his nose as he scans the poetry shelf. "They do not have my poetry book. I want to leave. I'm bored. This place is dusty. Your prince demands ice cream. Why are there so many books?"

"Um, because it's a bookshop."

"In my day, a bookshop wouldn't waste so much space with books. Where are the oriental tables and gilded couches filled with poets smoking opium and lamenting their lost loves?"

Drat our luck. We took out the opium den just the other week to make way for a coffee machine.

"Okay, who said that?" I glare at all three of them. Ambrose just looks confused. Pax draws his sword.

Pssst. Up here.

I crane my neck upward.

Perched on a narrow ledge above the door, next to a tiny trophy of a mouse head, is a huge black raven.

Hello, Bree. It's a pleasure to make your acquaintance.

"Argh!" I leap back in surprise. Edward ducks out of the way in time to avoid me falling through him.

"What's wrong?" Pax glares at the raven, his hand flying to his sword. "Is that bird giving you trouble?"

"N-n-no, but I think it's talking to me."

I am talking to you. I don't see anyone else around here with an awesome hoodie and magic humming in their veins, do you?

Shit. Okay.

206

I can hear the raven's thoughts. That's new.

"How do you know my name?" I have many, many questions, especially about the 'magic' part, but that's what comes out first.

The raven cocks its head at me again, then makes a croaking noise in its throat and takes off.

"I think he wants you to follow him," Ambrose says.

"Ravens are the messengers of the gods," Pax declares. "You should see what he wants, lest you anger Jupiter."

"I hope he poops on Jupiter," Edward adds with a smirk.

I gesture for the ghosts to follow me as I chase the raven back through the winding shelves to the other side of the main hallway, where a large room holds more shelves and a table stacked high with books and a stuffed armadillo. Behind the front desk, a girl wearing a killer skull dress rings up purchases for a customer while a guide dog sits alert at her feet.

A guide dog.

She's blind.

Mina Wilde, the murder-mystery-solving vampire slayer, is *blind*.

I reach out for Ambrose, my fingers brushing through his, causing that warm sensation to flow up my arm.

"Bree? Is something wrong?" he asks.

But I can't answer him, not with Mina at the counter and the handful of customers in the room. I can't tell him that here is someone who has the same experiences that he does, and that he's not alone.

I need to play this cool. I hover near the desk as Mina starts ringing up a stack of Stella Mey horror novels for a customer.

"So you're a big Stella Mey fan, are you?" Mina smiles as she rings up the books. "Me too. I love the way she twisted the vampire trope and made it her own. I just adored *Dusk*."

"I've never heard of her." The man's eyes gleam with a weird kind of hunger.

"Oh. Okay. Well, there you go. Your total is £18.29." Mina hands him a paper bag containing his books, and holds out a pamphlet. "While you're here in the village, why don't you check out the Argleton Shakespeare Festival—"

The customer scoffs. "Isn't he the fellow with the plays? Who needs that nonsense now that we have the telly?"

"Shakespeare? You mean that pimply fellow who wrote all those adulating plays for old aunty Lizzie?" Edward scoffs. "He never amounted to anything. Do people still care about him?"

Mina looks disgusted.

From the shadows of the office behind the desk, I hear a dark and gloomy voice say, "Take it, bird."

I'm on it.

The man snatches his receipt from Mina, mutters something that sounds suspiciously like 'this had better be worth it,' and storms out. The raven swoops down from the chandelier and chases after him.

A moment later, the customer bellows out, "Argh, that poxy bird shat on me!"

Mina covers her hand with her mouth, but I can see the laughter in her eyes. The man pokes his head back around the corner, and there's an enormous bird poop dripping down the side of his face.

The raven flutters back into the room and perches on the till, peering up at me with those fire-rimmed eyes.

Bullseye, the bird says.

I can't help it. *I* burst out laughing. Pax doubles over, guffawing. Romans love a good bird-poop-on-the-face joke. Edward makes a disgusted face. Ambrose just looks confused, and I'm laughing too much to explain it to him. I try to hide my laughter behind a book of Byronic verse, but Mina's head snaps toward me.

"Can I help you?"

Okay, I guess I'm doing this.

I hear the door slam as the man storms out, and I can't help laughing even harder. I approach the counter with the poetry book.

"Don't buy that guff," Edward scoffs. "Byron wouldn't know a rhyming couplet if it impregnated his mistress."

That sets me off even worse. I gasp for breath as I set the book down on the desk. "I'm sorry, I didn't mean to laugh, it's just...you know, *bullseye*, and he kind of looked like an angry bull..."

Mina's eyes widen, and I know she's wondering how I can hear the bird. Funny, I'm wondering the same thing. She hasn't acknowledged Edward, Ambrose, or Pax, nor any of the six other ghosts I've seen since I came in here, so I'm guessing she can't see them.

Duh. Of course she can't see them.

Even if she's a cool chick with a magical talking raven and three boyfriends, she can't talk to the dead.

She's not a freak like you.

"Sorry." Mina waves her hands around, looking flustered, before finally taking my book and ringing it up. "Blind girl moment. Can I help you?"

"I want books on military strategy," Pax says. "With lots of pictures of Druids being impaled on sharp sticks."

"I want every book she has about me," Edward says. "Start with that collection over there – *The Great English Poets*."

"Ask her if she's ever seen a manuscript come through here," Ambrose says excitedly. "It would be about yay big, and the lines will look odd, as if they were written using a frame of wood and string—"

I can't do this.

I swallow hard. I can't ask this girl for help. What was I *thinking*? Mina is totally the kind of person I'd love as a friend. I can't drag her into my ghostly chaos. Dani's known me my entire life, and she was still terrified when Pax cut the curtains and splashed food everywhere. I'm not ready for Mina to be terrified of me.

I hastily grab a couple more books without looking at the covers, building a wall between myself and Mina.

"Okay if I leave these here? I want to go upstairs and..." hide "...get some more books, and these are heavy."

"Sure," Mina beams. "Go right ahead."

I practically throw the books at her and scamper upstairs. Blissfully, this floor of the shop is empty. Hundreds of lamps haphazardly dot the room, and the shelves are wrapped in miles of twinkle lights. I assume it's got something to do with Mina's blindness – either that, or the hot, surly guy in the office downstairs has a thing for twinkle lights.

"Why did you run away from that girl?" Pax demands as we wander past the sociology shelves. I scuff my foot on the wooden floor. It almost looks like...chalk marks here. I wonder what that could be from?

"The poetry shelves are back downstairs," Edward adds. "Unless you think they have a special section reserved for members of the monarchy with particular special talents, because that would be the better place to look for material on me—"

"We're not looking for more books about your many affairs. We're going to the travel section, aren't we, Bree? Or...or maybe there's an occult section? There could be a spell that will enable ghosts to extend their ghost mojo, so Bree and I could go to Paris to see her parents..."

"We could ask that girl downstairs," Edward says. "Except that Brianna is too scared to talk to her."

"I'm not scared. I just—"

Pax draws out his sword. "I'll go down and make her talk to you."

"No, don't do that," I snap. "I've decided that I don't need Mina's help, and that's my final word on the matter. Now, if the three of you will shut up for a second, I'll find you some books."

"But can you ask about my manuscript—"

"Your manuscript is not here!" I yell, louder than I intended.

Ambrose reels as if I slapped him. His face collapses, and I hate myself.

"You're right, of course," he murmurs.

"Oh, Ambrose, I'm sorry. I didn't mean to snap. I'm just... this is a lot, you know? I just found out that I can hear that raven's thoughts. And it's clearly not a ghost. And he said something about magic and I...I just need a moment, okay?"

I'm dimly aware of some movement out of the corner of my eye – a shape behind the sociology shelf. Is it the raven? But I can't hear its voice.

Pax glares at the shelf and draws out his sword. "Stupid books, none of you are as good as our friend Ambrose."

"Pax, stop, please..." I grab his wrist before he can swing the sword and send books flying all over the shop. My fingers brush him, just grazing his edges before falling through him. My veins hum with fire. "We'll get you a military strategy book, I promise. Hold on a sec, I've got to check out the travel section first—"

"Excuse me, ma'am."

I whirl around, but the guy's not talking to me. He's talking to Mina, who leaps up from where she's crouched behind the sociology shelves. Has she been listening to me this whole time?

"Don't mind me. I'm just...uh...stroking these books." Mina shoves her hands into the shelf and starts shuffling them back and forth. Her cheeks redden. "If you don't show them a bit of love every now and then, they get ornery."

"Right. Yes." The man peers at her through horn-rimmed glasses. "I have a very important question that must be dealt with in haste. Do you have any books by Stella Mey?"

I take the opportunity to scarper out of there, the ghosts hot on my heels. The village square is surprisingly busy for a weekday. I see stallholders dressed in silly hats and clothing that looks straight out of a renaissance fair.

"What is this?" Edward stares around in wonder. "It looks like Covent Garden on a Friday night. Hey, do you think we can find a whore who can see ghosts? Or maybe we procure one for Bree and we can all watch—"

"This whole thing called feminism happened, and I don't have time to explain it to you, so just be quiet. This is the Shakespeare festival." I peer at a sign about a small bookshop next to the Rose & Wimple pub. "Oh, look, this bookshop has an original First Folio on display. Too bad we have to leave now—"

"Why does that poxy *actor* get a whole festival?" Edward pouts. "Where's my festival? Brianna, your prince commands you to give him a festival, filled with poetry readings and free opium for all, and some of this feminism, because that sounds kinky."

I try to keep a straight face as I head across the square. Ambrose hurries after me.

"Why are we leaving?" Ambrose asks. "I thought the whole point of coming here was to talk to that girl, Mina...oops, I just walked through the coffee cart...and you barely said two words to her—"

"The point—" I growl as I watch him stagger on the grass, smelling faintly of coffee "—was to solve Albert's murder. And if we want to have a hope in hell of doing that, we need to get to Basic Witch before it closes and your ghost mojo runs out."

BASIC WITCH IS Grimdale's New Age shop. Every self-respecting village has one, and ours is quite grand. It occupies a large Tudor cottage on High Street and is surprisingly one of the most popular shops in the city because of the number of local artisans who sell their products there. Despite the very welcoming statue of an orc by the door, I've never set foot inside. People think I'm weird enough – if they see me frequenting a shop like this, I'll never live it down.

Which is why I hesitate outside, my hand poised in midair, when a woman wearing head-to-toe Chanel rushes in front of me and nearly bowls me over.

"Out of my way," she snaps, swinging her enormous Hermes bag at me like she's swatting an annoying fly. I duck and the bag sails through the air where my head was only a moment ago.

We enter the shop behind her. I gag as my lungs fill with musky incense. Pax takes in a deep lungful, his eyes sparkling with nostalgia. "Mmmm, smells like burning villages in here."

Romans. Such a delightful bunch.

I head down an aisle filled with crystals, not really sure what to do. Hermes-Swinging Woman heads straight to the counter and slams a shoebox on top of the saint card display. "You buy weird old things, right?" she says to no one, because the counter is deserted. "These are Roman coins. Some medieval, too. You can punch a hole in them and string them on necklaces. How much will you give me for the box?"

I lean closer. Am I watching someone talking to a ghost? But then I see a thin head of grey hair bobbing behind the counter.

A short, hunched old woman pulls herself up onto a stool and peers disapprovingly into the box.

"Twenty quid," the old woman snaps in a harsh, croaky voice that reminds me far too much of Agnes.

"Twenty per coin?" Hermes-Swinging Lady's eyes light up with pound signs.

"No. Twenty for the box."

"But that's not even close to what they're worth! These are magical. They're imbued with, you know, ancient magic and stuff. Surely you have a client who likes old magic crap..."

"My customers buy pewter replicas for two-pounds-fifty. You can see yourself out." The old crone slides off the stool and hobbles back toward the storage room. Hermes-Swinging Lady glares after her, mutters something unladylike under her breath, grabs her box, and storms out.

I don't have time to wonder what all that is about because Pax is having an argument with an art display.

"No swords in the shop." I reach out and block his hand before he swings at a New Age painting of a man in a long flowing robe petting a wolf. The title of the piece is *The Druid's Lament*. My fingers brush his skin and stay there. I gasp. It feels almost like touching a real person except...except *better*.

What is going on?

Nothing makes sense. The guys remained in Argleton with me for over an hour without their ghost mojo pulling them back. And now I'm literally touching Pax. I'm holding his wrist back like he's a real person on my plane of existence, and it feels like sunshine pouring into my veins.

Why are all the ghost rules suddenly changing? Why now?

"This is a lie!" Pax frowns at the painting. He doesn't seem to notice that we are actually *touching*. "That's not what Druids look like! Where's his crown made of baby skulls? Where's his woad-painted skin? Where's the naked dancing with his under-wear on his head?"

"It's an artist's impression," Edward explains, stroking his chin the way he does whenever he discusses art. "They've romanticized the Druid, the way I romanticize women in my paintings. Every countess who sits for me wants to be depicted as Venus."

"Nothing romantic about dancing around muddy fields with your underwear on your head," Pax grumbles.

"It depends on what turns you on," Edward grins.

I leave them arguing about Druidic aphrodisiacs and head past a rack of saint cards to where Ambrose is engrossed in a round table with a display of beautiful pillar candles with herbs, petals, and even gemstones trapped within the wax. They're works of art, and I recognize them immediately as Maggie's work. In front of the candles are rows of healing balms, massage oils, and body butters with the distinctive Maggie's Bath and Body label.

"I thought the police were telling local businesses not to sell these." I pick up a candle and finger the beautiful amethyst nestled inside.

"I don't care what no police say. You don't want that one, missy."

I whirl around at the croaky voice behind me. The old crone had appeared from nowhere, her stooped frame looming just behind my shoulder. She leans against a gnarled wood staff.

How did she sneak up on me so quickly?

"Amethyst is all about promoting serenity." The crone nods to the candle in my hands. "You don't want serenity. That's not the stone for you."

"It's not?" I don't believe in this stuff, but who is this lady to tell me that I don't want serenity? Honestly, a little serenity sounds lovely.

The crone fixes me with a withering stare that freezes my witty comeback on my lips. She peers all around me, her eyes swooping before fixing on the spots where Edward, Ambrose, and Pax are standing. Beside me, Ambrose wilts.

"She's looking right at me," he whispers. "It's as if she can see me."

But that's impossible.

I'm the only person who can see ghosts.

Aren't I?

The old woman turns back to the table. I'm just about to move quietly away, assuming our weird exchange is over, but she whirls back around and holds out another candle.

"This one uses moldavite. It's a crystal alloy from a meteorite that landed in Moldova nearly fifteen million years ago. It has high vibrational properties."

High vibrational properties? I resist the urge to roll my eyes, but she's not done.

"This stone will amplify your powers, and enable you to reach even further beyond the veil."

She shoves the candle into my hands. It smells of lavender and cherry. I run my finger over the moldavite sticking out of the wax, admiring the dark cobalt colour and the shimmering planes. It's a beautiful crystal, even without its supposed magical properties.

I don't feel a thing when I hold it. No sparks or shimmers. *Nothing magical here, lady.*

"Fine. I guess...I'll take it."

She closes my fingers around the candle. "It is yours. Maggie would want you to have it, and I refuse to accept money for it. But I will be able to answer your question."

"What question?"

"You want to know if the balm in your purse was made by Maggie."

"How did you—"

"Show it to me," she commands. I don't dare to hesitate. I scramble in my purse for the crime scene bag and pull it out.

"I know it's not much," I say as I place the plastic bag in her tiny, wizened hand. "There was only a tiny bit left in the container the SOCO team removed for testing. You shouldn't touch it, though. It's poisoned with belladonna."

She unscrews the lid and raises it to her face, sniffing it disdainfully. "This is not Maggie's work. The ingredients are from a cheap, 'make your own bath products' kit – they're ten quid from any craft store. Maggie would never use these ingredients. Her products were made from ingredients she harvested from nature. The only thing in this pot out of Grimdale wood is the belladonna."

She can tell all that from a single sniff? "So someone else made this body butter?"

The old woman places the container back in my hand. "You should take that crystal with you everywhere. I think you might be surprised by what it can do."

But I'm not interested in the crystal. "Thank you." I slip the bag back into my wallet and notice Dani's sent me a text.

Dani: Did you meet Mina? And how did you go with the old witch?

I smile as I zip up my purse and turn back to the old crone. "Thank you again for all your help—"

But she's not there. The old woman has completely vanished.

22

AMBROSE

Bree goes back to the bookshop the next day.

At least, she tells herself she's going to the bookshop. All the way to Argleton on the bus, she mutters under her breath that she's going to go back in there and say something to Mina. But when we arrived in the village and set foot on the bustling town green, Bree takes off in the opposite direction, her fingers entwined in mine, pulling me along behind her.

Her fingers are *entwined* in mine. Like I'm a mortal, corporeal human, not a figment of an expired life. Like I'm real to her. This is a new sensation we only discovered this morning when Bree put her hand out to stop Pax from chasing after a duck. We've been fighting over who gets to hold her hand, but I won because Edward was being filthy, and Pax won't let Bree lead the way.

I can't believe it. Never in my life could I have dreamed this moment, that the veil around Bree would become so thin that we could touch each other through it, and that she'd feel like plucking the first wild strawberries of summer, or like the opening paragraph of a book you've been waiting to read.

It's not the same as two humans touching. It's better, somehow.

"The bookshop is back this way!" I tug on her hand. "I'm blind and even I know that."

I can't believe we're back here again. Yesterday we stayed in Argleton for over an hour before the ghost mojo started to drag us back. It begins as a stomachache – or what I presume is a stomachache because I haven't had a stomach for a hundred and forty-eight years. Then the ache becomes a tugging sensation that jerks your limbs about, and then the tugging becomes a *tearing*, like you're a piece of cork plugging a hole in a water-skin that's ready to burst, and the force of the water behind you is forcing you out. We don't know what happens after that because the pain is so excruciating that we always let go and bounce right back to Grimdale.

Before Bree's return, I could float all the way to the Babbage farm on the edge of Grimdale and stay there for fifteen minutes before I was pulled back. Pax can get a little further – almost to the eastern boundary of Grimdale wood. But he's out there most days slaying imaginary Druids. Edward can barely make it to the pub, but that's because he's too lazy to roam.

But yesterday, we got on the bus with Bree and we made it all the way to Argleton. I've never been so happy to visit a village pub and a grubby train station and a pigeon-infested green because they're completely different to the pub and train station and pigeons in Grimdale. Everything smelled different – different people, different pies at the bakery, different paper on the community noticeboard.

We got to have an adventure. All night I tossed and turned in my little secret bedroom, imagining what this could mean. Could Bree get me on an airplane? Would I actually be able to fly in one of those contraptions that explorers in my day only dreamed about? Could Bree and I see Paris together?

Climb the Alps together? Even make it all the way to the Americas?

At the moment, Bree is distracted by Albert's murder and her father's illness. She's not thinking about these strange things that have been happening. I don't want to push her. When she's ready, we will explore this new connection we have with her and figure out what it means. But for now, I'm content to be by her side while she...

...drops her hand from mine and vanishes.

"Bree, where are—" My words come out in a whoosh as someone walks through me. Ooof, it feels awful when you don't expect it. Like someone stabbing you with a thousand icicles.

"Are you okay, Robert?" I hear a woman ask.

"I don't know..." Robert puffs. "I got all cold and jittery all of a sudden. Maybe I'm coming down with something. It will be a shame to miss the Shakespeare festival."

Robert doesn't sound like he thinks that's a shame at all. "You're welcome, Robert," I murmur as I move slowly, using the tip of my stick on the grass to feel around for people's shoes. I don't want any more accidents.

"I may be a spoiled prince who cares for nothing but opium and art and sex, but I could have sworn the bookshop is in the opposite direction," Edward calls behind us.

"Oh, look, there's that shop with the First Folio on display! And the line isn't too long right now." Bree stops in front of me. "And there's a cake stall near the door. Pax, I'll get you a slice of lemon drizzle if you promise to make Edward and Ambrose shut up about Nevermore."

"I am at your service." Pax booms from beside me. The blade of his sword grazes my arm. I shiver.

Bree isn't serious...I hope.

"Thou art a chicken," Edward intones. "A feathered beast who—"

221

"Yes, yes, fine," Bree snaps. "I am a chicken and I'm stalling for time. But when else am I going to get the chance to see an original Shakespearean First Folio?"

"In a public latrine, being used for loo paper?" Edward scoffs. "His sonnets are excellent for scratching one's—"

"Yes, thank you for that, Edward."

"He's just jealous," I say. "Because in that one play, Shakespeare calls Edward's grandmother a bearded strumpet with a face that would sour grapes—"

"He was being mean!" Edward snipes. "It's not Grandmama's fault that women in my family have that skin condition."

"Maybe if you weren't always marrying your cousins..."

Bree stifles her laughter. She's reached the front of the line now. She pays her entry fee to a fellow at the door and enters the shop. The others decide to remain outside – Pax wants to sniff cakes, and Edward can't be bothered. But I won't pass up the chance to be close to such a beautiful and interesting book.

I follow Bree inside without paying the entry fee – a perk of ghost life. You need never be bored in the afterlife when all theatrical performances, art galleries, and museums are free. It's too bad that Grimdale's idea of culture is a community theatre production of Moose Murders.

I place my fingers on Bree's elbow and allow her to guide me as well as she can through the crowd. It's packed so tight that two more people walk through me, muttering about the cold drafts in the shop. By the time we reach the First Folio display, I'm trembling with pain.

But it's worth it. Bree stiffens beside me, her breath catching in awe. I can't see the book, of course, but hearing her reaction to it is more than enough.

"Oh, Ambrose, it's beautiful," Bree whispers under her breath. "It's this old book bound with crackly leather, and it's open to the first page of *Much Ado About Nothing*. There is this beautiful illustration of flowers…"

"What's that girl talking to?" someone asks behind me.

"I don't know. I guess Shakespeare attracts all sorts of crazies."

Bree stiffens again, but this time it's not out of awe. I want to go after those people and make them apologize to her, but I can't do that.

Instead, I turn back toward the book…or where I think the book is. My stick taps the bottom of the display case. I'm standing over a *First Folio*. Suddenly, I'm so excited that I can barely speak. I need to get closer. I have to know all its secrets…

"Ambrose, don't," Bree whispers, her fingers tightening around mine. "You can't touch it—"

Yes, I can. I'm the only person in this room who can.

All my life I've suffered from this tremendous sense of urgency. There's a huge wide world out there and if I don't hurry to explore it, I'll miss something. And then, my worst nightmare – I'm killed by the Tsar before I can find out how big the world really is.

It's why Bree and I are so close. Until I met her, I never knew someone with the same nervous energy as me, the same yen to experience everything that life has to offer.

And so when I bury my head inside the First Folio and sniff the musty, spicy odor of history and literature and all that grand stuff, I know Bree's behind me, trying not to laugh and wishing she could do the same thing.

I withdraw my head and sure enough, her fingers tighten around mine as we move away. "I just took a selfie with the book, but your story is way cooler. Tell me, what did it smell like?" she whispers.

"An old boot," I whisper back, even though no one except the other ghosts can hear me.

"Brianna, look what I found," calls Edward. I didn't even know he followed us into the shop.

Bree pushes her way through the crowd to a less-crowded corner of the shop. I feel her bend down to look at something in a display case.

"It's a Roman coin," she says without interest.

"I know that," Edward says. "But look how much it's worth. A single coin! And the tag says it was found in Grimwood forest, just behind your house."

"What?"

Bree leans in closer. "It says it was found by a Kieran Myers. Why is that name familiar?"

"Myers is the name of the real estate agent who visited Albert's house," I say. I'm proud to say that as a travel writer, I have a good memory for names and places.

"And her husband is a metal detectorist who's been in trouble before for taking treasures off other people's land," Bree adds.

"So why does Kieran Myers have his name on a Roman coin from Grimdale wood?" Edward asks.

"I don't know, but we're going to find out."

23

BREE

> Mum: Darling, have they had Albert's funeral yet? Do send a wreath of flowers for your father and me, would you? Oh, and could you ship me a box of Maggie's youthful shimmer serum and a couple of her sensual lavender body scrubs?

> I know you said she might've poisoned her husband, but she really does make the yummiest things.

I'm anxious to get back to Grimdale and find this Kieran Myers, but first I have to go back to the bookshop.

I like the bookshop. It contains a lot of strong smells that make Ambrose happy – old leather, the woody tang of paper and ink, the faint birdiness of the raven, and something I can only describe as 'hot men who like reading.'

And I like Mina. I didn't realize how desperate I am for friends – human, corporeal friends – until I saw her yesterday and realized we have the same taste in fashion and that she's cool and fun and blind, like Ambrose. I barely said two words to her and already I'm afraid that I'm going to fuck it up.

Hi, I'm Bree and I see ghosts. And one of my ghosts can't cross over until we solve his murder and make sure his wife isn't in danger. Can you help us?

Yup, I don't sound like a psychopath, at all.

But even after I buy a lemon drizzle cake and let the ghosts sniff it to their heart's content, they won't let me leave without seeing Mina. So I trudge up the steps of the bookshop and step inside.

Back so soon? The raven greets me with a dip of his wing. *Mina's in the main room if you want to talk to her. It's a good time because Heathcliff has stepped out for his lunchtime whisky.*

Heathcliff. Right, that's the grumpy owner. One of her boyfriends.

Who calls their son Heathcliff these days?

"Thanks," I whisper to the raven as I shuffle past, step around the ghost of a medieval scribe laden down with rolls of parchment, and enter the main room. Mina's behind the desk again, head resting contentedly in her hands as she listens to an audiobook.

I clear my throat.

"Hey, did you see what's going on in the square?"

Mina pauses her audiobook and looks up. I can tell that from this distance she can't see me, so I step closer, beneath the circle of light cast by an enormous antique lamp. Her eyes light up with recognition.

"Sorry. I didn't mean to startle you," I say quickly, before I lose my nerve. "I'm surprised it's so quiet in here. I would have thought this festival would attract lots of people to a bookshop."

"You'd think." Mina jabs her finger out the window. "They're all lining up at Rasmussen Books to see the First Folio. Our perfectly-ordinary *popular books* can't compete."

My cheeks heat up, remembering that not twenty minutes ago I was inside that shop watching Ambrose dunk his head inside the priceless tome. "If it's any consolation, I went there this morning, and your bookshop is much cooler. And you don't charge admission or have a gangly fellow follow you around the store to make sure you don't steal anything."

"Were you at least allowed to take photos?" Mina asks, her voice rising with excitement.

"Only if you pay an extra pound." I hold up my phone. "What can I say? I got my selfie with the big bad book. I'm a sucker for an Instagram pic."

"Can I see?"

I pass my phone over. Mina holds it under the light and leans her face so close to the screen that her nose almost swipes for her. "I love these! You should make that one your dating profile pic. You know, 'My Folio bringeth all the boys to the yard—"

"And they're like, 'It's better than thine—"

Mina laughs. She has a great laugh. "Verily, it's better than thine—"

"—I could teach you, but I must levy a fee'," I finish with a snort. "I'm Bree, by the way."

"I'm Mina. And this is Oscar." Mina indicates her guide dog. He peers up at me with hopeful eyes, his nose twitching, no doubt smelling the leftover slice of drizzle cake I have secreted away in my purse. But I know that you're not supposed to pat a guide dog while they're working, so I keep my hands pinned at my sides.

Ambrose, however, is not so deterred. "Oh, who's a beautiful boy? You are...you are a beautiful boy..." He buries his face in the dog's soft fur.

The dog tilts his head into Ambrose's embrace. He must be

able to sense the warmth of Ambrose's joy. Dogs can't see ghosts, but ducks definitely can.

Meanwhile, Pax has found a suit of armour in the corner and is taking swings at it with his sword and insulting the armour's mother. And Edward is over in the history section, looking for books about himself so he can relive the stories of his sordid affairs over again—

"Oh, sorry?" I realize Mina's been talking.

"I said, I remember you. You were in here the other day."

"Yeah. I live in Grimdale, just over the valley. Well, I've only just moved back. I grew up there but I've been travelling for the last few years – Canada, Germany, Vietnam, New Zealand. I don't like to stay in the same place for long, but my parents need me to cat-sit for them while they have a much-needed holiday in France. Grimdale is *boring*. It's dead. Deadly dead. No action whatsoever. We don't even have a bookshop. Hence why I'm back – I need more reading material."

I suck in a breath. *Stop rambling, Bree.*

"I'm an Argleton native," Mina says with a genuine smile. "I know all about village life. Maybe I can recommend something. What do you like to read?"

"Travel biographies." Ambrose's head pops up. "And, um, historical accounts of famous battles. Anything by or about Julius Caesar. I adore him. Um, and anything about over-throwing the monarchy." I glare at Edward, who is standing in front of the cover of a book on Queen Elizabeth II, trying to see what her crown looks like on his head.

"You wouldn't dare!" He storms over, waving his hands about. "Without the monarchy, who would be in charge? This riffraff?" he waves his hands at Pax. "Who would open public buildings? Who would pose for coins? Who would give sex-mad countesses the attention they deserve?"

He slams his fist down on the table of books. I gasp as a

stack topples over. My hand flies to my pocket, and I touch the moldavite crystal I gouged out of the candle. It's cool and hard in my fingers, like an ordinary crystal. Nothing magical about it.

I don't know why I brought it with me. It *can't* be the reason the ghosts can touch me. It can't be the reason their ghost mojo seems to be holding even more than yesterday.

But then what the hell is going on?

"I mean, *embroidery*," I say quickly as I plant my hand in Edward's chest and shove him back, grateful Mina can't see me flailing around. My fingers dig into Edward's bare chest, his skin warm and tingly, not quite living but... something else. "Anything about embroidery."

"That's...a diverse range of interests." Mina tilts her head to the side.

"Yes, well, I like reading. And apparently, embroidery." I force a laugh. "Anything to silence the voices in my head."

Mina finds me a stack of travel books that look amazing, and a couple of embroidery books that I purchase because I know it pisses Edward off. As Mina hands over the bag, I see a poster for the Shakespeare festival and ask, "Hey, are you going to the opening ceremony tonight?"

"I wouldn't miss it. My boyfriend is playing Macbeth in the production, and my mum is one of the three witches."

"Fun. I was thinking of heading along. It's no Burning Man, but it'll be good for a laugh." Before I can chicken out, I take out my phone. "Hey, what's your number? I'll text you mine. Maybe we could go for a drink sometime?"

"I'd love that."

Mina's smile makes my chest tight.

"Did you hear that, Bree?" Ambrose stands up and squeezes my hand. "She'd love that. See, you can make normal friends, too."

Right. Friends who are vampire-slayer amateur sleuths with

a harem of boyfriends and a talking raven. That's totally normal. Mina and I are made for each other.

24
BREE

"That was wonderful," Ambrose chatters away as he floats above his bus seat. "Argleton smells so different, doesn't it? I love that old bookshop and all the people bustling about for the festival. But my favorite part was holding Bree's hand. It felt amazing. Didn't it feel amazing, Edward?"

"I wouldn't know," Edward says frostily. "You wouldn't let me have my turn."

"I did, too! You wasted it by going after that dog who peed through your leg—"

I lean back in my seat on the bus, listening with half an ear while the ghosts argue. I managed to score the whole backseat, and even though the bus is crowded, British people would rather stand and risk face-planting when the driver takes a hairpin corner than sit next to a stranger, so the ghosts can sit beside me without the risk of anyone sitting in them.

Ambrose and Edward are the only ones sitting. My Roman ghost stalks the length of the bus, peering at people's phone screens to make sure they're not plotting to kill me. The tip of his sword brushes a guy's leg, and he itches the spot.

"Damn bugs," the guy mutters, his eyes never leaving his phone screen.

My ghosts are still invisible to other people, because even the most British of people would risk disturbing others to inquire why a huge man wearing a sheet and leather armour was brandishing a sword on the bus. But nothing else about today was normal ghost behavior. We spent two hours in Argleton, and the ghosts say they're not even feeling the first twinges of ghost mojo. And what about the way their fingers feel entwined in mine? What about how strange and solid and wonderful they feel?

What if they can now touch other humans, too? What if this sensation isn't just for me?

I take the moldavite out of my pocket and stare at it. It's not magic. It's just a lump of mineral. It can't be the reason why all this is happening. It's not even glowing. Surely if it was magic, it would be glowing or something?

But I can't get that old witch's voice out of my head.

This stone will amplify your powers, and enable you to reach even further beyond the veil.

The words chill me, not least because they imply that I *have* powers.

That the reason I see the ghosts is not that I had a near-death experience that day I fell off my bike, but because I'm *magical.*

I'm a freak.

It can't be right. The ghosts have gotten stronger even when I've been away. And surely they would have noticed these changes when I was a kid and hanging out with them all the time?

No, it's got nothing to do with magic space rocks and kooky old witches and veil-bending superpowers.

This has nothing to do with me.

Except...

Since I got back, nothing's been the same. The ghosts have been able to influence the Living world more than ever, without strong emotions. They made me a *cup of tea*. And when I was a kid, touching them never lit up my body the way it does now. They used to feel like passing through a cloud of steam, but now...

I glance over at them, my mind a whirlwind of emotions. I like being closer to them. I really like being able to touch them. I'm obsessed with the giddy feeling I get whenever we're together.

Even though we've been separated by thousands of miles, I've kept them with me every single day, inside my heart.

Ambrose's delight at the world woke me up every morning with the belief that today would be better than yesterday. I never stopped wishing he could be beside me when I saw the Great Pyramids or hiked the Inca trail or lost myself in a bustling Vietnamese market. He would have loved to have met all the interesting ghosts I encountered everywhere.

Whenever a boss refused to pay me or a hostel tried to rip me off, I channeled Edward's stubborn belief that the world should bend to his will. I borrowed his strength and confidence and forced myself to do all kinds of things I might have been too afraid to do, and to indulge in every treat I could afford without guilt.

And Pax...where would I be without his self-defense lessons and his love of baked goods? He taught me that I had to throw myself into each day as if my enemy might stave my head in at any moment. Any time I told myself that I shouldn't eat that exotic pastry or jump off that towering cliff, I asked myself what Pax would do, and I dived right in.

And sure, I've landed myself in a fair share of trouble, but I also found *myself*. I found Bree Mortimer is more than a freak –

she can be brave and confident and reckless and excitable and clever and wild and very, very stupid.

And I've had fun. More fun than I could ever imagine, except...I wished I could have shared all those moments with my childhood friends.

Is that all this is? Is this tightness in my chest, this tsunami that's tearing up my insides, simply nostalgia for the way we used to be? Or is it something more...

My phone beeps.

All thoughts of ghosts fly out of my head as I stare at the icon for a new video message from Mum. I experience the weird duality of excitement and dread that accompanies every update from their trip.

I want to see them having fun and enjoying their second honeymoon. But every time I see Dad, it's a reminder of everything he's already lost and how much I miss him.

I click on the icon, and the video plays. Mum and Dad are in a beer hall in Germany with a couple I don't recognise, huge steins of beer in front of them. The long tables are filled with people playing board games and doing puzzles. My parents are laughing as they try to play a game of Scrabble, but Dad can't place the tiles on the board. He keeps dropping them and getting them all muddled up.

"That is not a word," his German friend admonishes him, peering through his glasses at the jumble of letters.

"It's absolutely a word," Dad shoots back. "I am from the Pablo Picasso school of Scrabble. It means, 'the state of not being able to control one's hands,' and I feel it coming on again..."

Dad's grin widens as he raises his hand and slowly flashes his German friend a rude gesture, and they all crack up laughing.

The video ends, and the screen freezes on a frame of Dad

trying to pick up one of his tiles. He's smiling but his eyes...his *eyes*...

The horror in them freezes my blood.

I know that look because it's what I used to see every time I looked in the mirror.

He's trapped.

Just like me.

I was caged in by Grimdale and all the people like Kelly Kingston. I was doomed to be the freak they said I was. But I broke free. I escaped.

For a while, anyway.

Dad's trapped inside himself. He can't make his body do things it should do, and he's aware of every moment that's lost.

And suddenly, the idea of magic being real sounds amazing. Because if I was really magical, I could save my dad. I could give him back what the disease has taken.

But magic *doesn't exist*.

And I am a freak.

And Dad will never get better.

Ambrose and Edward are still arguing. I turn away from them and rest my cheek against the glass. The countryside rolls past me, miles and miles of rolling hills and fluffy-cloud sheep, pieced by the dark ribbon of Grimdale wood.

A tear escapes my eyes and rolls down my cheek.

"Bree?" Pax's head pokes between the seats in front of me. "Can we watch the moving picture box after dinner? Sylvie and Mike always watch Bake Off after dinner on a..."

Pax's voice trails off. "You are crying."

"It's nothing. I..."

I can't finish. If I say another word, the rest of the tears will spill over.

Pax reaches up and presses the pad of his huge finger against my cheek, blotting out the droplet. His touch burns through me, and I'm suddenly aware of how close he is and how solid he feels, and how the concern in his pale blue eyes makes the floor of the bus drop out beneath me.

"I'm fine," I lie. "I have something in my eye."

"You do," he nods in agreement. "You have sadness. But I will find a way to make it better."

25

PAX

I'm hovering over the couch, watching Nigella Lawson pull a Victoria sponge cake from the oven, when Ambrose wafts through the wall. "Pax, can you mute the moving picture box?"

"Can't. Nigella is about to make buttercream icing."

"I think Bree's upset."

No. That won't do. Bree's not allowed to be upset.

I glare at the magical knobbly stick on the arm of the couch, and press my finger into the large knob Bree calls the 'off button.' The moving pictures become a black screen, which matches my mood.

She was upset on the bus after seeing that moving picture about her father, and I thought I cheered her up. Which is good, because I want to do something for her, to make her see how special she is, and also because I have a very important thing to tell her. But the special thing I do for her must be extra special, and I can't think what it will be.

I am not good with women. I am a champion stabber, a world-class Druid slayer, a brilliant brawler, and a passable tenor. But when it comes to romance, I come from the 'throw them over your shoulder and fuck them until their legs turn to jelly' school of seduction.

Edward tumbles through the wall after Pax. "I just floated into Brianna's room to see if she was getting naked, but she's on her bed crying. We have to do something."

"Did you try comforting her?" Ambrose asks.

"Please," Edward smirks, sinking into the wingback chair by the fireplace. "Do I look like a moralist? That's more your department."

"I tried, but she told me she wanted to be alone." Ambrose is so miserable he doesn't even shudder as he stumbles through the liquor cabinet. Although that might have something to do with the essence of the four barely-drunk bottles of finest spirits he's just absorbed. He collapses into the fireplace. "I think we should do something to cheer her up. A grand gesture that she doesn't have to go through this alone. We're here for her."

That's my idea!

No one thinks I have great ideas, but I do!

"We're not here for her, though, are we?" Edward snaps. He sounds as bitter as the *Praefecti* after we were defeated by a ragtag bunch of upstart Celts. "We're not technically *here* at all. What can ghosts do?"

I touch my hand to my chest. *By Mars' merry mint stalk, we can do more than you think.*

And suddenly it comes to me.

"We will take her to one of those huge moving picture shows," I say. "A mooo-veee."

"A movie." Edward rubs his chin. "The flat theatre. This is an intriguing idea. I saw her on her phone this morning, watching an advertisement for a new Benedict Cummerbund movie. He's an actor that she likes. Normally, I wouldn't approve of Brianna consorting with actors, but if he is inside the moving picture machine and one of us is with her, he can't corrupt her..."

"But the nearest moovee theatre is in Crookshollow," Ambrose points out. "That's more than twice as far away as Argleton. Even with Bree's new powers, our ghost mojo will pull us back here before the movie even reaches the end of the first act."

"We could take turns," Edward suggests. "One of us escorts her to the flat theatre, stays until their ghost mojo pulls them away, then they pop back here, give the next ghost a quick high-light of the plot, and the new ghost returns to Brianna before she even knows we're gone."

"I'm not sure..." Ambrose says. "Maybe we should get Bree to talk about her dad—"

"It *is* a great idea." I beat my fist against my chest. Of course it's a great idea. I thought of it. "This is what humans do when they love each other. I see it all the time on The Bachelor."

"Bree?" we call out as we float upstairs together. "We want to take you to a moovee..."

26

BREE

"So this is a moving picture room," Pax whistles as we walk into the movie theatre and grab seats right down at the front. Hopefully, the movie won't be full of people and no one will sit on Pax's seat or come near enough to hear me whispering to myself. "Is this where the giant actors are trapped in the giant box where the magicians make them dance for our amusement?"

"Sure. Yeah, that's how it works." I don't even know where to begin explaining to a Roman how streaming services and movie studios work. I recline my chair as far back as it will go and set out our snacks – ice cream, pork scratchings, Walkers crisps, two types of M&Ms, and two giant tubs of popcorn (one for me and one to put on the ghost's seat so they can sniff it).

My skin prickles with unease. I shouldn't have agreed to this crazy idea. Going to a movie with the ghosts? Everyone's going to think I'm weird.

But they're so excited about it, and Pax is so proud that he came up with the idea. I didn't want to let them down. And I did really want to see the new Benedict Cumberbatch film – it's supposed to be a tear-jerker, and I could do with an excuse for an ugly cry.

Plus, it's nice to leave the house for a reason that isn't to help solve Albert's murder.

It's nice to do something normal.

Right. Because it's totally normal to go to a movie with three ghosts.

Pax tries to stick his head into the popcorn, but instead, he slams his face into it, sending kernels flying everywhere. I whirl around, worried someone saw the popcorn explode of its own accord, but the three other couples in the cinema are engrossed in their own conversations.

"No one is watching you." Pax grins at me, licking salt off his face.

"Can you taste it?" I whisper, leaning forward, surprised by how desperate I am for his answer.

I'm terrified of these changes, but I want my ghosts to be able to touch and taste and feel the Living world. I want more moments like today, where we can have adventures and they can hold my hand.

But wanting that is too close to wishing they were alive. And wishing for the dead to live again is a recipe for heartache.

Pax shakes his head. His shield clatters against his back. "I cannot taste. But I can feel the salt on my tongue. Gritty and familiar. Roman food is very salty. Maybe one day I'll cook for you."

"I'd like that."

"Oh!" Pax reels as the screen comes to life and the movie starts. "It's so big! They are like monsters! I can see right up that man's nostrils."

"Just remember that they're only projections. They can't jump out of the screen and hurt you."

I shift the popcorn and Pax sits down. Even though I've

been wanting to see this movie, I spend more time watching him than the screen. Every time someone leans toward the camera, he jerks away or growls until the camera moves away. At one point, Benedict's character gets into a bar fight, and Pax leaps to his feet and starts swinging punches at the air.

"That's what you get for messing with Buffalo Crumperbunts!"

"His name is Benedict Cumberbatch," I say.

Pax's smile grows wide with mischief. "Bumblesnuff Crimpysnitch."

"You're ridiculous."

"That *vappa* has insulted his honour!" Pax leaps to his feet. The popcorn bucket wobbles a little, but I don't think anyone else noticed.

"That's his boss, the antagonist," I whisper. "It's kind of his job in the film to—"

"Why doesn't Bonkyhort Cuttlefish simply pull out his sword and run the fiend through?"

"It's *Benedict Cumberbatch*. And he doesn't have a sword because not everyone solves their problems with stabbing."

"Why not? It is the most efficient method. If you stab problem, no more problem. See?" Pax dances up to the screen and draws his sword. "Take that, foul vappa! You have the breath of sour wine! How dare you sully the name of Bendynoodle Custardbath."

I can't help it. I burst out laughing. And once I start, I can't stop. Pax stops what he's doing and looks at me, and then he drops his sword and starts laughing, and the two of us are rolling around in tears.

Unfortunately, the current scene in the film has Bendysnack – I mean Benedict – discovering that his mother has been tragically killed, and I'm now chortling while the rest of the theatre is sniffling. The dirty looks of the other patrons burn into my

STEFFANIE HOLMES

back, and a guy two rows behind me hisses, "Will you kindly be quiet?"

Which is British for "fuck off and die."

I wipe the tears from my eyes and manage to compose myself. Unfortunately, Pax seems to take this as a personal challenge, and he spends the next ten minutes dancing around in front of the screen, pretending to fuck the villain whenever he's in shot, and tweaking Benedict Cumberbatch's nose.

I cry and splutter as I try to hold back my laughter. Pax's ghost mojo gets the better of him, and he floats away with a wave. I'm a mixture of sad and relieved. His antics have given me a stomach ache. I reach for the Walkers crisps.

A few moments later, Ambrose appears at the fire exit. Although, of course, he can't see where I am. "Bree?" He calls out.

"Ambrose," I hiss as loudly as I dare. "Over here."

Ambrose floats through the guy who griped at me about laughing. The guy wraps his arms around himself. "I wish they'd turn up the heat in here," he mutters to his girlfriend.

"Ambrose!" I call louder this time, wincing as five people turn and glare at me. I quickly slump down in my seat. Luckily, a few moments later, Ambrose finds his way to me.

"This is fun," he says after he has a good sniff of the popcorn and caresses the faux leather seat. "Are you having fun, Bree?"

"I am, although I think the film went over Pax's head a little."

"I believe it," Ambrose says. "Pax has explained to me what happened, but I'm more confused than ever. Is Butterscotch Cutiebrunch the grizzled army commander or the tough-as-nails pub brawler?"

"Neither." I cup my hand over my mouth and lean close to whisper the current plot into Ambrose's ear. My fingers graze his cheek, and my breath catches.

250

I'm *touching* Ambrose.

I can smell him, too – fresh and zesty and brimming with sunshine. My fingers linger on his cheek.

His body stiffens.

His long eyelashes flutter.

"Bree..." he murmurs.

If I were on a real date with a living guy, this would be the time when I'd lean in and kiss him. I'm desperate for it. I want to lick the sunshine from Ambrose's lips.

I tear my fingers away.

It hurts – it physically hurts to turn from him and straighten my body and focus on the screen. But I have to do it. Because I'm so tempted to see how far this strange new connection between us will allow us to go.

What happens if a human and a ghost kiss?

Nothing good. Nothing *normal*.

Beside me, Ambrose lets out his breath in a whoosh. Is he relieved? He's probably relieved. I sneak a peek at him. His sightless eyes are fixed on the movie. He has a little light sensitivity, so he'll be able to see the shades of light and dark moving on the screen. He chews on his bottom lips as he focuses on the story. He's managed to pull the popcorn container into his lap, but he doesn't try to eat it – he simply cradles it awkwardly the way a person who hates cats does when a cat sits on their lap.

See? Ambrose isn't thinking about jumping your bones. You're imagining all of this fire and sizzle.

I turn back to the screen and will my overactive hormones under control.

Ambrose is a surprisingly good movie-watching companion. He listens carefully and picks up the story, and he even sobs a little when Benedict makes a stirring eulogy at his mother's funeral. He doesn't lean closer or try to touch me.

Despite that – or perhaps because of it – I'm aware of every tiny movement he makes, and the electric pull of his leg only an inch from mine. I miss pivotal moments because I keep looking over at Ambrose, watching the way he worries his bottom lip or drums his fingers against the popcorn container when things get tense onscreen.

Not even a shirtless Benedict emerging from a waterfall can hold my attention when Ambrose is here.

I will myself to focus on the film. I manage it until I hear the popcorn rustling beside me. I turn to see that Ambrose has gone. His ghost mojo ran out, and he vanished without even saying goodbye.

Oh.

What do I...

"So that's Birdiebeak Cribblysnitch," Edward drawls as he slides into the empty seat. "Pax is right. He does look like me."

"He does not," I snap, hoping Edward doesn't notice the blush creeping into my cheeks. Because with his sharp cheek-bones and mop of dark hair, they kind of do look similar.

"If someone were to play me in a movie about my life, I should like it to be him, although he'll have to change his name. He is passably handsome, for an actor." Edward folds one leg over the other and drapes his hand over the back of my chair. His fingers dance on my shoulder, and a pulse of heat jolts through me. "But where are the buxom tavern wenches Pax promised? All I see are morose people wearing black. They look like they're at one of my poetry readings and the opium ran out."

"Can you shut up and watch the film? Did Ambrose catch you up on the plot? That man there is the lawyer's son and he—"

"Ambrose prattled on, but I didn't pay attention." Edward lifts one of those gorgeous eyebrows and looks at me in a way that makes my heart leap into my throat. "I know we're not here to watch the film."

"*I'm* here to watch the film."

"Please, Brianna. I am not clueless. This flat theatre is where modern people go to revel in lascivious acts." Edward runs his tongue along his upper lip, and I cannot swallow, I cannot breathe. My veins are filled with iron filings and his velvet-black eyes draw me in like two magnets aflame. "That's what happens in all the moving pictures I've seen. And I passed a couple in the back row who are heavily involved in a lascivious act, although I think you and I can outdo them..."

He leans in. The line beneath his bottom lip is outlined in shadow, and his burnt sugar and opium scent pulls me under his spell. He pauses there, his lips a breath from mine, demanding that I close the final gap between us, that I take this thing we've been dancing around for days and make it real.

And I want it. I want *him*. I want this sulky, spoiled prince and all the evil things he could do to my body.

But...

My hand comes up. My fingers splay across his bare chest. Every place where we touch is a tiny bonfire, spitting and sparking. "Edward, I'm not making out with you."

"Why not?"

"Because...a million reasons."

He sits back in his chair, that infuriating arm still draped casually over the top of mine, his fingers playing with my bare shoulder. His smile is a dare. "Name seven."

"Seven? That's a specific number."

"You said you could name a million. Well, I'm only asking for seven."

"A million is a figure of speech, like saying something is as hot as an oven." I stall for time. It's hard to think when his fingers dance sparks on my skin. "Okay, here's a reason: you're a ghost and I'm a Living. We're not even supposed to talk to each other, so what's going to happen if we kiss? It could blow a hole in the universe."

"That won't happen, because I *am* the universe and I don't blow anything until a lady has had at least three orgasms." Edward inclines his head toward his crotch.

"Edward!"

"For all we know, people like you walk around making out with ghosts all the time." Edward winks. "Maybe that's why the librarian at your school always looked so happy."

"Gross! I do not want to think of Ms. Potts that way!"

"Ma'am, I'm terribly sorry to ask, but could you please stop talking?" the man behind me whispers again. "It's hard to hear the film over your..."

He pauses as he takes in the empty chair beside me, the enormous pile of food, and the two tubs of popcorn. Edward takes the opportunity to lean in and kiss his nose, and the man clamps his hand over his face and quickly sinks down in his seat.

"You owe me six more reasons."

"Fine. Reason two is that I'm dealing with my dad's illness and Albert's murder right now, and I don't have time to think about lascivious acts. Reason three is that I don't want to play favorites between you and Ambrose and Pax, because you all mean too much to me to risk hurting you by choosing one of you. Reason four is that I am absolutely, one hundred percent not attracted to you in that way—"

Edward raises a dark eyebrow. "Oh, is that so?"

"It *is* so. You're infuriating and moody and selfish and...and dead! And I'm not going to fall for a guy who doesn't even have a pulse and then get my heart broken all over again when you leave—"

"That's it!" The man behind me stands up. "Either shut up or I'm getting the manager."

"It's okay," I mumble as I grab my coat. "I'm leaving. Right now."

"Bree?" Edward calls after me. "Please, talk to me. What did I do wrong? Bree?"

But I am already pushing my way out the theatre doors, desperately swiping at the tears burning in the corners of my eyes.

27

EDWARD

"What is this?" I hover on the end of the couch, where Pax sits riveted by his latest teevee obsession.

"It is a dating show," he says without taking his eyes off the screen. "This is how Livings find someone to marry. In this show, there is one man — him! The man with a face like a Druid's arsehole." He jabs a finger at the screen. "And all those women are competing for his hand in marriage."

"All those women?" I plop down beside him, intrigued. How is this ugly man making carnal mischief with all those beautiful women when Brianna won't even kiss me? And I can tell that she wants to. "With a face like that, he must be of royal birth – why else would such fine, buxom ladies give him the time of day? A duke, perhaps? Or an earl?"

"He is an actor."

"An *actor?*" I glare at the man on the moving picture box in disdain. "And he has these women falling over themselves to wed him? They must have a wager – the first to not drop dead of syphilis will win a fortune."

This absurd show gives me an idea.

Whatever it is that's giving us the ability to interact more with the Living world and allowing us to touch Brianna in a way we never have before...I want more.

My scepter stirs every moment I'm near her, reminding me that she is not a little girl who needs a friend. She is all woman, as beautiful as any countess, and twice as enticing. And maybe, just maybe, I can convince her that she wants me, too.

I wanted to tell her this at the movie, but those two see-through idiots upset Brianna so much that by the time I got to the movie theatre, she was immune to my charms.

It *had* to have been Pax and Ambrose who messed up last night. Everything was going so brilliantly. Our outing to Argleton proved fruitful. I saved the day by discovering that coin while Ambrose was busy sniffing musty old tomes, and Brianna managed to talk to that bookshop girl, so she was much happier. And we all took turns holding Brianna's hand while we looked around the market. It felt amazing to have her fingers nestled in mine.

How could such a simple touch make butterflies flutter in my chest when I once had an orgy on top of a pile of gold in the Royal Mint and didn't even break into a sweat?

And how did it all go so wrong?

What was that Brianna said about not wanting to choose between the three of us? There's no choice. I have the superior intellect, the most impressive ghostly powers, the most pensive and mysterious artistic side, *and* I know my way around a woman's body. I'm *obviously* the only ghost who can satisfy her.

And if I can get her away from the Roman oaf and the excitable Victorian, I'll prove it.

My plan forms in my mind. That cursed Shakespeare festival is on in Argleton tonight. Perhaps if Brianna were surrounded by actors, she would see how superior I am, and it would cheer her up.

But asking her means going into her room, where she's been hiding ever since we got home from the moovee. Ambrose thinks we should leave her alone. But I disagree. When you are sad about something – like your family disowning you and your halfwit brother being made the heir instead of you, to use a totally made-up example – a party is just the thing to pick up your spirits.

That's what Brianna needs – a night away from this house and from Grimdale, where everyone knows her as crazy Bree who talks to herself.

And maybe she would let me hold her hand again.

Or even something more...

It's worth risking her wrath by entering her room uninvited.

I float away from Pax and pop through the wall of Brianna's room. She's lying on the bed with her laptop open on her lap, scrolling through something. She doesn't seem to care that I'm there. "Albert gave me the password to his Facebook account," she tells me. "Alongside several dozen messages from that real estate agent about selling the house, Mr. Gibbons sent him dozens upon dozens of threats. Some of them are quite imaginative. It appears my old school principal was rather fond of Roman torture methods."

"What's a Facebook?" I ask. "Is it where some poet is reading from his own work, and it's so dreadful that you snap the book shut on his nose? Not that this has ever happened to me, of course. It's just something I've witnessed happening to other, less brilliant poets."

"Of course," Brianna grins. Her smile is opium and sunshine – warm and soft and addictive. It's all too brief before she returns her gaze to the screen. "Did you want something? Do you need the TV channel changed?"

"I wondered if you might like to attend the Shakespeare

festival in Argleton," I outstretch my hand, suddenly more nervous than I've ever been talking to a woman. "With me?"

Brianna's head snaps up. "Is the spoiled prince asking me on a date?"

"I thank you to use my full title – the spoiled but devilishly handsome and majestically endowed prince," I say pointedly. "And yes, I am."

She frowns. "But you're inviting me to the theatre. You don't like actors."

"Not when I was alive. Perhaps their manners have improved since then."

"I doubt it." Brianna cracks a smile that makes my chest tighten. "You know what? Sure. I'd love to go with you."

"Where are we going?" Ambrose floats through the wall, managing to avoid tripping over Entwhistle sleeping on the rug, but instead falls over a lamp into the corner of the bed. He doesn't slide through the bed, though. He grips the brass bedstead and puffs with excitement. "Did you see that? I can catch myself now. And trip over things! It's a miracle."

"Thank you, Ambrose," I mutter. "I'll alert the royal herald."

"Edward just asked if I'd like to go to the Shakespeare festival performance of Macbeth tomorrow night," Brianna says excitedly.

Ambrose's face perks up. "Oh, that sounds fun."

I glare at Ambrose, which of course he can't see. "This is actually just for me and Brianna—"

"Ambrose should come too. He'd enjoy another adventure out of the house." Brianna stands up. "And we should probably see if Pax wants to come."

"He won't want to come," I say feebly. "There are no gladiatorial battles or wild beast fights. No one gets their thumbs cut off or—"

But she's already disappeared down the hall.

"Pax?" Brianna calls out. "Want to go to the theatre tomorrow night?"

"As long as I can bring my sword."

My hands curl into fists at my sides. But I remain calm. I'm a lover, not a fighter. So my romantic date with Brianna has now turned into a group outing. I can work with this.

"I CAN'T BELIEVE we're stuck with the plebs." I frown at the man who just elbowed me through the ribs. The theatre is exactly as I remember it – unlike the movies, where every pleb and lord had the same padded seats, this theatre is circular, with three tiers of seats arranged around a stage, and a circular yard for the riffraff, which is where we are standing now, as if I am some commoner and not a prince of the realm. I point up at the boxes above the stage. "That's where I used to sit – in the Lord's Rooms – those are the best seats in the whole theatre."

"Didn't your neck get sore watching the actors from above?" Brianna asks.

"Darling, one doesn't come to the theatre to watch the play. One comes to give cunnilingus to Lady Sophia de Winter while her husband scarfs plums in the next room."

"You can be quite charming when you're not a chauvinist pig," Bree says to me.

I bow. "Thank you, m'lady."

"So maybe you should try it more often. Oh, look, I think Mina is over on the other side of the stage, with her boyfriends." Brianna waves. "Oooh, I haven't met the tall, suave one before. Or the dark-haired arty one. They are *beautiful*."

"They may be passingly attractive," I concede generously.

"But can they write a poem without using the letter A, or make a cup of tea?"

"Probably." Brianna waves again. "I don't think they can see me—"

"Bree!" a familiar voice calls out. We all turn around.

"Dani!" Brianna hugs her friend. I must say, I remember Dani fondly from Brianna's teenage years as the one who was always asking a million questions about us, and Dani is even more fetching as a girl. "I didn't know you were coming along tonight."

"Are you kidding? They're performing Macbeth and I'm a funeral director. I love a little betrayal and death." Dani holds up her hands to reveal two ice creams and two long bread rolls stuffed with fat sausages, something that looks like bean stew, bacon shavings, cheese, and a million other toppings. "Plus, the food trucks are delicious."

Brianna's eyes turn as huge as saucers as she admires the sandwiches. I lean in close to sniff the mixture of delicious scents.

"The world has come a long way since my drinking buddy, John Montagu, 4th Earl of Sandwich, didn't want to leave the poker game to get something to eat," I say as I prod the beans with my finger. They wobble a little, but Dani doesn't notice. "He asked his servant to fetch him a slice of roast beef between two slices of bread so he could eat it with his hands."

Brianna ignores me. "I'm assuming you're not trying to break a world record for eating your bodyweight in loaded hot dogs, so are you..."

"...here with Alice?" Dani's smile wobbles a little. "I am. She's in the bathroom. You can stand with us if you want. We got a sweet spot over by the minstrels."

"Minstrels are even worse than actors," I tell Brianna. The corner of her lip curls into a smirk.

"Thanks, but no. I'm not going to be your third wheel, but if the two of you want to grab a drink at the pub after, I might be persuaded." Brianna leans over and whispers to her friend. "I'm actually here with the ghosts."

"We're right here." I plant my hands on my hips.

Although at the moment, technically I'm the only one with Brianna. Pax is wandering through the stands, yelling and trying to rile up the crowd with Roman drinking songs. He thinks we're at gladiatorial games. Ambrose is deep in conversation with the ghost of a black-cloaked man wearing a white mask that obscures half his face.

Dani raises an eyebrow. "Brianna Mortimer, are you on a date?"

"Yes!" I say. "We like to take in a little theatre before our ghost orgy."

"It's not a date." Brianna's cheeks flush. She's so pretty when she's lying. "It's just a night out with my ghoulish friends. Edward's here now. He says something filthy and inappropriate."

"Oh, Edward." Dani waves at the spot where she thinks I'm standing, although all she actually succeeds in doing is knocking the theatre ghost's mask askew. "You were always my favorite. So you and the ghosts? I thought they couldn't leave Grimdale because of the ghost mojo?"

Brianna pulls the moldavite rock from her pocket and holds it up to Dani. "Ever since that old witch gave me this, they've been able to move further from the manor as long as I'm with them."

"How strange. It's just a rock, isn't it? You don't say bibbity bobbity boo or—" Dani's head snaps up. "Oh, there's Alice. I'd better go. But hang around afterward and we'll go for that drink, yes? I want to hear how you went at the bookshop, and all about your hot ghost date."

"It's a *not*-ghost date." Brianna waves as Dani makes her way back through the crowd. She turns to me and sighs. "I love Dani, but she wants me to try to put my past with Alice behind us, and I don't know if I can. Didn't your father try to force you to marry a French princess? What would you do?"

I touch my hand to her cheek, revelling in the warmth pooling through my body at the touch. It's been over three hundred years, but I don't remember touching living women feeling like my soul is on fire. "If you're me, you sulk off to your manor house in the country to host an orgy, which is absolutely something I could help you arrange..."

Brianna laughs. Her champagne eyes fizzle with heat...and a hint of fear. "What good are you?" she whispers.

"Come closer and find out." I stroke my finger along her jawline. Her eyelashes tangle together, her breath coming out in sharp rasps as she loses herself in the sensation of my touch.

Brianna laughs again, but her laugh is throatier, coming from deep inside her. She presses her cheek against my hand.

"You always make me laugh," she whispers, her eyes flying open, those deep, golden honey orbs focused on me, like she's seeing me for the first time. "You think you're this spoiled, selfish person, but you can be so, so kind. And the other night, at the movie, I wanted so badly to—"

"You must pay attention," Pax booms right in my ear. "The show is starting!"

"Fuck!" Brianna leaps back, clutching her heart. I jerk forward, and my outstretched hand passes through a man's head. A cold jolt bursts through my body, killing any amorous intentions, much to my scepter's disapproval.

"Oooh," the man holds his head. "I've got a killer ice cream headache, and I didn't even have any ice cream."

"I can't believe you did that, you poxface weasel," I mutter to Pax. Couldn't he see that Brianna and I were about to get lascivious?

I'm desperate to know what she was about to say.

"Bree? I'd like to stand beside you." Ambrose floats back over and takes up a place on the other side of Brianna. Luckily, even in the yard, British people don't like to stand too close to strangers, so we have enough space around us that we won't constantly be walked through. Brianna bites her lip, and I know she feels self-conscious being the only one in the yard standing off on her own.

But she's not on her own. She is accompanied by a prince of remarkable wit and intellect, and a couple of ghosts of no importance.

"Quiet, quiet, everyone!" Pax marches around the yard, bopping people still talking on the head. At least three of them threw their ice creams in the rubbish bin. The lights dim. I find my way back to Brianna and stand as close as I dare. An orange light flickers beneath a cauldron, and Brianna gasps as three gnarled, ugly witches dance around the stage.

"I'm glad Agnes isn't here to see this," Brianna whispers to me. "She would hex everyone in this theatre."

"This is boring." Pax lifts his fist as Macbeth comes out. He rotates his thumb down. "Kill him."

Brianna grabs his fist and yanks it down. "This is not that kind of show. There will be plenty of killing later, I promise."

"What's happening?" Ambrose asks.

"I don't want to wait." Pax's short tunic flaps around his bare, muscled legs. "I'm going to the bar."

"Can someone make Pax be quiet?" Ambrose pleads. "I have to pay attention to the dialogue."

A buzzing sound reaches my ears, and my eyes are drawn to a small box on the side of the stage which must have something to do with powering the lights. A daring and salacious idea pops into my head.

I stick my hand through the panel and grab onto the wires, and a jolt of pure pleasure wafts through my body. My scepter stands at attention, and with Bree and her strange rock so close, it feels better than ever.

"Aaaaah, now we're talking." My voice wobbles as the electrical charge courses through my body.

"Are you really doing that here?" Brianna snaps.

"Damn right I am."

A couple on the edge of the stage are making out, completely oblivious to the tragedy of acting being carried out on stage. I notice Brianna watching them, biting her lip.

She wants that.

She wants a human to touch her, to make her so crazy that she demands him anywhere and everywhere, even in the middle of a crowded theatre.

She deserves it. She deserves to be worshipped as a goddess, to have her body pleasured in every imaginable way...

And I can't give it to her. Not the way she wants. I can't be the handsome Living man she can parade around on her arm.

But maybe...

"You know," I whisper in her ear. "There are some wonderful things about being on a date with a ghost."

"Three ghosts," Brianna says without turning her head from the stage. "And we're not on a date."

"Fine, a date with three ghosts." I pull my hand from the electrical box and touch it on the underside of her wrist. She yelps, but doesn't move her arm away. "But one of those ghosts has his head in a cider barrel and the other is enraptured by the performance, and I have a mind to what we can do..."

"We're supposed to be watching the perforrrrrrrrrrmm-mm..." Brianna's protests dissolve into a low moan as I run my fingers down the inside of her wrist. For at least three count-esses, the inside of the wrist was extremely sensitive. One kiss there and they would fall to their knees for me.

Interesting that Brianna is the same.

"It doesn't feel like an electrical shock," Brianna gasps, bracing her other hand against the stage. "It's more like...a buzzing..."

"Precisely." I dance my fingers along her arm. Brianna peers up at me, her honey eyes pleading – no longer a child but all woman, in charge of her own pleasure and certain of what she wants.

She wants this.

She wants *me*.

And I'm always happy to indulge a lady. I move my fingers across her shoulder, over her collarbone, and dip down the front of her low-cut sweater, finding the little bud of her nipple.

Brianna gasps again as I roll her nipple between my fingers, and the hum of the electricity pulses through me.

Her nipple hardens.

I feel it.

I feel *her*.

My Brianna's body blossoming beneath my touch, falling open like the petals of a flower.

Oooh, that's a good line. I shall add that to a poem.

I swirl my fingers around her nipple, so softly, letting her feel the sensation of the electrical pulse coursing through us both. And then, when I see her and her lashes tangling together again as she sinks even deeper into the sensation, I take her nipple in my fingers and pinch it – not too hard, but enough that a tiny moan escapes her throat.

With my other hand, I brush my fingers on her cheek. "Stay very still, and keep looking straight forward, and no one will be any the wiser."

Brianna's jaw wobbles. I think that she's going to tell me to stop, that our friendship has boundaries that I'm trampling over with my opium. But she bites her lip in that utterly adorable way of hers and lifts her chin to the stage. Her eyes flick to mine, and even I can feel the heat burning inside their honeyed centers.

She wants this.

She wants *me*.

If I stop to think about this for even a moment, I will crumble. I will walk away from her and never return, lest I ruin the beautiful friendship that we share.

But I'm famous for doing things without thinking, and tonight, the only thing I want to do is my Brianna.

I move around behind her, pressing my chest into her back, letting the edges of my shirt open a little so my bare ghost flesh presses into her. She feels amazing, warm and tingling and so deliciously *alive*. I can't believe that after all these years of falling through objects and floating in walls, she is the one who makes me feel again.

She whimpers as I slide my hand out of her top. I move my fingers down her side, toying with the hem of her sweater. I press my fingers deeper into the box, searching for the energy I need to make this work. The theater lights flicker, but the audience is too engrossed in the performance to notice.

It takes me a couple of goes to grasp the hem of her tight leather skirt and slide my hand up her inner thigh. Brianna's breath hitches, and her fingers grip the edge of the stage so tight that her knuckles glow white. I dance my fingers in intricate shapes along her inner thigh, aware of the murmurs of the audience members around me.

We're doing this right in the middle of the crowd, while poor, dear, oblivious Ambrose stands beside us.

I used to love fingering a countess under the table during a state banquet, or going down on a duchess under her writing desk while she took dictation for her oblivious husband – all the naughty things people didn't know were happening right under their noses. And judging by the way Brianna squirms and presses herself back against me, she loves it, too.

I trace my fingers over her panties, teasing her, feeling the heat of her mound in my palm. She whimpers again. I hook a finger in the fabric and tug it aside.

My breath catches at the first touch of her wetness. She is shaven, her skin soft and supple and slick with wetness. For me. For *me*.

I want to drink all of her, gulp her down like a fine French brandy, losing myself in the magic of her beauty. I tease her folds, opening out her petals, committing every secret part of her to memory so I can immortalize her in a poem later.

"Edward…"

"I love the sound of my name on your lips…" I whisper against her ear. Her almond and pear scent invades my nostrils, sending me wild with desire.

I slip a finger inside her. She's so wet. I'm breathing hard – it's a reflex, because I don't require breath. But I'm so excited, so *elated*, to have my finger inside Brianna, to feel the way she constricts around me as my ghostly body hums with the electrical pulse.

I had no idea, but I've been waiting over three hundred years for this moment…and it was worth every moment.

"Eeeeeedwaaaaaa…" Brianna's breath vibrates as I slide my finger in and out of her. I curl another finger around and touch that tiny bud from which all a woman's pleasure emanates. I flick and swirl and drive deeper. She grinds her hips against my hand and I feel her, I *feel* her…and she is the most beautiful woman who has ever lived.

My name escapes her lips over and over in a hushed whisper, and it's all I can do to stop my silent flute from playing its final song. I didn't even think it was possible – death is supposed to render us impotent, to rid our bodies of the juices of our earthly desires. But my scepter is very aware of its earthly desires right now, and I have to look away from Brianna at that ridiculous Roman for a moment so I don't completely lose control over this situation.

"Let go for me, Brianna. Show these filthy plebs how a lady takes her pleasure."

Brianna tightens around my finger, and she lets out a final, shuddering gasp. Luckily, on stage, Macbeth has just killed King Duncan, so no one notices. Her body sags against me, but in her weakened state her powers must wane, because I find that I can't catch her. My hands fall through her, and she stumbles through me into the guy behind her.

"Ow, watch out." He glares at her. "Someone's had a few too many glasses of Shakespearean punch."

"Sorry, sorry." Bree steps away from him, her face beet red. She frantically straightens her skirt.

"Brianna, I—"

"Bree, are you okay? What happened?" Ambrose turns to her. "We're almost at my favorite part of the play, where Lady Macbeth's guilt gets the better of her. Please, come and watch with me."

"Sure, Ambrose." Brianna straightens her back and rests both arms against the edge of the stage, leaning in close so she can whisper to Ambrose. She won't look at me.

"Look, there she is! Lady Macbeth!"

The audience whirls around as Lady Macbeth flies through the upper galleries, wringing her hands and cackling wildly. She surreptitiously clips herself into a contraption and steps out onto a narrow platform directly over our heads.

"Oh, this is exciting," Ambrose exclaims.

"Out, out damned spot!" Lady Macbeth cries, and then she steps over the edge.

I don't know what I expect to happen. The theatre in my day used swings and winches and all kinds of contraptions to create dramatic effects. Lady Macbeth usually dies offstage, but this director had an eye for the macabre, so I expect her to fly around like a banshee, smearing herself with stage blood and wailing about her doomed husband.

That's not what happens.

The woman drops like a stone into the groundlings. People leap out of the way, and her body lands with a sickening crunch.

The theatre goes deathly silent.

And then someone starts screaming.

"What happened?" Ambrose nudges Brianna. "What's going on?"

"It's just a stage trick," Brianna whispers as she wraps her arms around herself. "Any second now she's going to get back up and keep reciting her lines."

"That may be so," I say. "But I'm pretty sure that wound in her skull is gushing real blood."

28

BREE

The actress' face is frozen with surprise. A dark stain spreads outward, encircling her like a halo.

Yup, definitely real blood.

Shit.

A lot of things happen at once. Her head flops to the side, her glassy eyes fixing on me. All around me, people scream and rush the exits, as if she's carrying the Black Death instead of being the victim of a horrible accident. And I...

I feel a strange tugging in my chest, like my heart is wrapped in a piece of string that's winding up and reeling in a great and terrible catch. I blink, not believing what I can see – a filmy shape rises from the actress's body and floats above her, still wringing her hands and moving her lips to recite the lines of the play.

Another ghost.

The masked theatre ghost runs to her, and I know he's trying to explain where she is and why she's suddenly able to float. Good, I'm glad she's got a friend, because I can't be the one who...

"Brianna?" Edward says tersely. "Why aren't you running in terror with everyone else?"

An excellent question. I open my mouth to tell him about the ghost and the strange tugging sensation that pulls me toward her, but no sound comes out. I'm jerked and jostled as people race around me to get to the exit. Mina's surly boyfriend drops to his knees beside the corpse, muttering something to Mina as he cradles the actress' head in his hands. I jab my finger at the new ghost, and Edward turns to look.

I've never seen a ghost appear before. It's *horrible*.

I feel it in my bones, the rending of her soul from its mortal tether. I feel her floating away. The string around my heart tugs frantically, like she's a balloon caught in the wind and I need to hold on to her for dear life. But why me? I don't even know the woman. Why does it feel like we're connected somehow?

"Brianna..." Edward tries to tug on my arm, but his fingers fall through me. "We should leave."

I'm frozen in place in the middle of the empty theatre. I can dimly hear police sirens growing closer. I know that I have to get out of here, lest they think I have something to do with this. But I can't tear my eyes away from the ghost of the actress as she floats across the stage, fingers clutching at the theatre ghost's cloak. My feet move toward her, dragged along by the invisible cord that binds us.

"Um..." I force myself to wave. "Hi."

"Hi?" She blinks at me. "Perhaps you can tell me what's going on. The theatre was full of people just a moment ago. I was doing my death speech. Why did they all leave during my death speech?"

"Didn't that nice fellow with the mask explain it?"

"I don't think he's very nice at all. He..." she frowns. "He said some nonsense about me being dead."

"I don't quite know how to tell you this, but...you did die.

During your speech. You launched yourself off that platform on the top gallery, but your safety harness wasn't attached properly or something, and you..." I sweep my hand behind me at her crumpled corpse, not certain if that's a good idea or not. "Everyone ran away in terror."

"But...that can't be." She floats down to inspect the body. "We tested that harness a hundred times. I know I put it on perfectly. This must be some kind of sick prank, but I didn't think even Rasmussen would stoop that low."

"Rasmussen? The owner of that swanky bookshop in town?"

"That's right, him!" She hops about madly. "He's been the bane of my existence, him and his First Folio. Even from the grave, he torments me!"

"Excuse me?"

"Oh, didn't you hear? Someone murdered him yesterday. And good riddance, too. The only problem is that I'm a suspect. But that Mina Wilde will figure it out—"

I turn to Ambrose. "Someone was murdered in Argleton and we didn't hear about it?"

This can't be a coincidence, can it?

He shrugs. "You've been a little preoccupied with your own murder mystery, Bree."

"Mystery, mystery..." the ghost's eyes dance frantically. "I had my own mystery to solve. I was supposed to do something tonight. It was important. Vitally important! I think it was about Rasmussen. But I can't remember..."

"It's the post-death amnesia." All ghosts experience it to some degree. It's why Albert can't remember who poisoned him or how he ended up in the cemetery, or why Pax has no idea exactly where on the battlefield he died or if his men liked him enough to give him a proper burial. "There's nothing we can do about it, so you have to live with it—"

"It's very important." The ghost grabs my neck. Her fingers slide right through me, cold as ice. "I don't remember all of it, but I do remember this. I came here tonight to tell Mina something. Do you know a woman named Mina Wilde?"

"I know her." *Sort of.*

"You need to tell her to look to the lily."

"What?"

"Look to the lily! Look to the lily! It's important, but I don't know why." The actress fixes me with a withering stare. "You promise me that you'll tell her."

"I promise." I nod vigorously. Anything to get the ghost's freezing fingers out of my trachea.

"Good." The ghost withdraws her hands. "I'll be checking up to make sure you do—"

"Mrs. Mortimer?" Wilson's voice echoes through the empty theatre. "What are you doing standing near the body?"

"Um, I..." My hand flies to my throat. My fingers are ice-cold. The ghost of the actress retreats into the shadows, but I can still feel the tether around my heart, binding her to me.

Wilson shoves me toward the exit. "Get out of here and wait with the others while we take statements. And if I find out that you've tampered with my crime scene in any way, I will throw your ass in jail. Got it?"

"Loud and clear." I half-walk, half-stumble out into the parking lot, where Dani and Alice and Mina and her boyfriends are waiting with the rest of the audience. My mind whirs. I can't believe I just saw a woman fall to her death. And the harness malfunctioning like that...was it sabotage? Was this another murder?

Why does death follow me? Why is my heart wrapped in the string of this ghost's soul? What is *happening* to me?

29

BREE

"I can't believe it. She threw herself right off that platform, in front of everyone." Dani refills both our cider glasses before sitting back in the wingback chair and raising hers to her crimson lips. "I know this sounds macabre, but I hope I get to work on the funeral, because I'm so interested in what happened. Was it suicide? Did her harness malfunction? Or was it..."

"Murder!" the ghost actress shrieks, storming through the room, wringing her hands wildly, and knocking over several knickknacks with the hem of her Lady Macbeth costume.

"Sabotage?" I say as I drain half my glass. After the performance was cut short by the dramatic death, Alice had wanted to go home, but Dani was keen to have a drink and talk about it, so we headed back to Grimdale Manor. Of course, we weren't alone. "The ghost seems to think so. She thinks her death has something to do with the murder of that other bookstore owner in Argleton the other day."

"I don't think so, I know so," the actress snaps, hands on her see-through hips. "I'll have you know that I'm a renowned

Shakespearean scholar, and so if I tell you something is true, then it's true."

"Ghosts, so melodramatic." Dani rolls her eyes.

"You have no idea."

"I resent that," Edward says from his chair beside the fire. "I am exactly the right amount of dramatic."

I deliberately avoid looking at him, because if I do glance over there I will catch him slouched over that chair, white shirt open to reveal the smooth planes of his chest, one leg draped oh-so-casually over the arms, and that infuriating smirk tugging at his too-pretty lips. If I look, my face will go beet red thinking about what he did...what *we* did...and Dani will see and she'll demand to know what happened and I'll have to tell her that I let a ghost finger me...

...and I liked it.

I really liked it.

I haven't been able to stop thinking about it since the police kicked us out of the theatre, the way his touch felt with the electrical current humming through him – not like an electric shock, which is what I expected, but more like the buzz of a vibrator...and he was so... and all those filthy things he whispered in my ear...

No. I'm not thinking about it. Focus on Dani and the very, very unsexy possible murder, and this new actress ghost and that strange tugging around my heart that's still plaguing me...

I close my eyes so I can resist the tug of Edward's smirk – a smirk I can sense even when I can't see it – and focus on what Dani's saying.

"—and what was that thing she said to you?"

"Look at the lily. I don't understand it."

"That's because it's not a message for *you*." The ghost wrings her hands in exasperation. "And could you not discuss it with every Tom, Dick, and Harry in sight? What's the point of delivering a message in secret if all of the village hears about it?"

"No one's going to hear about it. Most of the people in this room are just as dead as you are." I glare at the ghost. It's strange. She shouldn't have been able to follow me all the way home – her ghost mojo should have held her back at the theatre. But here she is, flouncing around Grimwood Manor, getting a death lesson from Pax on how to use the liquor cabinet.

"Sorry that you're dead," Dani says to the space where she thinks the actress is. "At least if you let me do your funeral, you'll be able to go out with a real party. So you're going to deliver the message to Mina?"

I nod. "If I tell Mina about the lily, then the ghost will cross over."

"Cross over? I don't like the sound of that." The ghost folds her arms across her chest. "Maybe I'll go back to that nice theatre ghost with the white mask. He knows how to treat a great stage actress."

"I'd actually prefer it if you did go back to the theatre, thanks." I glare at the new ghost, then turn back to Dani. "It's the right thing to do, even if..."

Dani raises an eyebrow. "Even if it destroys your new friendship before it even begins?"

Damn her. She knows me too well. "Yeah. I mean, when I told you that I saw ghosts, we'd been friends for years. And you're..."

Dani leans back in her chair and tugs on her tailored vest, which has a pattern of dancing skeletons. "I'm delightfully morbid. It's okay – you can say it."

"Fine. You're delightfully morbid. But I don't even know Mina that well yet, and she seems kind of amazing, and I'd love for Ambrose to connect with her in some way, if that's even possible. But if I walk into that shop and tell her that a ghost told me to tell her to look at a lily, she's going to think I'm crazy, just like everyone in Grimdale already does, including your girlfriend."

"Alice isn't my girlfriend," Dani says glumly, and I know she's thinking about her ruined date. "And you should give this Mina a chance. Maybe she'll surprise you. Didn't the witches say something about her slaying a vampire?"

"They were kidding about that."

I hope.

"So where are your three ghostly not-dates hiding? Pax, Edward, Ambrose?" Dani waves at the fireplace. "Hi, everyone."

"Ambrose is on the window seat. Pax is in the liquor cabinet. Edward is draped over that chair like a Renaissance painting of an indolent prince."

"Of course." Dani kicks her boots off and flops down on the sofa. She makes a face. "This antique furniture looks great and all, but it's not exactly comfortable. It's made for dainty limbs and tiny, pert little bottoms."

"I resent that," Edward says. "My limb is anything but dainty—"

"Edward says he agrees completely with everything you say," I finish.

"Liar." Dani grins as she swipes the cider bottle from the table and refills our glasses. "So, if you don't mind me asking, how did you enjoy your not-date? At one point I looked over and you had your eyes closed and were gripping the stage so hard—"

CRASH. CLATTER. BANG.

Phew. Saved by another calamity.

The actress shrieks and leaps into Ambrose's lap. "Save me, save me!"

Dani's neck snaps toward the ceiling. "What's that noise?"

"Oh, that's been happening a lot," I shrug. "My parents say that there's a bat living in the attic."

"A bat!" The actress shudders, collapsing into Ambrose's arms. He looks terrified, but awkwardly pats her on the shoulder.

"Dad named him Ozzy and they said to just leave him be."

"That's because they're too terrified to kick him out," Edward says with a shudder. "They are smart. Ozzy owns the attic now, but he's making sorties into the third storey bedrooms. Soon he'll have his own flag and he'll be setting up his family in my bedroom!"

The irony of a British prince complaining about a bat colonising the house makes me snort with laughter.

"It's best to give Ozzy his space," Ambrose adds from the window seat as the ghost sobs into his shoulder. He glances worryingly at the ceiling as the bangs and crashes recede. I look to Pax, expecting him to leap into action, sword drawn. Instead, I see the flash of a Roman sandal disappear behind the curtain.

"You can come out, Pax," I call. "I think he's stopped now."

"It sounds like he's having Ozzfest up there," Dani remarks. "Are you sure letting a bat live in the house is hygienic or—"

She winces as we hear a loud cracking noise. Pax dives back behind the curtain.

"—structurally sound?"

"I'm not sure at all, but if Dad's made friends with the bat, I'm not going to be the one to shoo it away." I glance into the corner of the room, where Edward has joined Pax behind the curtain, the pair of them together in terror. "Besides, the ghosts are terrified of him for some reason."

"Not for *some reason*," Edward says with a shudder. "For a legitimate, *specific* reason, which we can tell you about in great and explicit detail—"

"Not tonight," I say. "I've had far too much cider for that."

283

Dani's used to me making random comments to thin air, so she allows this whole conversation to pass over her without comment. "Oh, I was going to tell you that I have some news about our real estate agent."

"Annabel Myers?" I'd been intending to investigate her further, especially after we found that coin, but all the ghost shenanigans had taken up my time.

"The one and same. So Albert's body is in the freezer at work, waiting for an appropriate time for his funeral to be held. Obviously, with Maggie in jail, she can't be the one to manage it, so I'm waiting for their son to arrive from Australia. Basically, the entire thing is on hold. So imagine my surprise when I get a visitor asking about Albert's arrangements."

"Annabel?"

"Old Pointy-Toe Shoes herself. She was asking if I knew anything about Albert's estate. I told her the family wasn't ready for the funeral yet and referred her to the Fernsbys' lawyer, but she said that she'd already seen him and he wouldn't tell her anything. She wanted to know if the house sale was still going ahead. She was very insistent about it, said she had the perfect clients lined up but they couldn't wait."

"What did you say?"

"I said that I couldn't reveal private details about a client. She got really huffy and left."

"I mean, that's gross, but it's on-brand for a real estate agent. Albert didn't tell me that they decided to sell, though he might've forgotten because of his post-death amnesia."

"Or his dementia," Dani sips her drink. "I also combed through the Goat's social media pages to look at all the pictures from pub quiz night. No one in this town can take a picture. I've seen close-ups of more nostrils than I can count. But I can tell you unequivocally that Annabel and her husband Kieran were at pub quiz that night until closing. They show up in a lot of photographs, almost as if they're trying to establish an alibi."

"But we know that Albert was poisoned well before the pub quiz, and Pax saw Albert dancing into the cemetery himself, so they didn't need to prove they didn't move the body."

"True, but the police don't know what Pax saw. Plus, they had no way of knowing exactly how much of the poisoned balm Albert would use, or when he would use it. And Kieran's the scout troupe leader, so he probably knows all about belladonna. Oh, and do you know who wasn't at pub quiz? Principal Gibbons. He called me yesterday."

"He did?"

Dani nods. "His mother has been very sick, and she died peacefully in her sleep last night. He called to make arrangements for the funeral. Poor man, he's pretty broken up about it. He had a good cry and admitted that he's been an awful person lately because he's been worried about her and he's been taking it out on Albert and Maggie, but his mother left him a nice little nest egg, so he's going all out with the funeral."

"Isn't that a little callous?"

Dani shakes her head. "People grieve in different ways. Sometimes, when you see a loved one suffering, their death can feel like a relief because you know they're at peace. Having that money means he can honour her the way he wants to, and he can move on with his life without holding onto his grudge against the Fernsbys. My job is not to judge, and to allow the family the space to work through their emotions. I believe his grief is genuine, and I think we should focus on these other two as our main suspects."

"You are way too good at this."

"Five years in the funeral industry." Dani beams. "Oh, and all those true-crime podcasts I listen to. People in the death business have morbid tastes. Speaking of morbid...new ghosts.

Murders. Sabotaged equipment. Village gossip. Belladonna bath products. Your life is stranger than fiction right now, Bree."

Not to mention this new tugging sensation and this odd feeling that I've been made privy to something I shouldn't. "Tell me about it."

THE NEXT DAY, I have to spend the morning explaining ghost rules to a distraught actress, and then soothing an even more distraught Albert because I have no new news for him about Maggie. It's late afternoon by the time I set my three ghosts down in front of a Monty Python film and get on the bus to Argleton with my other ghostly retinue to chat with Mina.

Nevermore Bookshop is closed by the time I arrive, but I remember what the lady said about the sign, and I try the door. It opens easily, and I slip inside. I find Mina in the main room, arranging books on the table while the raven watches overhead. He raises a wing to me in greeting, and I nod in reply.

"This place could really use a dusting." The actress wrinkles her nose.

"I'm sorry," I say as I enter the room. "I didn't mean to startle you. I have something to tell you."

Mina's head snaps up. "Yeah?"

I look over my shoulder, but no one else is here apart from the ghost of the Victorian lady I saw last time, who's nodding at me. "Listen, I was at the theatre last night. I saw what happened to that poor woman. And I've heard around that you might be investigating these murders on the down-low."

"I wouldn't dream of undermining our constabulary," Mina

says in a tone that implies that yes, she very definitely is running her own investigation.

"I'm not here to bust your chops. The police couldn't organize a piss-up in a brewery. I might be able to help."

"How?"

"Okay, so." I hold up my phone. "First, I texted you the images I took of the First Folio. They might come in handy, since I assume the police have it in their possession now."

"They actually returned it today," Mina said, explaining that the First Folio is now on display at the theatre. "I don't know when I'd actually get to see it, so the photos will help a lot, thank you."

"You're welcome. And..." *I can't believe I'm doing this.* "Um... this isn't easy for me, and please don't think I'm a freak."

"Bree, I promise, you can't be a bigger freak than me. Just tell me what it is."

"Okay, let's say I happen to be closely acquainted with a... local expert in the Shakespearean period. Someone who very much like to talk to you but for specific reasons, cannot."

Because she's dead.

"Tell her I'm a renowned scholar!" The actress leaps up and down. "She doesn't know that many renowned scholars. She'll know it's me."

Mina tips her head to the side, interested. I continue. "And this...er, renowned scholar told me to tell you to look at the lily."

"The what?"

"The lily!" The ghost is trying to stomp her foot. "The lily! The goddamn lily! I wish I knew what it meant but it's very, very important."

I don't want to do this.

I don't want to be delivering messages for ghosts or solving murders or kissing men who died in the seventeenth century. I want to be a normal twenty-something woman. I want to go on dates with people who are visible, and hang out with my friends without them hearing me have one-sided conversations.

I want my dad. I want him to wrap me in his arms and tell me that everything is going to be okay.

Everything I want in life is out of my reach.

The moldavite rock in my pocket weighs a gazillion tonnes. The ghost shrieks, the sound like an air-raid siren in an old war movie. The cord around my heart tugs and tugs, and I think it's going to rip my heart out of my body. I'm barely aware of Mina in front of me, her eyes wide with concern.

"The lily. You must look at the lily. That's all I can tell you." The edges of the world glow with brilliant golden light that grows brighter and brighter until I can't see a thing. Nausea wells inside me. I need to leave this shop, *now*, before I hurl. "I have no idea what she means, but she seems to think you'll figure it out."

"Wait. How do you know—"

"Good luck, Mina."

I whirl around and race in the direction of the door. I slam into the table, knocking over a stack of books. Above my head, the raven croaks in distress.

You can see it, too, the bird says. *The shop filling with bright light. The ghost fading. The silver cord that extends from her into your chest...*

What? There's no silver cord. But I don't look down. I don't raise my hands to my heart because I can feel it there, tightening, tugging...

I cry out and stumble to the door.

"Come back," the ghost shrieks. "Something's happening to me. I feel all weak and floaty..."

Don't look, Bree. Don't look.

I push off the table and stumble to the door. The ghost

screeches, and even though I cover my ears, I can't block out the sound because it's coming from inside me and...

The shop bursts with light. I feel my way down the corridor and throw myself out the front door just as the ghost's screams go quiet and the cord around my heart snaps.

The light vanishes.

The world is okay again.

But I am very, *very* far from okay.

I lean against a fire hydrant and fight to catch my breath. I know exactly what happened inside that shop. The ghost crossed over because I completed her unfinished business. I've done everything I can for Mina's case. I delivered the ghost's message. The rest is up to Mina.

What I don't know is where that bright light came from, or why my heart is squeezed by the cord. I've seen ghosts cross over a few times before. They usually just fade and disappear. This was such a production that even the raven noticed.

What did he say about the silver cord?

And Mina...what must she think of me, stumbling around and mumbling nonsense about lilies and ghosts? I can't bear another moment of Mina looking at me with that confused, slightly terrified expression that people always use around me – the one that says, 'this girl is a freak, and we want to get far, far away from her.'

I wanted Mina to be different. But I don't think she is. Even the crime-solving blind bookshop girl with the three boyfriends and great taste in music thinks I'm too much.

Fine. I straighten my back, dust off my skirt, and start back toward the bus. No more Mina or visits to Nevermore Book-shop. I've done what I set out to do.

I have my own unsolved murder to crack, and my own ghostly demons to slay.

30

BREE

I pick up takeaways on my way home and eat them on a bench by the duck pond so I don't have to deal with the ghosts being attracted to the smell. My stomach is in knots as I unlock the front entrance. I know the ghosts will interrogate me, and the last thing I want is to talk about witnessing the actress cross over and the bright light and strange tugging around my heart.

But I can't put it off forever. It's late, and I feel awful that I haven't fed Moon and Entwhistle yet. I expect them to leap on my ankles as soon as I step inside the door, but they're nowhere to be seen.

The whole house is shrouded in quiet.

"Moon? Entwhistle? Ghosts?" I check the guest bedrooms, in the laundry baskets, and Moon's favorite hiding place – sandwiched between the couch cushions with only one ginger paw poking out. But they're nowhere, and neither are the ghosts.

Where are they all?

Panic rises in my throat, but then I hear Pax shouting. I

follow the sound to my old bedroom. My teenage sanctuary. Gingerly, I shove open the door. My heart leaps into my throat.

There's Pax, sitting on the end of my old bed, a piece of ribbon tied to the tip of his sword. He waves the ribbon around for the kittens, who leap at it, trying to slay it with their claws and teeth. His face is enchanted by their antics, his hard, aquiline features unusually serene.

He looks up at me then and his face falls, his eyes clouding with guilt. A horrible feeling settles in my stomach. Pax feels bad about being in this room, because he knows that I don't want to be in here. But this house is his home, too. I don't want him to feel like he can't go places or play with kittens.

"It's okay." I move to the turret windows. Far below, wind whips through the cemetery, rustling the oak and cherry trees and casting shadows on the faces of the two angels, so it appears as if they're talking to each other. *This place used to be peaceful to me...but now it's a walking nightmare. Would I give up seeing the three ghosts again to have that quiet back?* "I don't mind you being in here."

"You have returned." Pax keeps his face focused on the kittens. His shoulders are tensed. "You should have taken me with you. It is my job to look after you."

You can't save me, Pax. Not when I'm my own greatest enemy.

"I've been traveling around the world on my own for five years. I think I can go to a bookshop in the next village without being attacked by the Celts."

"If I could have gone with you on your travels, I would. But you didn't want me. You didn't want Edward or Ambrose, either."

"No. I didn't. I was young and sad and I needed to find myself. I needed to be normal for a bit."

"What about now?"

Pax still isn't looking at me, but I can't mistake the anguish in his voice.

I sigh. "Edward told you, didn't he? About what happened at the Shakespeare festival—"

"He hasn't shut up about it. He is most annoying. I told him that if he says another word, I will enact my favorite Roman punishment, where I peel his skin off and—"

I turn. "I mean, I don't have a problem with you peeling Edward. He probably deserves it."

Entwhistle's claws get stuck in Pax's tunic. Lovingly, softly, he plucks them out.

"So you have chosen him, then?"

My eyes flick to the graffiti I scratched into the plaster. *B + P + E + A = 4EVA.*

Young Bree couldn't imagine how complicated things would become.

"No. I...I don't want to choose anyone. That's the point. I had a moment of weakness last night. Edward was right there and he saw that I needed cheering up, and he...cheered me up. Because he's my friend and that's what friends do. The truth is, if you were all living and I could have an actual relationship with any of you, I have no idea who I would choose. I would not want to choose. But I am Living and you are ghosts."

"I don't know what I am." Pax glares at the tip of his sword. "Why is everything changing? Why does our ghost mojo suddenly go further? Why does it feel like this when I touch you?"

I yelp as he grabs my hand, crushing my fingers to his chest. The bees hum to life in my veins. I swallow back the moan of pleasure that wants to escape my lips.

"You feel it," Pax demands, cupping my fingers over his heart. "You feel what you do to me?"

"Pax, I don't—" but then I gasp.

Because I *do* feel it.

It's so faint that I think I've imagined it, but no...

There's a steady thud-thud-thud in Pax's chest.

A heartbeat.

"This isn't possible."

"By Mars' matrimonial peacemaker, it was a surprise to me, too."

"How long have you had this?"

He scratches his head. "I noticed it a couple of days after you came back. I've been trying to find the right moment to tell you."

"Since when does a Roman centurion care about the right moment?"

Pax frowns in mock offense, but his baby blue eyes are fixed on me with an intensity that pools heat in my belly.

I know I should remove my hand, but he feels so good, and the way he's looking at me holds me frozen. "What does this mean?" I whisper.

"I don't know what it means, but I am in agony." Pax grabs the edge of his tunic and lifts it. "This is my verpa. It hasn't been like this since I was alive. This is what you do to me."

I look down and gasp again.

Pax has his cock...er, his *verpa*...out. And he's hard as a rod.

And...huge.

So fucking *huge*. A great, veiny tree trunk, swollen and purple at the head. A droplet of pre-cum glistens on the tip, and more than anything in the world I want to bend down and lick it off.

So I do.

Because fuck it.

Because he's my friend, and he's hurting, and I know how to take the hurt away.

Because I will never, ever be normal, and maybe I'm tired of pretending.

I drop to my knees on the floor of my childhood bedroom, planting my hands beneath his thighs to pull him closer. I sink down over him, letting him fill my mouth. I stretch my lips wide and can only barely fit over the girth of him.

Pax's eyes are twin blue flames, burning only for me.

I've given a bit of head over the years in hostel rooms that smell like feet. The guys usually taste of pot and desperation. They're searching for themselves in the world, just like me. And for a night or two, we search together and somehow still come up feeling emptier than ever.

But Pax...I've never had to search for myself around him because he's always loved me for me. He's always protected me. And now, as I take him in my mouth, as deep as I can until I'm gagging on his length, I realize that he doesn't taste like other boys.

He tastes of sweetness, and blood, and oak leaves caught in the rain.

He tastes like home.

The warm, fuzzy feeling spreads through my body as I stroke him. There's still something about him, about all the ghosts, that isn't quite human. A lightness to them, a sense that what I'm feeling when I touch them isn't touching at all – at least, not in the way I'm used to. That they're not made of atoms, but small bright songs in the dark that have found their way to me.

"You feel amazing," he moans. "Your tongue, it is like silk..."

The head of his shaft hits the back of my throat, and barely any of him is inside my mouth. I curl my fist around him and pump him in time to each stroke of my tongue.

"Don't stop," Pax grunts. "Look at me."

I draw my gaze from his magnificent verpa to his face,

where twin flames burn into me, melting away all my doubt and fear. Behind his eyes, I can see the initials I carved into the ceiling all those years ago.

$$B + P + E + A = 4EVA.$$

"You are so good," he coos. "You are such a good girl."

Pax rocks his hips and fists my hair, but the pain only drives me faster, deeper. He throws back his head and lets out a ghostly howl that rattles the windows. The dark satisfaction in his eyes makes my clit pulse with need.

Pax's fingers tighten as he guides me deeper. He pumps his hips one final time and spills into me.

He tastes like the seaside. He tastes like Pax.

My Pax.

His shoulders sag and his body slumps back on the bed. The kittens have darted into the corner and are playing tug-of-war with the ribbon.

His heavy-lidded eyes watch me with something like worship. He holds out a hand. "Come here. Come down here with me."

I move toward him. "Do you believe me now? Do you believe that I haven't chosen Edward over you?"

"I believe anything those pretty lips want to say to me. Tell me that the stars revolve around the sun—"

"—they do—"

"—or that the Romans are weak, or that the gods don't exist, and I will defend your lies to my dying breath."

I take his hand, and for a moment, as our fingers touch, I can see the faint glimmer of a silver thread wrapping around us both. My heart tugs.

I blink, and the thread is gone.

"Pax." His name tastes strange on my tongue. It is the name

of my childhood protector, but what we did tonight was very much not a children's game. "I think...I think that something is wrong with me."

"Nothing is wrong with you. You are perfect." He tugs on my hand. "Come down here with me and I will show you just how perfect you are."

I shake my head. I can't do it. I want to but...lying beside him, seeing how far we can take this connection...it is too much like the end of something that I'm not yet ready to end. "That actress ghost crossed over tonight, and I *felt* her. In my heart. I felt the cord that tethered her soul to the mortal world unravel. I felt her *leave*. And I think...I had something to do with it."

He frowns. "But that is not how it works. She completed her unfinished business, and so she can cross over. You are not responsible for her, as you haven't been for the others we've seen cross over."

"This was different." I touch my hand to my chest. "I can't explain it, but—"

Rap-rap-rap.

I snap my head in the direction of the noise. "What's that?"

"Something's rapping on the window."

Rap-rap-rap.

It's just rain. When I'd glanced out earlier, the wind had kicked up, so maybe a summer storm was coming in...

No, not raindrops. The full moon peeks through the trees, casting a pale shaft of light across the room. The sky is clear. And that sound is too regular to be a natural phenomenon. It's as if something hard is tapping against the window...

Something like a bird's beak.

I creep to the window and pull back the edge of the velvet curtain.

The Nevermore shop raven stands on the sill, his dark eyes

ringed in orange fire. I pull up the window, and he flutters inside.

Pax is on his feet in a moment, his sword whirling wildly as he chases the bird around the room. "Get out of here, you foul fiend! You servant of Pluto!"

"Pax, stand down!" I wave my arms. "He's not a threat. He's just a bird."

I'm more than just a bird, thank you very much.

The bird worriedly peers over the edge of the light fixture. Pax backs into the corner and hovers over the beanbag chair, his arms folded and a look on his face that clearly says, 'One wrong move and we'll be roasting raven for dinner.'

"Meow!" Entwhistle leaps onto the arm of the chair beside him, his fur bristled and tail as big as a fox.

Keep all three of those bloodthirsty creatures away from me. The raven glares at Pax and the two kittens as he flutters down onto the bed. His talons sink into my Emily the Strange bedspread. I flop down beside it.

"Hello, again," I say, feeling kind of stupid talking to a bird. "What are you doing here?"

Hang on a sec. The raven bends his neck and uses his foot to scratch behind his head. *Ah, that's better. I came to introduce myself.*

The bird's voice lands in my head, like it was there all along.

My name is Quoth.

"Quoth, huh?" I think of the name of the bookshop and the famous Edgar Allan Poe poem. "That's on-brand."

You have no idea. The bookshop you visited brings fictional characters to life. The surly proprietor you met is actually Heathcliff from Wuthering Heights. I'm the raven from Edgar Allan Poe's poem, and one of Mina's other boyfriends, and you haven't met our other flatmate, the arch-villain James Moriarty—

That is...a *lot* to take in. "Oh, yeah, then who's Mina?"

The love of our lives.

I perk up at that. Yes, I know I'm having a conversation with a raven and hearing that Nevermore Bookshop is magical and brings characters from books to life, but there's something about knowing that just across the valley in Argleton, there's another girl who loves three not-quite-human guys. Like maybe she'd understand about me and the ghosts... "Wait, how are you one of her boyfriends? You're a bird."

I'm a shapeshifter. I have a male form, but I'm generally more comfortable as a bird. Usually. Except when there are two cats and a homicidal Roman in the room.

"Why are you talking to the bird?" Pax huffs. "Don't believe a word he says. Birds are dicks. They shit on Roman soldiers from a great height while we are marching, and we can't stop to wipe off the feces. Once, a bird shat right in my eye and I had to walk around with it crusted shut for the whole watch."

That was my great-great-great-great-great uncle. He always had excellent aim.

To Pax, he says, "Croak."

Pax waggles his sword. "That bird just insulted me, didn't he?"

"Please leave him alone, Pax." To Quoth I say, "If you're a shapeshifter, then prove it. Transform for me."

The raven hops up and down. *You know how in movies when shifters always appear in their human form with their clothes on? It doesn't work like that in real life. I don't particularly want to expose my dangly bits to your clawed friends over there, and you don't want your friend with the stabby stick in the corner to see you hanging out with a naked guy.*

"A fair point. But if you don't do it, I'm going to think I've imagined this whole conversation."

The raven huffs. But he unfurls his wings. At first, I don't see anything happening. There are no sparkles or "shazam!" sound. But then his wings grow outward.

"Croak!" the raven cries, tossing its head. His legs lengthen, his body contorts, and the sound of bones snapping and muscles twisting rends the night.

The raven tips forward off the sill onto my floor. What lands is a crouching man, his skin prickled with feathers that retract to reveal pale skin and lots of intricate, artistic tattoos. A waterfall of shimmering black hair falls down his back. He lifts his head and his hair falls away to reveal the most exquisite features and the same fire-rimmed eyes that first regarded me from the top of a bookshelf.

Mina is a lucky, lucky woman.

"Hello," he says.

Okay, so he's a shapeshifter.

Magic is real.

I should be more surprised. I should be terrified. But I'm not. It feels like something I always knew in my heart but desperately wanted to deny.

I did just give head to a ghost. I guess I've fully accepted that I'm a freak.

I move to the bed and drag off the duvet and toss it at him. Quoth wraps it around his middle and leans against the windowsill.

"Hello," I say. "Thank you for shifting for me."

"You're welcome." His smile is shy and dazzling. "You have questions for me, I think? You can lower your sword, Roman. I'm not here to hurt Bree."

"I'll be the judge of that," Pax growls, but he does drop his sword a little.

"You can see Pax?"

"I can see all the ghosts, same as you, but I can't hear them. It's a recent thing. I think it's because I died a few months ago and Mina made a deal to bring me back to life. Ever since then, I've been able to see ghosts."

Just like me. Interesting. "Does Mina know?"

"I haven't told her yet." Quoth holds his hands out to me in a gesture of supplication. "Please don't tell her. I'm...I'm waiting until the right time. We've dealt with a lot lately, and we've still got to solve Rasmussen's murder... But when I saw what happened at the shop tonight, I knew I had to talk to you."

I swallow. "And what happened at the shop?"

"You helped that ghost cross over. Only, what you really did was unwind a silver cord from her chest and then break it, and the ghost disappeared."

"No, I didn't."

"Yes, you did."

"No." I glare at the bird, then jab my thumb at Pax, as if to indicate we'd be having Kentucky Fried Raven for dinner this evening should he disagree with me. "I didn't."

"Fine, fine, you totally didn't use some powerful magic on that ghost. You and I are in complete agreement about that." Quoth winks at me before dropping the duvet, bending over, and transforming back into his raven. The bird hops along the windowsill.

I don't suppose you have any berries lying around you could give me? I'm starving—ow, hey!

The bird flaps its wings as I grab it around the middle and raise it to my face. "I am low on patience and possibly filled with magic I can't control, and I've got two kittens and a centurion in the corner who like to play with their food, so you'd better tell me why you came here. What do you want?"

"Croak!" The raven thrashes wildly.

I only came to tell you that you're not alone. I know it can feel so lonely being different. But you're not alone. Mina really wants to be your friend, and so do I.

I release him. The bird drops onto the duvet, his chest rising and falling and his wings thrashing as he struggles to right himself. "Thanks, birdie. Sorry about being rough. It's been a long, strange day."

I understand. Quoth hops onto the windowsill, sweeping one wing out and ducking his head in an adorable little bow. I nod in return.

"Hey, Quoth?"

Yes?

"Could you do a job for me?"

Is it dangerous?

I shrug. "I don't know. I know that your Mina is looking into the murders of Rasmussen and that actress. If you have access to Rasmussen's records, could you see if he's sold any artifacts on behalf of Kieran Myers? Especially if they're not 'official.' And can you bring me that paperwork?"

It would be my pleasure.

The bird swoops off. As I watch him soar behind the trees, back toward Argleton and his Mina, I notice a shadow moving on the edge of the graveyard.

No, not a shadow. Three shadows.

I lean a little further out the window, straining to listen. Someone giggles. There's a whisper and a clinking of glass bottles.

Someone's trespassing in the cemetery.

That's not out of the ordinary. The Grimdale Graveyard is often host to illicit teenage gatherings. Dani and I used to spend nights hanging out on Edward's grave, smoking our first cigarettes and discussing serial killers in our goth kid rite of passage. But we aren't the only people from Grimdale Comprehensive to use it as a hang-out spot, and I suppose the tradition has been passed to the next generation...

Or has it? The three figures move beneath a shaft of moonlight near Edward's grave, and I recognize Kelly, Leanne, and Alice, their arms laden down with alcohol bottles and snacks and what look like cans of paint.

"We're here." Alice sets her bag down on the plinth of Edward's tomb. "You dragged me out here in the middle of the night. Let's have a drink so I can get home to Mum."

Pax comes up behind me, his sword still drawn. Moon pads around his ankles, her nose twitching nervously as she studies the scene outside.

"Those are the mean girls from your school," he growls. "What are they doing here? Do you want me to decapitate them?"

"No. Not yet. Let's find out what they're doing here first." I lean forward, aware that without the lights on in my room, I'm completely invisible to them. I crack the window an inch so I can hear their conversation better.

Kelly is scolding Alice. "You're such a nana now. Why do you want to go home – your mum can't even talk to you. We're going to have way more fun out here. Remember all those crazy parties we had in the cemetery with Riley and his friends?"

"We're not in high school anymore," Alice says. In an excellent self-preservation move, she doesn't take the open bottle of strawberry vodka Kelly proffers. "And a man just died here. We should have some respect. Please tell me you're not going near the police tape. I don't want to mess up their investigation."

Leanne gulps down the vodka and sticks her tongue out at Alice. I can't tell in the gloom, but I bet the tip is bright pink. "Gross, no. We're not going anywhere near the crime scene. We're going to revive another one of our old traditions – showing creepy Bree Mortimer that she doesn't belong here. Remember all those things we used to leave at her house? That was hilarious. My favorite was when we drew ghost faces on all those tampons and then stuffed her letterbox with them. She cried when she found them." Leanne sniggers.

"My favorite is when you wrote her those letters from all those dead people we got from the gravestones here." Kelly opens a packet of crisps. "Remember how she used to skip to the letterbox to see if she got another one?"

Alice wrote those?

My cheeks burn with fresh humiliation.

I remember those letters well. I got one every few days for a couple of months. They were lovely stories from the ghosts of Grimdale cemetery, filled with historical details and questions about my life. So many lonely ghosts who wanted a friend, each one writing to me in their own distinctive handwriting. They told me to write them back and post my letters through a grating on the Montgomery Mausoleum. This I did diligently – spilling my hopes and fears and problems at school to these mystery ghosts even though Ambrose, Pax, and Edward all said it was a terrible idea. And they were right. Kelly Kingston shared the most embarrassing passages over social media, and that solidified my status as the school's freak ghost whisperer. I thought Kelly had been hanging out in the cemetery with her boyfriend Riley and stumbled on the letters, but it was actually a prank that Alice had masterminded.

I'm sorry, Dani. I don't think your girlfriend and I will ever get on.

"I remember well." Alice sighs as she accepts the vodka and takes a swig.

Beside me, Pax growls, low in his throat. I thrust my arm out to stop him from leaping out the window after her. I'm definitely fine with him peeling all three of those bitches, but I want to hear what else they say first.

Kelly dumps out the contents of her bag on top of Edward's

copulating cherub frieze. "I've got a plan for tonight that's even better."

"What is all the stuff?" Alice leans forward.

Kelly holds up a huge white object that flaps in the wind. "It's a wedding dress – can you believe it? I found it at the charity shop. It's very Ms. Havisham. And Leanne got us red paint from her boyfriend's shop. I thought we'd make it all bloody and then hang it from this grave, and then we could write some spooky messages in the red paint on the fence, or maybe on those ugly squirrel ornaments in their garden. This grave is right in Bree's sightline, isn't it, Alice? She'll see it and think it's a ghost. I'm brilliant, aren't I?"

"This isn't brilliant. It's childish," Alice growls. "I'm not doing it."

"Shut up, Alice. Of course you are." Kelly holds out a broom handle. "You keep this steady while I hang the dress and—"

Alice grabs the handle from her and tosses it on the ground. "You told me that we were going to the cemetery to relive old times. The three of us having a drink, talking the way we used to, like real friends. Not pulling some stupid prank."

"You're just saying that because you're in love with Ghost Girl's weird friend, the undertaker. Well, newsflash, you can't hang around with freaks and also with us," Kelly sniffs. "We have a reputation to uphold."

"You and your reputation can suck my lady balls. Just because Dani and I have a thing doesn't mean I care about Ghost Girl. I don't give a shit about Bree Mortimer, but I'm not going to desecrate someone's grave just so you can relive your high school mean-girl days. That's stupid."

"Suit yourself," Kelly simpers. She jams the broom handle into the dirt and drops the wedding dress over top of it. It looks pretty effective, the lace sleeves flapping in the wind. "Leave, then. Come on, Leanne, let's get this set up."

Alice folds her arms and glares at her friend. "It's a public cemetery. I'm staying right here. And if you set that up, I'm going to tear it down and call the police."

"Fine." Kelly glares at Alice as she picks up the stick and dress and marches away. "We'll stick it in her front garden."

Oh no, you fucking aren't.

"I'll crucify them!" Pax roars as he dives for the window. "I'll find a lion and kill it just so that it can become a ghost lion and consume their flesh over and over again before they're driven mad from the pain—"

"Wait, I've got this one." I race down the staircase. I pull open the side door, grab the garden hose from the implement rack, and sneak around the side of the house.

Kelly and Leanna have stepped over the low stone fence Dad laboured over for one whole summer. They hold up their paint-splattered doll and start hammering her into the garden bed next to Dad's mosaic – he made it as a present for Mum during his mosaic phase, and it includes the twelve signs of the zodiac. Giggling, Kelly and Leanne stand the white scarecrow upright in the garden, and then set about prying the lid off a can of red paint.

They're going to get that paint all over Dad's mosaic.

I see red. I now know what Pax refers to when he says that battle lust overcomes him, because I am not fucking human any longer. Pax yells behind me, but I don't hear a word. I sprint toward them, hose raised, and I don't know if I'm going to wet them or tear them apart with my teeth.

"Oh, look, it's Ghost Girl—" Kelly's smirk turns into a cry as a stream of water hits her straight in the face. She staggers back, arms flailing ungracefully, and trips over her bag of booze, landing ass over Louboutins in the herb garden.

"Get the fuck off my property, right now." I take aim with

the hose again. "You have to the count of three, or I call the police."

"This is silk, you bitch." Kelly splutters, tugging at her skirt as she climbs out of the garden. There's rosemary stuck in her hair. "You're the one who'll pay for assaulting us with that hose."

"One..."

"Come on, Kelly." Leanne tugs her friend's sleeve. "I don't want to get in trouble. And Riley will kill you if the police get involved."

"Two..."

"Fine, we're going." Kelly bends over to pick up her bag. I step onto the mosaic, keeping the hose aimed at Leanne, thinking she'd be the one to make a move on Kelly's behalf. Too late, I realize my mistake. Kelly grabs the paint can she and Leanne had gotten open and hurls it at me.

Red paint splatters all over me. I taste paint. The acrid stench of it flares in my nostrils, scratching the back of my throat.

"Bree?" Pax cries as he comes up behind me. "What did they do to you?"

But I don't care about myself. I stare at my feet, where the beautiful mosaic Dad made back when he could actually do things like that with his hands is now drowned in a river of red paint.

No. Please, no.

Tears prick at my eyes, but I won't give them the satisfaction of seeing me cry.

I don't have to worry about that.

Kelly whips out her phone and snaps a bunch of pictures.

"That's exactly how you want to look to the world, you freak show Wednesday Addams," Kelly smirks. "Grimdale was better off with you gone. The sooner you learn that, the better —argh!"

Kelly cries out as Pax shoves her hard with both hands. I expect his hands to go straight through her but with his new power, he hurls her into the air. She flies across the garden and topples arse over heels into Dad's koi pond with a huge splash.

"I'll save you, Kelly." Leanne races after her. She tries to grab Kelly's arm but Kelly is thrashing about so much that Leanne ends up completely drenched, too.

"Yussss!" Pax does a victory dance, flipping up his tunic to wave his bare Roman arse in Kelly's face. "That's what you get for hurting my Bree."

Kelly splutters as she tries to gain purchase on the slippery side of the pond. "What...what did you do to me? There are slimy fish in here! How did you...did you throw me all this way?"

"She didn't even touch you," Alice says dryly. "I was watching Bree the whole time. She was a good five feet away from you."

"Maybe it wasn't me," I say, my whole body shaking with rage and triumph. "Maybe it was one of my ghosts."

"Kelly, let's go," Leanne drags her sodden friend onto the grass. "I'm scared."

"You won't get away with this, freak," Kelly hisses. She and Leanne toss down their paint cans and other props and race out of the garden. Pax yells obscenities in Latin, but he doesn't go after them. He gathers me in his arms and crushes me in a bear hug.

Alice stands at the gate, her green eyes flickering over me. She opens her mouth, but instead of saying anything, she snaps it shut, turns on her heel, and stalks away.

31

BREE

"Of all the juvenile things to do." Dani stares down at the circular mosaic. She came with some special chemicals she uses in her embalming lab, and we'd spent two hours scrubbing at the stones under the light of the full moon. We got most of the paint off before it dried, but the mosaic will always have a pink tinge.

"I wish I could have seen Kelly flailing about in that pond." Satisfaction drips from Edward's tone.

"I wish we could help," Ambrose says forlornly. He and Edward and Albert are gathered on the front porch, watching us work. Well, Ambrose isn't technically watching. Pax stomped off in the direction of the old Roman shrine in the heart of Grimdale wood to ask Jupiter to curse Kelly Kingston.

"No," I grunt as Dani scrubs at some stubborn paint around Pisces' tail. My back ached, my arms ached, and I can still taste paint every time I swallow. "You don't."

"Yes, don't speak for all of us, adventurer. I, for one, haven't the constitution for manual labour." Edward lies back on the porch swing, one arm dangling lazily over the edge, long fingers relaxed, expressive. I try not to think of where those fingers were only the night before...

"Hey, are you wearing that stone again?" Dani sits back and wipes her brow. "A strange thing just happened. I think I can hear Edward."

"That..." I can't say that it's strange because so many unusual things have happened today. I think seeing a raven turn into a hot guy has made me stop trying to explain away everything weird. I take the moldavite out of my pocket. The little green stone shimmers in the light. "That's something. What do you hear?"

"Not much, just a whisper. Something about manual labour."

The crystal falls through my fingers and clatters on the mosaic tiles. Dani *can* hear Edward. I don't understand it. I don't feel anything when I hold it. It can't be magical, and yet...

Dani can hear Edward.

"You—" I jab my finger at Edward as I pick up the moldavite again. "Keep talking. What's he saying now?" I ask Dani as Edward flops onto his stomach and starts ranting.

"He's lamenting that he's no longer in a position to impose the death penalty, because those three girls deserve the harshest possible punishment. And now he's all offended because Ambrose said that if he really wanted to punish them, he should give them moldavite stones and force them to listen to him recite his poetry for hours on end..."

"Wow," Edward stares at Dani with a mix of awe and defiance. "She really can hear me."

"But you can only hear Edward?" I ask. "And you can't see him, or any of the others?"

"No. Just the whispers of Mr. Arrogant McKeatsFace here." Dani tries to give Edward a fist bump, but he thinks she's trying to punch him and puts up his hands in a pugilist's stance.

I place the moldavite on the tiles and back away to the edge of the garden.

"I'm better than Keats will ever be, and I'll fight anyone who says otherwise," Edward declares.

I glance at Dani.

"If he's talking now, I can't hear him."

"A power I wish I possessed," Ambrose says with a sigh.

"So you can only hear Edward when I'm holding the stone," I say. "You up for a few more experiments?"

"And have the chance to converse with a spirit from beyond the veil?" Dani's eyes light up in excitement. "Hell yes."

32
BREE

We move inside and try a couple more experiments – Dani holds the stone and Edward yells in her ear. Nothing. Next, we place the stone on the floor and let the ghosts try to pick it up, but they can't. I hold the stone and the ghosts touch things and move objects, and I move further and further away from them until they can't move any longer – nearly the depth of the house. Then we take the moldavite away and try it again. This time, I can only move to the next room before they can no longer touch things.

By then, it's past midnight and I'm still reeling from what Pax and I got up to and Kelly ruining the mosaic. Dani catches me yawning and declares it time to call it a night.

"I'll think of some more experiments we can try," Dani says as she shrugs on her coat. "But I think you have to accept that whatever's giving the ghosts their new powers, it's coming from you. The moldavite simply amplifies it."

That's what I'm afraid of.

The door closes behind Dani, and I'm alone with the ghosts. I hold up a hand. "I know that you all have questions. So do I. But I can't think about this now, okay? I just can't...Not until the mosaic is completely clean. I'm sorry, I know this is disappointing when you're learning new ghost powers—"

"We could never be disappointed in you," Ambrose says.

He leans forward and kisses me on the forehead, that same loving gesture he lavished on me as a kid. Only now, as his lips touch mine, the heat sears through me, and I find myself thinking about all these new powers that the ghosts possess, and how we might use them...

Ambrose's lips linger a little longer than what can be considered proper. When he pulls away, his blue eyes are bright and rippled with sunshine. He disappears down the hall, heading to his little secret room.

Edward steps forward, his eyes dark and dangerous. He takes my hand in his and brings my knuckles to his lips. His eyes, which are usually cold obsidian, smoulder with flecks of orange flame as he lays a kiss on my knuckles that manages to leave my whole body trembling with want.

"Invite me to your chamber," he whispers, his eyes locked with mine. "I will make you forget about what those vipers did."

"As tempting as that is," I wrap my finger around one of his dark curls, rubbing the silken strands, marveling at how impossibly real he feels, "I just learned that I'm the source of whatever is giving you guys these new powers. We don't know what this is, or how to control it. I could hurt you. I could..."

...*send you through the veil, the way I did with that actress...*

And then I'd be truly alone.

Edward steps back and bows. His eyes rake over my body, barely holding back his hunger. "If you change your mind..."

"I know where to find you." I swallow down the urge to fall into his arms.

"Goodnight, Brianna."

My full name on his lips sounds like a poem.

316

Pax says nothing as he follows me down the hall to the guest bedroom. When I step out of the bathroom, he's no longer visible, but a Roman sandal pokes out from the bottom of the curtain.

I drop my dressing gown and slide into bed, suddenly aware that I'm naked, alone, with Pax, and when I swallow, I can still taste ghost cum on my tongue.

"Goodnight, Pax."

The curtain shifts.

"Goodnight, Bree."

I pull the covers up. They rake over my bare skin, leaving trails of fire. I know Pax can't see anything, but I feel naked anyway.

"Pax?"

He pokes his head out, his face expectant. "Yes?"

"What we did before...all this excitement...I just want you to know that..."

"I am disappointed."

My heart thuds. He's disappointed. Did I do something wrong?

"Oh?"

I hate how small my voice sounds.

"I am disappointed," he continues. "You made me come so hard that I saw the gods behind my eyelids, and then the birdie knocked on the window before I could return the favor."

Oh.

Oh.

"That's okay," I say quickly, my blood molten lava. "I mean, we probably shouldn't be doing this stuff anyway. We're playing with magic that we don't understand..."

"Your lips are magic. Your tongue is magic. *You* are magic. Next time," he growls, "you will be the one screaming my name."

Pax fades back into the curtain, and I sink into the blankets, warning my throbbing pussy and the ache in my belly to calm the fuck down so I can sleep.

"It doesn't look too bad," Ambrose says as we all stand around the zodiac mosaic in the morning sunlight.

"You can't see it," Edward points out.

"I know, but I'm trying to think positively."

I clutch my mug of tea to my chest. It's not so bad. Dani and I got the worst of the paint off last night. There's a little around the edges of some of the stones, and the grout is pretty much permanently going to be red, but it's really not too bad.

But as I stare at the mosaic that my dad spent a whole summer making during his arts and crafts phase, I can't help but think about how nothing is permanent. I thought my dad would live out his days going to old man rock concerts, annoying Mum with endless vague questions, trying new hobbies, and filling the house garden with strange and wonderful creations.

That was the plan. That's what my dad has worked every day of his life to achieve. And now...it all has to change.

It makes me think about these terrifying new powers that seem to be coming from *me*. What if I can't figure out how to control them? What if I hurt someone, living or dead? What if I accidentally send the ghosts away?

Nothing is permanent, not even death.

A warm hand falls on my shoulder, shooting tingles down my spine. I turn to face Edward, his usually haughty expression drawn with concern.

"They shall pay for hurting you," he says, low and menacing, and even though I know he's a ghost and he has no royal powers anymore, I can almost believe that he could order Kelly Kingston's head on a spike.

I have to admit, it's a nice image.

"I'm angry enough to stab them, but stabbing is too good for them," Pax growls as he paces around the mosaic. "We Romans employ many creative ways of dealing with our enemies. We have this punishment where we stuff a person into a sack with a snake and a monkey and then throw the sack into a river."

"No stabbing," I say firmly. "And while I think the animal sack has a certain savage poetry, no way am I subjecting a poor innocent monkey to Kelly Kingston."

Pax peers forlornly down at his sword.

"We could haunt them," Ambrose suggests, his face hopeful.

"Yes!" Edward pumps his fist in the air, then seems to remember that he's supposed to be a prince. He immediately switches to rubbing his chin. "I mean, that sounds interesting, peasant."

"No," I fold my arms.

"What is haunting?" Pax asks.

"Do you remember that dreary writer Poe Bree studied in high school?" Ambrose asks. "He was obsessed with hauntings."

"I tune out all discussions about poetry," Pax says. "Nothing compares to traditional Roman war poems. 'Upon thy bloodied battlefield, I scatter thy bones—"

He drops to his knees, thrusts his sword into the air, and continues to recite at the top of his lungs "—where Mars' brave men plowed their swords into their enemies and jiggled them around—"

"Now look what you've done!" I yell at Ambrose.

"I didn't mean to!"

"—and pulled their guts out through their arseholes—"

"Oh, I like that line," Edward says. "It has a lovely rhythm. Now, if you could make it a rhyming couplet—"

He must see the look on my face, because he thrusts his hand around the Centuiron's neck and covers Pax's mouth before he can start a second stanza.

"Remember all those horror movies we used to watch with Brianna? Where the innocent family moves into the creepy house and then the ghosts make them so miserable they have to call in a priest? That's a haunting." Edward strokes his chin. "I think the explorer is onto something. We could go to this Kelly Kingston's house and haunt it so bad that she'll be too afraid to hurt our Brianna."

"But how can we haunt them if they can't see us?" Pax asks, getting off his knee.

"Simple. Bree comes with us. She hides in the bushes outside and holds her stone and *boom*, we are ghosts from horror movies who can move objects and tear up the curtains and whisper spooky things." Edward looks extremely pleased with himself.

"This is a bad idea," I say.

"It's really not," a new voice says.

I whirl around. Albert stands on the path, staring down at the mosaic with disgust. "I saw what happened from the window, and I agree with Edward. Your dad worked so hard on this mosaic, and those girls need to learn a lesson. Your ghosts should haunt their asses."

"Welcome to team 'haunt the bitches'?" Edward grins.

"It's a terrible idea," I plead, sensing that I'm losing this battle. "Knowing my luck, the stone won't work, and Kelly will find me lurking in the bushes and will have even more ammunition to make my life miserable."

"That's not going to happen." Pax clamps his hand on my shoulder. "You must let us solve a problem for you for once. All my life I have tried to protect you, but I've never been able to do anything when those girls hurt you. And now..." he flexes his huge arm muscles. "Now I can feel the bloodlust coursing through my veins at the thought of revenge. Now I feel *Roman* again."

It would be nice to see Kelly Kingston afraid...

I think of all the horrible pranks they pulled on me in intermediate and high school, all the times they left me out or called me Ghost Girl or sniggered every time I raised my hand in class until I was too afraid to say anything at all. I think of how alone I felt because of them.

You don't believe in ghosts, Kelly. Well, you're about to.

I try to suck in a deep breath, but all I can taste is paint. "Fuck it. Let's haunt their asses."

33

BREE

"I can't believe I've resorted to haunting my childhood bullies," I mutter as I sink into the begonia garden beneath Kelly's front window. She's living in a little annex off Riley Jenson's parents' house. Riley's parents are rich enough to afford a brick Victorian on the corner of Grimwood Crescent but – thankfully for my purposes – not rich enough to afford security cameras.

"Sssssh," Pax booms. "If they hear you, it will destroy the haunting."

"Your prince commands you to hold that crystal nice and tight," Edward says. He tries to crack his knuckles the way Pax did, but all he manages to do is make a face. "Ow. This hurts."

"How can that even hurt?" I groan as I take out the moldavite and hold it in my palm. "You don't have knuckles."

"I'm excited about this." Ambrose rubs his hands together. "Let's get in there. I can hear them talking."

The three ghosts take deep breaths and dive through the wall, their limbs disappearing into the bricks. They've been practicing controlling their new abilities and can now turn on and off the ability to touch things at will, which is nice for them, but also terrifying because we still have no idea why this is happening.

I spent half the day today trying to get Annabel Myers on the phone, and the other half googling the magical properties of moldavite, which has left me more confused than ever. The internet agrees that the crystal itself isn't magical – it enhances the magic of the user. The words 'celestial energy', 'inter-dimensional conduit', and 'facilitates journeys to other lives' are now burned into my brain.

I don't want to be an inter-dimensional conduit, thank you very much. I just want to be a normal person. With three invisible friends.

Who are maybe more than friends now.

Maybe.

I crouch down in the flowerbed, straining to hear as I clutch the little stone to my heart. The three witches told us that they saw the girls having lunch at the pub, and they were going to have drinks at Kelly's tonight, so I was pretty confident they'd be here. But I was relieved to hear Alice's barking laugh as Leanne tells a story about some lady at her tennis club who never wears underwear beneath her skirt.

"Hey, I have an idea. Let's go into London this weekend." Kelly's voice grows loud, excited. I hear the windowpane sliding up, and flatten my back against the hard brick. My heart races. *She's right above me.* "We haven't been anywhere except the pub in ages. I'll get Riley to give me his credit card and we can spend up large on Oxford Street, have high tea at the Savoy, maybe go to a spa..."

I can't believe I let those ghosts talk me into this. She's going to see me. She's going to—

"I can't this weekend." Alice's voice comes from further back in the room. At least their conversation is easier to hear with the window open. "I promised Dad I'd take him to the museum."

"Blow it off," Kelly scoffs. "It's just your dad, and you work at that stupid museum. You can take him any time. Bor-ing."

"It's not a stupid museum. It's the museum where my dad worked for ten years as chief curator of Roman coins. I'm hoping it will stimulate his memory. I promised him I'd take him, and I'm not missing it. Go to London without me."

"You're no fun anymore." Kelly moves away from the window. Her voice is sullen, loaded with meaning. This is an argument they've had before.

My heart leaps into my mouth. Slowly, I turn around, trying not to crunch any twigs, and raise myself on my knees to peer over the windowsill.

Kelly perches in a Nina Campbell armchair, her long legs crossed, a Prada slingback dangling from the toes on one foot and a Champagne glass clutched in her pink, manicured talons. She looks like she's auditioning for the next season of Footballers' Wives. Leanne lies across the sofa, picking at a loose thread in her Alice Temperley jumper, trying to look like she doesn't care that Kelly's face is red with anger. Alice, who was sitting on an ottoman beside the fireplace, throws down her magazine, tosses her golden blonde waves over her shoulder, and stalks over to the bar.

"Whatever. I'm going to get another drink."

As Alice slams glasses and smashes ice, a ghostly hand attached to a dapper Victorian frock coat reaches out from inside the cabinet, grabs the rim of her glass, and makes it float through the air in front of her face.

"What's this?" Alice backs away from the bar. "Kelly, is this some kind of a joke?"

My heart leaps into my throat.

The haunting has begun.

34

PAX

Ambrose makes the glass dance around Alice's head, sloshing alcohol in her face until she screams and jerks away. The other two haven't noticed anything spooky yet, but that will change in a moment. I glance out the window to make sure Bree is watching. I very much want her to enjoy every moment of this.

And then I grab the curtain with both hands and rustle it.

"Hey, Leanne, would you close the window," Kelly snaps. "The wind is picking up and it's making the curtains jerk, and Alice think that she's seeing things, like glasses floating through the air."

"I'm not seeing things!" Alice reaches for the glass, but Ambrose jerks it out of her reach. "If you'd turn around and look, you'd see that it's floating all on its own."

"Right. I turn around and you, what, throw your drink in my face?" Kelly sniffs. "No thanks. I'm not falling for another one of your ghost jokes. Bree pushed me last night and I won't hear either of you say otherwise. Now, I want to do something. I'm so bored, I can't stand it here. Even Bree Mortimer sounds like she's having more fun than us. Do you realize how pathetic that is? Our lives are way better than hers, so why does she get to go travelling when Alice won't even get on a train to poxy London—"

"So go to London without me. Problem solved." Alice's eyes dart to the door. She tries to step around the glass, but Ambrose moves it between her and the only escape route. "I really think you two should turn around and see this—"

"London by myself isn't fun! Who wants to get a mani or go to high tea by yourself—"

"Life isn't only about fun, Kelly. Some of us care about people other than ourselves, and we have responsibilities —argh!"

Alice dives for the door, but Ambrose is faster. He tosses the whole glass at her, and vodka and cranberry splashes all over her silk wrap dress.

"Guys, please don't fight," Leanne begs. She gets up and moves toward Alice. "Kelly didn't throw the drink at you. She was all the way over here—"

"Then who did?" Alice snaps, shaking her dripping hair. "Because I didn't throw it at myself. And why is that curtain doing that when there's no breeze?"

She points a shaking finger right at me. I stop making the curtain dance, poke the hilt of my sword into the fabric, and start to wiggle it around.

"Look at me," I call out. "I'm a big scary ghost! Woooo!"

Kelly's looking at the curtain now. She narrows her eyes. "Is that a...horny ghost?"

"It kind of does look like a giant dick getting hard behind there," Leanne licks her lips. "I'm sure it's just a trick of the light or something, but imagine if ghosts *were* real and they were actually hot dudes? A ghost could eat me out under the table while I'm at one of Simon's boring work dinners and he'd never know."

"You're not scaring them. You're *titilating* them," Edward leaps out from behind the bookshelf and frowns at me. "Allow me to show you how it's done."

He storms across the room and walks right through Kelly Kingston.

"Oof." My belly churns just watching him do it. Walking through people is terrible. It makes me feel sicker than the night Marcus Flavius and I decided to get drunk on Egyptian wine...

"Owwwwww." Edward doubles over, clutching his head. But I'm more interested in Kelly. She wobbles on her feet, her expression turning from sanctimonious bitch to terrified in less time than it takes a Roman legionnaire to cut his toenails after his first day marching in Roman sandals.

"Did...did anyone else feel that?" she whispers, hugging her arms around her body. "It's turned ice cold."

"I don't feel anything," Leanne says.

"The only thing ice cold around here is your heart," Edward cries out. Kelly's face twists. She heard him.

"Did you hear that?" Kelly grabs Leanne's arm and shakes her. "Someone said that I'm...that I'm..."

"Ambrose, go!" I yell.

Ambrose stalks through the room, sweeping his cane in every direction. The ball on the bottom raps against the floor, and the girls scream and scramble out of the way of his path. He knocks over stacks of books and a lamp, and sends Kelly's bottles of colored potions she uses to paint her nails flying everywhere. I check that Bree's watching, and she is, her eyes wide as her arch-enemies cower before our might.

I flip my sword over and chop at the curtains, tearing them to ribbons. When I'm done with them, I move onto the fancy chair, ripping chunks of stuffing from the cushion.

Edward knocks books off the bookshelves. "Urgh, whoever put together this collection has appalling taste. Byron? What a hack. Dan Brown? Never heard of him. And what the devil is a Harry Potter?"

Ambrose catches a wine glass on the metal ball of his cane and moves it slowly through the air, right in front of their faces.

"Th-th-that's not possible." Kelly trembles. "Alice, do something!"

"Why do I have to do something?"

"You're the brainbox who went to Cambridge."

"I didn't read in Occult Studies." Alice squares her shoulders and plasters her mouth into a brave line. She claps her hands. "All right, ghosts. You have our attention. What do you want?"

I gesture to Edward. He steps forward and whispers in Alice's ear, "Leave Bree alone."

Alice stiffens.

"Bree?" Kelly screeches. "Bree Mortimer sent you?"

At the window, Bree's shaking her head frantically, her hands over her mouth as she struggles not to crack up laughing.

"Yes," Edward intones, making his voice wobble. He does sound quite fearsome. "We are the spectral servants of Bree. We pushed you into the pond the other night, and we're here to tell you to stop hurting her or else..."

Edward jams his hand into the electrical socket, and the lights go completely dead.

"Aaaaaaaaah! Ghoooooooosts!"

We leave the three girls clutching each other and screaming for their mummies. We go out the front door – much more pleasant than walking through a wall – and meet Bree on the street. She has twigs and bits of leaf in her hair. She throws her arms around me, pressing her tiny body against mine. I let myself relax and allow her touch to permeate me. I like feeling the curve of her body in mine, the way her heart thuds against her ribs, the swell of her sweet bosoms as she...

If Bree can feel my little soldier pitching his tent beneath my tunic, she's too busy laughing to comment.

"I can't believe it." Tears of happiness roll down Bree's cheeks. "That was amazing. Did you see Kelly's face when Edward walked through her? She was *shitting* herself. And Ambrose, when you threw that drink at Alice – inspired!"

Ambrose takes a deep bow. "I am particularly proud of that bit."

"Hey," I grumble. "What about me? I was the commander of this sortie into enemy territory—"

"I could never forget you, my Pax," Bree peers up at me with those intense honey eyes. "You've always protected me. When you tore up the curtains, I think I've never loved you more than at that moment—"

I've never loved you more.

The words soak into my body like sunshine. I bask in them, the most beautiful words anyone has ever spoken to me.

For years we had to watch Bree endure Kelly Kingston's taunts and pranks, and we were never solid enough to do anything about it. But now Kelly will live in fear of Bree and her spooky men, and that is as it should be. The world is set to rights.

And Bree loves me.

I peer down at her face, and I want to tell her that I love her, too. That I have always loved her from the moment she first stretched her tiny baby hand out to me. From the moment she *saw* me. But now the love I felt for a frightened child and a struggling friend has blossomed into something more...and I want to tell her what it means to me that she feels the same, but I have no words for love, no words that will do justice the big, warm, joyous bulge of my heart. And as I'm trying to figure out what to say, I see Bree's face.

She's *terrified*.

"Bree?"

She covers her mouth with her hand, her eyes wide with fear.

I move to hold her again. "You do not need to be afraid. Those girls will never bother you again."

"I'm not..." she jerks away from me, and I cry out at the sudden loss of her. "It's not that, Pax. It's just that...I have to go."

"But we should celebrate. We should go to the pub and sniff some roast beef. Or do you have any other enemies who need haunting?" I reach for my sword. "We have twenty-five years of revenge to catch up on. We should get started now."

"Er, no, that's fine. Thank you, all of you, for doing this for me." Bree won't look at any of us. "It means the world. But I need to go back to the house for a bit. I'll, um, I'll see you all later..."

"Bree?"

She whirls around and bolts away. I move to go after her, but Ambrose grabs my arm.

"Don't," he whispers. "Let her run."

"But she said that she loves me." I struggle against him.

"Yes," Ambrose's eyes flutter shut. "She loves all of us, old bean. That's the problem. Loving us is breaking her heart."

35
EDWARD

"You don't have to do this if you don't want to," Brianna says as she sits on a park bench opposite the real estate office. She twists her hands nervously in her lap. "I can't get her to answer my phone calls, even though I've left a million messages with her secretary."

"Are you kidding? There could be all kinds of illicit things up there." I rub my hands together in anticipation. "I'm honoured you would consider me for this most important work."

Honestly, I'm elated that Brianna has chosen to speak with me at all. She hasn't talked to any of us after last night's haunting. I very much want to speak with her about what happened at the Shakespeare festival, and make certain she knows that I'm up for another round whenever she wishes, but Ambrose is adamant that we give Brianna space.

"Bree's always needed time alone to think," he says. "Let her do her thinking, and she will come to us when she's ready."

"That is such a nineteenth-century attitude," I admonish him. "Trust me, a melancholy woman does not wish for *space*. She wishes for a fine, princely man to give her a jolly good rogering."

I am not enamored of this 'wait and see' attitude, especially since the last time Brianna decided on something she wanted, she banished us and we had to live in the attic for two years, and then she ran away.

But she found me with my hand in the toaster this morning and asked me to join her on a covert mission to Annabel Myers' office, and I could not refuse her.

I float through the office wall, sucking in my breath as the wall's weight settles in my chest before lifting again. Annabel is sitting at her desk, eating a chicken wrap that doesn't even look appetizing enough to sniff, and scrolling real estate listings for Santorini online while she talks on one of those magical rectangles that modern Livings are so obsessed with. Her signature spike-toes heels have been tossed carelessly beneath her desk.

"...don't worry, darling," she purrs into her magical rectangle. "This has all worked out for the best in the end. With the old couple out of the way, we don't even have to waste our money buying the place – all we need to do is wait until the girl next door is down at the pub and then we'll go back and finish the job. If we cover up the hole, no one needs to even know we were there. Rasmussen's death might slow things down, but once we have the stuff we can find another dealer. And then it's goodbye to crummy Grimdale and hello Santorini. Let me send you this gorgeous villa..."

Interesting. I notice some twigs sticking out of her rubbish bin. I bend down and hunt around. Sure enough, a whole bunch of belladonna twigs, leaves, and berries have been thrown in the basket.

Next, I peer over Annabel's shoulder. On the desk in front of her is a broken old ceramic jug. Annabel moves the jug aside and taps her pen on a printout of a map for Grimwood Crescent. I recognise the cemetery and Grimwood Manor and the Fernsbys' home bordering the edge of the woods. And right in the

middle of the woods, on the boundary between the two properties, is a big red X.

Like a treasure map.

Oh, exciting. This is just like back in my Living days, when
Bunny Westminster read in a mouldy old book that one of my
ancestors hid treasure behind a mirror in the palace, so we went
about the place smashing all the mirrors and found nothing at
all except a few disgruntled spiders.

Actually, come to think of it, that might've been the incident
that resulted in me being kicked out of the palace—

"Argh!"

Pain shoots through my body.

I look down, trying to figure out what happened. Annabel
swirled her chair around to grab her coffee cup from the bookshelf, and propelled herself right through the center of my
being.

The indignity!

The disrespect!

My whole being courses with sickening nausea, sending me
reeling right through the wall and into her boss' office next
door. Imagine my shock to see him bent over his desk with a
burly man behind him doing some quite imaginative things
with an eggplant.

This place really does remind me of my Living days.

"Douglas, will you turn the heat up!" Annabel yells from the
adjoining office. "I've just had the most frightful chill."

"Sure thing!" Douglas croaks out as he urges his friend to
switch to the cantaloupe. I decide that even some things aren't
meant for princely eyes, and duck through the wall.

"Are you okay?" Brianna's delicate features crinkle in
concern. "You look paler than usual."

"She sat *in* me," I murmur, clutching my stomach. I quite
like Brianna's concern for me.

"Oh, you poor thing. Did you find anything good?"

"You mean besides Douglas and his cantaloupe?"

Brianna makes a face. "I don't even want to know. I mean, about the Fernsbys?"

"I am an even better detective than I am a notorious rake. There are remains of a belladonna plant in her rubbish bin. Also, I found out that Annabel and her husband are digging up something in the woods – a treasure! – right on the property line between Grimdale Manor and the Fernsby property. They've been trying to buy the property off the Fernsbys so they could own this treasure outright, but instead, they've decided to dig it up and take it to the island of Santorini, which honestly looks like a place we should consider going now that we can move about, because there are a lot of beautiful people who look like they enjoy an opium pipe—"

"Edward..."

I lift an eyebrow. "You know, you'd look beautiful in the Santorini sunset. We would rent a villa by the ocean and I would paint you in all your naked glory, and then we'd make love on the rocks—"

"*Edward.*" Brianna manages to sound both annoyed and tempted. "What else did they say about this treasure?"

"Just that they're going to wait until you're out of the house, and then they'll go back and 'finish the job.'"

"This is it. Kieran walked through the woods all the time – Albert says they often saw him on their morning walks. He's not allowed to detect on their land, and he's already been in trouble once, so Kieran and Annabel were trying to legally get their hands on that treasure. Whatever's out there must be worth a fortune. Did they say what it was?"

I shake my head. "There was a broken old jug on her desk, but that can't be it. It didn't even have any booze in it."

"Maggie was interested in selling the house because they

needed the money, but Albert didn't want to sell." Bree covers her mouth with her hand. "Would they really murder dear Albert so they could get to this treasure?"

"People kill for less. Why, my cousin the Earl of Dorchester once beheaded a man for blowing his nose on the curtains."

Brianna makes a face. "Rich people are weird."

I sweep a hand. "Weird, yes. And yet, still superior in every way. Allow me to escort you back to the manor. We have a treasure to hunt."

36

BREE

" It's hard to be certain, because I'm looking at a drawing I made based on Edward's instructions, which are in turn based on another drawing he saw only briefly in Annabel's office," I say to Albert, frowning at the map as I step off the woodland path. "But I think it's just down here."

"I think you might be right. I just remembered something – there's a strange arrangement of stones on the slope where Maggie used to harvest feverfew flowers for her migraine balms. Peter Agincourt, the archaeologist at the Grimdale Roman Museum, took a look at it for us a few years back and said he thought it was an altar to the Roman god of war. Apparently, the Romans and Celtic tribes fought a huge battle right here!" Albert gestures to the trees with a far-off look on his face.

I gesture to the trees. "Then lead the way, my good sir."

Albert sets off between the trees. He's got the floating thing down now. As we walk, he talks about Maggie. He's spent every moment of his afterlife trying to get to her, or wafting around the house smelling her things. He only agreed to help me today because I took him to Argleton and stood outside the police station with my moldavite for an hour so he could visit with her. He has a full report about the size and stench of her cell, the faded lustre of her hair, and the fact that Linda Bateman came to visit her and offered to dedicate the first-place ribbon for the Bake Off to her when she won, but the police wouldn't let Maggie carry it back to her cell.

I walk alongside Albert, and I listen. I don't say anything because Albert's love fills the whole wood and also because the hill is steep and I am too busy trying not to die.

I left the ghosts in the house – Pax is watching Bake Off episodes, Ambrose is excitedly turning the pages of a travel memoir for the first time ever, and Edward's enthusiasm for treasure hunting evaporated once he realized digging would be involved. When I asked him if he wanted to come with us, he said, "Brianna, if I must endure nature then it should at least be as part of a hunt or to roll in a field of wildflowers with a beautiful naked duchess," in that haughty Edward voice of his, so I stuck my tongue out at him and left him with his head in the fridge motor.

I know Pax and Ambrose would have come if I told them what I was doing, but I remember that coin in Rasmussen's shop with her husband's name written beside it. I'm not a fool. I can guess what she's found. We're in England, after all. You can't kick a stone without uncovering some ancient burial ground or Victorian rubbish dump. But whatever's out there must be seriously old and valuable if it's worth killing over.

I need time to prepare for what I might uncover.

Nothing is permanent. Not even death.

"This is the spot." Albert circles a beautiful old oak tree. Feverfew flowers dot the slope as it extends down through the trees toward the gully and the public walking path. "We used to come here often on our walks. Maggie loved this tree. Why, I can't count the number of times I laid her down in the grass and we made passionate love right here."

I leap away as if the grass is on fire. "Ew, Albert, I don't need to hear that."

"Er, right. Yes." His faraway expression hardens as he points to something near the stones. "Look. The ground's been disturbed there."

I drop to my knees and inspect the dirt. Albert's right – it's definitely been disturbed. Someone has dumped a bunch of twigs and dead leaves on top to try and hide it, but it's obvious that the dirt has been turned over.

I pick up the garden trowel I brought with me and start to shift the dirt toward me, the way I see people do on *Time Team*.

My fingers brush something – a flat, curved surface that doesn't feel like the other stones scattered beneath the tree. I clear around the object and manage to pull it out of the ground.

It's a squat, rounded pot with a jagged edge where a triangle section is missing. There are carvings on the outer face – horses and men with spears, I think?

I bet this is similar to the pot on Annabel's desk.

I turn it over and scratch away at the dirt crusted to the base, and notice a short inscription. It looks like Latin.

Latin...

Pax.

My stomach drops into my knees as I realize what I might be holding.

Pax's legion fought an important battle here against the Celts. This could be from his campaign. I know nothing about Roman archaeology (I did visit Rome, but if I'm being truly honest, I spent more time knocking back grappa shots with a group of Australian tourists than looking at museums), but this could be like a food pot from the army camp, or some kind of offering to Mars, the war god. Or...or...

It's not a grave. It can't be a grave. Pax says he didn't receive a proper Roman burial. That's his unfinished business. That's why he's still here.

Don't jump to conclusions, Bree. The Ancient Romans ate, slept, and shat all over Grimdale. This pot might have nothing to do with the one *resident Roman soldier who you accidentally—*

I turn the pot over in my hands. If I take this to Pax now, he'll get his hopes up, like the time we found remnants of what we thought was a Roman road when Dad tore down an old toolshed, but it was actually just part of my great-grandfather's BBQ pit. I can't tell Pax about this until I'm absolutely sure...

There is someone who could shed some light on this pot and why Annabel might've wanted it.

"Are you going to keep digging?" Albert asks.

I shake my head. "This pot is old. I don't want to risk damaging anything. Besides, I don't have to dig this up to prevent Annabel from stealing it. Stay here and guard this spot. I'll be back in a jiffy."

I pull off my hoodie and use it to carefully wrap the pot. I cradle it in my arms as I make my way back to the house. I hunt around in the shed until I find my bike, and I dust the cobwebs off the handlebars, place the pot inside the basket, and cycle off into the village.

The bike is rusty, and the ribbons I'd tied to the handlebars are now an unappealing color, but I make it to my destination without going ass over tits. I tie the bike to a tree and walk up the steps of the Grimdale Roman Museum with the pot tucked under my arm.

"*Si vales bene est, ego valeo.* Welcome to the Roman Museum. If you want to see the toga exhibit, I'm afraid—" Alice's words freeze on her lips as she looks up and recognizes me. "Bree? What are you...I mean, why are...I mean, can I help you?"

She says the words in a stiff, formal voice. Her eyes dart to the open door behind me.

She's afraid of me.

I kind of like that.

I place my balled-up hoodie on her desk.

"Can you look at this and tell me what it is?"

"This is a hoodie from some vampire goth band," she says in that same forced voice.

"Oh, gee, I can see the four years you spent studying at Cambridge paid off." I fold down the edges of the hoodie to reveal the pot. Alice's expression changes instantly. Her features soften and become reverent. She leans in close, turning the hoodie to examine the pot from every angle.

"It's an olla," she says. "It's a Roman cooking pot."

Disappointment surges through me. A cooking pot? That could belong to anyone. And it doesn't sound very valuable, not worth Annabel buying a house over. "Can you tell me anything else about it? Like, maybe what year it's from?"

"I can't tell you an exact year – the Romans weren't nice enough to conveniently write the date on everything. But don't look so disappointed." She blinks, and her mouth twists as if she's worried that angering me will make me unleash my ghosts. "This pot is actually very interesting, especially if you're into morbid things, which I know you are. See this edge?" Alice points to the missing piece. "This hasn't broken off in the ground. It's actually been struck with a sword. This pot has been deliberately broken. The Romans would often ritually break objects in this way before they placed them in a grave. You're probably looking at a pot that once held a funeral offering. Probably for a soldier, judging by the pictures on this pot."

A funerary offering for a soldier.

My heart thuds. The blood rushes to my ears, and it takes me a moment to realize Alice has asked me something and I haven't answered.

"I'm sorry, can you repeat that?"

Alice makes a face. "I asked if you found anything else nearby?"

"I didn't really look," I say. "But the ground's disturbed and I believe someone has already pulled coins and maybe other objects from the site."

"They did?" Alice's face frowns. "Isn't this on your land, though? That's illegal."

"It's Albert and Maggie's land, and yeah, they knew that."

"And they haven't reported any coins or gold objects found, because we'd be notified. That's also illegal." She narrows her eyes. "Kieran Myers wasn't involved, was he? I see him detectoring along the public path sometimes."

I tilt my head to the side and grin. "Are you sure you didn't study the occult at Cambridge? Because you're psychic."

Alice blanches. She stares down at the pot. "Hey, so, listen... I'm sorry about what Kelly and Leanne did with the paint. I didn't know they were planning that, or I wouldn't have been with them. And that day I came to dinner, I was rude to you. I can be a bit abrupt when I'm nervous. And you were having a whole conversation with thin air. But I was wrong to say what I said and run off like that."

I'm stunned. "You were nervous? About your date with Dani?"

Alice doesn't look up from the pot. "Um, yeah. Of course. But also about seeing you and going to your house and hanging out. I've kind of always wanted to be friends with you both. But I guess I blew that."

Hang on a second... "With us? You want to be friends with *us*? You were *horrible* to us at school!"

"Duh, of course I was. Kelly decided she didn't like you and Kelly was my only friend, so I had to follow along." Alice looks up at me then, and I fancy I see something like pain in her vivid amber eyes. "I was so jealous of you and Dani. You always looked like you were having more fun than everyone else, and you didn't have to constantly try to please Kelly just to stay on her good side. You didn't care what anyone thought of you, and I always cared too much."

That's not how I remember high school at all. I remember every insult ever hurled at me like a knife wound in the back. I remember many, many nights sitting on Edward's mausoleum with Dani, smoking weed and cussing out Kelly and Alice and Leanne for the mean things they'd done, and wishing we could get the fuck out of Grimdale. I remember especially the brave face Dani put on as she fought to wear the girl's uniform at school and be her true self.

I think about Dani telling me that Alice is different when she's away from the others. I never believed her. I didn't think people could change.

Everyone has always called us freaks. I've been 'Ghost Girl' since kindergarten. But here's one of the cruelest girls from high school, telling me that she envies me? I have to grip the edge of her desk so I don't keel over.

"We would have let you hang out with us," I say quietly. "If you'd asked."

She shakes her head. "No, you wouldn't have. And I don't blame you. I'm sorry about your dad, by the way. I've been meaning to say that since I saw you back in the village. My mum was on the pub quiz team with your parents. She told me about his diagnosis. I remember he used to build the sets for the school production. He was a good guy. I'm sorry he's sick."

Fuck, this is too much. Tears prick in the corners of my eyes. "Yeah. Me too."

"My dad's sick, too. Dementia. It's the reason I'm back in Grimdale. My mum can't cope. I had this amazing internship at the British Museum, but I just couldn't leave them alone, you know..." Alice stares at her dirt-encrusted hands.

"I'm so sorry," I say. "It's not easy."

"At least your dad still gets to keep his mind," she says. "Some days, Dad thinks I'm his mother. Some days, he thinks I'm this old teacher from high school who he hated. Those days...they fucking suck."

I swallow back the tears. "Sometimes...sometimes I think that would be better, you know, if he could forget. All my life, my dad's built things with his hands. He's played the drums in that silly covers band at the Goat every Friday. He tried to learn the guitar and Mum nearly divorced him. He's so fun and creative and practical. And for him to lose that, and see himself losing that...I worry that he won't see himself anymore."

"Yeah," Alice says. "I get that."

We both fall silent for a moment, lost in our joint misery.

Alice sighs. "Let's take a closer look at that pot again."

I lean over the desk as Alice turns over the pot. Her whole face lights up.

"There's an inscription on the bottom."

It's strange to see her like this, so genuinely excited about something that isn't tormenting me. She picks up a tiny scope and uses it to examine the inscription.

"Yes, as I suspected, this is from the grave of a second-century AD Roman soldier, probably from Hadrian's expansion. His name was Pax Drusus Maximus, and his friends remember him as a great fighter and an even greater drinker, and his body was carried off the battlefield and given a proper Roman burial."

Pax.

I found Pax's grave.

I can't believe this. Never in a million years did I expect this to happen. Not only have I found Pax's remains, but his men gave him a proper burial. All this time, his funerary rites had been performed as they should have been, but his spirit didn't know, so he couldn't find peace.

Pax can cross over...he can...

He can disappear from my life forever...

The thought of it is too horrible to consider.

"I need to sit down."

"No time for that." Alice pushes out of her chair. "You need to show me where you found this pot."

37

BREE

My heart swirls around my throat as I lean against the oak and watch Alice move dirt aside with her paintbrush.

This is Pax's grave.

Pax's *grave*.

If I show this to him, then he will finally be able to cross over.

After almost two thousand years of being a ghost, he'd be able to walk the fields of Elysium.

I should be jumping for joy. And yet...

...if I show Pax this grave, I'll never see him again.

He'll never again stand at the foot of my bed, watching over me while I sleep.

He'll never again stab things that make me sad or crack his silly, crass jokes that make me laugh until I can't breathe.

We'll never get to go further than we went that night in my old room. I'll never get to know what it might've been like to...

I can't even finish the thought.

The reality of it stabs at me, over and over again, in time with Alice's controlled brush strokes. This grave is a bomb ticking down to the moment where I lose one of my closest friends forever.

I hate myself for being so selfish. This isn't about me. It's about Pax and his immortal soul. *He was never supposed to be here. He was always supposed to be in Elysium. Every second I've had with him has been a gift.*

I have to turn away from Alice to wipe away the tears streaming down my cheeks.

"You've definitely got a grave here – probably a centurion, because it looks as if all his men contributed something." Alice swipes her hair behind her ear, leaving a streak of dirt across her cheek. "There are a lot of grave goods here, and some pretty remarkable coins. I'm going to call my old professor. She's an expert in the Roman history of Grimdale. She's probably going to want to excavate this grave."

"What will that mean?"

"Oh, the usual once the archaeologists get involved. Lots of people in silly hats traipsing around the garden and wanting to use the loo."

Alice goes off to make her call. I inch closer to the hole she's dug. I gasp as I glimpse the dark bones poking from the dirt. They look like ribs, and that's the...the edge of a skull.

Bile rises in my throat. But I know what I have to do. I lean down and brush off a little dirt near the jawline of the skull. I squeeze my eyes shut as I reach in and hunt around in the dirt until I feel it – the unmistakable coolness of a metal object. I pull the object out and hold it up to the light.

A gold coin placed in his mouth.

Payment for the ferryman to carry him across the river to Elysium.

Those are Pax's bones. His *bones*. Bits of him that have been left in the ground because he's dead.

He's *dead*.

My beautiful, possessive, bright, funny, stabby, baking-obsessed, slightly unhinged centurion is dead. He died nearly two thousand years ago, and I've been kidding myself that I have a future with him. I've been kissing him and touching him and now...

"Bree, are you okay?"

I jump as Alice's hand rests on my shoulder. I quickly shove the coin into my pocket.

"I'm fine," I gasp. "I just...bones freak me out. I have to—"

Before Alice can say anything more, I race off to the house. I don't even make it up the back steps before I throw up in the rose bushes.

Pax only just came back into my life, and now...how am I going to live without him?

38

BREE

I have to tell him.

I *have* to.

It's the right thing to do.

The coin in my pocket weighs a hundred pounds. My legs are lead weights as I drag myself through the house. I don't remember making a cup of tea, but the next thing I'm aware of, I'm slumped in the window seat in the snug with a steaming cuppa in my hands, dunking my gingernut biscuit again and again until it's a soggy mess as I watch Alice lead a whole Indy of archaeologists (that's the correct collective noun for a group of archaeologists – fight me) down the woodland path to the gravesite.

How will I live without him?

What will I do without his hugs and his insanity and his Bumblyshorts Snugglestack jokes?

Grimwood Manor won't be the same. But then, everything is changing anyway. My strange new powers. This...whatever it is simmering between me and the ghosts. Albert's murder. Dad's Parkinson's...

As if on cue, my phone rings. My dad's smiling face pops on the screen. My heart thuds in my chest.

I prop the phone up on my mug and press ACCEPT. "Hi, Dad."

"Hi, Bree-bug," he says. "How are things?"

Terrible. Heart-rending. Apocalyptic. I give the British answer. "They're good. Where's Mum?"

"Oh, your mother and her new friend have gone shopping in Berlin. They invited me to go, but even in Europe, one handbag kind of looks like another."

I laugh. I can't help it. Fresh tears leak from my eyes, and I lean out of the frame to wipe them so he can't see. But of course, he's my dad. So as soon as I move back into frame, he leans forward, his eyes dark with concern.

"Bree-bug, are you okay? What's wrong? Is it about Albert and Maggie?"

And just like that, I'm a little kid again after my accident, afraid of the ghosts I see everywhere, desperate to have my father's arms wrap me in a tight, safe hug.

"No, it's not about the Fernsbys, although that's so sad." I swallow, but I can't keep fresh tears from toppling down my cheeks. "Dad, what if you...what if you have to tell a friend something that could make them really happy, but it also meant that you'd never be able to see them again?"

"You tell them, of course," he says kindly. "It's not up to us to decide the future for someone else."

"I know." I shove my hand in my pocket and feel the edges of the gold coin next to the moldavite crystal. "I know it's the right thing to do. I just need to get myself together first."

"Oh, Bree. I'm sure that whatever it is, this friend will understand that it's hard for you. Otherwise, they're not a real friend, are they? And never say never. When you left, your mother cried for a month straight. She was so certain that you'd never come back to Grimdale after the horrible time you had. She thought she lost you forever."

"She did?" I can't imagine my forthright, strong mother crying about anything.

He nods. "Don't tell her I told you, but she was distraught. It's not easy to say goodbye to your child, especially when you know they were unhappy with you, and there was nothing you could do about it. We felt so helpless when you had all that trouble after your accident, and we worried that we wouldn't be there for you if something happened. But then we started talking to you on video chat, and we saw how happy you were living your wildest dreams, and we both realized that we can love you just as much from afar, even if that means it hurts sometimes. We had to let you spread your wings, and when you were ready, you'd come back to us. And look at you now, hanging out in the snug like you used to."

Nothing is permanent. Not even death.

"And another thing..." Dad looks down at his hand, which is clenched against his chest – another symptom of his Parkinson's. "We could have seen you anytime. We could have shut down the B&B for a month and visited you in Australia or Bali or Attica. Sometimes, us old folks get stuck in our routines, and we don't see there's a big, wide world out there for us if we're brave enough to embrace it before it's too late."

We both stare at his hand.

"I just wish...I wish there was something I could do for you." I ball my hands into fists as another wave of tears fall. "Ever since you told me, I feel so helpless and angry. It's not fair that you got this disease. It's not *fair*."

"Honey, don't cry." Dad folds his arms and shoots me a mock glare. "I forbid you to cry. Do you see me crying about it?"

"But—"

"No buts. Sometimes things don't work out how you

thought they would. That's life. When I was your age, I was going to be the new drummer for The Who, and that didn't exactly happen. But I have your mum, and you, and our beautiful house and my hobbies. And right now I'm discovering a love for travel. Do you know why we went to France in the first place?"

"Because the French bakery on High Street closed and Mum was craving a pain au chocolat?"

"Because for five years I've watched my brave, beautiful daughter explore the world, and she made me realize that all those things in life I wanted to do are still right here for me, if only I'm bold enough to take the first step." He flexes his arm. His words grow quieter the more he talks, which is a common symptom of Parkinson's. "Because of you, Bree-bug, I don't see this diagnosis as the end of all good things. It just *is*. I'm not going to sit around lamenting the things I can't do. I've had a full, beautiful life, and I've got so much more to enjoy."

Oh, fuck.

"Dad?" I sniff.

"Yeah?"

"I miss you."

"I miss you too, Bree-bug. Every single day. But that's how I know how lucky I am – I have a beautiful daughter to miss."

We hang up and I flop back on the cushions, his words playing over and over in my mind. I roll over and something hard digs into my thigh. The moldavite crystal. I pull it out and hold it in front of my face, watching the way the light plays off its delicate green swirls.

I hurl the stone across the room. It clatters against the bookshelves and drops to the ground. Entwhistle bats it under the table.

"It's not fair!" I scream as tears streak my cheeks.

It's not fair that my dad has this stupid, evil disease. It's not fair that he's worked so hard his whole life, and just when he was going to settle down and enjoy his retirement, he has to deal with this. It's not fair that this disease is taking away all the things he loves.

It's not fair that Pax died on the battlefield when he was so young, and that he didn't get to find a wife or have a family or delight the world with his wonderful...Paxness. It's not fair that he's had to linger here for two thousand years because he didn't know that he'd had a proper burial, that his men loved him enough to honour him even amongst the carnage.

It's not fair that we have to say goodbye.

It's not fair that I can talk to the dead, but I can't save the people I love.

39

BREE

"Brianna, are you in here? I've been looking for you everywhere. Ambrose found a book in the library with a chapter about me, and I want you to read it aloud…" Edward flops through the wall onto my bed. He runs a hand through his mussed dark hair to keep it out of his eyes, and he jerks when he sees me. "Brianna? You're crying. What's the matter?"

"Go away," I sob into my pillow, aware that I'm acting like a complete fool.

"And leave you here upset? Don't be ridiculous. Talk to me."

"I don't want to talk."

"That's fine. There's so much else we can do to take your mind off—"

"I told you to go away," I glower at him. "What happened to obeying my personal boundaries?"

Edward waves a see-through hand. "I own this house. These are my walls, and if I want to waft through them to check on my muse, then that's precisely what I'll do."

"Fine." I roll over in bed and face the opposite wall. I can't deal with his ridiculousness right now. I have so much that I should be dealing with. The archaeologists are already down in the woods, digging up the grave. I should tell Albert what's going on. I should tell Dani to ease off on Mr. Gibbons.

Instead, I'm back in bed, running my fingers over the coin and trying to work up the courage to tell Pax that he can cross over.

"Brianna," Edward's soft voice grazes my earlobe, demanding my secrets. "What's this about? Is it your father?"

"Go away."

"Is it Albert's murder? I thought we had made tremendous progress on that."

"I don't want to talk about it."

"You used to say that all the time as a kid, and it was a lie and we both know it. When you lie, your nose twitches. Is your nose twitching?"

"No." I touch my nose. *Maybe a little.*

"I thought so. So tell Edward what it's about, and I'll order Pax to fix it, and he'll stab whatever hurt you until it can't hurt you anymore. He's rather good at stabby, and I am rather good at ordering people around."

Pax can't fix it. He'll never stab anything for me again.

"It's the same thing it's always about." I bury my face in my hands. "All I want is to be normal, but it's never going to happen for me."

Something rolls on the bed beside me. The moldavite. I peer over my shoulder. Big mistake. This close, Edward's dark eyes capture me. His lip curls at the corner into that infamous half-smirk. He holds up a hand and strokes my hair, and I don't know how, but it makes me feel calmer.

"I found Entwhistle and Moon rolling it back and forth between them," he says, those fathomless eyes of his twinkling with mischief. "They are most displeased that I ruined their game, but I figured you would want it back."

"Why?" I glare at the crystal in disgust. "If it's any kind of magic, it's a curse. It's done nothing but bring misery."

"Now, that's simply not true." Edward's fingers tangle in my hair. He places his palm against my cheek, and despite myself, I lean into his touch. He feels so good. He flicks a finger under my eyes, blotting away a tear before it can fall. "What about the night of the Shakespeare festival? When you shuddered under my touch, that wasn't because you were miserable."

"I—"

"And what about when you took Pax in your mouth? What about when you swallowed his Roman cum?" Edward's voice hardens as he strokes my cheek. "You weren't miserable then, were you?"

"H-h-how do you know about that?"

"I had my head in the light fixture at the time. I saw everything." Edward leans closer, the shadow beneath his bottom lip darkening. "The way you made that delicious little groan in the back of your throat when he thrust into your mouth, it was enough to make a ghost mortal again."

It takes all my self-control to jerk away. "That's it exactly. You don't understand. I'm not supposed to be sucking off a ghost, especially not my childhood friend. Especially not after what you and I...I'm not supposed to *want* these things. I'm not normal. This power has done something to me, made me even more of a freak—"

"Of course you're not normal, Bree Mortimer." Edward's voice drops to a register that stirs in my stomach and makes my toes curl. "You've never been normal. You're extraordinary. You're remarkable. Quite possibly enchanted. I saw it from the moment you were born."

"From the moment I was born, huh?"

"Well, perhaps not quite the *exact* moment. I couldn't bear to be in the house with Sylvie in labour. All that screaming.

All those *fluids*." He shudders. "Pax and Ambrose and I hid in the attic, and I came down when she handed you to Mike. He held you in his arms and said it was a pity that you couldn't really see him yet, because he was such a handsome-looking fellow. And you opened your eyes right then and stared straight at me. At *me*. And I felt like you truly saw me, even then."

His voice shakes with wonder.

I shake my head. "I didn't see you. That was before my accident. I was just staring at the wall or something."

"I'm not so sure." Edward leans forward again, and his lips part a little into one of his best smiles – the one that feels like a secret he's desperate to spill. "Sometimes, we'd visit you while you were crying in your crib. When we leaned over, you would stop crying."

"That's not true."

"It is true. And when you got older, you would hold things out to us – toys, bits of food. Once, you threw a book through Ambrose."

But how... "Why have you never told me this before?"

"And have you believe that you're some kind of freak?" Edward slinks closer, and the air between us charges with electricity. "You already hated yourself, and it broke our hearts to see it. We didn't want to contribute to that pain. We all agreed that we'd never mention it to you."

"B-b-but you're telling me *now?*"

"In my life, I could have my pick of women. Or men, when the mood took me. Queens, princesses, actresses, artists, they all fell at my feet for the chance to bed me." Edward moves across the bed, so close that a single breath would press us together. His long limbs dangle off the end of the bed, and his white shirt pulls open, revealing that pale triangle of smooth skin. He is my friend. He is a weapon. He is a Swiss Army knife, packed with six different ways to ruin me. "And yet, you, Bree Mortimer, you're the only one I ever truly *wanted*."

He called me Bree.

Edward's finger traces a line beneath my chin, leaving a trail of fire on my skin. I'm standing on the edge of a cliff, and I know all that awaits me at the bottom is a bloody, gory mess.

Nothing is permanent, not even death.

I tilt my head into his impossibly warm, impossibly corporeal hand. I swallow down the jumbled emotions. Maybe it's true that this can't last. Maybe I am about to crash land in a whole pile of hurt. But fuck it.

Fuck it all the way to Elysium.

I take a breath, close my eyes, and I fall.

I fall into Edward. And just like this spoiled, surly prince has done my entire life, he catches me.

Only this time, it's his lips that catch me. No, they *capture* me. Capture me and crack me open.

I taste burnt sugar and opium as his tongue dips between my lips. This is Edward, who – if the history books and his own boasting can be believed – has kissed a thousand horny countesses, instigated orgies, fornicated in throne rooms, and done every wild and depraved thing I can imagine (and several I can't). And now he is kissing *me*. He groans into my mouth, like I am special, like I'm everything he's ever wanted.

I can't believe this.

His fingers snake through my hair, and they feel like real fingers, but better. Hotter and needier and tinglier. Edward leans over me, laying me back on the bed, his lips more urgent. His hand sweeps over my body, the featherlight touch testing, exploring. We don't know what this power will allow us to do, but it certainly let me have some fun with him and with Pax before, and right now I'm so confused and sad that I'm ready to fall right over the edge with him.

Edward's fingers stroke over my nipple through my shirt, rubbing it with the pad of his thumb until it pebbles. Then he rolls it and pinches it, a little hard, but that little bite of pain makes me melt into him, desperate for more.

"Can I remove your clothing?" Edward asks, his mouth cocking. "I want to see all your beauty."

"I can do it." The ghosts may be able to touch now, but they don't always have fine motor skills. I lift the hem of my shirt and—

Edward's hand closes over my wrist. He lays it gently back against the duvet. "No, no, Brianna," he scolds me, those dark eyes rimmed in fire. "Don't deprive a prince of the joy of unwrapping his present."

He works slowly, rolling the hem of my shirt up and kissing and stroking every inch of revealed skin. He trails kisses down my arms, spending time on the insides of my elbows and wrists until my hairs stand on end. He rolls me over and kisses my back, then down the backs of my legs as he slowly rolls off my jeans. He bites my ass as he tugs at my thong, but he doesn't pull it off completely.

Instead, he flips me over again. His lips skim the edges of the fabric, kissing and nibbling over my stomach and my inner thighs. My heart spins like a pinwheel as his warm mouth moves closer.

"I've been wanting to taste you since the moment you walked back into Grimdale," Edward breathes as he gently tugs off my panties.

"Edward, I—"

Whatever I was going to say flies out of my head as Edward dives between my legs. The heat of his tongue melts against me as he finds just the right spot. I roll my hips into him, and he groans as he slides his hands under my ass to raise my hips up to him.

How is he doing this? It shouldn't be possible?

I don't care anymore. I don't...

Those fathomless black eyes never leave mine. He watches me as I watch him eat me out, devouring my heart and soul as his lips and tongue devour my clit.

He's not human. That much is obvious because this isn't the fumbling wet mess I'm used to from human men. This isn't needy and hopeful and lost. Edward's lips are solid, his tongue warm, but that ghostly hum still burns through me – that electric charge that draws us together, that lights every part of me on fire whenever he's near.

Ghost sex is so much better than regular sex.

My hands tangle in his hair.

"That's it," he urges, altering the strokes. "Show me how you like it, Brianna."

"I love when you say my name like that," I moan.

"It's such a beautiful name." He does something with his tongue and I lift off the bed, it's so fucking good. "A beautiful name for an extraordinary woman."

I like Edward calling me beautiful. And extraordinary. I like it a *lot*.

But then, he pushes a finger inside me as his tongue does that thing, and I'm glowing with ghost mojo inside and out. The warm, delicious ache that's been pulsing inside me since the first time I saw him again bursts open with a rush of pleasure. I scream and curse and yell as his tongue draws out every last tremble from me. Only when I sink back into the sheets, utterly spent, does Edward draw back and flash me his spoiled prince smirk.

"And now that I've got my present unwrapped, there are so many things I've been dreaming of doing to that delectable body of yours—"

He's interrupted by a huge shape bowling through the wall

and landing on top of him. Pax grabs Edward's throat and slams him into the mirror with such rage that the glass cracks. Edward winces as Pax's blade dances dangerously close to his eye.

I can't scream because Edward took my voice. "P-P-Pax?"

"You're upsetting her. I heard her crying. I will rip every not-bone from your body and use them to pick my teeth—"

"Pax, look at her," Edward gasps out. "She's hardly upset, is she?"

Pax turns to me. His eyes blow out as he sees me lying naked, the sheets tangled around me. He glances at Edward, then back at me, his Adam's apple working as his eyes drink me in with his customary wild abandon.

I should shrink beneath such a gaze – the wild, untamed need of a man who hasn't touched a naked woman in nearly two thousand years. But this is Pax, *my* Pax, and although he may be terrifying in his want, I know he'll never hurt me.

I'm more afraid of the want that burns inside *me*.

Pax drops Edward, who lands hard on the floor. Pax just continues to stand there, jaw open, staring at me while a thousand emotions play across his face.

"We were in the middle of something." Edward picks himself up and pulls his linen shirt back onto his shoulder. "You could join us, if Brianna agrees?"

A million warnings crash into my splintered mind. I ignore them all. I want them both. I want to keep Pax forever and ever. I want so many things that I can never have.

But I can have this night.

I hold up my fist. Pax's eyes widen as I lift my thumb up into a thumbs up. The ancient Roman symbol from the gladiatorial ring. *Let him live.*

Let him love again.

The smile that bursts on Pax's face could light the whole

world. He leaps onto the bed, and his weight nearly flips me off the mattress. He grabs me and crushes me against him, and his lips smash on mine.

Pax's kiss is so different from Edward's – they're both experienced lovers, but Edward is all about enjoying himself, drawing out the pleasure until you're a quivering mess of need. But Pax kisses the way he does everything else – with single-minded savagery.

And I am *here* for it.

His mouth slants over mine, and his kiss steals the air from my lungs. My knees go weak, and if I weren't already lying down, he'd have to hold me upright.

White hot heat punches through me, obliterating the ache in my heart. This could be my last night with Pax, and even though I know he has no idea, it feels like he knows because of the way he's kissing me. Like a condemned man devouring his last meal.

It's like he's determined to tear out a piece of my soul to carry with him for eternity.

A piece I give willingly. And I'd give so much more if only to have more kisses like this.

His fingers curl around the back of my neck, his grip as strong and firm as he's ever felt. Although every touch I share with the ghosts also has this fragility about it – at any moment I could go back to not feeling them.

Pax's other hand curls possessively around my hip, and I move against him, my body unfolding around him, our bodies fitting together as he floats above me. Every place where skin touches ghost skin, he burns so good.

Our tongues rage against each other, battling for domination. I'm happy to bend to him, but I know he craves the satisfaction of the fight. I rake my hands along his spine, for the first time feeling the bumps and ridges of his hard muscle. Pax's not-quite-human skin shimmers beneath my fingers, and I can grasp him and hold him, no matter how tenuous and shaky the connection.

Pax breaks our kiss, and I look down to see three silver threads stretching out of my chest. One enters Pax's chest, the other snakes through the open V of Edward's shirt, and the third stretches into the wallpaper...

"What's going on?" Ambrose cries from the other side of the wall. "I'm hearing all kinds of strange noises. Is Bree okay?"

Edward's lips trail their fire across my thigh. I must be crazy because I call out, "Ambrose, please, come in."

"Are you sure? Unlike those other two, I respect your personal space."

"Get in here, adventurer, before you ruin the mood," Edward snaps.

Ambrose wafts through the wall. I reach out and touch his wrist. My fingers tingle where they touch him. I steer him onto the bed. He kneels beside me, looking unsure of himself and rather overdressed in his impeccable frock coat.

"What's going on?" Ambrose asks nervously.

"What's going on, my dear friend, is that I have removed Bree's garments, laid her down upon the bed, and drank in her exquisite pussy until she quivered beneath me," Edward says in that insouciant tone of his. "And now, I believe you and Pax have some things you'd like to do to her."

A thousand emotions pass over Ambrose's face – shock at Edward's crass words, confusion, concern (probably for my womanly virtue, although he needn't worry – my ship of womanly virtue sailed out of harbour a long time ago). His azure eyes darken, and as he turns back to me, I can see only one emotion remaining.

Desire.

Sweet Ambrose. The ghost who understood my love of

adventure, my need to run, my fixation on being anywhere but here. The friend who let me dream of a world where I could truly be myself, even if that world could never include him.

Ambrose reaches out with a trembling hand and touches my cheek, and in that touch is a promise, a need, a longing that's so pure it tears my heart to shreds.

I turn my head so that my lips graze his fingers. "I want you," I whisper. I don't think many people have said that to him before. Ambrose's eyes flutter shut, his long eyelashes tangling together as a deep, needful sigh escapes his full lips.

"What..." he swallows, even though ghosts don't have saliva. "What does Bree look like?"

"She is the most exquisite creature I've ever seen," Edward the poet breathes.

"And her bosoms are amazing," Pax adds helpfully.

Ambrose's face changes. His tentative fingers brush my cheek, but now they are hungry, desperate. He strokes across my jaw and down my neck, rubbing my collarbone with his thumb in a way that shouldn't be hot at all but makes me want to jump on him and claw his clothes off.

My moan breaks something in him. He pulls away, his hand hanging in the air, his lips parting with uncertainty.

"I've never..." His eyes close. He hangs his head. He's embarrassed. "Not with a woman."

I grip his wrist and bring his hand back to my cheek. "Then let me be the first."

"Can he touch you?" Edward asks, taking on the role of directing this...whatever this is. The ghosts may not also get on, but they have been living together for longer than I could even contemplate. They understand each other. Edward understands that with his debauched history he can ask for what Ambrose and his Victorian sensibilities cannot.

My breath catches. "He can touch wherever he likes."

I lie back on the bed, and Ambrose floats over me. His fingers brush over my skin – feathering over my chest, my breasts, my arms, my face. His face is rapt with wonder as he explores me, as he sees me in a way he's never been able to see me before, an adventurer stepping into uncharted territory for the first time.

I cannot describe the feeling of his exploration. The closest I can say is that it's like pulling on a silk dress, so soft and supple and perfect against my skin. Ambrose strokes the inside of my thighs, and the ache that burns inside me for him grows and grows until I'm growling and thrusting my hips toward him.

"You should kiss her," Edward says. "Kiss her everywhere. She enjoys that, don't you, Bree?"

"I enjoy that very much."

Ambrose bends over me, his body floating just above mine, the air between us a buzz of pure energy. Behind him, Edward watches while Pax unbuckles his leather armor and shrugs off his tunic. I can see the three cords extending from my heart into theirs, squeezing a little as they shimmer and glow.

I don't know what the cords mean, or why I'm seeing them. But right now I don't care.

Ambrose brushes his lips to mine. His kiss is different from Edward and Pax. He is not savage or desperate. He does not play a game with me, stepping into a role that he believes he must play. Ambrose is completely himself, completely in the moment – excited and nervous and warm and wonderful. Racing ahead and then slowing down to enjoy every new sensation.

He tastes exactly the way I expect Ambrose to taste, like wide open spaces and fresh air, like the first page of a brand new journal, like ink pens and spice markets and sea salt on the breeze. He tastes the way I felt the day I first stepped onto an airplane with my belongings strapped on my back, like I'm standing on the edge of a cliff, heart in my throat, throwing my arms out as the wind pulls me over, trusting that the world would catch me.

Ambrose's lips leave mine, and I moan in protest until I feel him kiss my neck, my collarbone, my breasts. His kisses trace new paths over my skin – Ambrose doesn't follow where Edward led, but forges his own path. I watch him, transfixed by his exploration, by his wide eyes and the wonder in his voice as he exclaims over every part of me.

And when he reaches the mound between my legs, Edward leans in and places his hand over Ambrose's fingers. "Brianna, open those beautiful legs for us."

I obey. Of course I obey. I'm so aching and needy for Ambrose, I want to shove his head down there myself.

Ambrose's face is rapt, his hair loose of its stays and flopping over his eyes. Edward leans in and whispers in his ear. Ambrose's cheeks grow beet red, but he nods with understanding.

He bends between my legs.

The first stroke of his tongue is exquisite. Edward's hand strokes Ambrose's back, and he whispers encouraging words to him in a way that feels almost perverse.

I expect Ambrose to shrug Edward off, but he comes alive under his instruction. His mouth on my pussy is no longer hesitant, unsure. He's lost in the moment, in this new adventure that we get to share together. He tries different strokes – slow circles, fast and hard little jabs, little cat laps that make me grind my teeth with need. He pushes his tongue inside me and moans with pleasure.

"I told you she tastes amazing, friend," Edward coos, his fingers playing with the ends of Ambrose's hair.

Ambrose keeps going, alternating lighter strokes of his tongue with hard and heavy, leading me right to the edge and then pulling back so my legs quiver with the need for release. I can't believe he's never done this before.

Satisfied that his student is applying his lessons, Edward lays beside me, his hand cupping my cheek. The sensation of the two of them touching me makes the whole room spin. I've never been with three guys before.

And three ghosts? That's also a first.

Their touch is so, so warm, so close to Living and yet, something different – something both more and less at the same time. Tingly, needful, yearning. I find myself pulled toward him, drowning in those hungry icicle eyes. "We want to make you feel good. We want you to see how special and unique and amazing you are."

"That's what we want," Pax growls in my ear.

"Does this please you?" Edward asks.

Why be normal when you can have three ghosts pleasuring your body?

"Um, yeah." I roll my eyes at him. "It pleases me very much."

Edward leans in, tipping my head toward him as he claims my lips with his. His hand grazes the back of my neck, quietly possessive and self-assured. He doesn't need to hold me down. He's so certain I won't run, not when he's doing wicked things to my mouth and Ambrose is between my legs...

And Pax...

The bed groans as Pax lies on the other side of me. He's naked now, his sword laid at the foot of the bed where he can easily grab it. His strong arms go around my waist, and he pulls me back against him, skin on ghost-skin. With this much of us pressed together, I can feel how different he is from a normal guy. That much muscle should feel like a solid wall, but there's a springiness to him, as if I might breathe wrong and accidentally slip through him.

Everywhere we touch is on fire.

His huge hands cup my breasts, those rough fingers grazing my nipples. The silver cords tangle through his fingers. His hands, at least, feel solid, protecting me, worshipping me.

And all the while Ambrose continues his slow, deliberate strokes on my clit.

My vision swirls, and the room disappears, and although I'm still in my body, still being pleasured by them, I'm carried along in a wave of their memories. I'm marching across foreign lands at the head of a mighty legion. I'm debating the meaning of existence with my fellow libertines while tendrils of opium smoke curl around us. I'm hopping off a train in a far-off city and smelling this new and exciting place for the first time.

I'm inside their memories. I feel everything they feel – the excitement, the anticipation, the sheer indulgence of *life*. And then I see myself – first as a girl, then a surly, black-clad teen, and then the day I returned to Grimwood Manor, my head hung, my eyes dull. I see myself as they see me, and the love they feel for me swells and aches inside me.

Ambrose's tongue drags me back to the present. I blink away the memories as he teases my entrance with his finger.

"She's so wet," he whispers. "So warm."

"Just you wait until you get your ghost prick in here," Edward murmurs, his teeth nibbling my bottom lip. "It's going to feel amazing."

"Can we even do this?" I ask. "Can ghosts and Livings…"

"We're going to find out."

"Me first," Pax growls.

"Why do you get to go first? I'm the prince. I should go first—"

"I've never done this before," Ambrose says. "I should go first so you can walk me through it—"

"I'm the oldest," Pax declares. "And I have a sword. It will be hard for you to pleasure Bree if I cut off your verpa."

Edward pales. "The Roman makes an excellent point." Edward places his hand firmly on my stomach, pressing me back against Pax. The Roman's teeth dig into my neck as he rolls me onto my back and yanks my legs apart, pulling my thighs back to impale me...

...impale me...

...what?

...what's going on?

"It won't work." Pax's voice shudders as he drags my thighs back again, but even though the tip of his cock rubs against my clit, he can't get it inside me. "My verpa keeps going *through* you, not inside you. We're not...we're not solid enough."

"That's nonsense. Come to me, Brianna. We'll show them how it's done." Edward pulls me on top of him. I plant my knees into the bed, straddling him as he gazes up at me with those dark, obsidian eyes.

"Lower yourself down," he urges, his voice ragged with need. "Nice and slow. I want to feel every inch of me inside you."

I rise up on my hips and press down, but the same thing happens. Edward's not solid enough. He can rub against me, but that's it.

"It won't work." Edward's voice wavers with distress.

"I do not care!" Pax declares. I yelp as he grabs me around the waist and flips me down on my back on the bed. "By Jupiter's blue balls, I have waited thousands of years for a woman like Bree. I won't waste a moment of this night lamenting what we cannot do."

And with that, he dives between my legs again.

I lose count of the number of times they make me come.

Edward and Pax take turns to show Ambrose all their 'tricks.' Since they were both manwhores when there were alive, they have a *lot* of tricks.

Ambrose is a quick study.

At some point around 3AM, I lose all feeling in my legs. The ghosts run a bubble bath for me and carry me into the bathroom (it takes all three of them, and it was more of a 'drag' than a 'carry' – they aren't quite solid enough for that kind of effort yet. But I appreciated the gesture). When I'm done in the bath, I crawl into bed between the three of them, and they pull the blankets up around me.

"Remember when we used to sleep like this sometimes?" Edward says as he drapes his arm across the pillow behind my head. His fingers dance lightly over my skin as those anthracite eyes regard me with curiosity. "If Brianna was having a bad night, or there was one of those horrible storms outside, we'd tell stories or jokes or just hold her until the storm passed."

"It wasn't quite like this," Ambrose says. "Bree was just a kid."

"I know that," Edward says frostily. "I'm not a pervert. I'm just *saying* that even though some things have changed, other things are still the same, and I like those things."

"I like those things, too," Ambrose snuggles down beside me. "And I also like the naked things."

Pax lies down behind me and pulls me into him, pressing my back into his chest and crushing my ribs with the force of his embrace.

"This is my favorite part of sex," he whispers into my ear. "This is the part I've missed the most. The cuddling. I'm so happy that I get to cuddle with you."

A sob threatens to escape me, but I manage to hold it down. I grip his arms and just enjoy the warmth of his ghostly body around me, grateful for the magic that brought all three ghosts to my bed and gave us this night together.

I'll tell him tomorrow.

40
BREE

Tomorrow comes, and I wake with a start to find Edward attempting to do his hair with my comb, Pax standing at the window, eyes fixed on the world outside, surveying the forest for marauding Celts, and Ambrose floating a foot above the bed, sound asleep. A warm rush floods my body at the sight of them. They're so familiar to me and yet, after last night, I feel like we've found a new side of each other to explore.

Who knew that my ghosts were capable of...of that?

My gaze lands on Pax. He may be on duty, but he's humming a little song under his breath. I think about the way he looked at me last night as he did those incredible things to me, like I was a goddess and he would fall at my feet to worship me, and it all comes crashing back to me.

I have to do it.

I have to say goodbye.

I'm going to miss him so, so much, but my dad's right. Pax has already given me the most precious gift I've ever received – his friendship. His love.

He deserves a gift in return.

He deserves to be free, to be at peace. He's watched over me my whole life. He's given me the strength I need to watch over myself.

But first, I have something else I need to do.

I crawl out of bed, grab my phone, and head into the hallway. Edward follows me, but I motion for him to leave me alone. I head out to the mailbox and find an envelope tucked inside, sealed with a red wax stamped with a bird's footprint. Inside are documents showing hundreds of artifacts moving between Kieran Myers and Rasmussen's shop, from areas all over the county, many of which I know to be private land.

Gotcha.

A piece of rubbish flutters out of the envelope. I almost don't pick it up, but then I see a note attached.

I found this in the rubbish bin at the real estate office, along with a bunch of belladonna leaves. There is plenty more there if the police want to take a look. Quoth.

The piece of rubbish is a scrap of packaging from a 'make your own bath products' craft kit.

I call Dani and tell her what Alice and I found yesterday, and the package I had just received.

"This is everything we need," I say. "We can go to the police and clear Maggie's name."

"Just remember not to get your hopes up, Bree. This is real life, not an Agatha Christie novel. You only have circumstantial evidence," Dani says. "You can prove that the Myers were stealing artifacts and treasure from the Fernsbys' property, but not that they killed Albert. But it should be enough for Hayes and Wilson to look more carefully at them."

"I understand that, but if we're going to do this, I have to get Alice to talk to the police. Wilson already thinks I'm weird –

she's not going to take me seriously without Alice's expert opinion on the artifacts."

"Leave Alice to me," Dani says. "I can convince her."

"Convince her brains out?"

"You're disgusting," Dani laughs. "Accurate, but disgusting."

I hang up with Dani and head to the kitchen just as I hear an ominous crash.

"Oops." Pax looks up guiltily as I walk in. Broken shards are scattered around his sandals. "We were trying to surprise you with a cup of tea, but the mug slid off the end of my sword."

I stare at those brightly-coloured floral shards, and every good feeling from the night before flees my body. I have to bite down on my lower lip to stop myself from bursting into tears.

Pax has broken my mum's favourite mug, but I can't even get angry about it.

I'm keeping a huge secret from him, and it feels horrible.

Together with Edward and Ambrose, he gave me the best sex of my *life*. Last night they showed me what life could be like if I embraced this strange connection between us, if I could learn how to control these new powers.

I could be crazy Bree the ghost slut, with my three spirited lovers.

It's starting to sound like a good idea.

I look down at my chest. The three silver cords are there, stretching from me to them. Pax's cord jerks wildly. My heart clenches.

Last night is never going to happen again. Pax's time is running out.

Nothing is permanent. Not even death.

"ARE YOU READY FOR THIS?" Dani asks as we run up to the police station.

"Am I ready for the love of my life to be free from imprisonment? Am I ready to know that with those vicious killers behind bars, my Maggie will be safe?" Albert thumps his hand against his heart. "Gosh darn it, I'm ready."

"She wasn't talking to you," I whisper to Albert as Dani rushes up the steps to squeeze Alice's hand.

"Hmmmph. Well, if you don't need me, I'm going to the cells to visit my wife." Albert disappears through the brick wall with a flourish.

"New ghosts, so temperamental," Edward simpers. Ambrose rests his head on my shoulder and squeezes my hand. Ever since last night, he's been so cuddly, always reaching out to touch my hand or stroke my cheek or run his fingers through my hair. I love that we're having this secret PDA and no one even knows.

Pax storms along behind us as the rear guard, his eyes flicking everywhere, watching for ninja Celts. I can't look at him.

We have to get through this first. Then I will figure out how to say goodbye.

The four of us join Alice and Dani on the steps. Alice's cheeks are flushed from cycling over from Grimdale. "I can't believe you talked me into doing this," she says. "I need a drink."

"If we get through this, we can get a cider at the Goat," I say. "My treat."

She fixes me with a fiendish glare. "That sounds an awful lot like something friends do. Don't think this makes us friends."

"Oh, I know. We're still sworn enemies." I shrug. "While we drink, the ghost of a Roman centurion is going to stand behind you, and he'll stick his sword through your gut if you try and hurt me."

"You're very weird, Bree Mortimer." Alice sucks in a deep breath. "Come on, then. Let's get this over with."

Alice spins on her heel and storms inside. Dani stares after her with that adoring expression I remember from high school. I nudge her inside and follow along after, Quoth's documents tucked under my arm. The ghosts crowd in behind me.

At the front desk, I tell the duty officer that we have information for Detective Hayes about Albert's murder. He tells us to wait while he gets someone, and a few minutes later, Wilson steps out and ushers us into an interview room. Alice and I sit down, and Wilson flips on a tape recorder and starts explaining that our interview will be recorded.

"You don't even know what we're here to say," I point out. I didn't realize this would be quite so...formal. Alice sinks down in her chair. She looks downright terrified.

Wilson sighs. "I heard lots of stories about you this week, Bree Mortimer. I have a feeling I'll need the tape. Do you consent to this interview being taped?"

"I thought Hayes would interview us."

"Hayes is busy." *Hayes is busy chasing real leads* – she doesn't say it, but the implication hangs in the air. "Do you consent to me recording the interview?"

"Yes. Fine. Whatever." I glance at Alice, and after a moment, she agrees. I'm too nervous, so when Wilson asks us what we want to discuss, I burst out, "Maggie didn't murder her husband. We know who the real killers are. And we can prove it."

I shouldn't have said that, because Dani's right – we can't prove it. I wanted to be calm, cool, in control. I wanted Edward's poise and Ambrose's composure. The three ghosts stand along the wall, Pax stabbing the air enthusiastically with his sword. I suck in a deep breath, certain that we're about to get kicked out.

Wilson's eyebrows shoot way up. "I'm listening."

I outline everything I learned about Annabel and Kieran, and lay out the documents that Quoth brought, telling them that they were shoved anonymously through my mailbox, which is at least partially true. Alice chimes in with her evidence from the dig, and explains the laws around taking treasure from private property without the owner's permission.

"Kieran and Annabel knew they were in the wrong," Alice says. "Kieran has been in trouble over this before, and these documents point to a long history of selling stolen artifacts. The artifacts that we've pulled from the site on the Fernsbys' property aren't just grave goods – they're golden statues, jewellery, and coins offered to the Roman god Mars and the Celtic god Neit. These are extremely valuable items, worth many times the value of the Fernsbys' property. I believe that the Myers tried to buy the property from the Fernsbys without disclosing to them that they had found the grave. When the Fernsbys declined to sell, the Myers decided to simply take the goods, but they could have never excavated the site without the Fernsbys catching them, especially since Maggie often foraged for herbs and wild-flowers near that site. So they devised this plan to get rid of the Fernsbys and – while the village was distracted with the murder – secret away the treasures, sell them, and move to Santorini."

"I bet if you check the rubbish in Annabel's office," I say, "you'll find traces of belladonna and a 'make your own bath products' kit in her rubbish bin. Just a hunch, of course."

Wilson leaves us waiting while she consults with Hayes. The detective comes in and asks us all the same questions again. They dispatch some officers to find the Myers. We wait some more. Alice looks as pale as the ghost of a seventeenth-century royal rake she doesn't know is sitting right beside her, nervously fidgeting with the sliver of glass wedged into his behind.

After what feels like forever, Hayes and Wilson dismiss us from the interview room and have us wait outside while they bring Maggie up from the cells. When she arrives, she's not in handcuffs and she's clutching a plastic bag containing her possessions.

"I'm free to go! I can't believe it." Maggie practically skips out of the station doors. Albert's ghost trails behind her.

"You did it, Bree. You freed her!" He tries to hug me, but his arms fall right through me. He is a newer ghost, and I think even my enhanced powers don't work quite as well on him yet. "I can't believe you did it."

"I can't believe it, either."

"Bree, I can't thank you enough for what you've done." Maggie throws her arms around me, unaware that she's just fallen through her husband. She kisses me on the forehead. "You know, it's strange, but even though I know Albert is gone, I felt so calm in jail, like I knew he was still here, watching over me. Does that sound crazy?"

"It's not crazy!" Albert jumps up and down. "I'm right here, my darling. I've been with you through this whole ordeal. It was my idea to have Bree solve my murder. It was—argh!"

He breaks down in a wheezing cough as a police officer marches through him on the way to the cafeteria.

"It's not crazy at all," I smile at Maggie.

"Well, I've got a busy day ahead of me." She glances down at her watch. "There's still a couple of hours left to submit my scones for the Bake Off judging. I have to call Linda immediately and get an entry form. I need to get baking!"

"That's my Maggie!" Albert grins. "She'll win that competition, just you wait!"

"Not so fast," Wilson says. "We have a bit of paperwork for you to fill in, and then I'll give you a ride back to your house."

While Maggie and Wilson go over the paperwork and Maggie texts Linda Bateman, we watch as two officers drag in Annabel and Kieran Myers. Wilson looks over at me, and gives me the faintest of nods.

We step outside. Dani and Alice walk ahead, hand in hand, discussing what they're going to get for lunch at the pub, when something occurs to me.

"Albert, you haven't crossed over."

"What?" He looks confused. "Crossed over where?"

"You stayed behind as a ghost because Maggie was in danger from whoever murdered you." I touch my hand to my chest. I should be feeling the silver thread inside me tugging, right? The way it did for the actress ghost? But the only one I can feel is Pax. I frown at Albert. "We caught the baddies. Kieran and Annabel won't be able to hurt Maggie now. So then why are you still a ghost?"

"Yes. You should be drinking wine in Elysium," Pax punches his fist in the air. "The gods have cheated you."

"Maybe it's because I don't want to go?" Albert looks at me pleadingly, as if I'm behind this. "I don't want to leave Maggie. Even if we can't truly be together, I want to be beside her as she lives out the rest of her days. I'll be so lonely without her, and you heard her back there – she can sense me! Maybe you could even teach her how to see me and—"

I shake my head. "That's not how it works. Trust me, I've

seen enough ghosts in my life to know that you're not supposed to be here anymore. The only reason for you to still be sticking around is..."

I trail off as I realize the horrifying truth.

"...is if we haven't caught the killer. Because we were thinking this was about Albert, when it's been about Maggie all this time. We've got the wrong murderer. Again." I leap to my feet. "And I think I know exactly who's responsible."

41

BREE

"Are you sure that this is the place?" Ambrose says as he touches his hand to the white picket fence. "You have to be certain. I don't want to haunt the wrong house."

"I'm absolutely positive." I tap triumphantly on a wooden sign attached to the gate. "Only one person in this village would have a 'Kiss the Baker' sign."

"Let's go! Pax is ready for haunting!" Pax stretches his hands out to crack his knuckles, but Edward gets there first.

"Hey!" He grins. "I did it!"

"You did." Pax slaps him on the shoulder with such force he sends Edward sailing through the gate. "You're practically a Roman!"

"Kill me now," Edward mutters as he dusts himself off and limps after Pax and Ambrose.

"You're already dead," I mutter under my breath as I watch the three of them disappear through the wall. I pull out the moldavite crystal and squeeze it hard, but all I can think about are those bones in the woods and the horrible tugging of Pax's silver cord around my heart.

"Boooooo!"

"Whooooooo!"

From inside the house comes the sound of crashing objects and torn curtains. A few moments later, Linda Bateman runs out, her blouse only half-buttoned, her face and hair covered in flour, a bunch of leaves and sticks in her hand, and an expression of utter horror on her face. I step out in front of her, as if I were just walking along the street. "Mrs. Bateman, what's wrong? Are you okay—"

"I did it!" She grabs the collar of my shirt and shakes me so hard my teeth clatter together. "I killed dear old Albert. I killed him with this!"

I jerk my head to the side as she thrusts the belladonna into my face.

"I killed him, but it was an accident. I meant to kill Maggie. I grabbed the wrong balm at the Bake Off planning meeting – my eyesight isn't what it used to be and I thought it was the one Maggie uses on her tennis elbow. I returned it the next day when I brought over some paperwork for the marquee rental."

And left a little flour on the windowsill, I think.

"I thought she'd use a little dollop and go mad and then her baking would be *terrible*. I didn't know Albert would slather the whole jar over himself. I just wanted to win *so badly*."

"You've never won the Bake Off before," I say, remembering. "Maggie always took the title."

"Twelve years in a row she's won! It's nepotism – she's the organizer. She shouldn't even be allowed to enter. I just got so sick of her and Albert acting like they're God's gift to the village when Albert gave terrible investment advice and Maggie craved personal glory. My cakes are so much better than her scones."

"Your cakes are exquisite," I say, because she's got that belladonna awfully close to my face and, well, it's true.

392

"Thank you, my dear. I was going to win this year. I deserve to win! But Maggie texted me to say she was out of jail and entering the competition at the last minute, and I knew I had to act." Tears stream down her cheeks. "I was just baking a special belladonna cupcake to give her as a welcome-back present when the most horrible thing happened. G-g-ghosts! Terrifying, ugly ghosts—"

"I resent that. I am a frightfully handsome ghost." Edward says as the ghosts appear around me.

"It's going to be okay, Linda." As I speak, a tightness grows in my chest, and I look down and see a thin silver cord extending through my shirt – not Pax's cord, but someone else's. I try to grab it, but it falls through my fingers, like the way the ghosts used to do. "I...I...can help you..."

But she shoves me aside.

"Out of my way!" she cries, waving her belladonna cupcake around. Crumbs fly everywhere. "I have to get to the police station and confess what I did! It's the only way to save my immortal soul!"

A grin twitches at the corner of my mouth. "Is that so?"

"Oooooooh," Edward whispers in her ear, a wicked grin on his face.

"I can't bear it! I can't bear another minute of the horror!"

Linda races down the street and trips over the curb. A woman with a baby stroller stops to help, but Linda shoves the woman away and makes a run for it. The tugging of the silver cord grows more intense as we follow her down Main Street, wondering if she's going to run all the way to the Argleton station, when she throws herself in front of a cruising police car, crying that she wants to make a confession. They're confused, but they get Linda and her cupcake in the back of the car and drive away.

I look up at my ghosts. "You guys are getting far too good at this haunting thing. What did you do to get her frightened enough to confess?"

"Oh, it was simple, really," Ambrose says. "We had Edward read some of his poetry."

Edward beats his chest proudly. "Some of my best work."

"Why are you holding your heart like that?" Pax demands.

"You can't see it?" I ask, opening my hand around the glimmering silver cord. My voice croaks from the tightness. It feels like it's closing off my heart.

"See what?"

"The silver cord." I close my eyes against the discomfort, then open them again as I realize what's happening. "We have to get back to Grimdale Manor. *Now.*"

I RUN home as fast as I can, the silver cord extending from my chest quivering. The ghosts trail behind me, excitedly swapping haunting tips with each other. I hope they don't expect this to become a thing. I shouldn't use my ghoulish friends or new powers as weapons.

I arrive just as Maggie steps out of DS Wilson's car, her hands free of cuffs and a broad smile on her face. She must have finished the paperwork and she's now free. "Bree! I'm so happy to see you. DS Wilson here tells me that you were instrumental in my release."

She throws her arms around me. I'm too distraught to enjoy the warmth of her arms around me. I look over my shoulder as Albert emerges from the car behind her as Wilson pulls away. His body is surrounded by a brilliant glowing light, and the thin silver cord wrapped around my heart extends into his.

"Albert?" I whisper.

Maggie shudders. "I know, honey. I can feel him with us, too. He'd be so proud of you."

Albert floats over. His features are disintegrating as the light breaks him apart and the silver cord vibrates. I reach into my pocket and squeeze the moldavite. "Bree, it's my time. Don't fight it. You were right all along. Now that Maggie is safe, I will go where I'm supposed to be and wait for her. In no time at all, we'll be together again."

"A-A-Albert?"

I whirl back to face Maggie. Her face is gone white, and she's staring right at the spot where Albert's ghost is floating.

"Maggie?" He reaches out a fading hand to her.

"I can see him," she whispers, raising her own hand. "It's Albert. He's faint, but...he's here. He's here with me."

"Maggie, you can see me?" Albert's voice wobbles. "Lovey, I'll always be with you. Not even death can separate us. I'm your man for eternity."

Wow.

I step back as the two of them gaze at each other, their fingers touching but not touching. The love radiating from their faces makes my heart clench even worse. The silver cord vibrates.

"He..." I swallow, try to find the words. "He's been with you since his death. He needed to protect you from Linda. But now you're safe and he has to...he has to go..."

"Thank you," Maggie whispers. "Thank you Bree, for giving us this last moment together."

Tears stream down my cheeks. "I'm so sorry, Albert."

"Nothing to be sorry about. You listened to me when no one else would. I wanted to tell you how thankful I am. What you have is truly a gift."

It's really not. But I plaster a smile on my face. "I'm just happy to help, Albert. Where are you going? What can you see?"

"I don't know, but it feels wonderful – like a warm bath and a cold beer at the same time. I can hear...my father calling me, my brother's laugh, it's wonderful..."

Albert's body is gone now. He exists only as a shimmer of silvery light. He bends down and lays his light across the top of his wife's head. "Goodbye, my love. I'll be counting the days until we meet again."

"Until we meet again." Maggie blows him a kiss, her cheeks wet with tears.

My chest constricts as the silver cord snaps. The light envelops Albert completely.

And then the light is gone.

"That was beautiful," Pax says, wiping a tear from his cheek. "I have something in my eye. A piece of dust. It is most annoying."

"Oh, yeah, I hate when that happens." My throat is dry. I cough and step back from Maggie, but I have to hold onto the gate for support because my legs aren't working. "Right. Yes. Maggie, I'll let you get on."

As we move up the path toward the house, giving Maggie some time to digest what she saw, I say, "Ambrose, Edward, will you excuse us? I need to show Pax something in the woods."

"But don't you want to enjoy your victory?" Ambrose asks. "Hayes and Wilson will no doubt want to ask you a bunch of questions. And you should go to the pub and gloat and make everyone buy you a drink—"

I shake my head. "As lovely as a good gloat sounds, this can't wait."

42

BREE

"How much further?" Pax demands as he follows me down the familiar path. "We are getting close to the boundary of the cemetery. I do not go into the cemetery. That is where I lost my men. That is where my bones lay, forgotten by time, without a proper Roman funeral to welcome me across the river Styx..."

I keep facing forward. I don't want him to see the tears streaming down my cheeks. "I know you don't go in the cemetery. What I need to show you is right over here, I promise."

I turn off the trail and head toward the altar. The archaeologists have put a cover over the grave to keep out the weather, and they've left some of their tools stacked up against the tree. Every step is agony. The cord tugs and jerks, and it feels like I'm mashing my organs against a cheese grater.

At last, I draw up beside the grave. My whole body trembles. My heart is being squeezed so tight I don't know how I'm still upright.

"You're crying." Pax steps toward me, arms wide. "I will make it better."

I hold up my hand and shake my head. "You can't. Not this time. Do you feel anything?"

"Feel anything?"

"In your body?" I touch my hand to my chest. My heart slams against my palm. It's going to explode through my ribcage. I can feel the edges of Pax's cord shimmering around my hand. The magic hums and trembles. "Anything different?"

I refuse to look down. I refuse to watch the cord snap. I have only moments left with my Pax. I want to cherish every one of them.

Pax wrinkles his brow. "I feel mild irritation because I am missing the Grimdale Bake Off judging to stand under a smelly old tree next to an altar the Celts stole from my god, and I feel concern because you are sad, and I do not know why and you will not let me make you not sad."

"Oh, Pax." The tears flow freely now. I can barely get the words out, I'm sobbing so hard. "I am so sad, but happy, too. Look."

I reach down and tug away the tarp, revealing the ditch containing the grave. I gasp. They've uncovered most of the skeleton now. From just the bones I can see that he was a giant of a man. A warrior. A centurion. More pots and other items are buried in the dirt around him. Here and there is the glint of gold.

"This is..." I break into a sob and have to start again. "This is your grave."

Pax stares down into the hole. His body goes rigid. He doesn't say a thing.

"Kieran Myers found it – he and his wife were stealing the coins and gold items to sell. That's why they were trying to buy the house, so that they would rightfully own this treasure. And when Albert was murdered and Maggie in jail, they decided to just take the chance and dig it up. You've seen all the archaeologists traipsing through the yard? Well, they're preserving the grave and all the objects because they tell a beautiful story. The story of a beloved commander who fell in battle, and even though they were beaten and forced to retreat, his friends and fellow soldiers got together to give him the proper funeral rites and to bury him with honour. They did this for you, Pax. They loved you."

"I can't believe it," he murmurs. "All this time...all these centuries...I didn't dare hope that I would be able to go to Elysium, but I had everything I needed right here."

"Pax..." I step closer, my hand reaching for him. I don't know how much time we have. I draw an object from my pocket and place it in his hand. "This is the coin they placed in your mouth to pay the ferryman. This is it. This is what you've been waiting for. You can cross over now. You can be free. I'm so happy for you."

His head snaps up, and I see the emotion burning in his eyes. He glares at the coin like it might burst into flame at any moment. "If you are happy, why do you cry?"

"Because I'm going to miss you, so so much." I hold my arms out, longing to hold him one final time, even if it hurts so bad I might pass out. "And because not all tears are ones of sadness."

"No," he growls. "I don't want to go if you are crying."

"I think it's too late for that."

Something in my chest *snaps*. The pain blooms hot inside me, rising through my chest into my head, pressing my brain against my skull until I'm sure it's going to ooze out my ears.

"Bree?" Pax calls, but he sounds far away. Shimmering silver light pours from his eyes, his nostrils, his ears. Tendrils of silver coil around him, glowing brighter and brighter until they make my head pound, but I don't look away. I have so so much to tell him.

"I hope that wherever you go, you get to break bread with the gods. I hope there is endless wine and so many things to stab and women to make love to and cuddle—"

"There is only one woman I want," he growls. He reaches for his sword, but as he pulls it from his belt it dissolves into silver shimmers.

A gnawing, twisting feeling snakes in my gut. "You've been one of the best things to ever happen to me, and I'm so sorry for all those years I made you live in the attic, and for all the time I've been away. I love you, Pax. I never told you that before, but it's true. I love you and I'm going to miss you so much—"

The light grows stronger, and the warmth of my love for him grows and grows inside me, until I'm overwhelmed by it. Until every breath I take feels like I'm breathing him. Through the sadness of losing him, I can see that this is the way it's meant to be.

Pax was never supposed to be here.

Every moment I've had with him has been a gift.

I have to learn to let go.

No matter how much it hurts.

"Goodbye, my soldier." I reach for him, desperate to touch him one final time, even if what we had is never really touch. Pax is practically all light now. He reaches for me, and his fingers close over mine.

His fingers close over mine.

His *solid* fingers.

Real, *human* fingers.

The whole world shudders.

"Pax, what's happening?" I stare down at his fingers in mine. This isn't a trick of the moldavite. This is real. His fingers are *real*. The whole wood groans. "Pax, let go of me. I think you're dragging me into the underworld with you."

Pax's face twists with pain. "I cannot let go. You are the one holding me."

"That's not—" but I look down again, and I see something that makes my heart stop.

The white light surrounding him...it's not coming from the heavens, or from Hades beneath the earth, or from some deep place inside him.

It's coming from *me*.

It pulses through my skin like starlight. The light hovers around my chest, my heart. Instead of the silver thread snapping, it winds faster and faster, as if my heart is a spindle spinning off more life for him. The light encircles us both, and it has weight and substance.

Pax throws his head back and roars as the light folds over him. I hear the crack of bones breaking, reshaping. But this is impossible. Pax doesn't have bones.

"Bree?" he calls out. "What are you doing to me?"

I'm not doing anything. What's happening?

"Pax?" I cry. "Pax?"

The only reply is a howl of pain.

The light squeezes me, pressing my skin against my bones, and I feel something I don't expect to feel – a miraculous wonder, like when someone gives you a houseplant and you remember to water it, and it grows a flower and you feel like a god.

Am I a god now? Maybe I'm one of the ones who gets punished for using too much power by being turned into a duck.

The light begins to fade. The clamp around my heart loosens, and my throat opens so I can breathe again.

I'm still holding Pax's hand.

I dare myself to lift my head. My eyes are closed. I'm too afraid of what I might see.

"Bree?" a gravelly voice whispers.

I open my eyes.

Standing before me, his fingers still entwined with mine, is Pax, solid and enormous, and very much *alive*.

TO BE CONTINUED

How will Bree and her ghostly men solve this mystery? Will Bree find out more about her strange powers? Find out in book 2, *If You've Got It, Haunt It*

http://books2read.com/grimdale2

What do you get when you cross a cursed bookshop, three hot fictional men, and a punk rock heroine nursing a broken heart? Read book one of the Nevermore Bookshop Mysteries – A Dead and Stormy Night – to get the story of Mina and her book boyfriends.

http://books2read.com/adeadandstormynight

(Turn the page for a sizzling excerpt).

Can't get enough of Bree and her boys? Read a free bonus scene from before Bree left on her travels, as well as her playlist, along with other bonus scenes and extra stories when you sign up for the Steffanie Holmes newsletter.

http://www.steffanieholmes.com/newsletter

FROM THE AUTHOR

I hope you enjoyed Bree's story. This has been such a fun book to write. I'm a bit obsessed with ghosts and hauntings (if you're a member of my newsletter, you'll know this), so it's been wild to create this world where ghosts aren't these scary apparitions, but rather they're just like you and me...except hotter.

Our three ghosts are all fictional – they don't exist historically, although the details about their costumes and memories are as real as I can make them.

Pax's name means 'peace' in Latin. It's not a traditional Roman name, but I thought it was too fun not to use. He uses the word 'verpa', which is a vulgar Latin word for penis. And his insult – vappa! – means scum! (It refers to wine that's gone sour). His views on Druids are his own and not shared by the author.

Ambrose is based on one of my own personal heroes – the Victorian adventurer, James Holman. Holman became mysteriously blind in his early 20s, and when this curtailed his naval career he first put himself through medical school and then set off on a series of adventures across the world. He was known as the 'Blind Traveller'.

Using a cane to rap on the ground, Holman was able to learn about the spaces around him through echolocation. He would walk holding a rope, which was then tethered to a carriage, so that he remained on the road. He wrote books about his travels using the frame with strings that Ambrose describes.

Holman's books were at first well-received, but he then became a bit of a novelty and wasn't taken seriously as an adventurer. People even said that he couldn't really be blind. He rode elephants in Ceylon, fought the slave trade in Fernando Po Island, helped chart the Australian outback, and was captured in Siberia by the Tsar's men on suspicion of being a spy. He was not killed, though, but ejected to the frontier of Poland.

His final manuscript – an autobiography encompassing all his travels – was never published and likely did not survive. He died in obscurity and is buried in London's Highgate Cemetery – the very place for which Grimdale Cemetery is based. Jason Roberts wrote a wonderful biography of Holman called *A Sense of the World* and I highly recommend it.

You might not know this, but I'm legally blind. Unlike Ambrose, Mina, and Holman, my eyesight didn't disappear one day or fade over time. I was born with the genetic condition *achromatopsia*, which means my eyes lack the millions of cone cells required to recognise colours and perceive depth. I'm completely colour blind, light sensitive with poor depth perception, I squint and blink all the time, and I struggle to make eye contact. I'm so short-sighted I'm considered legally blind.

I love being able to write stories where people like me get to have adventures, save the world, and discover that they can be sexy and have their happily ever after.

There are so many people who've supported me and believed in me, even when I struggled to believe in myself. My family – my Mum and Dad and sister Belinda.

The writers with whom I've celebrated and commiserated –

the peeps on Dirty Discourse, the fab ladies of Romance Writers of New Zealand and SpecFic Slack, the Badass Authors, and my reverse harem babes. Thank you for teaching me that when one of us succeeds, it lifts everyone up.

To my friends, the Bogans – my extended family, my brothers and sisters of metal. I apologise for the volume of our shenanigans that end up in my books. (That's a lie.)

Always, to my cantankerous drummer husband, who is everything. Every hero I write is a piece of you and what you mean to me.

And lastly, to you, my readers, for going on this journey with me. I love you more than words can say.

A portion of the royalties from the sale of this book are donated to Parkinson's New Zealand. Thank you for the work you do!

Every week I send out a newsletter to fans – it features a spooky story about a real-life haunting or strange criminal case that has inspired one of my books, as well as news about upcoming releases and a free book of bonus scenes called *Cabinet of Curiosities*. To get on the mailing list all you gotta do is head to my website: http://www.steffanieholmes.com/newsletter

I'm so happy you enjoyed this story! I'd love it if you wanted to leave a review on Amazon or Goodreads. It will help other readers to find their next read.

Thank you, thank you! I love you heaps! Until next time.
Steff

EXCERPT
A DEAD AND STORMY NIGHT

Uncover the secrets of Nevermore Bookshop in book 1, *A Dead and Stormy Night*

http://books2read.com/adeadandstormynight

Wanted: Assistant/shelf stacker/general dogsbody to work in secondhand bookshop. Must be fluent in classical literature, detest electronic books and all who indulge them, and have experience answering inane customer questions for eight hours straight. Cannot be allergic to dust or cats – if I had to choose between you and the cat, you will lose. Hard work, terrible pay. Apply within at Nevermore Bookshop.

Yikes. I closed the Argleton community app and shoved my phone into my pocket. *The person who wrote that ad really doesn't want to hire an assistant.*

Unfortunately, he or she hadn't counted on me, Wilhelmina Wilde, recently-failed fashion designer, owner of two wonky eyes, and pathetic excuse for a human. I was landing this assistant job, whether Grumpy-Cat-Obsessed-Underpaying-Ad-Writer wanted me or not.

I had no options left.

I peered up at the towering Victorian brick facade of Nevermore Bookshop – number 221 Butcher Street, Argleton, in Barsetshire – with a mixture of nostalgia and dread. I'd spent most of my childhood in a darkened corner of this shop, and now if I played my cards right I'd get to see it from the other side of the counter. It was the one shining beacon in my dark world of shite.

I don't remember it looking so... foreboding.

Apart from the faded *Nevermore Bookshop* written in gothic type over the entrance, the facade bore no clue that I stood in front of one of the largest secondhand bookshops in England. A ramshackle Georgian house facade with Victorian additions rose four stories from the street, looking more like a creepy orphanage from a gothic novel than a repository of fine literature. Trees bent their bare branches across the darkened windows and wisteria crept over grimy brickwork, shrouding the building in a thick skin of foliage. Cobwebs entwined in the lattice and draped over the windowsills. There didn't appear to be a single light on inside.

Weeds choked the two flower pots flanking the door, which had once been glazed a bright blue but were since stained in brown and white streaks from overzealous birds. A pigeon cooed ominously from the gutter above the door, threatening me with an unwelcome deposit. Twin dormer windows in the attic glared over the narrow cobbled street like evil eyes, and a narrow balcony of black wrought iron on the second story the teeth. A hexagonal turret jutted from the south-western corner, where it might once have caught sun before Butcher Street had built up around it.

When I used to hang out as a kid, the first two floors were

given over to the shop – a rabbit warren of narrow corridors and pokey rooms, every wall and table covered in books. The previous owner – a kindly blind old man named Mr. Simson – lived on the remaining two floors, but for all I knew, the new owner used that space as an opium den or a meat smoker.

At least the flaccid British sun peeked through the grey clouds, which meant I could make out these finer details of the facade. The buildings on either side of it were cloaked in the creeping black shadow that now followed me everywhere. I squinted at the chalkboard sign on the street, hoping for some clue as to the new owner's personality, but all it had on it were some wonky lines that looked like chickens' feet.

This place is even more drab than I remember. It could use a little TLC.

That makes two of us. I squinted at my reflection in the darkened shop window, but I could barely make out the basic shape of my body. At least I knew I looked fierce when I left the house, in my Vivienne Westwood pleated skirt (scored on eBay for twenty-five quid), vintage ruffled shirt, men's cravat from a weird goth shop at Camden market, and my old school blazer with an enamel pin on the collar that read, 'Jane Austen is my Homegirl.' Combined with my favorite Docs and a pair of thick-framed glasses, I'd nailed the 'boss-bitch librarian' look.

That is, if you ignored the fact that I pushed my nose up against the glass to see my reflection, and twisted my head in order to see all the details of my outfit because of the creeping darkness in the corners of my eyes.

Please, Isis and Astarte and any other goddess listening, let me get this job. I can't deal with any more rejection.

I smoothed my hair, sucked in a breath, pushed open the creaking shop door, and stepped back in time.

As the shop bell tinkled and the smell of musty paper filled my nostrils, I became nine years old again – the weird outcast kid whose mother was banned from school events after swindling the chair of the PTA with a Forex trading mastermind program that was really just a CD-rom of my mother comparing currency trading to doing the laundry. (It was his own fault for getting swindled. Who even uses CDs anymore?)

As soon as the school bell rang I'd sprint into town, duck through this same door and escape into another world. I'd curl up in the cracking leather armchair in the World History room with a huge stack of books and read until my mother finished her shift and came to collect me. Books became my friends – characters like Jane Eyre and Dorian Grey the perfect substitutes for the kids who were horrible to me. When I was older and the guys at school sneered at me and fawned over my best friend, I fell into books again – this time to fall in love with the bad boys, the intelligent boys, the boys filled with anger and lust and pain. Dark horses and anti heroes like Heathcliff and Sherlock Holmes, and melancholy authors like Edgar Allan Poe spoke directly to my soul.

Mr. Simson barely said a word to me, but he never seemed to mind the fact that I read every book in the shop but couldn't afford to buy any. Sometimes he'd even let me riffle through the boxes of rejects before he sent them away for recycling. People would come into the store and try to sell Mr. Simson stacks of airport books – James Patterson and John Grisham paperbacks that no one buys secondhand. When he refused their generous bounty, they'd creep back at night and shove the volumes one by one through the mail slot, so Mr. Simson always had stacks of them lying around. I would smuggle the books home to our housing estate – If Mum caught me reading she'd lecture about how men didn't like smart girls and we'd have a big row – and read them under the covers at night or hidden in my textbooks during class.

It was in Nevermore Bookshop where I first discovered punk

music. I found a box of battered 1970 zines in the Popular Music section, and I lost myself in faded photographs of bored teenagers with bleached mohawks. None of them fit in, and they didn't give a shit. I was in love.

Teenage Mina threw herself into punk music and fashion, bought a second-hand sewing machine, and started cutting up all her clothes. Fashion became a way to express myself, and opened up a world that was bigger and brighter and more fun than the council estate and my shitty school and lack of tits and the tiny village of Argleton.

When you don't have any friends and have an entire bookshop for research, you get a lot of schoolwork done. At the end of my last year at secondary school, I was offered four scholarships to prestigious universities. But there was only one thing I wanted – to become a punk-rock fashion designer. The next Vivienne Westwood, thank you very much. So when I was awarded a place at New York's infamous Fashion Institute, I packed up my Docs and sewing machine and left Argleton behind me for good.

Or so I thought.

For four glorious years I lived in New York City, working my arse off, living it up with my best friend Ashley, and learning everything there was to learn about the fashion industry. Last year I finished my degree and Ashley and I landed the same year-long internship with Marcus Ribald, our favorite designer of all time after Vivienne.

Then I noticed a faint blur in the corner of my eye and I fell down the stairs three days in a row. I would reach for my coffee cup and knock it over, or sign my name on a document and miss the line completely. I thought it was nothing – I walked through life constantly hungover and running on coffee and discounted day-old hot dogs, which I assumed explained the pounding headaches that stabbed me day and night. But I kept pushing, kept working, kept drinking. I was living the dream. Nothing could stop me.

Wrong. All it took was a harrowing doctor's appointment and Ashley's betrayal to stop me.

Bye bye internship. So long, crappy rat-infested apartment I secretly loved. Nice to know you, dreams of future success and dressing celebrities for the red carpet. Now I was back in Argleton, sleeping in my crummy old room and getting nervous about a job interview as a bloody *bookshop dogsbody*.

I stepped into the gloomy interior. My boot landed on a thick carpet in the wide entrance hall, flanked on either side by tall shelves crammed with books. A small line of taxidermy rodents peered down at me from tiny wooden shields nailed along the moldings. *I don't remember those.* The new owner sure had strange taste in interior decor. But then, he had written that acerbic job ad...

I ran my fingers along the spines of the books, moving carefully to avoid tripping over the stacks of paperbacks littering the floor. Must and mothballs and leather and old paper caressed my nostrils. The air practically *sweated* books.

"Hello?" I called, coughing as dust tickled the back of my throat. *Was the bookshop always this dusty?*

Hello, beautiful. A voice croaked from behind me. I whirled around, a retort poised on my lips. But no one was in the doorway. I twisted my head to peer into the corners of the room, but I couldn't penetrate the shadows.

Where did that voice come from?

"Hello?" I called out. *The first thing I'm going to do if I get the job is brighten this place up a bit.*

Something rustled in the dark corner above the door. I glanced up. My eyes resolved the shape of an enormous black bird perched on the top of the bookshelf. At first I assumed it was stuffed, but it unfurled a long wing and flapped it in my face.

"Argh!" I flung my arm up, slamming my elbow into a stack of books, which toppled to the ground. The raven croaked with satisfaction and folded its wing away.

What in Astarte's name is a raven doing in here? It'll poop over the books. I wonder if it's roosting in the roof somewhere? We'll have to find that if we want to chase it out...

"Croak," said the raven with an accusatory tone, as though it had heard my thoughts.

"I guess you kind of suit the place." I glared at the bird as I bent down and fumbled for the books. "A raven in Nevermore Bookshop. Once upon a midnight dreary—"

"Croak." The raven's yellow eyes glowed. Something in that croak sounded like a warning.

"Fine. Fine. I didn't come here to quote poetry to a bird." I stood up and rubbed my throbbing elbow. "I want to talk to the boss. Do you know where I might find him?"

As if it understood the question, the raven dropped off the shelf, swooped past me, and flew around the corner, disappearing through an archway on the left. I followed it into what would have once been a drawing room and was now a jumble of mismatched shelves and junkstore furniture. In the middle of the room were two heavy oak tables – one holding a large globe, the other a taxidermy armadillo. Books stacked so high it looked as though the armadillo was building itself a border wall. Old cinema chairs and beanbags under the window formed a reading area, and the large lawyer's desk that had served as Mr. Simson's counter still took pride of place beside the grand fireplace, although the brass plaque on the front now read "Mr. Earnshaw."

The raven swooped around me and perched on the desk lamp, its talons clicking against the metal. It took me a few moments to register the man hunched over the desk – the dark, wavy hair that spilled over his shoulders obscured his face, and his black clothes faded into the wood behind him.

"We're closed." A gruff voice boomed from inside the hair.

"Your sign still says open."

"Well, flip it over for me on the way out," the voice managed to sound both exasperated and uninterested.

"Um, sure. Mr. Earnshaw, was it?" I waved. He didn't even look up from his paper. "I saw the job ad you posted on the Argleton app, and I wanted to—"

"App?" The head snapped up. Eyes of black fire regarded me with suspicion from beneath a pair of thick eyebrows, deep set in a dark-skinned face of such remarkable beauty I sucked in a breath.

The new proprietor was younger than I expected him to be – Mr. Simson had been an old man even when I was a girl – and far too handsome to be working in a bookshop. His exotic features and sharp cheekbones belonged on the cover of a fashion magazine. The defiant tilt of his chin and twitch of his haughty lips concealed a storm raging inside him.

Danger rolled off him in waves. Danger... and desire.

Thick muscles bulged at the seams of his shirt. He'd rolled the sleeves up to his elbows, one thick forearm graced with the tattoo of a barren, gnarled tree and some words in cursive script below.

Even though he was an Adonis, this Mr. Earnshaw also looked like a complete wanker. He scrunched up that perfectly-sculpted nose, his lips curling back into a sneer. "What the devil is an app?"

What kind of weird question is that? "Um... you know, an application for your phone, so you can get the bus timetable or talk to your mates or—"

"Don't talk to me about *phones*," Earnshaw snapped. "People spend too much time on their phones."

Right. I'd forgotten the part in the job ad about hating ebooks. *This guy must be one of those weirdos who eschews technology.* "Oh, I agree. I mean, phones should only be used for calling people. And checking social media. That's it. I would never read on mine," I blubbered, shoving my phone behind my back. "I mean, studies have shown it can cause long-term eye damage and—"

"No matter how long you keep talking, it's not going to change the fact that we're closed. What do you *want?*"

"I'm applying for the assistant's job." I fumbled in my purse for the envelope I'd carefully sealed, trying to avoid accidentally showing him the ereader tucked behind my makeup case. "I've got my resume in here for you with all my qualifications and—"

"I don't need that. If you want the job, tell me why I should hire you."

"Right, well..." This was the weirdest interview I've ever been to. Earnshaw's eyes stabbed right through me, turning my insides to mush. I opened my mouth, but then he blinked, long black lashes tangling together over those eyes – they were like black holes, gobbling whole universes for lunch. A shiver started at the base of my neck and rocketed down my spine, not stopping until it caressed me between my legs.

Now I wanted the job more than ever, just so I could stare at this specimen all day. Bloody hell, I always did have a thing for surly bad boys. I blamed Emily Brontë. The brutish and untamable Heathcliff ruined me for nice guys.

"If your answer is to gape at me like a bespawling lubberwort," he growled, "then you can take the job and shove it where the sun don't shine—"

"That's *not* my answer." My cheeks flared with heat. *Who even is this guy? Adonis or not, how'd he get off talking to customers and potential employees like that? No wonder the place is deserted.* "I was just collecting my thoughts. You should hire me because I'm a hard worker. I'm punctual. I have some retail experience, as well as design expertise so I can do graphics and window displays—"

"I don't care. Why do you want to work *here?* No one wants to work here. That was the whole *point* of the ad."

I racked my brain for an answer to that question. *What does he want from me?* "Um... I guess because I used to hang out in the bookshop all the time as a kid. I know where all the books go and I've personally helped Mr. Simson fix that till on at least two occasions." I pointed to the ancient contraption the raven was pecking.

Earnshaw glared at me, his eyes flicking over my face as though searching for something. He didn't say a thing. The silence stretched between us until even the raven got bored of hunting for worms in the credit card machine and stared at me, too.

Is he waiting for more?

"And... um, I have all sorts of useful skills." I scrambled for anything that might endear me to this strong-chinned man. "I have a fashion degree, so that's probably not useful. But I am a Millennial, so I can do the store's social media. I could build a website—"

You can see it, can't you? That strange voice said. *It's obvious. She's the one he told you about.*

Earnshaw grunted. I narrowed my eyes at him. *Does he hear it, too?*

Just hire her already, that voice said again. *She's pretty.*

"Hey!" I glanced over my shoulder, looking for the owner of the voice so I could kick them in the nuts. But there was no one else in the room.

Was it Earnshaw? But the voice didn't sound like him, and

judging by the way he was still staring at me, he already thought I was nuts. *Maybe he didn't hear the voice after all?*

Besides, the voice sounded like it came from *inside* my head.

Please, don't tell me that on top of everything else, I'm now hallucinating voices—

I like her, the voice interrupted. *I bet she'll bring me treats. Berries, smoked salmon, maybe even a mouse.*

I peered over my shoulder again. *Are they hiding in the hallway? Behind the beanbag stack?* "Who's there?"

Earnshaw's head whipped up. "Who are you talking to?"

"You didn't hear that? I think that raven told me I'm pretty."

I was kidding, but Earnshaw's eyes narrowed. He reached out and clamped an enormous hand around the raven's beak. "Don't be ridiculous. Ravens don't have opinions. You didn't leave the door open, did you? We're supposed to be *closed.*"

"No. I..." My shoulders sagged. *Who am I kidding? This is hopeless.* "I guess I'll just be going now. Thank you for your time and—"

"You start tomorrow," Earnshaw glowered. "We open at nine. Be here at eight-thirty, but don't let anyone else in. If you're late, the bird gets your paycheck. Welcome to Nevermore Bookshop."

TO BE CONTINUED

AGATHA CHRISTIE MEET BLACK BOOKS

Book boyfriends may do it better, but they're more trouble than they're worth.

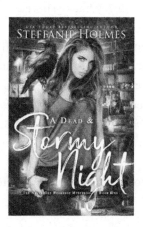

After being fired from my dream fashion job, I return home to my village under a cloud of failure and take a job at the quaint Nevermore Bookshop. I'm hoping for an easy few months while I get my life together.

But this is no ordinary bookshop.

A mysterious curse on Nevermore brings infamous fictional villains from classic literature to life in the real world.

My "easy" job involves rescuing customers from a 6foot4, grumpy, tattooed Heathcliff, drinking tea and evading the authorities with suave villain Moriarty, and making art with Edgar Allan Poe's shy, cheeky, raven shifter, Quoth.
As if that isn't crazy enough, my ex-best friend shows up dead with a knife in her back, and I'm the chief suspect. I'm going to have to Agatha Christie this shiz if I want to clear my name.

Oh, and those three fictional villains?

They like to share...

The Nevermore Bookshop Mysteries are what you get when all your book boyfriends come to life. Join a brooding antihero, a master criminal, a cheeky raven, and a heroine with a big heart (and an even bigger book collection) in this spicy cozy fantasy series by *USA Today* bestselling author Steffanie Holmes.

READ NOW:
books2read.com/adeadandstormynight

OTHER BOOKS BY STEFFANIE HOLMES

Nevermore Bookshop Mysteries

A Dead and Stormy Night

Of Mice and Murder

Pride and Premeditation

How Heathcliff Stole Christmas

Memoirs of a Garroter

Prose and Cons

A Novel Way to Die

Much Ado About Murder

Crime and Publishing

Plot and Bothered

Grimdale Graveyard Mysteries

You're So Dead To Me

If You've Got It, Haunt It

Ghoul as a Cucumber

Not a Mourning Person

Stonehurst Prep Elite

Poison Ivy

Poison Flower

Poison Kiss

Kings of Miskatonic Prep

Shunned

Initiated

Possessed

Ignited

Stonehurst Prep

My Stolen Life

My Secret Heart

My Broken Crown

My Savage Kingdom

Dark Academia

Pretty Girls Make Graves

Brutal Boys Cry Blood

Manderley Academy

Ghosted

Haunted

Spirited

Briarwood Witches

Earth and Embers

Fire and Fable

Water and Woe

Wind and Whispers

Spirit and Sorrow

Crookshollow Gothic Romance

Art of Cunning (Alex & Ryan)

Art of the Hunt (Alex & Ryan)

Art of Temptation (Alex & Ryan)

The Man in Black (Elinor & Eric)

Watcher (Belinda & Cole)

Reaper (Belinda & Cole)

Wolves of Crookshollow

Digging the Wolf (Anna & Luke)

Writing the Wolf (Rosa & Caleb)

Inking the Wolf (Bianca & Robbie)

Wedding the Wolf (Willow & Irvine)

Want to be informed when the next Steffanie Holmes story goes live? Sign up for the newsletter at www.steffanieholmes.com/newsletter to get the scoop, and score a free collection of bonus scenes and stories to enjoy!

About the Author

Steffanie Holmes is the *USA Today* bestselling author of the paranormal, gothic, dark, and fantastical. Her books feature clever, witty heroines, secret societies, creepy old mansions and alpha males who *always* get what they want.

Legally-blind since birth, Steffanie received the 2017 Attitude Award for Artistic Achievement. She was also a finalist for a 2018 Women of Influence award.

Steff is the creator of *Rage Against the Manuscript* – a resource of free content, books, and courses to help writers tell their story, find their readers, and build a badass writing career.

Steffanie lives in New Zealand with her husband, a horde of cantankerous cats, and their medieval sword collection.

Come hang with Steffanie
www.steffanieholmes.com
steff@steffanieholmes.com